D1210627

The List
2nd edition

C. D. Baker

The List by C. D. Baker
© 2002, 2015 C. David Baker
All rights reserved.

ISBN: 145640668X
ISBN 13: 9781456406684

2nd Edition

Cover art by Amy Pak

Dedication

In memory of Philadelpia's gracious daughter, Eleanor Caldwell

Acknowledgments

I WOULD LIKE to express my gratitude to my enduring wife, Susan. Her discerning eyes did much to improve the story and her willingness to quietly suffer the obsessions of the author is very much appreciated.

I owe much to my friend Alan Crippen, founder of the John Jay Institute, Philadelphia, Pa. for his guidance and insight.

I am grateful to the many patient curators and guides of the numerous historical sites of Philadelphia. Among these are Elaine of the Betsy Ross House, Kate of St. Peter's Church, and Sarah of the Arch Street Quaker Meeting House.

This second edition contains corrections and improvements offered by astute readers for which I am thankful.

Finally, I offer a special thanks to Doug and Beverly Schmitt of PrestonSpeed Publications for their confidence and encouragement in the publication of the first edition. Their vision was a short novel that might reveal the history of the times within a memorable story drawn from actual events. They continue inspire me with their love for the past, which is only exceeded by their hope for the future.

Table of Contents

Introduction

HOW INSPIRING IT is to a person whose heart inclines toward others first, whose conscience is shaped by things greater than himself, and whose character has been forged on an anvil of pain. Imagine, then, how remarkable it would be if a whole empire recognised the qualities of selflessness, devotion, and integrity as virtues and fostered them amongst its people.

There was once a people who respected just such things. She was an ancient civilisation rooted in the green, well-watered lands of Britain and nurtured by Christianity for more than a millennium. She was imperfect, of course, and struggled within herself to grow and mature in ways that were good and true. But grow she did. Many of her most courageous sons and daughters eventually sailed across the wind-swept Atlantic to begin new lives in the endless reaches of a fresh New World. Mother England sent them gladly, and not empty-handed. For with them came their birthright of liberty, a heritage granted to them by the blood of their ancestors.

Indeed, the brave colonists who came to America carried the guarantees of the Magna Carta—a document resulting from a confrontation in the year 1215 between free Englishmen and their tyrannical King John in an English meadow. The King was forced to put his seal to the document and, in so doing, he reaffirmed and codified many of the liberties previously assumed in English custom.

Among other things, the Magna Carta established the legal precedent that a ruler had authority only so far as he did not violate the trust he had been given, and guaranteed that taxes would be levied only by consent of the governed.

This foundation block of liberty was an important step in the progressive growth of the English Constitution, a series of documents and customs that provided an orderly society a pathway toward ever-increasing freedoms. Among the many notable events that contributed to the development of this Constitution was the English Civil War during the 1640s, which ended in the execution of King Charles I by the people's ruling representative body, the Parliament. But liberty is a living thing and change is its breath of life. The balance between liberty and order would shift again in favour of authoritarian rule as the monarchy returned to prominence once more. However, by 1689, the Glorious Revolution and the English Bill of Rights helped re-establish many of the liberties that had been eroded.

From their very founding, the American colonies were part of this evolution of liberty. As in the motherland, the great debates over freedom's definition continued among people of integrity and intelligence. American colonists struggled to identify and declare their legal rights in the context of a new land, far away from their ancient Anglo-Saxon home.

By the French and Indian War of the 1750s, many Americans had grown weary of the Old World's feuds and entangled alliances. Some began to see themselves as a new people in a New World and they had little patience for matters of empire. And the years following the expensive war became increasingly tense as the British government attempted to recoup its losses by taxes deemed illegal by many.

In response to Parliament's efforts to exact taxes, the colonies began to resist. This, in turn, prompted a series of heavy-handed reactions by an insulted and indignant King and Parliament. The alarming activities that followed drove many of the colonists beyond all patience, for it was becoming painfully clear that their inherited rights were being threatened. They contended that their liberties were actually drawn from a source even deeper than their Constitution. They argued that their rights were first rooted in natural law—they were gifts from the Creator and affirmed by nature, not grants from government or from custom. It was apparent to many that King George III and the Parliament, like King John of old, were rapidly becoming corrupt and tyrannical—resulting in a violation of the sacred Constitutional compact and a violation of those natural rights to which all men are entitled.

But not all the colonists agreed. An equal number saw themselves as the extended arm of gracious empire, gathering the bounty of new lands for the benefit of all. Their hope was the maintenance of order and tradition. They urged patience as the Constitution and the government adapted to the challenges of the New World. These voices, too, were committed to defending their rights as Englishmen. Some even agreed with their fellow colonists that their rights were natural rights. But they believed the best path to true freedom was the one most familiar—due process within the established order of things. These loyal subjects of the crown trusted their government to ultimately abandon its despotic course.

A decade of debate among principled men did little more than delay the inevitable. The events that shaped the 1760s and 1770s are familiar to most: tea parties and protests, Committees of Correspondence, retaliatory laws—and the sound of muskets. Finally, discussion gave way to shouting and to shooting as "Rebels" and "Tories" staked out their ground. Born of blood and soul-searched genius, an inevitable line was then drawn that forever divided the great empire. This line was the Declaration of Independence. Now it was war that called upon each man of character to search his conscience and follow duty, with or without enthusiasm.

Far from a struggle between alien peoples, the American War of Independence was, instead, a war between cousins. Its forgotten paradox is the quiet misery of those whose hearts beat sadly for their foes. Its remarkable virtue is the unparalleled devotion to principle that cost so many so much. Its sad irony is the gut-wrenching dilemma of consciences in conflict.

When a civilisation wars against itself it may be tragedy enough. But civilisations are simply collections of families. So when families are divided, the tragedy is made worse.

The story that follows is a story about a divided empire and the competing forces that ultimately founded a new nation. But it is also the story of a divided family seeking common ground while honouring conscience. The story draws upon the untold dilemma of families all across the former colonies who were caught in a whirlwind of conflicting values and who desperately sought ways to reconcile principle and love, friendship and loyalty, religious faith and political ideals.

Our story is the second volume in the 'Bookends of Liberty' series (following *Swords of Heaven*) and is set in Philadelphia during the winter of 1777-1778. It is written with respect for historical accuracy, though I recognize the inevitability of inadvertent error. Some of the characters were real people, though the author has taken liberty in speculating on their personalities. With few exceptions, references to weather and natural phenomena are based on public records or personal journals of the time. Joseph Galloway's list is a fact of history, as are the military events, and the citywide events that are described. All dates referenced are accurate.

It is the author's hope that the reader will enjoy an imaginative experience of life in the period. It is further hoped that the reader will understand that his or her life is now different because of what has happened in the past. Though that principle is true generally, it is *particularly* true for our story.

C. D. Baker

On a green and distant island, a lion raged and roared and bared its claws against thirteen rebellious cubs. Her wayward litter had dared to growl and snap and leave the lair. But oh, if lions could but fly. She might have soared atop her mighty sea and hovered high above her wary brood to see more clearly what wrath she had provoked. She might have heard her young ones' anxious whisper, "Mother England." Perhaps from this better vantage she might have found another way.

But, alas, lions do not fly.

CHAPTER 1

A Gathering of Clouds

KATHERINE BROWNE COULD keep a secret well. Yet even she had her limits in the heat of Philadelphia's summer of 1777. "Penelope!" she cried.

"Mother's looking for us again."

Her brother lifted a finger. "Listen. We'll hear my name next—the *whole* name."

"Thaddeus Henry Browne!"

Waiting impatiently for her fourteen-year-old twins, Katherine stood on her stoop and wiped her hands on her apron. Her mobcap was soiled with ash from a smoky hearth and her apron was black with soot. She blew a wisp of red-brown hair off her smudged brow and folded her arms as she tapped her foot impatiently.

"You two. I thought I made it clear that you are not to go to the shambles until you've finished the morning's chores. Thaddeus, you've more wood to cut and stack, else we shan't be eating this evening and you know what happ—"

"I know, mother. I—"

Katherine took a long stride and twisted one of the boy's protruding ears. They were always an easy target. "You'll not be interrupting me."

"Aaah—alright, mother."

Mrs. Browne let go of the boy and drew a deep breath. Her morning had not gone very well. The chimney had clogged and smoke had filled the kitchen in her cellar. Distracted by the domestic disaster, she had not noticed when her daughter had slipped away. Her pottery would now need to be cleaned, and her daughter's help was required. "You, Penelope. Have you any idea what miseries I've suffered without your help? Where did you go?"

Penelope, or 'Penny,' as some called her, was a feisty red-headed girl. The apple of her father's eye, she was a handful of trouble. She was as spirited and impulsive as her twin was steady and careful. The girl looked at her feet in hopes of deflecting her mother's anger, and commented: "They are too big, I think. Do you agree?"

Katherine rolled her eyes. She was not unfamiliar with this game. "What?"

"My feet."

"No, dear," answered her mother wryly. "I think they suit you."

Penelope hesitated, uncertain if her mother's dry wit had just nipped her a bit. "Uh, does that mean—"

"It means I am not playing. Now, young lady, you've a kitchen to help me clean, and you, boy, you've work as well."

Today was Saturday and the weekly livestock auction had drawn a huge crowd to the New Market shambles just a few blocks away. More than that, Thaddeus' good friend, Webster Yates, had told the Brownes that a fresh batch of prisoners was to be set in the stocks at noon.

Thaddeus completed his work as the bell of St. Peter's chimed for noon. His own church, Pine Street Presbyterian, never rang for anything. Its single bell had been donated to Washington's army to be melted down for musket shot. At the time, his father had said, "The bell that drew us to the liberty of our soul now whistles in defence of the liberty of our land."

Thaddeus disagreed.

Before the last bell had finished echoing over the wood-shaked roofs of Union Street, Thaddeus was pleading with his mother to release him. "Mother, I've done my chores. The wood is stacked and I've carried in nearly a half cord. That's two weeks' worth."

Mrs. Browne nodded. She was perspiring and sooty. She looked around her kitchen and at the stack of wood piled at the far end of the cellar.

Penelope was muttering and grimacing as she heaved an iron kettle off the table. "Can't he help me finish?" she pleaded.

"You've your tasks and he his," answered Katherine.

Thaddeus looked out the cellar doorway that opened to the street and watched as a flurry of chattering folks hurried along the brick sidewalks. Thaddeus waited for his mother's answer.

"First," Mrs. Browne began, "I need you to take this bottle of brandied raspberries to Mrs. Jones on Third Street by Spruce. The new cobbler's wife."

"The Welsh family?"

Katherine sighed. "Aye, boy, the Welsh family. They are new to the neighbourhood and in some distress."

"Of course you want to help them. They're Anglicans, like you wish you still were," said Penelope.

Mrs. Browne turned a hard eye towards her daughter. "I'm content to attend your father's church."

"Most at St. Peter's are still loyal to the Crown, like you." Penelope folded her arms and turned a hard eye to her brother. "And like you."

Thaddeus bristled. "Aye, and proudly."

Katherine stood between her twins. She shook her head in desperation. *Cursed trouble-making rebels have brought me nothing but problems,* she thought. Katherine Browne was a staunch Loyalist. Raised in an Anglican family to value order and tradition, she wanted no part of the rebellion, which had divided her country, her church, and her family. "Enough. Can we have no peace, even in our own cellar? Now, Thaddeus, take this bottle to Mrs. Jones and tell her I shall come to call next week. Then you may leave for the shambles."

With a smug smile, Thaddeus escaped up the shallow stone steps onto the sunny street above. He shook bits of bark and chaff off his linen sleeves and wiped his knee-length breeches clean. He paused to pick some dirt off his woollen stockings and beat his three-cornered hat against his hip. Dusted, wiped, and ready to go, the lad turned up Union toward the cobbler's.

Philadelphia's cobblestones clattered loudly beneath the iron shoes of prancing horses and the well-worn rims of hurried carriages. The hot sun shone brightly above the busy city, but all was not well, for a storm was howling in the councils of the King's generals.

Some thirty thousand souls lived within the simple grid of streets designed nearly a century before by the English Quaker, William Penn. It was his hope that this "city of brotherly love" would be a wonderful, peaceful place of shady trees, colourful gardens, and quiet homes. Honest, simple, pleasing to the eye, Philadelphia had become the second largest English-speaking city in the British Empire. This "Athens of the New World" sat comfortably at the edge of the wide Delaware River and teemed with the bravest and the best of many lands and many faiths. Here liberty and order were treasures valued as much as the stores of plenty piled atop the busy port's crowded wharves.

Eagles then roamed the skies above this tidy city and sometimes soared high above narrow King Street, which ran north and south parallel to the river's edge. The right side of King was lined with shipyards and wharves and docks. The left was crammed with sheds, boathouses, and workshops for sail makers, carpenters, caulkers, and smiths. Parallel to King ran first Front Street, then Second, then Third, continuing in like manner all the way to the western edge of the city.

About two miles beyond the last street was the Schuylkill River, which marked something of a western boundary to the city's expanding reach. The land between the Schuylkill and Philadelphia's cobblestones was green and generous, and supported magnificent orchards and pastures. Many of the city's wealthiest residents owned summer mansions and stables in this most pleasant region.

William Penn had a great affection for trees. In fact, he named his colony 'Penn-*sylvania*'—Penn's Woods. It was no doubt this same affection that led him to give the east-west streets of Philadelphia such names as Pine, Spruce, Sassafras, and Walnut. Running perpendicular to the Delaware River, these streets intersected the numbered north-south streets at perfect right angles, forming thereby neat squares or city "blocks."

On one such block resided the family of Dr. Archibald Browne. To be more precise, the doctor's family lived on Union Street, between Second and Third. Union Street would have annoyed William Penn, for it bisected the original block bordered by Pine and Spruce Streets. Of course, knowing he was living on a street that interfered with the planned order of things gave Dr. Browne a secret pleasure. Indeed, Archibald had lived much of his life "at the edges," as his wife often remarked. It was not as if the man were rebellious or lacking in conscience; rather, he was simply more willing than most to follow his nose into places and situations others might avoid.

The neighbourhood of Union Street was a pleasant one. Most of its row houses were of good quality, red brick, typically narrow and built within the past thirty years. Two-and-a-half stories were common and nearly all had a single-gabled attic room as sleeping quarters for the children.

These were the "trinity" homes, so called because each of the three levels had the same square footage. Naturally, in home building as in theology, some strayed from doctrine and were built with three and a half stories. It was not that the builders were un-Christian, but the extra story offered advantages in space and, as Mrs. Browne often noted, in pretence. Steeply pitched roofs were the overwhelmingly popular design, with a few gambrels here and there, the latter being something similar to what others called a hip roof or Dutch roof. A gambrel roof, such as that on Dr. Browne's house, allowed for a little more headroom in the attic where the children slept.

Most of the neighbours were artisans or professionals—reasonably well-educated people like the Brownes, but not members of the gentry, or even the lower gentry. In years past, the neighbourhood had been home to the offices of the Free Society of Traders and served the many craftsmen working along the river slightly "downhill" from the homes. For this reason, the blocks around the Brownes were known as "Society Hill."

Thaddeus arrived at the Joneses' and entered the cobbler's simple shop. Like most shops, it operated in the front room of the first floor. Behind it was a small parlour. Young Evan Jones was busy repairing the heel of a gentleman's boot. He hoped someday to rise above a cobbler's life and become a shoemaker.

"Good day," said Thaddeus.

"And to you, young man," Evan answered in his Gaelic brogue.

The lad handed the man the bottle of fruit. "My mother sends a gift to you and your wife. She shall call on you next week."

"M'thanks to your mother," said Evan. "She's a Presbyterian now?"

Thaddeus shrugged. "Not in her heart." The boy stepped back to the street. He walked at a restrained gait until he rounded the corner, then he dashed toward the market. Summers at nearby New Market were delightful, to be sure, even in times as uncertain as these. Set along Second Street just a block south of Union, the market was the meeting place of the curious, the bored, the gossips, and the children. The lad charged onto Second and nearly toppled his old friend "the Grackle."

The Grackle was a fixture at the Newmarket shambles, just as he had been some thirty years ago at the older market on Market Street. He peddled the handiwork that he whittled with the row of knives that lined his belt. His given name was Josiah Byrd, but his peculiar looks had earned him the nickname "Grackle" from the lips of his very own mother.

Josiah was a free Negro. He was the son of slaves who had worked the indigo fields of the Carolinas in the service of a pious Anglican minister named Samuel Byrd. The reverend Byrd, it seems, had fallen under a "conviction of conscience" by the preaching of another minister in the revival called the" Great Awakening" nearly forty years prior. He had claimed that "fits and starts of the soul" came over him "like the waters washing the world of Noah." He had declared his soul was rekindled with the "fires of righteousness," and he set free Josiah's family of twelve. "Go," he had said, "like the children of Abraham; go and cover the earth." So Josiah's family found their way to Philadelphia.

Philadelphia, however, was a large slave-trading city. Two wealthy Quaker gentlemen successfully conspired to return the family into bondage through coercion and a false claim. All, that is, except for Josiah. It seems that Josiah had a knack for playing the dimwit, the weak-of-mind. He could roll his eyes and slobber and look for all the world like a pitiful wretch. Believing the man would bring little in the slave sale, the good brethren passed him by.

"Uh—Master Thaddeus," grunted Josiah, as the two collided.

"Beggin' your pardon, Grackle. I ought be more careful."

The Grackle laughed. His teeth glistened in the sun. Thaddeus thought the old, white-headed man looked like a frosted jack-o-lantern, because of the large empty spaces staggered between each tooth. "You be more careful? You be the most careful boy I knows."

Thaddeus grinned. He knew he took great care in nearly everything he did. His father would turn bright red as he waited for the boy to make decisions, but he would turn purple when he tried to change the boy's mind on any point. "Right again. And you, my friend, are the wisest, I think."

Josiah Byrd's eyes shone like the sun. His irises were not the brown most common to his race, but were yellow, like rings of gold. It was these gold-coloured eyes shining against his shiny black African skin that had earned him his nickname. It was said that all of Carolina heard his mother scream when her baby first looked at her. Josiah laid one of his huge hands atop the young Browne's shoulder and smiled. "Wise? I wish so."

Thaddeus nodded and bade a hasty farewell. He ran toward the south end of the market where the stocks were usually set. He trotted along the long rows of merchants' stalls filled with summer produce and with meats, tinkers' pots, and pewter. He elbowed his way past ox-carts filled with fowl cages and tethered hogs, pausing only to pull up his stockings or straighten his tricorn hat. The bleats of sheep and the honking of geese filled the air. At last he saw a crowd of citizens chanting and yelling oaths at a hapless row of sad faces staring out from the wooden collars of the stocks. Craning his neck in search of a friend, Thaddeus heard his name do hr strained his eyes to find the familiar figure of Webster Yates waving to him.

Pressing between the elbows of those around him and smiling as he approached, Webster soon reached Thaddeus' side. He was the son of Whittaker Yates, the neighbourhood apothecary and good friend of Dr. Browne. A bit short for thirteen and round as a plump robin ruffled in the rain, Webster had the black hair and small features of his mother who had died giving birth to him.

"Look, there," said Webster. His brown eyes were wide with anxiety as he pointed to the stocks. "They're filled with folks we know. John Withers, Israel Newcommer, Nigel Forbes—"

"John Withers?" blurted Thaddeus, incredulously.

"Aye."

"But—but he's a trader from Christ Church. Father knows him. What's his crime?"

Webster grew quiet and nervous. "He wouldn't take the oath."

Thaddeus darkened. "That blasted oath. Father spoke of it a few weeks ago. I think this colony has gone mad... all this rebel talk of liberty. I swear these Whigs to be hypocrites."

"Shh." Webster put a stout finger on his lips and looked from side to side. He led Thaddeus by the elbow to an alleyway. "You must be careful what you say. You'll be tarred for certain."

Thaddeus stiffened his jaw. "Did your father take the oath?"

Webster looked from side to side. He leaned to Thaddeus' ear and whispered, "No; but tell no one."

A loud cheer distracted the two for a brief moment. Another man was being locked in a stock. He was bent over and his throat and wrists were held in the cut-outs of the bottom half of the wooden yoke. A militiaman then closed the hinged top over him and locked the two parts with an iron padlock. The captive was weeping.

"Your father is a good King's man, like me," said Thaddeus. " I wish I could say the same for my own or for Cameron. Father served the King against the French less than twenty years ago and now he sides with the Whigs. My

C. D. Baker

brother joined the Continentals after the were Hessians paraded through the city this winter."

"*Please*, Thaddeus—can we speak of this later?" begged Webster.

Thaddeus nodded. The patriots in Philadelphia were growing more anxious as the war gained momentum. Since Washington's surprise victory at Trenton on the Christmas just passed, their hopes were aroused. The springtime campaigns of this year brought news of Washington's Continentals engaging the British general, William Howe, across the river in New Jersey. It was reported that his army was pressing Howe, but news of another British campaign had suddenly filled the taverns with rumours and fears. The English General Burgoyne had arrived in Quebec in May and was threatening a dangerous British advance into the colonies from the north. Should he and Howe join forces in New York all might be lost.

Thaddeus was a disciplined lad and prudent. Though opinionated, he was usually careful. He whispered, "Well, I'll just say that my brother was so excited by the sight of those captured Hessians, he joined up."

Thaddeus and Webster left the alley and soon found themselves standing in the midst of an angry mob that was hurling eggs and spoiled fruit at a long line of frightened Tories in the stocks. These Loyalist prisoners had refused to take the oath of allegiance to the new American nation. The day before had been the first anniversary of the signing of the Declaration of Independence and the patriots were still celebrating and easily incited.

A bill passed into law by the Pennsylvania Assembly in Philadelphia's State House only weeks before required every white male inhabitant of the former colony to take an oath of allegiance to the new government of the United Colonies or forfeit a number of rights and privileges, including the right to a jury, and the right to buy and sell land, among others. All Loyalist office holders were dismissed and replaced with oath takers. Also, those who refused to take the oath were disarmed—a fearsome disadvantage to any person, especially a citizen in a nation embroiled in a civil war.

On the other hand, for a fee of one shilling—about one-third of a day's wage for an ordinary labourer—each male resident declaring his allegiance was issued a certificate guaranteeing him the rights and privileges of American citizenship.

A brown egg flew through the air past Thaddeus' ear and landed squarely on Joseph Smith's nose. The man howled and the crowd laughed. A maidservant ran quickly to him and wiped his nose and mouth free of the dripping yoke. She had been hired by four of the victims as their "face-saver." Although all that was at risk was one's dignity, suffocation from the rotten garbage was feared as a very real possibility.

A volley of rotted cabbages flew from a wet crate to the stocks. When the missiles landed, a great cheer rose up and Thaddeus turned toward the flushed faces all around him. His heart sank. He had known many of them for all his life and could have called them by their given names. Instead, he secretly knew them by other names, such as 'rebel,' or 'Whig,' or 'traitor to the Crown.'

Of course, not every Tory was seditious and not every Whig threw eggs. Instead many hearts were simply heavy with sadness. Many 'Loyalists' had great sympathy for the 'rebel' cause but could not bring themselves to turn against their King. And many 'patriots' loved their British past, yet had joined with the rebellion while grieving its necessity.

Thaddeus groaned. "When the rebels win I fear for good men like these. If I can do only one thing in this war, I hope it is to keep men of honour from undeserved suffering."

Webster was shocked. *When the rebels win?* He thought. He was sure his friend had gone mad. After all, he reasoned, Britain ruled most of the New World. She had the mightiest army and navy in all the earth. Defeat was preposterous.

The crowd again roared its pleasure as another barrage of garbage found its pitiful marks. Then a small company of Continental soldiers entered the marketplace to the lively fifes and drums of 'Will You Go to Sheriff Muir.' A handsome young officer in a smart blue coat tipped his tricorn hat and smiled from a stately horse. The mob in the shambles cheered. Behind him fluttered the new American flag, sporting its proud red and white stripes and its circle of stars in a blue field. The American Congress had only just approved it for the navy three weeks before and the city was in awe. The white-shirted soldiers formed a friendly but imposing line between the prisoners and their countrymen. The officer smiled and raised his hand. The man had a quality of bold confidence that quieted the marketplace. The mood became almost reverent. "Good citizens of these United States."

A rousing roar rose up. The officer smiled proudly and nodded to the crowd. "Good citizens. I am Captain Allen McLane and I am proud to serve you."

Another cheer filled the air.

"We are no rabble. We are men of law and it is for the rule of law we fight. Your sons, husbands, and fathers serve bravely for the order of a Republic, not for anarchy." He nudged his mount along the line, slowly. His face was friendly and inspiring. "Our fair capital city shall soon be hosting two men of note. It is our hope that your behaviour will not make them wonder about the goodness of our cause. The Marquis de Lafayette shall be taking quarters at Mayor Powell's home not more than a few blocks from here. And with him is General Baron Johann de Kalb, that most fat and furious Bavarian."

The mob laughed. It was rumoured he was neither a baron nor a general, but it seemed to matter little. As for the Marquis, the ladies of Philadelphia swooned at the mention of his name. The handsome young Frenchman was said to enchant whole cities with his charm and grace.

"And your faithful representatives in the Congress do labour at your own State House. We need not discourage their duties with such a show as this. Look here. You pummel these Tories like they were common thieves and hooligans. The law does not call for this and decency ought not allow it." He pranced about on his horse and then changed his tone. He barked a firm command to his sergeant. "These men shall be released at once. Give them safe passage to their homes."

The surprised crowd muttered complaints and a few hollered catcalls at the soldiers. But in a few moments the stocks were opened and the suffering Tories were slumping their way out of the market as fast as their wobbling legs could carry them. Despite a few lingering grumbles, the crowd then agreed to follow the officer in a spirited 'Huzzah' for the Stars and Stripes. The fifes and drums played a cheerful tune and a happy mood lifted the marketplace until the crowd dispersed.

Thaddeus and Webster shrugged and mumbled a reluctant respect for the American officer. They then decided it was time to find some other neighbourhood lads. Perhaps they could find Braddock Nester, the feisty Quaker. Braddock's father was part of the "fighting Quakers," a group of dissenters who supported the patriot cause and whose members had been cast out of their meetinghouse. Elizabeth Ross, the widow of John Ross—and the seamstress who had sewn the new flag—was also part of this group, and she now worshipped with the congregation of her deceased patriot husband at the Anglican Christ Church.

Braddock often travelled with Timothy Thomas and Richard Davis. Mrs. Browne was not particularly fond of the three, though she knew the Thomas and Davis families from church. Dr. Browne was not as offended with the lads' coarse ways as was his wife, but he, like her, did not care for their lack of basic manners. Nonetheless, Thaddeus had played with these three since he was a sprout, spending hours at Scotchhoppers or playing chuck-farthing, prisoner's base, and fives. Lately, however, the three had been distant and even insulting towards Webster especially, but also towards Thaddeus.

The two walked along the busy rows of peddlers' stalls and standing oxen. Chickens clucked and geese honked, horses whinnied and snorted, and sheep bleated. The boys' noses filled with the strong smells of the urine of oxen, the manure of horses, tobacco, sweated leather, and hay. Auctioneers sang their cadence from their blocks as chests and barrels, carts, kegs, baskets, and wheelbarrows of foodstuffs and dry goods, livestock, and ale were bought, sold, and traded in what seemed to the untrained ear to be sheer confusion. It was a place like no other.

Seamen in groups of twos and threes strutted in their rolled-up pants, well tarred, flat-brimmed hats atop their heads. They were a fearsome sight to Webster. His father had often warned him to avoid the wharves at night. "Press gangs will steal you sure. They need short men for the low quarters—and your wide bottom will plant you well on deck."

Amidst the sailors and rough dock workers preened the ladies of wealth. Shaded by their parasols and hand fans, they bade their servants pick through the best of the cabbages and turnips and other fresh vegetables. Thaddeus was glad his mother was more modest in her ways. She carried herself with a dignity these strutting birds could only hope to imitate. Their scurrying servants—some of whom were Negro slaves, some indentured whites—were flushed-faced and dripping. The sleeves of their simple dresses were rolled up to the forearm and the buns of hair atop their heads were covered with floppy straw hats or cloth caps.

Thaddeus suddenly saw Braddock's towhead bobbing at the riverside of the shambles. "There," he pointed. "Come on, Webster, let's go."

Thaddeus trotted toward his three friends with a grin spread wide across his face. Webster was panting and had lagged some distance behind. "Ho, ho, Brad, Tim—Richard!" cried Thaddeus. "I've not seen you for—for maybe a fortnight or more." He tipped his tricorn hat back on his head and smiled.

Another boy was standing with the three. He was bigger than the others and stood wide-legged, arms folded and his chin lifted up like some strutting cock-bird. Thaddeus' friends shifted awkwardly on their feet and stared at the ground. "So," began the stranger. "You'd be Thaddeus and that fat one is Webster."

Thaddeus was suddenly uncomfortable. "Aye. And who would you be?"

The boy smiled. "I am Gilbert Oakely. What of it?"

Thaddeus remembered his manners and extended a reluctant hand toward Gilbert.

"I'll not shake the hand of a traitor." He slapped Thaddeus' hand away and pushed his hat off his head.

Thaddeus was generally not one for impulse. Some even described him as a bit mulish. More often than not he was like his mother, slow to anger and reserved. But he was not afraid to speak bluntly and to the point when the occasion required. And he was his father's son as well. He leaned his face into Gilbert's. "So, you'd be another hero of liberty, eh?"

"What of it?"

"Then why aren't you chasing Redcoats with my brother? You'd be about fifteen. They'd gladly have you."

Gilbert paused. He had thought the smaller Thaddeus would cower at his bluster. He paused for a moment and licked his lips, then turned to the other three hollering for all to hear. "This little Tory thinks the rest of us are cowards." He looked for reinforcements and pointed to some German boys walking by with a milk cow and a cart. "You there, do you speak English?"

The Germans were taken by surprise. They had no interest in some English street squabble and their religion forbade them to engage in conflicts of the world.

"I know that one," pointed Timothy. He was anxious to keep Gilbert as a friend. "He's Ezra Kolb, one of those Mennonites from Germantown. My mother buys cheese and cabbage from his father."

Ezra stepped forward. "*Ja*. I shpeak sum English."

Gilbert circled him and smiled. The German was probably only thirteen or fourteen, but was a head taller than all of them and had the shoulders of a full-grown man. His round face was edged by brown bangs, which peeked from beneath his straw hat.

He would do, Gilbert thought. "Good. I'll keep it simple for you. This traitor says you are a coward."

Ezra shrugged and looked at his cow. He chuckled, innocently. "I am no cow—dis is de cow."

Braddock, Timothy, and Richard roared. Braddock pointed to Webster with a big grin. "And he is a pig."

The boys howled and the Germans smiled, albeit politely. Thaddeus protested. "What are you doing, Brad? I thought maybe you had a ball for a game of fives; I—"

"Fives? We'd not be playing handball any more, Thaddeus. You're now a traitor."

Timothy and Richard folded their arms and glared at Thaddeus and Webster. Gilbert put an arm around Ezra and spoke very slowly. "Listen again. He said your *mother* is a *cow*."

Thaddeus' mouth dropped open and he turned his eyes to the German whose face was suddenly red and tight.

"N-no—I said no such thing. I—"

Mennonite or not, Ezra Kolb rolled up his homespun sleeves and began to stalk poor Thaddeus. Thaddeus held his hands out and tried to explain the misunderstanding, all to the delight of the unholy foursome leaning against the German's cart.

Young Webster was not a particularly brave boy, so he found peace-making a tempting option. As noble as his gesture was intended to be, however, it was not handled very well. He came behind the Kolb lad and reached his hand toward the towering Teuton's muscled shoulder. At the touch, Ezra wheeled about and planted a solid fist into Webster's surprised face. The poor, well-meaning chubbling staggered backwards, crying in pain, and fell to the street.

Thaddeus watched Webster crash to the cobblestones. He barely had time to react when the angry German spun back around and ground a hard set of knuckles into his own face. The lad fell back a step or two but was caught by the suddenly sympathetic hands of Richard. Thaddeus grit his teeth and set his jaw. Even mules can be provoked. He charged the Anabaptist with a yell. But Ezra caught the angry boy with ease and tossed Thaddeus away like a cat throws a mouse.

Good Webster climbed to his quaking feet and took a deep breath. He stepped toward the combatants in another admirable effort to end the fight but it seemed to all the others that he was about to "double-up" on Ezra. That was, of course, a foul and he was pounced upon by Ezra's heretofore silent friends. In moments, the street was a mass of screaming boys and flying fists encircled by a cheering, laughing mob.

Then, with a loud Indian yell and blazing green eyes, Penelope Browne joined the mêlée. The girl was no lady. There was simply no escaping that fact. As hard as her mother had tried, she seemed to "lack the natural proclivities granted others." Or so her aunt had once concluded. Long-armed and leggy, the lanky miss entered the swarm with fists and feet flying. Nor was she averse to inflicting a good bite. Girls, it seems, were not bound by rules.

Ezra bellowed as the redhead sunk her bared whites into his forearm. It was enough for him to sound retreat. The Germans hurried away and Penelope then turned her fired eyes toward Gilbert and his companions. Webster and Thaddeus stepped to her side and the three stood shoulder-to-shoulder, ready for more. Gilbert shrugged and boasted that he had never stooped to fight a girl. He walked quickly away.

Thaddeus exhaled slowly and turned toward Brad, Tim, and Richard, who lingered nearby. Sheepishly, Richard spoke first. "I—we are sorry. I think the war is changing us." The group paused for a moment, and then shook hands, apology accepted.

As his friends turned away, Thaddeus looked at his sister. "Mother says you shouldn't fight," he grumbled. He was not all that happy to be rescued by his sister.

Penelope waited.

"But—thanks for your help—again. "Thaddeus smiled and embraced his twin.

Penelope grinned and winced. "Ouch. Is my lip bleeding?"

Webster examined it. "Aye, Penny. It's a good cut, too. You'll need some chickweed ointment and a compress, and—"

"Our father is a *doctor*, Webster," interrupted Thaddeus.

"And I'm his apprentice, so I think she is in good hands."

"Uh, yes, of course." Webster laughed a little, but his red face purpled in embarrassment. He was always flustered when pretty Penny was near.

A familiar voice turned all heads. "Children?"

The three turned to see Dr. Browne panting behind them. "I was minding my own business over a pint of good English ale, just over there, when I heard my name being shouted by some patient of mine. 'Dr. Browne,' says she. 'Come at once. Some Mennonite is pounding your son.'

A Mennonite of all things. I could hardly believe it. How could you lose a fight to a peace-maker?" A smile urged the corners of the man's lips upwards. But now his back hurt. Running was no easy task for him. He had lost his left leg to a tomahawk in Quebec in the last war and he now walked with a wooden leg.

Looking at their father was suddenly difficult for the Browne twins. His father's horsehair wig had slid to one side and forward, his tricorn was tilted precariously atop the dislodged wig and his spectacles were cocked sideways on his nose. Penelope thought he looked like a madman loosed from the basement of the city hospital.

"By your looks I must be quite the sight. Well, I like to see you laugh. However, Penny, your mother will not be pleased this evening." He lifted her chin gently, and then held her hands lightly in his own. He had the special touch of a caring physician. "Your lip is split and swelling and I think you cut nearly every one of your knuckles. She's a gracious woman, my pumpkin, but your wounds won't spare you chores. And she'll be embarrassed at church."

"But you say Presbyterians are fighters. You always say it," countered Penelope.

Archibald laughed. "Aye, my deary." He turned to Thaddeus. "Now you, boy, are another story. You ought not to be provoking the German lads. They're simple, plain, good folk. I don't care what Dr. Franklin thinks of them. I like them. Picking on an Anabaptist is—well it just isn't a fit thing to do. They don't know how to fight. Next time go find yourself a Lutheran, or one of those Reformed fellows up-town. *They'll* give you a fight to remember."

"I think this one knows how to fight," groused Thaddeus.

"Enough. The matter is over. And what of you, Mr. Yates?"

Webster was rubbing his jaw with one hand and holding a kerchief on his nose with the other. Wanting very badly to seem brave, he simply grunted and gave a thumbs-up.

A familiar voice was suddenly heard. It was Mrs. Browne. She had come to shop but had heard about the commotion from the family's annoying neighbour, Mary Franks.

Archibald answered. "Aye, mother. Your children are fit and sound." The doctor paused to look at his wife. Some would have called her plain, but Archibald thought she was the loveliest woman in the city, perhaps in all the colony. Tall, thin, willowy and well bred, he felt fortunate that her father had arranged their introduction seventeen years prior. Her narrow, angular face was strong, yet tender. *A woman of grace*, he thought. And grace was a particular treasure for a good Calvinist like he.

Katherine sighed and studied the bruises rising on the three children. Her eyes lingered on Thaddeus as she prayed he would not join the war. They moistened as she thought of her eldest, Cameron. She hoped a few cuts and bruises would be the only thing he'd suffer. When her wet eyes met Penelope's, though, she smiled and shook her head. "The world shall never endure the likes of this one."

Charity was as much a part of the woman a warmth is of a Christmas hearth.

Katherine turned to Webster. She lifted his chin and stroked his hair. At her touch, the poor, motherless lad closed his eyes. A tear dripped down the boy's cheek and Mrs. Browne held him for a caring moment. "We are in difficult times, good Webster, but you are not alone."

She wiped her eyes with a kerchief as a hay cart rumbled across the cobblestones. She drew a deep breath and took her husband's hand. "I fear for all of us," she said with a trembling voice. "We are a family divided and we are standing in the centre of a storm. May it never be that we lose sight of each other as the night grows darker." The woman leaned against her husband and wept.

CHAPTER 2

The Storm Begins

THE MAN FULL of Trouble was Dr. Browne's favourite tavern. He would come to dine on the inn's specialities: spit-roasted beef or venison. Hunters from the "Neck," the lands south of the city, brought a regular supply of whitetail deer and occasional rabbits, or even turtles from the bogs. Archibald loved to smell the meat sizzling on the iron spits. Of course, the proprietors were outspoken patriots and boycotted mutton, as did their comrades in the other colonies. Sheep needed to be preserved at all costs so the army could be supplied with uniforms and blankets.

"I tell you it is so, Colonel," said John Wood as Dr. Browne entered the tavern door. John was a clockmaker and co-owner of the tavern. "The New York militias swear that they sailed on the 23rd of July and they headed southward."

"Your militia reports are never right," replied a voice from a far corner. "It makes no sense. Howe is to join with Burgoyne coming from Quebec and attack the colonies from north to south."

Colonel Braithewaite Jones slammed his pewter tankard on the table and swore an oath. "Hear me, Goodman Wood: I am the dock-master and responsible to defend this city. Washington has sent no word to me of any change." Jones was John Wood's partner and would have taken a contrary position no matter what the point.

John Wood shook his head and scowled. The title 'Goodman' was reserved for men of low standing or lacking in prestige, just as 'Goody' was for women. Coming from his partner it was an insult. He threw up his arms and stormed out of the tavern.

Confusion reigned in the early days of August. It was true that General William Howe, the commander-in-chief of His Majesty's armies in North America, had set sail from New York City, where he and his army had been quartered. The manoeuvre made no sense to the American generals and Washington was baffled. However, militia units relayed regular reports from fisherman off the sandy shores of New Jersey that confirmed that the British navy was sailing southward. It seemed suddenly possible that Howe was moving to take Philadelphia.

A calm voice entered the conversation. "Joseph Galloway is the cause."

All eyes turned to see a confident, elderly man smoking a clay pipe. "That pestilent fellow has the ear of Howe and has turned the strategy of the King."

"Galloway? How is it possible for that rake to turn a King?" said Colonel Jones.

"I've a friend, a merchant in New York who is a Tory and present at every grand ball the general attends. It seems Galloway has convinced the British that Philadelphia and the whole of this region is filled with loyal subjects impatiently waiting to form an army in support of the crown."

Dr. Browne listened carefully. He knew Joseph Galloway. The man had been an outspoken champion of the rights of Englishmen in the First Continental Congress some four years ago but had withdrawn his sympathies for the colonists when the more extreme patriots gained influence. "And what of it?" Archibald asked.

"I have learned that he assures General Howe a British presence in Philadelphia could encourage thousands of able-bodied men to join the Loyalist regiments and likely double the King's forces. With such numbers they would be able to squeeze Washington between Howe and Burgoyne."

Archibald nodded. "Seems a possible explanation. Galloway is a man of sway."

"Aye. 'Tis true enough. He is also a man of deep conviction and passionate for Parliament and the King. Philadelphia is his home and the British are convinced he knows us well."

Dr. Browne knew his son, Thaddeus, would be excited about such news and his heart sank. He could not bear Cameron's enlistment even under the American flag. To envision Thaddeus dying for the King and Parliament was more than he could endure.

Lightly oiled by English ale and American rum, Archibald decided to set politics aside. He reached into his pocket to retrieve his spoon as the server arrived. As with most folks of "middling" means, the Brownes owned no forks. It was a matter of some complaint for his wife, as the more fashionable of the city were now acquiring them. Even the Continental Army had been issued wire forks to help with the foraged beef or pork they roasted over their open flames. But since most meats were stew meats, spoons and knives were generally all that were needed. Furthermore, since Dr. Browne was aware that disease was somehow spread through unwashed utensils, he insisted that his family use their own spoons.

The serving maid appeared with a smile and a poplar wood bowl of hasty pudding. The pudding had been sweetened with molasses and brushed with butter. Archibald smiled again and sucked the pudding off his spoon slowly, rolling his eyes with delight. Meanwhile, three large leather jugs, called "black jacks," were set on the table to be shared by all. The doctor took the jug in two hands and nodded his thanks. He leaned his head back and drew a long, satisfying draught. "Kill-devil. That New England rum shall be the end of us for sure." The table roared. "Someone pass the applejack."

Applejack was a drink of cider blended with brandy. It passed through a flock of fingers toward the doctor as a diner from the end of the table announced, "John Adams drinks one full tankard of hard cider at each day's rising." He took a hearty swig. "The Whigs are on to something."

More diners crowded along the table leaving Archibald squeezed shoulder by shoulder along his bench. The hungry diners licked their lips as a huge pewter platter heaped with steaming chunks of beef and venison was placed on the table. A large, two-pronged fork and the long carving knife were plunged into the rare, roasted meat. An elderly Quaker man was granted the honour of carving. He cut and sawed like an Italian sculptor." Doctor Brown," he said, as he waved a slab of dripping beef, "may I serve thee?"

"Indeed, and with thanks." Archibald did not like most Quakers. He thought they were, at best, saints in matters of religion, but devils in matters of politics and business. The Quaker smiled and plopped the beef on Archibald's trencher. The ale-maid grunted and hefted a large potato pot atop the table along with twifflers of corn pudding.

A bit more oiled with rum, Archibald then said, "Nature gave Mother England neither corn nor potatoes." He licked his lips. The potatoes were cooked with butter, sugar, and wine, and topped with cinnamon. The table was soon graced with a basin of boiled cabbage, a clay bowl of boiled beans, and a basket of fresh-baked bread.

When the diners were finished, a large, perspired workman shuffled out of the pantry carrying a heavy contraption made from a half-barrel. He set it on the floor with a bang and lifted off a wooden lid. The patrons climbed from their benches and crowded around, staring at a milky substance from which cold air was steaming toward their dumbstruck faces.

"Citizens of a free Pennsylvania," said Colonel Jones. "I've a treat just new from New York. For six-pence a scoop, come taste what you shall ne'er forget. It is called 'iced cream.'"

Archibald Browne was first in line. Americans, whether Whig or Tory, had one thing in common: They loved sugar and anything sweet.

If only such a common delight such has iced cream could have spared them all for what was to come.

--→▰◉ ◉▰←--

It was a sultry Sunday morning in late August when a group of riders charged through the streets of Philadelphia. "The army's coming! The army's coming!"

Thaddeus and his father were returning home after attending an elderly woman ravaged by fever. Dr. Browne whispered to his son, "Find out whose army."

Thaddeus sprinted past a small flock of lazy chickens, scattering them in all directions. He charged past a couple of wandering hogs, two dozing hackneys, and a milk cow. At last he arrived at the shaded grounds of the State House where he begged information from a nervous young Continental soldier pacing by the stables. Chatting briefly with the soldier, he returned to his father.

Archibald was waiting impatiently on the street. "Yes, yes?"

Thaddeus caught his breath. "*Your* army."

Dr. Browne stiffened a little. He answered curtly. "You might have said, 'Washington's army,' or the 'American army,' or perhaps, 'Cameron's army.'" Archibald sighed. "What else have you learned?"

"It seems the King's army has landed somewhere south of Wilmington and is expected to move to Philadelphia."

Archibald groaned. "I feared it would be so. Go on."

"Washington is marching toward them in haste and shall come directly through the city tomorrow."

The doctor nodded and stared at the empty street. *Things are about to change,* he thought. He closed his eyes. "Boy, say nothing of this to your mother. I shall tell her after a restful lunch." The two walked toward home and arrived just as Penelope and Katherine were returning from morning prayers. Services at Pine St. Presbyterian started at nine o'clock, as they did at St. Peter's, the Anglican church next door. The Presbyterian reverend dismissed his congregation for a lunch interlude at the same time as the reverend Coombs of St. Peter's. It was an agreement that protected each congregation from the noisy chatter of parishioners parading down the sidewalks.

Penelope grumbled and wiped perspiration from her brow. She was required to carry a parasol and hand fan in a dutiful but futile effort to keep her skin from tanning. Penelope chafed at such bridles. "It is as hot as the fires of eternal Hell in that brick oven."

Thaddeus understood. He wished he could go to St. Peter's for lots of reasons, not the least of which was that St. Peter's was cooler in the summer, due to its higher ceiling and bigger windows. The boy pulled at his woollen coat and scratched his knee-length stockings.

As Mrs. Browne opened the front door, Cromwell dashed out for a day of mousing. Cromwell was a wily grey tabby cat found by Katherine one cold winter several years ago. Dr. Browne did not share his wife's affection for cats, but was often willing to forego his own preferences in favour of his wife's joy. In return, Mrs. Browne agreed to name the pet after one of Archibald's heroes, that champion of English liberty, Oliver Cromwell.

Mrs. Browne closed the door and walked through the front room where her husband had his office, then into the rear room that was used for her sewing, spinning, and weaving. She proceeded to the corner of what her family called "the loom room" and descended the stairway that led to the cool of her cellar kitchen. There she prepared a quick lunch of berry preserves and day-old bread. She added some cider, a few strips of salted pork, and some milk cooled by ice stored in the small sub-cellar.

The others relaxed in the garden behind the house. The well-manicured apple tree that grew in one corner provided welcome shade on days such as these. Its branches were trimmed to allow the sun to reach the vegetables and herbs planted in neat rows nearby. Cabbage, turnips, beans, beets, asparagus, parsley and the like served the kitchen well enough, and for the doctor there were rows of medicinals, such as clary-water, feverfew, chickweed, chamomile, and others. A short hedge of black currant lined the fence to the south side, and a hedge of sweet and pungent "lad's love" to the rear. Since the Brownes lived at the end of their row, there was a narrow strip of yard bordering the side alley. This was filled with delights for both eye and nose, and had even yielded play toys for the children when they were young.

C. D. Baker

Penelope had found great amusement in searching for the shapes of monstrous faces in the centre of peonies, or displaying the image of the 'Old Lady's Washed Feet' within the petals of the heart's-ease. Thaddeus had squeezed many a helpless bloom to make coloured inks from nectars and saps, and he had gathered leaves and petals to craft tiny boats to float in Dock Creek.

Summers were a joy for these garden-bred twins and Katherine took a special pleasure in her flowers, spending hours bent over her gardens, weeding and harrowing her beloved little friends. She planted tall and varied hollyhocks in the spreading shade of another's chestnut tree. She added happy-faced daisies, purple mourning-brides and pink sweet peas. Was that not a tapestry enough, she tended buttercups and peonies, morning glories, johnny-jump-ups, and sunflowers. It was a glorious place. Of course, it was fenced all the way round to keep wandering hogs from rooting it up and chickens from snapping off tender shoots.

Archibald paused at the sundial and made sure no neighbourhood rascal had turned it again. Its inscription had been taken from the Song of Solomon:

> *Awake, O north wind; and come, thou south;*
> *Blow on my garden that its fragrance may drift afar.*

A bee landed on the man and he shooed it lightly away. A few doors away, Mrs. Mary Franks, the milliner, kept several hives, but shared their honey with no one. Dr. Browne saw her over the short, backyard fences and turned quickly away. He could not imagine a better way to ruin a summer's Sabbath than by having a "fence chat'" with Mary Franks. The man walked toward his daughter. "Penny," he said. "Do you recall the hours you spent playing here?"

Penelope smiled. When she was very young she had indeed spent many a summer's day enjoying the colour and aroma of the garden. "Aye, father. They were good times. I pressed flowers in my primer—I still have many of them—and blew up morning glories to pop at church."

Dr. Browne laughed. "I always thought it was Thaddeus. I should have known." He lay back on the grass beneath his apple tree and smiled. Katherine came from her kitchen with the family's lunch. "And you loved my Jack-in-the-pulpits. You'd pinch them and make them 'preach.'"

The family lounged about the garden, refreshed and drowsy. Katherine and Penelope, of course, remained protected from the sun. They were compelled by taste to guard their soft complexions and keep them milky-white. Though Archibald respected the particular strength of his own dear wife and daughter, he agreed with the prevailing understanding of his times that the female gender was, in general, designed as the weaker one. He accepted some, but not all, of the numerous customs society prescribed that was intended to express this principle and to clearly differentiate the sexes.

Archibald thought that a creamy, porcelain complexion was a harmless and pleasing statement of the ideal. Furthermore, he liked the way hooped dresses accented the natural difference in a woman's shape, and he agreed that long hair was a biblical mark of femininity. But there was more.

Most girls, including Penelope, were required to endure the discomfort of backboards in their younger years. These were designed to assure straight posture, which, in turn, served to remind them of their need to be "upright." Her father, however, did not require that she suffer the agony that others did by having their feet bound within tiny shoes.

On the other hand, Penelope, like her mother, would not enjoy the benefits of university, though her father happily hired a private tutor for her betterment. Also, regardless of her personal competence, or the love of a caring father, it would be Penelope's likely destiny to live her public life within the identity of either her father or her future husband.

Yet Katherine and Penelope understood that these proscriptions were not intended to be cruel. They shared the common view that a woman's natural weakness could make her dangerous to herself and even to the world around her. Lucifer, after all, had recognised this fact of the creation and had chosen to tempt Eve, not Adam. It was Eve who then allied with the devil as a co-conspirator against the stronger Adam. In all his natural strength, poor Adam could not avail against the two. Therefore, it was a reasoned conclusion that the virtue and honour of men, as well as the civilisations they ruled, were in constant jeopardy from the frailties of these weaker vessels.

The family dozed for a short while, carried to their pleasant dreams by the happy songs of birds and the drone of busy bees. The conversation of a few passing neighbours awakened the family and the doctor stirred. He rubbed his eyes and checked the sundial. Their time was nearly spent and they'd be returning for afternoon services shortly.

Knowing the church would be filled with talk of the army's imminent arrival, Archibald called his family to order. "We've news before we go," said Dr. Browne. "While you were at worship, riders came through the city and announced that General Washington's army is coming."

Katherine stood up. "Cameron?"

"My thoughts, too. But it seems the British army is landed near Wilmington and wants to take Philadelphia for the winter. I fear a fight is coming." He looked at his quiet family and a deep sadness filled his face. "We need to pray in earnest for—" he hesitated. He secretly prayed for American victories but wanted to respect his wife and son. "We need pray for our Cameron."

Katherine trembled. "Husband," she said slowly, "we must also pray that we see him."

Archibald thought for a moment. He was wise to the pain of unrealised expectations. He knew the army would be hurrying towards duty and Cameron would surely not be dismissed to visit his family. But as difficult as the world often was, it was surely not empty of hope. "Dear Kate, it is a good prayer. We shall pray we see him, if only for a moment."

⇢⇒⊙ ⊙⇐⇠

The night was a restless one for not only the Brownes but also the whole city that was anxious. It seemed that the street watch were shouting their reports more loudly and more horses clip-clopped atop the cobblestones than usual. Katherine spent much of her night on her knees, begging God to protect her son in the battle sure to come. "And if I might humbly ask Thee," she prayed, "Thy servants would be grateful if we could but have a glance of our brave son."

By the first crowing of the city's roosters, the morning candles and oil lamps had been long lit. Archibald thought the dawn was a particularly bold one, and it seemed to burst upon the city with an urgency befitting the day to come. In the first hour of daylight, an advance company of mounted men charged along Second Street and assembled at the shambles. Crowds of curious onlookers raced down Union to see them. Dr. Browne gathered his excited family and began to hurry them down the half-block to Second, where they turned to the right, into the marketplace.

A weary-looking officer barked some orders to his men and they dismounted. The crowd pressed around them, bringing cheese and milk, morning bread and jams. The grateful men ate ravenously. Whittaker Yates, Webster's father, was a Loyalist, though not a zealot. He had refused to take the oath, but admitted sympathies to the patriot cause. Generally timid and extremely cautious, he rarely dared adventure. On this morning, however, the man could not remain in his apothecary. He craned his long neck in search of his good friend, Dr. Browne, and upon seeing the doctor he called loudly. "Archibald, old fellow."

Dr. Browne turned to see a long arm waving high in the air and Whittaker's smiling face towering above the crowd. He chuckled and waved to him. Whittaker was probably the tallest man in Philadelphia. Long-legged, long-armed, long-necked, and long-suffering, the man was indeed a good friend. Penelope and Thaddeus worked hard to not laugh each time they saw him. He was spindly and lanky, awkward and a bit clumsy. He walked excessively upright so as not to lose his wig and tricorn. Penelope was an imaginative girl and claimed she sometimes dreamt of poor Mr. Yates as if he were a daddy long-legs, smiling.

Whittaker's wife had died giving birth to Webster, and he had never remarried. She had been a cheerful, squat little woman and the two had laughed and sung in every season. Archibald and Katherine used to take tea with the pair and both had been truly saddened at the woman's death. It was grievous that the midwife had failed to call on Dr. Browne that awful night. "Good morning to you, sir. And to you." As was the custom of those times, Mr. Yates "made a leg," by setting his right leg out stiffly and bowing slightly as he tipped his hat.

Dr. Browne and Thaddeus returned the "leg," as Katherine and Penelope offered the courtesy of a "sink," or curtsy: clasping their hands together at their waists, they put one shoe at right angles to the other, and dipped downwards with a straight back and lowered eyes.

All courtesies exchanged, Whittaker called for Webster to hurry and join them. "Dr. Browne," Whittaker began, "I am told the army is to arrive by mid-morning."

"So I've heard as well."

"They would have crossed upriver from New Jersey yesterday and I suspect they'll come through Germantown and on the Germantown road into the city."

"Agreed."

"I think the officers may pause at Christ Church."

Archibald shook his head. "No. Judging by the look of these poor souls, I think the army is in some hurry. I think they'll not be pausing anywhere."

Whittaker thought carefully, and then nodded. "You've made good sense, again. Surely they'll come down Second Street, then directly past us and through the shambles. Look there." He pointed to a crew of men suddenly pulling sheds and booths away from the market centre. "See. The way is being cleared. These cavalry shall clear all of Second Street."

Katherine's heart was pounding. "One look at my son— just one look."

Whittaker craned his neck in search of a good vantage point from which to observe the passing troops. "Archibald, we could gather up-town a bit. Wider walks and—"

"I think not. We've more interest in Cameron than anything else. I've reasoned that he would most likely look hard up Union as he marches by. He's a clever lad; I think he may even work his position to the right edge of his column."

Katherine nodded and smiled. "Aye, he is a clever one. He'd think of that, wouldn't he?"

The men agreed it was a sound plan and they pressed their way back to the southwest corner of Second and Union. Webster soon found them, and there the group formed a tight ball that could not be jostled out of position, waiting in the heat of the morning as the crowd thickened around them.

About ten-thirty a faint cheer was heard in the north. An excited titter rippled through the neighbourhood of Union Street. Anxious men lifted to their tiptoes and impatient children raced up Second Street toward the noise. The cheers grew louder and closer and the sudden shrill of fifes drew tears to all. "They're coming!" shouted a wild rider as he charged past. "They're coming!"

A smart company of advance dragoons trotted their mounts calmly down Second and urged the cheering onlookers back to the walkways. The sweet song of the fifes now floated lightly toward them like a symphony of songbirds, and the steady, measured, rat-tat-tat of the snares kept perfect time with the tramp of feet thumping ever closer. Katherine's eyes blurred with tears as she strained forward to see her boy-soldier.

"There!" cried a voice. The crowd at Union began to cheer and hurrah. Hats raised to the sky as men, women, and children rallied their voices for the column of white breeches and the patchwork of vari-coloured coats and hunting shirts sweeping toward them. The noise became deafening as the first line passed Union. Penelope cheered wildly, whooping and screeching like a savage Indian. This was *her* army. Archibald cheered as loud as the lump in his throat would allow and applauded each young face that brushed by him.

"Dear God," said Katherine. "Look at that one. He's so tired and pale, and the other is so old. He should be reading

Scripture to his grandchildren, not bearing arms. Look, husband, look. That one carries a musket, but I swear he cannot be eleven years. What madness is this?"

The American soldiers were weary and worn. Their uniforms were threadbare and some marched with no shoes. But behind each gaunt face were eyes set forward in duty and purpose. These brave bearers of liberty's torch marched proudly beneath the snapping furls of their new nation's flag. Brawny yeomen, shop keeps, and preachers; English, Irish, and Scottish heirs to the rights of free men stepped in determined unison with Germans, Dutchmen, Swedes, and a sprinkling of Africans. Boys as young as ten snapped the snares, while those as young as twelve shouldered the musket.

In Cameron's own regiment, there were one ten-year-old, three twelve-year-olds, two thirteen-year-olds, and one seventy-three year-old. Old men, young men, patriots all, now hurried past the Brownes. Dr. and Mrs. Browne strained to see the colours of Pennsylvania's Second Regiment.

"Whittaker, are you looking?" cried Katherine.

"I see Virginia and—and there is a Rhode Island; a Connecticut follows."

The stream of men marched at a quick pace, and the urgency on the faces of officers reminded all that these men were rushing into a storm. Dr. Browne studied the sad but resolute faces passing by and prayed for them. He remembered the horror of war from his own time of service to the King and wished they all could be spared. He believed the American cause was just and necessary, but he could not avoid a reluctant and even sympathetic understanding of the position of their foes.

A large hand suddenly fell on Dr. Browne's shoulder. Archibald was startled and spun around. "Josiah!"

Upon hearing the name, the whole family turned. "Josiah Byrd!"

The man smiled. "I am looking, too. He's a good boy, your Cameron."

Penelope and Thaddeus patted the old man's back and Katherine welcomed him with a smile and a quick curtsy. Together they stared ahead, waiting for Whittaker to see the regimental colours from his high advantage.

Archibald said, "Josiah, I need to tell you again that the powder horn you carved for Cameron was—was the most beautiful I've seen."

The Grackle smiled awkwardly and shuffled. "Thank you. I was happy to do it." Josiah had presented Cameron his hollowed ox-horn the day the lad had bid his family farewell. It had been a sad day for all and Katherine had been barely able to contain her tears until she read the words the man's gifted hands had inscribed. Josiah was unlearned but not illiterate. His deft fingers had carved an inscription that looked like the work of a writing-master:

> *The Lord is my rock and my fortress, and my*
> *deliverer; my God, my strength in whom I will trust.*
> *Psalms 18:2*

C. D. Baker

Penelope suddenly shrieked. "Look, Mr. Yates, look!" She had climbed on Thaddeus' shoulders and was pointing to a block of men approaching them from about one hundred yards away. Whittaker shouted, "The Second Pennsylvania."

Katherine's heart stopped. She cared not one whit that her daughter's petticoats were tangled and flapping above the cheering crowd. She wanted only to see her son. Tramp-tramp-tramp sounded the march of hard leather on the cobblestones. The Georgians passed by, then a company of sharpshooters in their fringe and buckskin. At last, the banners of Cameron's regiment were seen fluttering proudly under the Philadelphia sky. Many of the lads were from the city and the street went wild. The fifes and drums struck up 'The Brickmaker March,' and the brave boys of the Pennsylvania Second Regiment passed by Union Street.

"Cameron! Cameron!" Katherine gasped and clutched her breast. There was her boy—*her* boy.

Cameron was one away from the column's edge. He had lost his coat but was wearing the heavy linen shirt his mother had sewn for him months ago. His knee breeches were torn but the boots his father had bought him were well polished. His right hand gripped the strap of his musket anxiously as he craned his neck and strained his longing eyes toward Union. When he saw his mother's frantic charge toward him, he broke rank and tumbled out of the column and into her arms.

"Mother, dear mother!" the sobbing boy cried. He ignored the shouts of his officers and embraced the weeping woman. He wiped his eyes and looked up to see his father pushing and shoving his way toward him. The seventeen-year-old laughed for joy.

Ahead of the one-legged doctor rushed the twins, crying his name. In another moment the whole family was embracing and weeping, "Cameron. O thanks be to God for Cameron."

A firm hand seized the lad by the shoulder and pulled him back into the flooding river of patriots. "Private. In the line, lad, in the line." It was Captain Roger Staynor of Cameron's Company D.

With a desperate lunge, Cameron struggled to touch his family one last time, but it was not to be. He cried out for his own and stretched his fingers toward them, but he was quickly swept away between the surging shoulders of his comrades.

CHAPTER 3

Redcoats in the City

"IT IS GOD'S will," answered Dr. Browne. He had received news of the war and was troubled. He closed the front door and walked slowly to the chair by the fireplace. It was a dreary day in mid-September, but no fire flickered in his hearth. He looked sadly at the doorway separating his office from the back room where his wife was busy weaving cloth on her loom.

"Was that the weaver's man, husband?" Katherine asked.

"Aye. He brought his payment for your work." The weaver commissioned private work from many of the city's housewives, from which he made a variety of blankets, garments, and other textiles for sale around the world. He and his workmen were famous for their news mongering and they travelled throughout the city, passing information more quickly than any corner gossip. It was just such a bit of news that Dr. Browne had received.

"I hope he paid us in the King's sterling," said Katherine over the rhythmic thumping of her pedals and shuttle.

Dr. Browne looked helplessly at the fistful of Continental dollars he held. He had other thoughts on his mind, however. He removed his spectacles and cleaned them with a small rag.

His silence caught his wife's attention. The loom became quiet and the woman walked carefully into her husband's office. She faced him and waited.

Archibald picked aimlessly at a bit of yarn snagged by a splinter on his wooden leg. The cheerful red trim of his room did little to brighten his spirits on this miserable day. He stared aimlessly across the room and out of his two front windows, moodily watching the torrential rain that was washing the brick and cobblestones of Union Street.

"You have news?" asked Katherine.

The man nodded and rose. "Yes," he answered slowly. "Two things. Old Goody Peters is suffering with fever again."

"She's the one you attended on the Sabbath last month."

"Yes. She is a wise woman. She gave me some good thoughts for my 'commonplace.'"

Many men gathered wise sayings and sound advice throughout their lifetimes and wrote them in what were known as "commonplace books." These commonplaces were greatly cherished by both the compilers and their descendants.

Archibald chuckled. "I told her that her wisdom was payment enough—and she agreed." He walked to his desk and thumbed to the last page in his commonplace. "She told me last week that 'time is like a little mouse. When noticed, it hurries; when not, it creeps.'" Archibald paused and turned back a number of pages. "Here she told me how to resolve a dilemma of conscience. She said, 'When the conscience is strained by conflicting beliefs, seek to find the one of *highest* virtue and yield to that.'"

Katherine agreed. "Aye, husband. She is wise indeed. But you said you've news of two things?"

Archibald nodded and set his book down. He filled his nose with the damp, musty air of his book-filled room and rubbed Cromwell's neck. "Howe has defeated Washington along the Brandywine Creek—about thirty miles south-west of here."

Katherine waited, suddenly nervous.

"I've no news of Cameron, though I do have some of his regiment. His captain, that Staynor fellow, has family on Chestnut. It seems Cameron's company was guarding a place called Chadd's Ford—and was overrun."

Katherine gasped. Dr. Browne rose and held her tightly. He assured her that they would soon learn if the boy had been wounded, captured—or worse.

Penelope and her tutor, Mr. Gregor Robertson, suddenly appeared in the loom-room doorway. She had been studying in the upstairs front parlour and was bleary-eyed and bored. The tutor, a stern, icy-eyed Scot, waited respectfully for Dr. Browne to console his wife, then cleared his throat.

Archibald turned. "I beg your leave, but my wife is troubled by news of the war."

The Scot's face darkened. "Tell me not of defeat."

"I am afraid it is so."

"Ach. That cursed, crabbed race of red-coated leeches. That swarm of vulgar locusts—"

Penelope nodded her head and added, "Those encroaching spawn of tyranny, those—"

"Enough," said Mrs. Browne. "I am so weary of this war. I do not need my daughter spewing vile indecencies. Some of these 'encroaching spawn' are sons or husbands of dear friends of this family. I dare say a few may be cousins to us as well. Mr. Robertson, is this what you teach my daughter?"

The teacher bowed curtly. "I beg your pardon."

Dr. Browne led the old Scot toward the door. "You are a good man, Mr. Robertson, and a good instructor. These times draw sentiments from us that can easily offend or wound others. And for some, these times have worn their patience into a thin fabric." Archibald closed the door.

Thaddeus entered the room. "Father, does this mean the British army will take the city?"

"You'd hope so, wouldn't you," scowled Penelope.

"Enough, girl. Thaddeus, I do not know. It seems likely to me. Washington's army can not fight in this rain and is in retreat." Dr. Browne turned to his daughter again, wanting very much to change the subject. "I see you have two books in your hand."

Penelope hesitated. "Mr. Robertson said I ought replace my old primer with the latest one. He presented it as a gift to me. He said we ought to destroy the old one."

"Why so?" asked Mrs. Browne, suspiciously.

The girl looked at her feet and rocked nervously.

"Well?"

"There's been a change, that's all."

Mrs. Browne looked troubled. "A change? I should like to see the change."

"Perhaps a better time, mother, perhaps—"

"This is a fine time."

Penelope looked at her father with pleading eyes. He answered sternly, "Do as your mother asks."

The girl nodded and opened her old *New England Primer*. It was a wonderful little book that had belonged to her mother and had guided both Penelope and her brothers in their very young years. About eighty pages long, it contained the Lord's Prayer, the Apostles' Creed, morning and evening prayers, the alphabet with rhymes, and a syllabarium—a dictionary of pronunciation containing words such as abomination, mortification, and purification.

Of course, before learning her primer, she had studied with her hornbook—a simple piece of wood with a sheet of coarse paper bearing the alphabet, some syllables, and the Lord's Prayer. As little children, Penelope and her brother had carried them around their necks on leather cords. From her hornbook she had gone to the *Primer* and the discipline of the backboard for Mrs. Browne, under the influence of her great aunt, Margaret Shippen Howell, had insisted that Penelope develop "an upright carriage, a sound and rigorous mind, and the virtue of elegance." Strapped to the long, oak board, like many of her generation and others gone by, she had studied the Psalms, the New Testament, and then the whole of the Bible which, by her thirteenth year, she had read through for the third time.

Penelope had also been taught the art of fine penmanship, or knotting, as it was called, by a writing-master, and her father had insisted she also learn a bit of Latin, some basic geography, and the etiquette of proper dance. Mr. Robertson had been her tutor since she had begun the Psalms, and now instructed her from *Cocker's Arithmetic*.

Thaddeus regularly complained that his sister enjoyed great leisure in her learning compared to the rigours he endured. He suffered long hours under the willow wand of Schoolmaster Smith at the Quaker school. However, he was not bound to a board.

Penelope opened her old primer to the alphabet rhymes. A few stiff rose petals slid from the corner-worn pages and fell to the ground. She picked them up carefully and placed them neatly in the supple crease of the comfortable book. She then handed it to her mother. "Look here, at the rhyme for the letter 'K'."

"You need not show me, daughter. I remember it well:

> *'King Charles the good,*
> *No man of blood.'"*

Archibald groaned.

Thaddeus leaned forward.

Penelope opened the new primer to the letter "K". "Uh, it reads differently now. It says:

> *'Queens and Kings*
> *Are gaudy things.'"*

Katherine Browne was displeased. Pursing her lips, she said, "I hope you see, daughter, the difference between the two books. The first is filled with pressed flowers and familiar words. It boasts tradition and has weathered the tests of time. This new thing is—a new thing. It has no past, no seasoning, and no character. It boasts only anger and poor wit. It is a fitting thing for your rootless cause." She spun on her heels and disappeared behind a slamming door.

Fear soon gripped the city. Washington's aide, Alexander Hamilton, had been sent to warn the American Congress residing in Philadelphia that General Howe was approaching the Schuylkill River. It was not a complete surprise. A week or so earlier all bells had been ordered removed from public buildings in case the British could not be stopped. Among those removed was the State House bell, or Liberty Bell, as it had come to be called. The bell had been made twenty-six years earlier in Whitechapel, England, and commissioned by Philadelphia's Quakers to commemorate the fiftieth anniversary of William Penn's Charter of Privileges.

The Quakers were not so pleased that it had proclaimed the signing of the Declaration of Independence. Cracked and imperfect, like the new nation it represented, it was now a symbol that was worthy of rescue. Few patriots could imagine anything more repugnant than the Liberty Bell being melted into shot by the purveyors of tyranny.

Hamilton's news, however, made this suddenly a very real prospect.

Frantic and confused, the city's patriots now ran hither and fro, removing books and papers from the State Library, as well as court records, money, charters, and sundry accounts from various other places, and sending them some fifty miles to the north, to the cities of the Lehigh Valley, for safe keeping. Hamilton's information also prompted the members of the American Congress to make a speedy escape from the city. The capture of the colonies' delegates would be a blow the new nation could not survive. So, on Thursday, the eighteenth of September 1777, Congress abandoned the city and moved westward to the city of Lancaster, and then to York.

It was about one o'clock in the morning on September 19th that the Browne family was aroused by the shouts of citizens who were filling the streets. A wild rumour was flying from block to block that the British were about to enter the city.

"Dr. Browne?" cried a voice from the street. "Come at once. You need to leave the city."

Archibald rolled from his feather bed in the rear room of the second floor. He stumbled though the front parlour and opened a window to the street. "What? What say you?"

"Howe and his army are here."

The doctor paled and stared at the torches flaring up and down the street. His wife lit the oil lamp by the washbasin and carried it into the parlour. She looked at her husband in the dim light. The room's shadows were long and eerie and the terrifying cries from the street made her shiver in dread. Archibald steadied her and called up the stairs to the children. "Come all to the parlour. Wife, some candles."

In moments the family was huddled around a small table in the front room. The parlour was generally reserved for pleasant, social occasions and for dining with special guests. On this dark night it seemed hollow and cold. The doctor looked calmly at the three faces staring back at him. He asked all to sit on the wooden chairs he gathered from the room's outer edges. He wrapped his shoulders with a thin blanket and shivered slightly. His shaved head seemed small in the subtle light of the candles, but his clean-shaven face loomed large as he leaned closer to the table. "First, we shall pray the Lord's Prayer." He began, and the others followed. "Our Father, which art in heaven, hallowed be thy name, thy Kingdom come—"

When they had finished, Archibald paused for a moment, and then recited the Apostle's Creed, which he followed with a short prayer of his own. He then asked his family to recite the 46th Psalm:

> *God is our refuge and strength,*
> *An ever-present help in trouble.*
> *Therefore we will not fear, though*
> *The earth give way*
> *And the mountains fall into the*
> *Heart of the sea,*
> *Though its waters roar and foam*
> *And the mountains quake with*
> Their surging—

Calmed by the reminder of providential care, the Brownes relaxed and soon chuckled at the chaos outside their sturdy door. "Have you thoughts, children?"

Thaddeus answered first. "I think we are about to see a lot of change."

Penelope agreed. "Yes. The Tories shall have their vengeance."

"And why shouldn't they?" countered Thaddeus.

Mrs. Browne shook her head. "No, boy. Vengeance breeds the same. They should not because it is not right."

Thaddeus grumbled. "I tell you, mother, the rebels have made us pay a price."

"Rebels? It's your King and Parliament that's turned traitor against us," snapped Penelope.

"You read too much of that Thomas Paine. You ought to be reading the reverend Seabury or Joseph Galloway. You are the rebel."

"No more," said Dr. Browne. "No more of this. Each of you sit quietly and listen to me. I need to make some decisions for this family." He stared at his twins until they settled themselves. Content that peace had been restored, he continued. "I am well-known as a Whig; your mother is a known Loyalist. Because I took the oath of allegiance, the family has not suffered under the free government. But I shall not hide behind your mother's hoops when the enemy takes this city."

Katherine's face tightened. With a steady voice she asked, "Are we leaving the city, husband?"

The family held its breath as the doctor stared, deep in thought. "If we stay, our lives shall be changed. My conscience may bind all of you to trouble. If only I leave, you shall be at the mercy of Howe's army and his mercenaries. They will be like grinning wolves gloating over helpless prey.

"If we all leave, then you shall be subjected to a winter of misery in a strange place, and I shall ever afterwards believe myself a coward who abandoned his home to tyrants. Oh, I can not bear to yield my world to them." The man folded his hands and closed his eyes in prayer. He remained silent for a long while, as his family waited. At last he settled into his chair and spoke calmly. "We stay and we serve God in this place."

Katherine spoke tenderly and took his hand. "Brave Archibald, it makes me proud to call you husband. I do not share your cause, but I share this home with you. It is our home and we need to stay until God makes it plain to us to go."

The matter was settled.

⤙⤙⧫ ⧫⤚⤚

Sunday dawn brought a day of quiet. The rumours of the night before had evaporated before the dawn's mist had cleared. Though nearby, the British army had not entered the city, at least not just yet. But as Dr. Browne put it, "smoke precedes the dragon's fire."

Before leaving for church, Archibald arranged his family at the front door and carefully examined them, as he did each Sabbath. He made certain that both Katherine and Penelope were properly dressed. They were clothed very similarly, though Penelope had a penchant for bolder, brighter colours. Each wore a linen shift under her whalebone corset. The shift was a comfortable undergarment that could be tightened at the wrists and neck by simple drawstrings, serving as an undergarment in the day and a sleeping garment at night. The corsets, or stays, were much more confining and served to support the shape of a woman's hips and waist. Both of the Browne women had been put in corsets at about seventeen months of age.

Over the corset was placed a hoop, or pannier—a cloth covered basket that rode along the hips. The new fashions did not require the Brownes' to be nearly as wide as in times past. Over their hoops they wore their cotton petticoats, ruffled ones for Sunday, and atop all of this, each woman wore her gown. Mrs. Browne preferred a simple, light blue sack, as it was called, with ruffled shoulders and a square-cut neck. It was amply adorned with ruffles and lace. On the other hand, Penelope preferred her green caraco dress that she belted with a dramatic red sash.

Their hair was pinned up and placed neatly beneath their hats. Penelope boasted a bright blue velvet bonnet with a red plume. Katherine was ever so proud to sport a straw hat designed by Philadelphia's own hat maker, Mrs. Sibylla Masters. (Mrs. Masters had received an English patent—the first American to do so—for using palmetto and straw in her hats.) Each wore long, brown gloves and carried a fashionable fan. Their black, thin-leather shoes were clean and supple.

Dr. Browne frowned. "Penelope, have you been switching shoes?"

"Yes, father, faithfully."

The man looked closer. "The soles are wearing unevenly. Look at your mother's. They are perfect. I think you need to pay more heed."

"Yes, father."

Archibald was tempted to make a comment about the size of her feet as well. He turned to his son, instead. "Now you," began Archibald. "A quick look at you."

Thaddeus stood erect as his father circled him. "Good, good. Hair well greased..." Though others might have thought the boy somewhat plain, Dr. Browne thought the young man was handsome, despite his oversized ears. His round face was earnest and even. Nearly the height of his father, he had a proud bearing, like his mother, and looked particularly genteel in his Sunday clothing.

Thaddeus always took care to dress properly. He fancied himself to be a gentleman and even wanted to wear a wig. Boys from the gentry wore theirs by age twelve, but Archibald's hostility toward his own "vanity bush" ensured that the boy had not been granted permission to own one. Over his cotton dressing gown, a soft, one-piece body garment which was worn for both sleep and as underclothing, the young man wore blue breeches that were tight fitted to boast a man's muscular thigh. Below the knee he wore white silk stockings of a very fine weave that were secured to the breeches with red garters.

On his feet were heavy-soled black shoes that sported large silver buckles. Of course, like the women's, his shoes were not made with a left and right foot, as in later times, but could be worn on either foot. Thus they had to be regularly alternated from foot to foot in order to insure even wear. Thaddeus wore a ruffled cotton shirt whose ample sleeves protruded some inches from the sleeves of his brown velvet coat. The coat was cut away and fell to the back of the lad's knees. Its standing collar came high on his neck and its wide lapels were generously bordered by red brocade. For Sunday he set aside his tricorn hat and donned a leather flop hat, pinned up on one side.

Content that his family was presentable, the doctor smiled, and put on a number of the mourning rings he customarily received as gifts at the many funerals his profession called him to attend. Peeking outside at the drizzly day, he bade them all put on goloe-shoes, or overshoes, to protect their feet from puddles. Then, with all ceremony completed, the Browne family walked the block and a half to Pine Street Presbyterian Church.

The church, a simple, red brick building in the Georgian style—designed by Robert Smith, the renowned architect—had been built nine years prior, in 1768. It stood on the same side of Pine Street as St. Peter's Anglican church, but was separated from St. Peter's by Third Street and by each church's respective graveyards. The wigged, pinch-faced reverend, George Duffield, greeted the Brownes anxiously. "Aye, and peace to you all," he said, as he clasped hands with Archibald.

The family settled quickly into their customary pew. The twins could not help but twist their heads and gawk at the mere smattering of bowed heads scattered throughout the sanctuary. The booming voice of the reverend Duffield turned them forward. "Grace to you and peace from God our Father and the Lord Jesus Christ." The reverend hesitated. He pursed his thin lips and sucked a deep breath through his long nose, slightly enlarging his nostrils. Dr. Browne leaned forward, certain something was troubling the reverend Duffield.

Silent prayer was invoked, then a psalm was sung. The Book of Common Order was followed reasonably well, though Pine Street did not mind deviating from it from time to time. The Ten Commandments were recited by the congregation, a number of general confessions offered, and the day's first sermon preached. Then, after two more psalms and a prayer, the congregation was dismissed for lunch.

When they returned after lunch, the reverend Duffield led his small flock in the Apostle's Creed, and then baptised three infants and a new convert. The congregation sang two hymns from Isaac Watt's hymnal and listened to a long reading of several chapters of Exodus. The good reverend delivered his final sermon with a passion that Penelope imagined might shake the plaster off the walls. He railed against tyranny, injustice, imprudence, and false piety. After administering the Lord's Supper, the reverend released his folk with a simple benediction: "The Lord bless thee, and keep thee; the Lord make his face to shine upon thee, and be gracious to thee; the Lord lift up his countenance upon thee, and give thee peace. Amen."

The Brownes had begun to stand when the reverend Duffield lifted his arms. "Brothers and sisters. Please, I've something more to say."

The curious flock settled themselves and waited. The minister adjusted his robes and stepped from behind his wooden pulpit. "Nearly two hundred of the brethren have fled to York, or Reading, the Lehigh Valley, or New Jersey. The McAllisters have gone to Virginia. Elder Murray is en route to the Alleghenies. Some of you are leaving on the morrow.

"I have spent hours in prayer and have sought the counsel of my peers at the Buttonwood Church and at Second Presbyterian. Our common counsel is for our flocks to depart, and us with them. The King's army wages war against us as if we are the Presbyterians of Cromwell. All of London calls this war a "Presbyterian Rebellion." For this cause they shall be without mercy toward us. This church will be either their stable or their brothel. The passage of the Quebec Act makes it clear that they are in league with the Roman Catholics and they shall surely bring their popish allies against us. I tell you, King George of Hanover is drifting the way of the Stuarts.

"Each man must seek the peace of his own soul in this matter. I have been summoned to York to act as chaplain for the Congress. It seems the reverend Jacob Duché of Christ Church is suspected of timidity and shall not be continuing in that capacity. Should any of you choose to remain here in

Philadelphia, I counsel you to seek Christian fellowship at other churches. The reverend Coombs at St. Peter's has sympathy for our cause. Many of his own serve with Washington. I stood by him as he buried a patriot soldier, Captain Shippen, killed at Princeton near our own college. If you must stay, perhaps you ought to consider St. Peter's—the worst you'll need upon our return is a good scrubbing. Now I pray you the protection and guidance of an all-wise Providence."

The subdued congregation stirred. The reverend Duffield walked among his brethren, offering comfort and prayer. Each sad soul bade his shepherd a heart-heavy farewell. At last, the reverend stood in his doorway and watched quietly as the last of his flock disappeared in the rain of the grey Sunday afternoon. The faithful minister then gathered his Bible and his musket, mounted his old mare, and trotted briskly away.

--->===) (===<---

In the hours that followed, every man had to make a decision. The city's patriot mayor, Samuel Powell III, chose to remain, and news of his decision served to calm many. It was a courageous gesture, for Mayor Powell was known to be a close friend of General Washington and many other prominent patriot leaders. But thousands of others chose to flee. Wagons of every sort and description were soon groaning and tilting their way along the city's crowded streets toward the ferries bound for New Jersey or toward the roads leading north to Allentown, Bethlehem, or Easton. The refugees bundled what they could on carts, hand-wheeled litters, back-racks, and barrows as they flooded toward the presumed safety of other parts. Though it seemed that half the city was on the move, it was more like twenty-five out of every hundred residents.

Actually, John Adams had called Philadelphia, "that mass of Toryism." Indeed, many, many citizens were Loyalist or neutral. And with the arrival of the British, many Loyalists who had abandoned their homes earlier would quickly return—Loyalists like Joseph Galloway. In the meantime, those Tories who had spent the last year in quiet submission now began to strut and swagger along Philadelphia's streets. Little groups appeared here and there singing, "God Save the King." Union Jacks appeared from windows. The pendulum had swung.

The day the reverend Duffield bade his congregation farewell; the American army was retreating west, away from Philadelphia. It had lost a battle named the "Paoli Massacre" and had suffered heavy casualties.

By September 23, Colonel Braithewaite Jones had hastily ordered all decked vessels to leave the city docks and cross the river to Burlington or to Fort Mifflin further south. All small boats were to be taken across the river and hidden in New Jersey creeks. He then ordered anything that might be used by the British army or navy to be burned or floated away. With that, he closed his tavern and abandoned the city.

General Howe and the British army occupied nearby Germantown on September 25th. The long stretch of houses and sheds was home to a large and industrious German population and was situated about two miles north of the city proper. General Howe took his comfort in a nearby Loyalist's mansion and sent a message to Philadelphian Thomas Willing, a man respected by both sides, urging all the city's residents to remain quietly in their homes as their King's army prepared to liberate them.

For the Brownes, the blinding swirl of these dark, chaotic days was unsettling. Neither they nor their neighbours understood what changes to expect. Was Archibald at risk for his patriot sympathies? Would the family be required to quarter British soldiers? Would there be food enough, firewood, security?

It was damp on Friday morning, September 26. Dr. Browne peered out his office window at the crowd of happy citizens racing over the slick cobblestones and brick toward Second Street. Cromwell leapt silently to the windowsill and stared out of doors. "Quakers," Archibald grumbled. "Miserable self-serving, self-righteous, drab-dressed, busybody wheedles of Toryism."

"What's that, husband?" called Katherine's voice from the loom-room.

"I said the street is full of Quakers."

"Father, the British army is coming," said Penelope.

Archibald closed the shutter and returned to his reading. His wife re-pinned her hair as she entered the office and then drew a shawl around her shoulders. "Archibald?"

The man set down his book and stared into the fire. The chill of autumn had settled on the city. The leaves of the tall hardwoods lining the streets were tinted with colour and would soon be boasting bright yellow, orange, and crimson. On this day, however, the air was cold and wet, the leaves hung limp and stale, and the house of Dr. Browne was gloomy and grim. "I suppose Thaddeus is cheering with the others," grumbled Archibald. "I sent him to tend the Carson boy hours ago."

Katherine laid a hand on her husband's shoulder. "You've given him the right to follow his own mind."

Penelope stormed into the office. She was covered with soot from work in the kitchen. Her green eyes blazed. "Father, the city is taken. I've been listening through the cellar door. The Loyalists are rushing from their holes to welcome that— that—that cursed Howe and his—"

"Penelope," scolded Dr. Browne. "Hold your tongue. Washington's army is only about twenty miles away. The British army may not hold the city for long. You—"

"What is that?" said Katherine. The family ran to the windows and listened. The crowd outside had thinned, but those who were passing had stopped. Everyone waited; then it was heard again. Thud. Thud. Then another.

"Cannon," whispered Archibald. "Cannon from downriver."

Katherine shuddered. The family strained to hear more, but all became quiet. Satisfied that the brief cannonade had ended, the street began to move again, and once more was heard the anxious chatter of passing people as they came and went beneath the windows of Dr. Browne. Katherine returned to her loom, Penelope to her kitchen, and Archibald to his desk. All were lost in the duties of their tasks when suddenly a fist pounded furiously on their front door.

"Open! Open in the name of the King!"

⊷══◑ ◐══⊶

Thaddeus was pressed within a throng of the King's loyal subjects along Second Street near Market. He had administered a proper dose of herbs to his father's patient and then raced towards the sounds of shouts that were rising from the city's north end. The day was gloomy and the city's spirits were sagging from ten days of rain. But the sounds of the British army approaching from Germantown filled some hearts with gladness.

Thaddeus looked at the joyous faces beaming all around him. He saw Schoolmaster Smith in his broad-rimmed Quaker hat waving and cheering with other grey-clad brethren of his meetinghouse. He saw Rebecca Franks, and Samuel Whiting,

Eliza Singer, Robert Huddel, and Benjamin Plumstead. Then, towering above them all, he saw Whittaker Yates, his father's friend.

"Mr. Yates," said Thaddeus.

Unaware of the Browne lad, Whittaker and his son Webster elbowed their way to a good vantage on Second, in front of a silversmith's shop. Thaddeus ploughed his way through the ever-enlarging crowd and finally reached them. "Ah, good fellow." beamed Whittaker. Thaddeus and he shook hands and tipped their hats.

"This is a good day!" exclaimed Webster. "A good day for the King."

Thaddeus laughed. It felt wonderful for him to be able to enjoy his freedom of speech and he did so loudly. "God save the King," he shouted.

As old friends reunited, a cheer raised up-town. It grew louder and louder. Whittaker stretched his head over the others and smiled. "They're coming."

To the snap and tatter of snare drums, the regiments of General Howe marched toward the breathless Thaddeus Browne and his cheering compatriots. Under the command of Lord Cornwallis, these smartly dressed and well-ordered companies stepped in unison down Second Street. Ranks of clean, well-tailored red coats swept by, carried by shiny black boots. Near the front trotted a company of green-vested light dragoons on prancing horses. With them rode Phineas Bond, Jr. and Enoch Story of Philadelphia. These two proud Loyalists waved and cheered their comrades along the street and called on every young man to enlist in the Pennsylvania Loyalist Regiment.

Thaddeus felt a surge pulse through him unlike any feeling he had ever known. "Mr. Yates, I *must* join."

Whittaker nodded and laid a hand on the lad's shoulder. "Speak of it later, son." The man looked nervously at his own young Webster. Though only thirteen, he knew the army could take him.

"What a wondrous relief," cried a woman from behind.

Whittaker turned to see Mistress Mary Franks, the milliner from Union Street. He smiled although he had no affection for the black-haired busybody. Her husband served in the Loyalist Regiment and was coming home. Whittaker wondered to himself whether her husband wouldn't rather swim the stagnant marshes of Delaware than return home to the likes of her.

Thaddeus cheered loudly, Webster at his side, but he did not fail to notice that the streets were filled mostly with women and children. *Why are there not more men of fighting age?* He had no time to answer his own question, for a band marched by playing "God Save the King" and those on the sidewalks applauded loudly. Many sang along:

> *"God save great George our King,*
> *Long live our noble King,*
> *God Save the King!*
> *Send him victorious,*
> *Happy and glorious,*
> *Long to reign over us,*
> *God Save the King."*

Behind the band marched several companies of grenadiers in their "bishop's hats." Proud, precise—huge giants of men— these grenadiers stepped in perfect order. Their uniforms were spotless and without a single tear or lost button.

Officers in their finest regalia smiled affectionately at the happy faces cheering them. Boasting gold epaulettes and plumed hats, adorned with gleaming swords and dashing sashes, these gentlemen of property manifested a dignity and intelligence that set them far above even the most disciplined of infantrymen.

"Father," said Webster, "this is only Cornwallis' men? What of the rest of General Howe's army?"

"Aye, lad. I'm told he's some fifteen thousand strong, maybe twenty, especially if you count the Hessians. He's maintaining his main strength near Germantown, where he thinks Washington shall strike."

No sooner had he answered Webster's question then companies of blue-coated, moustached Hessians passed. The sons of farmers and simple townspeople from the central German state of Hesse, they were often pressed into service by powerful landowners, and liberty was always a tempting option. Many had already deserted the British army to fine homes in the friendly Pennsylvania countryside or with other Germans living in and near the city. In fact, there were so many German-speaking people in the area that the Congress had ordered a copy of the Declaration of Independence to be printed in their language.

Thaddeus and the Yates waited patiently as the last of the soldiers passed by. Behind them, however, lumbered a huge column of wagons loaded with ammunition, clothing, food, and sundry supplies. Behind the wagon column came something Thaddeus had never considered—the wives and children of many of the soldiers, both English and Hessian, as well as laundresses, seamstresses, and women of other services. These camp followers, as they were called, were unwashed and weary, stumbling between the great numbers of horses, oxen, and sheep.

The boy sat on the curb and reflected on the historic occasion he was witnessing. He could not escape the contrast between this grand army of the King and the poor wretches of General Washington that had hastened through the city just a few weeks before. The British did not march in bare feet nor did they hang their uniforms on half-starved skeletons. Their men were rested and flushed with healthy colour.

But the lad was wise and had noticed more. For though the King's well-fed army was fit and polished, it lacked spark and vigour. Marching past this day were no jaws set in defiance, no shoulders hardened with purpose, and no bleeding feet striding boldly toward a righteous prize.

CHAPTER 4

Shadows on the Cobblestones

"Open the door."

Archibald Browne narrowed his eyes. His wife hurried from her loom and stared nervously at her husband. The doctor rose from his desk and promptly handed his wife the loaded musket that he kept standing in the corner. "Back there," he whispered.

Katherine nodded and retreated to the doorway of the loom room as Penelope burst from the cellar stairway. "What's all the noise?" she blurted.

Her mother hushed her and the two waited as Dr. Browne approached the front door. He reached for the latch with one hand and held a cocked pistol with the other. A fist on the other side pounded again as Archibald flung it open. "Hold fast," Dr.

Browne bellowed. He aimed his pistol directly at the forehead of a well-dressed citizen. "Speak your piece."

The surprised man froze with his mouth open. He was standing with a group of coarse-looking ruffians, each carrying rope or a musket. One of them bolted from the others and disappeared around the corner of the house.

"Speak, man!" roared Archibald.

"We are m—m—making arrests of known tr—traitors to the Crown," he stammered.

"Under what authority?"

The man had no answer. A repugnant, unwashed fellow pushed to the fore, shouting: "We need no authority other than this." He aimed his musket directly at the doctor's head.

Archibald was no stranger to combat. The doctor quickly reasoned that his lighter trigger could easily fire first. His eyes narrowed.

A crash echoed from within the house and a shot rang out. Penelope screamed. Fearing other ruffians had forced their way through the rear door, Archibald turned and charged across his office to the rear room. "Kate, Penny?" he cried.

"Steady, you," growled a snarling intruder. "Stand steady, else —"

"Easy, lad," said Dr. Browne calmly. "I shall just set my—" A body flew atop Archibald's back and drove him hard into the wood framed loom. His pistol flew across the room and his face crashed against the unforgiving corner of a maple beam. His cracking spectacles cut the skin beneath his eyes and he shattered a tooth. Blood spilled from his mouth and streamed down his chin as he was yanked to his feet. His wig was tossed away and he was struck in the face over and over until he slumped onto the floor.

Were that not enough, he was again hauled to his feet and beat about his head and body.

Katherine had been pinned to the ground by a heavy boot across her neck and Penelope was held in place by the gaping mouth of a musket barrel pressed hard against her temple.

Coughing and nearly unconscious, the doctor was bound by ropes and dragged through his office toward the front door. Katherine was slapped and Penelope shoved against a far wall. Then, with a facetious salute, the rogues left the women to their fury and dragged Archibald into the street. Despite a scalding torrent of abuse and threats from the Browne women, the laughing men dumped the half-conscious doctor into an ox cart laden with a forlorn group of others similarly trussed. With the slap of a long rod, the ox lurched with the cart through a light rain up Union and disappeared around the corner of Third.

Mrs. Browne quickly gathered her composure and stormed back into her house, Penelope in tow. Her face tightened with purpose. "Girl, find me a weapon."

The men had stolen the pistol and a musket but Dr. Browne had always recognised the necessity of a free man's house to be adequately stocked with firearms. 'No arms, no liberty,' was an early entry in his commonplace.

Penelope charged down the cellar stairs and quickly returned with her mother's rifle, a musket, and a pair of powder horns, cartridges, a bag of lead balls, and a canister of wadding. "Here."

Kate Browne pulled her mobcap tightly against her head and reached for her weapon—a Pennsylvania Rifle given to her by her father at her wedding—a strange gift, perhaps, but for those who knew the man, it was no surprise. She checked the flint, skilfully primed the flash pan, and loaded the spiralled barrel with a heavy measure of powder and a well-made lead ball. She slid the ramrod hard against the ball and patch and drove it to the barrel's bottom with a determined grunt. She turned to Penelope. "Is your musket loaded?"

"Aye," answered Penelope. Her face was still covered in soot, but her eyes glowed with fury.

Katherine snapped the girl's musket from her grasp like a seasoned, battle-hardened sergeant. Her eyes flew across the flint, the flash pan, and the firelock. Muskets fired their lead ball straight out the barrel so were not as accurate as the spiralled shot of the rifle. But this was a dependable Philadelphia-made musket and would do. Dr. Browne had wisely stocked up on pre-measured cartridges from Krider's gun shop just months before.

The girl stood at attention, a full cartridge box hanging from her shoulder. Mrs. Browne flung the weapon into her daughter's hands and charged out the door.

Penelope said nothing as she trotted behind her raging mother. She couldn't imagine where they were going or what they would do when they got there. Her heart was filled with anger, but also with a newfound respect for her mother. The woman had always been strong, but had chosen to live a life marked more by deference and submission. Katherine was no broken mare but a noble female who loved her family and her traditions enough to restrain any competing demands of the self within her. Penelope suddenly understood the grace and power of her mother's chosen humility.

The pair of armed women marched west on Union to Third Street, where they turned right. They stormed up Third with such determination that groups of open-mouthed pedestrians sprinted out of their path. They crossed Spruce and turned left on Walnut, where they frightened a huddle of self-contented Quakers chatting in front of their almshouse. The grey-clad brethren scattered to the four winds. The two gave no heed to the lively music of the marching bands just a few blocks away, nor did they care to notice the glad-hearted revellers waving their Union Jacks in celebration. They could only see the bloodied face of Archibald as he was tossed upon the cart like a sheep for slaughter.

A block and a half away, two British soldiers saw the armed women marching toward them through a drizzle. The soldiers were stationed at the corner of Fifth and Walnut because it comprised the rear of the Pennsylvania State House property, the centre of governmental and military affairs for the colony. The Fifth Street Jail was nearby. The two watched the Brownes stomping their way closer and closer. Alarmed, the soldiers laid their muskets across their chests and advanced.

Katherine spotted the pair and nudged Penelope into an alleyway. "Quick. Follow me." Mrs. Browne and her daughter raced through the muddy alley and ducked into a leaky tanner's shed. There they squatted midst crates of hides and putrid smelling barrels of tanbark slurry.

Penelope held her nose and her eyes watered. Not far away crept the sluggish, debris clogged, horrid waters of Dock Creek. It reeked with the city's raw sewage and the pollution of tanneries, papermakers, and slaughterhouses. The girl retched.

"Shh," Katherine whispered.

The Redcoats raced past the alley and could be heard pushing their way into shops and workhouses along Walnut. Katherine licked her lips nervously and listened. "Seems they have moved down the street." She relaxed a little and wiped from her face the water that was dripping through the roof of the poorly shingled shed. Katherine checked Penelope's musket again. She had instinctively protected her powder by shielding her hammerlock in the folds of her dress, as her father had taught her as a child during a difficult adventure in St. Kitts. But no one had taught Penelope, and her powder was wet, her flintlock splashed with drops of water. Truly, Providence is a kind overseer.

Penelope followed her mother's eyes and looked down at her musket. She groaned. "I–I am sorry, mother."

Katherine bit her lips, then burst into tears. The two held each other for a long while. "Oh, dear daughter. We need to find another way. First, we—we need to go home." Their fury abated, the two now considered the prospect of their retreat with anxiety. Slipping out of their hiding place, the two crept through the shadows of the dreary alley toward the brighter light at its end. Suddenly, a familiar figure dashed by them along Market. It was the Grackle.

Katherine poked her head carefully around the corner. "Josiah," she cried hoarsely.

Her old friend stopped and cocked his head. Glancing nervously from side to side, Katherine waved one arm and called again. "Josiah!"

The man stared, open-mouthed. He rushed toward her and slipped into the alleyway. "I only just heard. 'Tis news all over Union Street that Mr. Yates be beside himself lookin' for you. I heard of it at the shambles, then heard 'bout some Quakers scared by two woman with guns."

Penelope hugged the old black man. "Oh, it is good to see you."

"And you. But you be in great danger. Soldiers are in the neighbourhoods searchin' patriot houses for arms. Tories are arrestin' Whig men—like the doctor. Dear Mrs. Browne, we needs get you home safe."

Katherine nodded. Giving her daughter some quick instructions, in a moment each was grunting and grimacing as they slid their cold, wet firearms upward from the bottom of their dresses, along their legs, against their corsets, and finally out the top. Penelope's musket was a bit shorter than Kate's rifle, but each suffered the discomfort of a cold muzzle end resting against an ear. The women stood perfectly erect, each holding her weapon hard against her side.

"Penny, your backboard was good training after all. Josiah, I think my daughter and I are ready to go home."

The Grackle smiled. His golden eyes shone and he nodded. "I'll keep a little back to keep an eye."

Kate nodded and looked at her daughter. "Be brave, girl. Now, follow me." Mrs. Browne stepped onto Walnut as nonchalantly as their predicament would allow. The two walked quickly and oddly as a result of the hidden weapons. With lips murmuring in prayer, Katherine led Penelope east on Walnut, toward the river. At Third they turned right and hurried toward Union. But they had not even reached Spruce when a voice suddenly boomed from the women's right. Turning, they saw a lone, high-hatted grenadier swaggering toward them from across the street with long menacing strides. Katherine felt a chill rise through her and she hastened her pace. The soldier quickened his steps and easily barred their escape. *So close*, poor Katherine thought.

The grenadier was a huge man, as they all were: the army required every grenadier to stand at least six feet tall. He was dark-eyed and strong-featured and his face belied the fatigue of a day's march. He was without patience or courtesy. His breath reeked of rum. "You wenches come with me," he ordered. Shoving the two sideways into an alley that lay empty and dark at their backs, he stalked them as they retreated deeper into the shadows of the narrow passage. Farther and farther they backed until Katherine finally stopped and stood her ground.

"I'll—I'll not take another step," she said. "I am Mrs. Katherine Henry Browne, a loyal subject of our King. I am related to the loyal families of Shippen, Howell, and Seabury. Philadelphia's own Joseph Galloway is known to my kin—"

The grenadier laughed and drew a dagger from a sheath within his high boot. He pushed Penelope hard and slapped Mrs. Browne in the face. "Shut yer mouth. I've no care for you or your friends. I'm a Dublin man and I care e'en less for your cursed King." The man reached for Katherine and pulled her toward him by her hair.

Josiah had not failed to keep his watch. Like a cat stealing upon an unsuspecting rat, he began to creep down the alley. His callused, bare feet padded silently atop the cool mud as he drew closer and closer. His yellow eyes stayed fixed on the grenadier's back as his trembling fingers danced along the knife handles lined along his belt.

Penelope saw the Grackle coming from the corner of her eye but had the discipline to stare only at the soldier's face. And Katherine simply strained within the Irishman's grasp and maintained a loud, insistent chatter.

Josiah's fingers began to lift a long knife from his belt, but he hesitated. With sweat pouring down his cheeks, he glanced from side to side and spotted a broken wooden wagon tongue lying within easy reach. Leaning forward, he took a firm hold.

Then, as swift as the strike of a Pennsylvania rattlesnake, Josiah sprang forward and swung the beam with all his might, smashing it against the side of the grenadier's head.

The Irishman's legs buckled and he staggered sideways as his high hat tumbled from his battered head. His eyes rolled white and he teetered, but did not fall. Josiah waited for a moment, but as the man recovered his balance he had no choice but to swing a second ferocious blow. This one landed hard against the man's forehead and the soldier collapsed backward into the alley's mud like a felled tree in wet woodland.

"God forgive me," muttered Josiah. He tossed the blood-splattered beam away and knelt by the man. "I've killed him." Josiah wept. "The shamble's full of talk of what these men do. I—he sure was to bring harm to you and the young mistress; I—"

"Shh," Katherine said gently. She hugged the old man. "Thank you, dear friend."

The Grackle nodded. He was a kind man by nature. He was more apt to pick flowers with children than to brawl. But he was no stranger to the sad facts of a world in darkness and was capable of doing hard things. "Take the girl and go quickly. I'll finish here."

Katherine hesitated and looked anxiously into Third Street. The parade would be ending soon and the city would be filled with people again. "What..."

"Mistress, *please*. I know what to do." The man spoke with confidence and just a hint of impatience.

Katherine nodded and pulled her daughter by the sleeve. Penelope was aghast. She had seen dead people before, but she had never actually seen a person die. The war was suddenly very real.

The two quick-stepped out of the alley and turned toward Union, ignoring the sounds of the British army's fifes, bassoons, clarinets, and drums. It was just past noon and the parade had reached the New Market shambles just blocks away. They knew they *must* hurry home. Their legs grew heavy and each step seemed to add a hundred yards to their goal. Their lungs heaved and they sweated with effort. Penelope wanted to cry out, but, at last, she and her mother collapsed through their doorway and fell into the safety of their home.

⊷⊫◉ ◉⊯⊶

It was mid-afternoon when Thaddeus returned. After the parade he had spent time chatting with soldiers at the shambles. Now he was hungry and anxious to tell all of the day's events. Expecting a good lunch of stewed meat and boiled potatoes, he was disappointed to see his mother and sister well-dressed and preparing to leave. Where's lunch?"

Penelope growled, but Katherine answered calmly, "We have terrible news."

Thaddeus looked carefully at his mother, then at Penelope. He removed his hat and waited.

"Your father has been arrested."

Thaddeus was stunned. "Arrested? For what?"

"For supporting liberty," exclaimed Penelope.

The boy groaned.

Penelope began to cry. "They beat him. They knocked him to the floor and beat him. And they threw mother down and—"

"Who?" roared Thaddeus.

Mrs Browne took the lad by his shoulders and spoke calmly. "I did not recognise any."

The lad paced. "What do we do?"

Before Katherine could answer, a knock sounded on the door. The women turned white but Thaddeus stormed to the door and flung it open. "Mr. Yates."

Whittaker ducked through the doorway. He bowed slightly as he tipped his hat. "Ladies. It is a relief to see you well." Whittaker handed his wet overcoat and flop-hat to Thaddeus. He folded his hands behind his back. Mr. Yates could be either fun loving or serious; today, he was deeply worried. "Three hours ago I learned from that abominable Mary Franks that Archibald was arrested—and with some resistance."

"It is true," said Katherine.

"I took the liberty to dispose my attorney, Mr. Benjamin Fielding."

"He is the husband of a niece to my aunt's friend, Sarah Moore. He is a Loyalist, but not without Whig sympathies, I believe?"

"Yes, he is that man. He is respected by all sides and was helpful to me in keeping my shop during the past year. He has agreed to help Archibald and is already at the jail. I was chased away."

"Did you see my husband?"

"No. It was confusion greater than any I have ever seen. Wagons full of good men are being emptied into crowded cells with no regard to their status. I saw Stephen Williams,

Owen Cranberry, Thomas Huddings—many others. Some are valued patients of your Archibald and patrons of my shop. That new cobbler—Evan Jones—was there as well."

Katherine nodded. "I am deeply grateful to you, Mr. Yates, but I need to see my husband."

Whittaker shook his head. "I think he would not want you to come there. It is a mob. The soldiers are frightened and are handling all sides roughly. There are only a few officers and there is little law. I think it is dangerous."

"Then I shall go with her," said Thaddeus.

Whittaker shook his head. He surveyed the three pairs of eyes fixed on him and reluctantly yielded. "I object, but since you insist, I shall come with you."

With that, the Brownes and Whittaker Yates walked briskly to the Fifth Street Jail. They passed revellers—many of who were now drunk—and soldiers wandering lustily about the streets. These showed little regard for common decency and had not the least bit of shame in using the middle of the streets as their privies. The sounds of broken glass informed the foursome that looting had begun.

"Mrs. Browne," said Whittaker as they walked quickly down Walnut. "You understand these troops are just the vanguard of Howe's army. Once Washington is beaten in Germantown, all of the British regiments and all of the Hessians shall enter the city proper for winter quarters."

"I should think that some order might follow these—these ill-disciplined advance companies?"

C. D. Baker

"I agree. General Howe has a particular affection for us colonists and I doubt he would stand for what is happening now."

Their pace slowed as they approached the jail. The scene in front was terrifying to all of them. Drunken citizens had formed an angry mob that pelted the jail with rocks and bricks. A hasty gallows had been constructed in the centre of the street and numbers of noosed ropes were draped over the beam. A straw-stuffed likeness of Washington was burning in the waning light of the grey day. Determined to see Dr. Browne, the four bravely waded into the seething crowd and toward the jailhouse door. A line of nervous soldiers guarded the chained door.

"No, you may not enter. Are you mad?" shouted an officer.

Katherine pressed the young lieutenant. "My husband is in there. I need to see him."

A flurry of rocks and clumps of mud flew against the walls nearby. Katherine shouted louder, "I must see my husband."

The officer was sympathetic. He took Mrs. Browne by the elbow and rounded the corner. "My lady, can you not see what is happening? I must control this—this despicable mob. They want the rebels hung. General Howe ordered your city to be treated with respect and *all* of its citizens to be treated with courtesy. If I open the doors to you, your husband's life shall be put at risk, along with many others."

Katherine hesitated. She looked into Whittaker's pleading eyes and reluctantly agreed.

⋆⊷⊷⊷⊷ ⊷⊷⊷⊷⋆

Katherine invited Whittaker and Webster to dinner that evening. She also invited poor Mrs. Jones, the cobbler's young wife, who was with child and expecting to deliver in several months. Her husband had been dragged away while she watched and she had spent the day in tears. Thaddeus was sent to find Josiah.

Too weary to carry the meal from the cellar to the second floor parlour, Katherine and Penelope served their guests at their trestle table in the kitchen. They ate a quiet, simple meal of boiled chicken, roasted corn, and white bread. Katherine had an ample supply of ale and brandy, and fresh milk from the neighbour's cow. They were nearly finished when Thaddeus and Josiah came down the stairs.

"Greetings, Mr. Byrd." Whittaker stood, cracking his head against a low beam.

"Ah, Mr. Yates, and young Webster Yates." Josiah seemed forlorn and heavy-hearted. Katherine and Penelope looked at the man with imploring eyes. They dared not ask him anything.

"You look like a man that could enjoy a hot meal," said Katherine. A hint of nervousness made her voice tremble a little and Thaddeus noticed. He looked carefully at his mother.

The Grackle eased himself stiffly on to the bench. "Yes, I've a fierce hunger." He paused for a moment, and then said carefully, "I had a strange day, but all is laid to rest."

"Ah," answered Katherine. "That is good." She knew what he meant.

Webster broke the odd silence that followed with a wild chatter about the parade of soldiers and the Loyalists who seemed to now fill the city. No one seemed interested.

Mrs. Browne served a sweet-cake and an apple tart with a pot of coffee. "Father would be pleased to see the coffee," remarked Penelope. Coffee had become the Whig drink of choice. The brown beverage was a protest against English tea as well as the assorted taxes and monopoly foisted on the colonies *because* of it.

"Out of respect for your father's suffering, we shall be drinking coffee until he is home."

"And what of Cameron's suffering?" Penelope had a bite to her question.

Katherine said nothing.

Whittaker thought it best to avoid risk to the women's reputations by staying the night. He was a single man, unrelated by blood or marriage, and it was not a fitting thing to do. Josiah agreed he ought to leave as well, though the Brownes protested loudly. Josiah, after all, lived in a cave some four or five miles away, but the man could be stubborn and he bowed himself out the door. Mistress Jones thanked her hostess and joined the others as they left for home.

Exhausted and worried, Katherine undressed and prepared for bed. Standing in her corset and linen shift, she prayed for Archibald. She wondered what horror he was suffering in that awful, crowded jail. No doubt he was sleeping in excrement, pressed against others, and shivering in the cold. She wept for him.

Penelope and Thaddeus knocked lightly on her door.

Katherine wrapped herself in a velvet robe her husband had bought her in New York some years before, raised the wick on her lantern, and opened her door.

"Mother," said Thaddeus nervously. "The streets are filled with drunken brawlers. I think we need keep arms handy and stay together."

Katherine agreed. She reached under her bed and carried her dry, loaded rifle to the front room of the second floor and stood it in a corner by the window. "Penelope, get the other musket. The mob carried off your father's pistol and the downstairs musket."

"That pistol was father's from the French war."

"Aye." She turned to Penelope. "Why are you waiting?"

Penelope rocked on her feet and hesitated. "It—it is downstairs in the cellar."

"Yes?"

Thaddeus chuckled. "You're scared?"

The girl shrugged. She didn't dare tell her brother of her fears of the dead grenadier. She shuddered as her mind's eye saw the lifeless soldier lying so horribly still in the mud. She imagined his ghost greeting her in the dark haunts of the cellar, lit only by the dying embers of the fire.

Mrs. Browne understood. "Thaddeus, I think we should check Mr. Yates' repair of the back door." Holding her lantern aloft, Katherine led the twins down the dark, turning stairway to the loom-room. It was nearly eleven o'clock in the night and the sounds of boisterous brawlers were still echoing in the neighbourhood. Most of the noise seemed to be coming from Second Street, probably from the shambles. They checked the back door and found it firmly barred. Before dinner Mr. Yates had nailed it fast so no one might pry it open in the night. The three chuckled as they each put a finger in the black hole their mother had fired through the frame.

The cellar was eerie. It was filled with long shadows cast by the flickering coals of the dying hearth. Thaddeus stumbled into the table bench, then into a box of potatoes, and finally into a keg of rum before finally reaching the door to the outside. He made sure the sturdy lock-beam was set in place. Penelope retrieved the musket from its pegs above the hearth and hung the powder horn from her shoulder.

Walking across his father's office to the front door, Thaddeus took it by its handle and gave it a good shake. Certain that it was locked, he moved through the dark past his father's desk, suddenly stopping and turning towards his mother. "Mother. Others may know the man of this house is gone. Some may not know I am here. Look, father's wig." He bent to pick it off the floor. "Why not get his wig-stand and his coat and set him up at his desk?"

Penelope was confused. "What? What do you mean?"

"The shingle out front says, 'Dr. Archibald Browne.' It is not surprising that a doctor might be at his desk late in the night. If we keep a dim candle by his desk, it shall look like he is sitting by it."

Mrs. Browne liked the idea. "You are clever, like your grandfather. Penelope, fetch me the wig-stand. Boy, there is his coat."

In a few minutes "Dr. Browne" was hard at work at his desk. Mrs. Browne decided she needed to check the view from the rainy street so she tiptoed out the door. Pleased, she began walking back, but her heart suddenly stopped as her eyes fell upon a dark figure hunched at the corner of her house just yards away. Clutching her robe by her throat, she darted for the open door. She burst through the door and slammed the door behind her. Quivering, the poor woman leaned into the safety of the corner and called for her twins.

Thaddeus and Penelope could see nothing from the windows and they dared not venture out the door. They comforted their mother and led her to bed, but they determined to keep a vigilant watch through that fearful night. Thaddeus positioned himself in the centre of his father's office, away from the light of the desk candle. He faced forward on a stout wooden chair and laid his own musket across his thighs.

Penelope sat with her back to his and stared through the office, past the loom, and into the silver light of the rear window. She sat vigilant upon a cushioned chair, the musket cradled on her lap as if it were a precious newborn child. There the two sat as the hours crept by.

St. Peter's had no bell. The twins did not know what time it was when they both stirred from a sleepy drowse. The street was quieter than it had been but Thaddeus was certain he had seen shadows rushing by from time to time. Penelope did not know if she had been dreaming or if she had truly heard the crunching of early autumn leaves in the garden at the rear of the house. They reassured each other that all was in order and sat as still as frightened rabbits.

It was in the darkest hours just before dawn when Thaddeus and Penelope leaped from their chairs. A brick crashed through the glass in front of Thaddeus and bounced hard across the pine board floor.

"What?" cried Thaddeus.

The two ran to the window and saw two dark figures running down Union. The one behind was yelling something indiscernible. The taller silhouette was bounding away about thirty feet ahead of the first. Thaddeus flung open the door as his mother tripped down the stairs. "Children?"

The twins thoughtlessly bolted out the door and charged onto the cobblestones of Union. The dark figures ahead of them were sprinting down the middle of the street, only dimly visible by the city's lanterns. Unbeknownst to Thaddeus, Penelope set her musket against her shoulder and took careful aim as the one caught up to the other. She paused as the two figures suddenly clasped hands and began to laugh. The girl growled, then pulled the trigger.

"Whoom." Penelope staggered backward in a cloud of smoke.

"No!" cried Katherine from behind.

A startled Thaddeus raised his musket and took aim. He laid his sight on the taller silhouette but heard one of them call his name.

"Thaddeus? Thaddeus? Do not shoot."

"Who's there?"

"Mr. Yates. Whittaker Yates and Josiah Byrd."

The Brownes were dumbstruck. Katherine and her children peered through the darkness in horror. She turned to Penelope. "Why in God's good name did you shoot at Mr. Yates or Josiah?"

"I–I didn't know—"

"Enough. Get into the house."

Thaddeus wasn't so sure. "Mother, take Penelope and lock the door. I want to be certain. Someone threw a brick through the window, and then ran. It was these two."

"Yates and Josiah would never do such a thing."

"Exactly, mother. Now do as I say." Thaddeus had never given his mother an order before, and she had never taken one.

Katherine Browne looked at her fourteen-year-old and sighed. *He's become a man,* she thought. "Son, be careful." With that, she and Penelope retreated quickly to the house.

Unable to see clearly, Thaddeus wisely moved away from the centre of the street and took cover behind a thick-trunked chestnut tree. He waited.

"Thaddeus?" cried two voices.

They sounded just like Mr. Yates and the Grackle. The boy stepped out carefully and kept his musket under his eye. "Come closer."

"Don't shoot, young Master Browne." The man's voice echoed in the silence of the pre-dawn hour. Thaddeus thought it had to be Josiah. The two shadows moved slowly toward him, arms raised.

"Come closer."

The two obeyed. "It is Whittaker Yates."

"Why did you throw a brick and run?"

"We can explain all that. But the street watch is sure to come soon. Can y'not take us to your home?"

Thaddeus looked around. Indeed, the Loyalists had raised companies of citizens' patrols and they acted like roving mobs.

"Josiah Byrd, what verse did you inscribe on Cameron's horn?"

"Psalm eighteen, verse two."

"Whittaker Yates, what medicinal do you recommend for—for arterial contraction?"

"Ergot."

Thaddeus lowered his musket. "Good heavens. I'm sorry. Come quick to the house. But you've got some explaining to do."

The Grackle and Whittaker each breathed a sigh of relief and hurried toward the lad. With a few chuckles and some heavy sighs the three moved quickly to the Browne house.

Mrs. Browne and Penelope had been waiting nervously in the doorway. When Katherine saw the arrivals she cried out in joy. "You two. Mr. Byrd and Mr. Yates—such an unlikely pair of street vandals. Come in and dry yourselves."

In moments the cellar kitchen was filled with the warmth of a crackling hearth and the conversation of friends. "God above, I heard your shot whistle between our ears."

Whittaker's narrow-set eyes twinkled in the firelight and he shook his head. "I tell you, I am no man of adventure, but I have never felt so alive as when that musket roared at me."

"If it had been mother's rifle, I fear you'd be dead," quipped Thaddeus. "Now, really, whatever were you doing throwing bricks at our window?"

Josiah Byrd began to giggle like a schoolboy. His eyes watered and his mouth stretched wide between both ears. He couldn't speak and finally just pointed at Whittaker.

All eyes turned to the blushing Mr. Yates. His small eyes were swollen and bloodshot, his bird-like nose was as red as a radish, and a large wad of bread crust was lodged between his front teeth. "Yes, well. I–I spent the night across the street in Drinker's Courtyard. I thought from that vantage I might spot troublemakers and chase them away. Or I might be able to summon a patrol to help. So I watched from my cover behind a boxwood, and after your upstairs lanterns were out, I saw a figure moving about your side-alley. The figure moved from front to back all night and vexed me so. I moved up the street and down the street. I watched him slip behind your house, where he would hide for a time, then move to the corner. Sometimes he crossed the street and hid behind John Wilkes' oak. He almost stumbled over me once.

"Archibald's lamp made me curious and it drew him as well. I chose to keep a distance, but after some hours he could no longer avoid a peek. I watched him creep under the window and lift his eyes to look within. It seemed to me that he was making his move to your door and—

"Well, I picked up a brick and gave it a heave."

Katherine turned to Josiah. "And you were the one hovering by the house."

Josiah nodded and winked at Whittaker.

"What a grand comedy," laughed Katherine. She leaned over to Josiah and hugged the embarrassed man. "And you as well, Mr. Yates." She embraced the apothecary and wiped her eyes. "Thanks be to God for both of you."

"I think you crashed through Naphtali," blurted Thaddeus.

"Aye?"

"The window has twelve panes in the lower half and twelve in the upper. Father had us name each pane of the lower for a tribe of Israel and each of the upper after a disciple."

Whittaker laughed, loudly. "Your father is a clever fellow. Next time I should aim for Judas."

CHAPTER 5

Changing Times

SATURDAY'S DAWN HAD barely broken when Mrs. Browne was standing at the door of the Fifth Street Jail with Whittaker Yates. The morning air was chilly and damp but patches of blue sky brought a welcome relief to the dreary days of endless rain.

The sun peeked through the breaking clouds and began to light the puddles spotting the sidewalks and streets. Katherine lifted her face to feel the warmth of the sun as its brilliance burst from behind a passing cloud.

"I am afraid that your husband's case shall not be heard until Tuesday, possibly Wednesday," stated Benjamin Fielding, the family's attorney. He was a formidable lawyer, having received his education at London's prestigious Middle Temple. Stout, hard-eyed, and sharp-tongued, the seasoned counsellor was a good ally in troubled times.

Katherine nodded. "Thank you. I have no doubt you are doing all you can. Were you permitted to see my husband?"

"Yes, I was. I *insisted* on it. He sends his deepest affections to you and to your children."

"And the conditions of his confinement?"

Mr. Fielding paused. He looked at Whittaker and tapped his cane angrily. "Deplorable, Mrs. Browne. It is an outrage."

Mrs. Browne pressed him further. "And the condition of my husband?"

Mr. Fielding moved toward his waiting carriage. He walked proudly, like a puffed rooster strutting through a yard of his lessers. "I say this to you: he is a brave man. His spirit is indomitable and his eyes clear with righteous rage."

"But is he in health?"

The man stopped and turned. "I feel only shame to be serving the same King as these rakes, these contemptible cowardly dogs, these canker-worms of lawlessness that dragged your honourable husband from his own home without cause. I assure you that the vulgar toadies who trespassed your home like encroaching hogs shall be brought to a swift and most satisfying penalty." Mr. Fielding bowed and tipped his hat, then disappeared into the shadows of his carriage.

Katherine was not satisfied. "It seems Mr. Fielding uses drama to avoid a direct answer."

⊷⊜ ⊜⊶

The Brownes spent Saturday afternoon doing chores. They knew they needed to stay busy and that there was nothing like a good day's work to bring peace to one's mind. Josiah stayed close and helped Thaddeus chop wood in the rear garden. Winter would be fast upon the city and the need for firewood was enormous. Wood sellers had been through Philadelphia over the last few weeks and Dr. Browne had wisely purchased more than what most others might this early in the autumn.

Penelope was busy on the loom while Mrs. Browne travelled the shambles in search of ink powder, paper, some badly needed thread, and sundry foods. The market was filled with news. It seemed that the Pennsylvania Hospital and the Bettering House—the city's largest poorhouse—were being filled with wounded British soldiers. The basement of the hospital had been a merciful home to the mentally ill. To make room for the soldiers, however, these had been released into the city's streets.

She also heard it said that Washington was moving his army toward Philadelphia from parts west and north. Since Howe's main army was poised in Germantown, it was certain that another battle for the control of the city was inevitable.

Sunday was an adventure for the Browne twins and a homecoming of sorts for Katherine. Since Pine Street Presbyterian was closed, Dr. Browne had approved the family's attendance at nearby St. Peter's Anglican Church. Mrs. Browne had been raised in the Anglican church, or Church of England, as it was also called. She was proud to be a member of a church so rich in history and tradition, although she admitted displeasure at the likes of George Washington, George Mason, and so many other prominent patriot leaders also claiming membership. She had attended Philadelphia's Christ Church with the aunt who raised her, and it was there she had learned the creeds, liturgies, and prayers that had sustained her during the times she had accompanied her father in his life of adventure in the Caribbean, Africa, and Europe.

Katherine led her family into the large brick church and felt an immediate comfort upon entering the familiar environment of the spacious sanctuary. St. Peter's had been built just sixteen years before to relieve Christ Church, its overcrowded mother church. The building had been designed by the famous Scottish-born architect, Robert Smith, and built on land donated by Governors Thomas and Richard Penn. Its white-painted interior was elegant and refined. As with all Anglican churches, the altar was placed at the east end of the sanctuary so that the congregation could celebrate the Lord's Supper while facing east, the direction of His Second Coming. Above the altar was a wondrous Palladian window. Balanced and orderly, the design of the grand, clear-paned window said much about the nature of worship offered up by the congregation.

Mrs. Browne led her family up one of four corner stairways leading to the gallery, or balcony, which surrounded the church on three sides. Like the main floor, the gallery was built with pew-boxes, though here all faced the centre of the sanctuary.

The Anglicans believed that God related to his people as families rather than as individuals, so the church was designed so that people sat as family units. From the gallery, worshippers enjoyed a comfortable view of the altar to the east and of the pulpit mounted high on the west wall. The pulpit from which the priest preached was shaped like a wooden wineglass in order to symbolise the Sacrament of Holy Communion. Thus, Word and Sacrament, two chief duties of the clergy, were visually combined.

The twins walked respectfully behind their mother and sat quietly among the strangers filling the pew-boxes around them. As at Christ Church, about a third of the members of St. Peter's were staunch patriots, another third were staunch Loyalists, and the remaining third were, as John Adams called them, "mongrels." Mrs. Browne preferred to call them "neutrals."

In the gallery alongside of the raised pulpit was a group of pews reserved for slaves. These seats were crowded with black faces eager to worship the God of their masters. Though not a slave, Josiah Byrd sat with these whom he was proud to call his friends. Thaddeus smiled and waved to the Grackle before turning his eyes to the ground floor where those willing or able to rent pew-boxes sat. Pew-boxes were rented according to one's ability to pay, and the more expensive boxes were positioned with the better views. It was rumoured that Betsy Ross paid $50 for the one she had at Christ Church, while the wealthy Mr. Robert Morris paid $6,000. Of course, Widow Ross had a pillar blocking most of her view.

While waiting for prayers to begin, Katherine strained to see if the church's black-tiled aisle contained the graves of men and women of virtue and character, as did the floor at Christ Church. She was a little disappointed to see none, though she knew Archibald would be relieved. The ancients of Christendom believed that some mysterious quality was present in the remains of the righteous dead, and that by walking atop their bones, the living might draw from a residue of the departeds' character. Archibald and his Presbyterians railed against the notion as "popish superstition" and "black magic." Katherine wondered.

The reverend Coombs welcomed all and proceeded to lead his flock through the Prayer Book of 1662 and the Holy Scriptures. As it was the day before St. Michael's Day, he read from the Book of Joel, chapter two, verses fifteen to twenty-eight.

He then turned to the Psalms, the creeds, and the prayers, after which he began the first sermon. Katherine's mind drifted to her husband languishing in the awful jail. Near tears, her heart grabbed hold of one of the verses the parson had read: "Be not afraid, O land, be glad and rejoice. Surely, the Lord has done great things."

After the service, in the cool courtyard of St. Peter's, the Browne family made their way through a throng of well-wishers and greeters. Most were pleased to see the doctor's family now worshipping with them, and many delighted to see Katherine returning to the church of her childhood. Her mother's family was well rooted in Philadelphia's Anglican society and she was quickly surrounded by Townsends, Whites, Abercrombies, Shippens, Wilcoxes, Willings, and Howells. Thaddeus was delighted to be re-acquainted with cousins, family friends, and smiling men of means and stature. Most were Tories and now outspoken in their passions, but most showed genuine sympathy for the Brownes' present distress. What Whigs remained were quick to leave for home to enjoy a quiet lunch until the afternoon services began.

For Penelope, lunch was over far too quickly. Standing by her mother and brother outside the church once again, she watched the approach of Mary Franks, the busybody of Union Street, who was buzzing from person to person. Finally reaching the Brownes, she fluttered her face with a silk fan and said, "Oh, dear Lord above, it is such a joy to welcome you."

Thaddeus dutifully bowed with a properly executed 'making of the leg' and tipped his Sunday hat dramatically.

Penelope grimaced as she "sank" a quick curtsy. "A pleasure, Mrs. Franks," she said.

The woman was giddy with the news of her husband's arrival at Germantown. He belonged to the Pennsylvania Loyalist Regiment and would, no doubt, be allowed to spend some time with his spouse once his company was quartered in the city. She was bubbling with other news as well. Leaning close to Katherine, she tittered, "Have you heard about the reverend Duché?"

The reverend Jacob Duché, the rector of both Christ Church and St. Peter's, until recently had also been the chaplain for the Continental Congress. "No, Mrs. Franks, I can not say I have," answered Mrs. Browne.

The woman's face brightened. Gossip was as tasty to her as the sweet dainties she feasted upon each evening. "Well, he was arrested this very morning at Christ's Church, just after morning services. Poor, poor, wretched man. We must pray for him."

Katherine had little patience for idle talk, but this time she succumbed. "Go on, Mrs. Franks. For what was he arrested?"

"Well, you must have heard about his antic last year, when he had the audacity to strike all references to the King from the prayer book the Sunday before that abominable Declaration of Independence was signed. It seems one's sins do find one out. I spoke with my dear niece from Christ Church at lunch and she says the slippery eel put them all back in this Sunday morning. He took one look at the King's soldiers filling his boxes and he changed his tune. But the turncoat was found out and marched away."

Katherine was not terribly impressed with either the information or Mrs. Franks. "Ah, yes. Is that all?"

Mary Franks huffed a curt "Aye" and stomped away.

"Katherine Henry Browne?" A well-dressed gentleman addressed Mrs. Browne with a magnificent bow and tipped a striking, blue velvet bi-corn hat. The man appeared to be in his early sixties. He was distinguished and intelligent, well bred and articulate. He looked at Katherine and her twins from large, sad eyes and spoke from thin lips pursed tightly around a small mouth. His chin was receded and his nose long and straight, but his bearing was one of self-assured dignity.

"Mr. Joseph Galloway," said Katherine.

"It is a pleasure to see you again. Your Aunt Margaret Howell was such a dear. I was grieved to learn of her passing some years back."

"Ah, dear Aunt Margaret. Yes, yes. And are you well?"

"Well enough in times as these. It is good to return from New York. Would that the colony was filled with women of such grace as you. If it were, I doubt its men-folk would be so apt to undo the world."

Katherine blushed. "I read your 'Plan of Union' with great interest and admiration," said Mrs. Browne. "I share your vision of an American Parliament united with Britain's."

Mr. Galloway was impressed. He raised his eyes and smiled. "We should talk of it further. All hope is not lost, but these conspiring revolutionaries are a stubborn, stiff-necked lot of idealists. I fear order and sensibility may be things of the past."

Thaddeus was in complete agreement with the man. He bowed and extended a hand. "Sir, I am Thaddeus Browne, son of Dr. and Mrs. Archibald Browne, and this is my sister, Penelope."

The man bowed respectfully and greeted each. "Red hair. A sure sign that a Scot or Irishman's been about." Galloway laughed. "It is indeed a pleasure. And now I must attend to others, so I bid you all farewell and Godspeed."

The Brownes turned to Whittaker Yates standing nearby. "Do you know of his position? Howe has made him the chief civilian administrator of the city. He is in charge of the police, public order, all of that. He is military liaison; he issues licenses, warrants, and all such things. He's ordered a census to begin tomorrow and is publishing General Howe's offer of amnesty in all the city newspapers.

"Amnesty?"

"Aye. Any who would pledge allegiance to the Crown once again are forgiven. They can then have a license for business, buying and selling, and the like."

"Archibald would never—"

"No, I suppose not."

"Joseph Galloway has the ear of Howe. He has been an intimate friend of Ambrose Serle, Howe's secretary. Some say it was Galloway who convinced the general to leave New York and occupy Philadelphia. Howe was convinced he needed more troops to win the war and Galloway promised him thousands of Loyalist recruits from the area."

Katherine and her twins listened carefully. Joseph Galloway might be the friend they needed.

⇢═◉ ◉═⇠

The early days of October were cool, but bright. The Browne's attorney, Benjamin Fielding, had worked diligently for the past week to free Dr. Browne from his jail. Unfortunately, the British were preoccupied with the anticipated battle with the rebels near Germantown.

Each day Katherine dutifully marched to Fifth Street and called to her husband through the barred and well-guarded gates. But sadly, he could not hear her. Archibald was cold and aching. His bruises were uncomfortable and his spirit was wounded. He yearned to hold his wife and embrace his children. Instead, foul-smelling men coughing and sneezing in the damp hold pressed him on all sides. The food he was given was ample. Boiled beef, mutton, some seasonal vegetables like squash and pumpkin, and baskets of rye bread were generously provided. And he thought some of his guards were sympathetic, even kind.

On the third day of his captivity a handful of captured American soldiers were thrown into the dark cell. Malnourished and weak, suffering from scurvy and dysentery, the pitiful wretches collapsed into the arms of their patriot brethren. With no instruments or remedies, Dr. Browne felt helpless. He spent hours encouraging the brave lads with words of hope, and in return some offered him news from the army, news Archibald was desperate to hear. The men near him had been taken prisoner in the battle near Paoli but none knew of Cameron's regiment. Two young lads were Virginians and one was from New York. A few were from the Carolinas. Just days later, the Virginians were lost to fever.

In desperation and anger Archibald cried out to the guards, "I tell you again, I am a doctor. I am needed to serve any that are sick. You cannot keep me here for matters of conscience. I am entitled to the rights of a free Englishman."

On most days the guards would politely smile and ignore him. Occasionally, one might quip something about "that rascally Whig," but none listened. Or they didn't until the evening of October 4th.

Indeed.

October 4th meant little to the men bound in the dark, damp, dreary jailhouse, but for two nations gripped in war it was an important date. The day before, General Washington had made his move against the defences of General Howe near Germantown, some five miles north of the city. The days of October 3rd and 4th were foggy and wet. The fog was so thick that confusion prevented an organised attack. Sightless and lost, the American regiments executed their orders poorly and by October fourth they were in retreat. Philadelphia would surely be the winter home of the British army.

As the American army fell back toward the area of Whitemarsh and beyond, caravans of wounded men from both nations flooded the city, as well as prisoners of war. Late on the night of the fourth, Archibald's cell was so packed with groaning men that none could sit. Standing back-to-front in disordered rows, the men could barely breathe. The stench of human filth caused the newcomers to vomit. City men, once proud and prosperous citizens, wept openly in their despair. The seeds of hatred were now well watered in their anguished souls.

That night Archibald found himself pressed alongside a man who seemed familiar, even though he could barely see him in the dim light of the single torch smoking nearby. The man's face was grizzled with a three-day beard and he was powder burnt and bruised. He wore a torn, brown coat and tattered breeches. He had no shoes. "Sir, if I may—I wonder if you know of my son's regiment?"

The man grumbled.

Dr. Browne persisted. "Sir, my name is Archibald Browne; my son is Private Cameron Browne in the Second Pennsylvania."

The man stared at Dr. Browne blankly. "You are Cameron's father?"

"I am," said Archibald.

"I am Captain Staynor, Company D of the Second Pennsylvania—your son's company."

"God be praised," said the doctor. "Can you tell me of him?"

"Aye. He's a good soldier, brave and dutiful, always in good spirits. You should be proud. Last I saw him he was firing on Hessians by the Wissahickon Creek. We were lost in that cursed fog and were surprised by them. I ordered him and the others to fall back; then I had my head banged. Next I know, I'm in a wagon with my hands tied."

Dr. Browne laid a hand on the young captain's shoulder. "Thank you sir."

The next afternoon a swaggering Benjamin Field escorted a greatly relieved Archibald Browne to a waiting carriage. The doctor was dismissed with many of his compatriots on orders from Lord Cornwallis. Though preparing for a counter-attack, the British army was in confident command of the city and its environs, and the British high command believed it was time to show mercy to the civilian population, even the Whigs. Furthermore, the city jails were desperately needed to house the many hundreds of American prisoners being carted in from the battle of Germantown.

The brief carriage ride to Union Street was one the doctor would never forget, and liberty was now a joy that he would ever treasure as nothing before. Mr. Fielding steadied him as he stepped from the carriage toward his own front door, and in a moment he was weeping in the arms of his sobbing wife, telling her of Cameron.

Archibald was then taken to the cellar, where his wife quickly heated water for a much-needed bath. Like most others of his time, the man normally took his rare bath with a great deal of reluctance, but on this cool autumn afternoon, he eased into the warm waters of his tin tub with a smile as big as Josiah Byrd's. Katherine had recently made a barrel of soft soap—from the hearth's ashes and the accumulated grease of a few months cooking—that she used for the monthly clothes washing. But instead of giving the happy doctor her common "washing soap," she handed him a chunk of hard bayberry soap, scented with lavender, that she had bought two weeks ago in anticipation of this very occasion.

The man soaked for nearly two hours. He slept much of the time as Katherine quietly adding newly heated water. Finally, he stared at his wrinkled fingertips and laughed. "Time to get out, else my brain will shrivel next."

"Ah, but not so fast," laughed Katherine. She took his long razor. "You are due for a head-shave. Your wig awaits."

With a sigh and a groan, Archibald endured a few nicks and scrapes, and soon was shaved, dried, and dressed in his clean under-linens, good stockings, well-washed breeches, and favourite shirt. Then, with skilful hands, he placed his wig upon his freshly shorn head and put on his pea-green coat. With a happy smile and a light step, he proceeded to his desk to make many an entry in his commonplace. After all, with much suffering comes much wisdom.

⊶⊷

The Browne family was thankful to be together once again; but for others, misery reigned. The Pennsylvania State House had become the literal dumping grounds for wounded American soldiers. They were laid atop each other in every room, on every staircase, and even out-of-doors. In this same building where black ink had boldly declared liberty, the blood of patriots now pooled dark and red.

It was not that the British were without mercy or were deliberate in their neglect. Their own physicians were hard-pressed to manage some 3,500 sick and wounded of their own. Every hour more wagons groaned into the city with suffering Redcoats and Hessians bound for converted churches, stables, private homes, and warehouses. Pine Street Presbyterian was now filled with wounded; its burial grounds held the remains of some three hundred Hessian dead.

Dr. Browne and his apprentice son knew where duty lay. Katherine and Penelope followed, along with other women, bearing bandages, liniments, cool drinks, and food to the American soldiers at the State House. Each new day Mrs. Browne studied the faces of the groaning mass of men in fear that she might see Cameron. Some days she hoped she might find him, for then she would know he was not buried in some distant grave. On others, she hoped not, for the suffering of these afflicted and wounded was nearly beyond her ability to endure. But she did endure it, knowing that each of them had a worried mother of his own.

The doctor and Thaddeus worked feverishly day and night. The jittery British guards were charitable enough to offer assistance when they could, often helping to move an American soldier from place to place. The hovering gravediggers, however, seemed all too willing to thin the ranks of the makeshift hospital, and carried the dead away with cruel jokes and words of contempt.

Dr. Browne laboured with his colleagues from the city. He, like they, followed the "medical bible" of military and surgical procedures written by Dr. John Jones, a renowned Continental Army surgeon. His book, entitled *Plain, Concise and Practical Remarks on the Treatment of Wounds and Fractures*, had been published in 1775, and the counsel found therein had saved many lives. Archibald and Thaddeus spent many hours stitching torn flesh with crooked needles and waxed thread. They plunged their forceps deep into tissue in search of hidden musket balls, and skilfully lifted pumping arteries to the air for knotting.

Fractures were bound and splinted, and eyes hastily patched. Limbs were removed with the most awful collection of saws, cleavers, and knives. But the most difficult procedure for Thaddeus to assist with was the trepanning of fractured skulls.

The victims of such an injury often suffered severe head pain and dizziness. To relieve these poor wretches, Dr. Browne had been taught to open the skull. "Thaddeus, help that lad to the chair," barked Archibald.

Thaddeus wiped the sweat off his brow and helped a hobbling, disoriented young corporal to a wooden chair, into which he was strapped. A board was then tied to the chair-back and his head securely wrapped against it.

"Scalpel."

Thaddeus handed the doctor his blade with a quivering hand. Archibald wiped his bloodied hands on his apron. "Give the patient a lead ball to bite on and come behind me. We need to split the skin along the skull at the approximate location of the fracture. Here."

The poor soldier bit bravely on the lead ball but screamed.

"Easy, lad. Now Thaddeus take these retractors and pull the scalp away to expose the bone. Aye. There it is." The doctor wiped blood off the exposed skull and pointed to a crack. "We need to remove the split area of the bone and ease the pressure against the brain. Hand me my trephine."

The trephine was something of a hand drill or small hole saw. By twisting its wooden handle, a circle of teeth would grind against the skull and cut out a round piece of bone. The bone was then carefully removed.

"There. Look, boy, can you see the membrane over the brain, the *dura mater*? Good. I shall take my scalpel and open it, carefully. Good. See the fluid pushing out? Now, I wipe it away—I need another rag—there's one. Fine. Now, Thaddeus—

Thaddeus?"

The boy had fainted flat on the floor.

With a disdainful shake of his head, Dr. Browne proceeded to fill the hole in the soldier's skull with dry lint and wrap it securely in place with a bandage that he tied under the trembling man's chin. He patted the young private on the shoulder and wiped his hands.

"Next."

⇢⊨◉ ◉⊨⇠

By the middle of the month it seemed certain that no counterattack by the Americans was likely. Washington had pulled his forces further north and west, creating a semi-circle some twenty miles distant. Advance sentries and pickets wandered at the edges of the British line, however, though little engagement occurred. Despite General Washington's disappointment at Germantown, he had not lost his civility. It seems that a dog was found wandering near the general's headquarters at the Peter Wentz farm near the village of Skippack. The dog's collar bore the words, "General Howe." Amused, Washington, always the gentleman, sent the dog to its heartbroken owner under a flag of truce. It was no wonder that Lord Howe had an abiding affection for these coarse, backwater frontiersmen called Americans.

General Howe moved his headquarters from Germantown into the city. He occupied the mansion residence of the Deshler family at Market Square, on Market Street, in the very centre of Philadelphia. From there he would oversee the military occupation of the city as well as direct the regiments still guarding the north at Germantown. Furthermore, he needed to supervise efforts to reopen the Delaware River to traffic. The Americans had succeeded in preventing shipping from entering or leaving the city, which could prove disastrous, as winter was fast approaching. Howe ordered batteries of artillery to be placed along the riverfront and to maintain a steady fire on any approaching American vessel. In addition, he and his generals began an earnest campaign to clear the river of American defences.

For days, the Brownes stayed busy, tending to the wounded. The doctor was anticipating hard times ahead, for the air was colder than usual for late October and he feared the onset of a most difficult winter. Though he quietly cheered for every success of American resistance along the Delaware, he could not help but wonder if his family would be better served if the river were open. Without shipping in the fall, there would be such shortages in the city as few could imagine. Even if the river were to be opened by Christmas, that might be too late. The Delaware often froze and nature could certainly block ships as effectively as Mifflin and Mercer, the two American forts guarding the river just south of the city.

"Thaddeus," stated flatly Dr. Browne one Friday morning. "Today and tomorrow I want you, your sister, and your mother to stay home from the hospital. I have been thinking carefully about the coming months and I think we need to make some provision.

Have you seen Josiah?"

"Aye, he's selling chestnuts in the market."

"Ask him if he would be willing to work for hire for us."

"Yes, father. Doing what, exactly?"

Penelope and Katherine joined the pair in the office. Archibald spoke solemnly. "Whether the devils open the river or not, we shall suffer shortages as you have never seen. Washington has no choice but to choke his enemy, even at the cost of our misery. He needs to keep the outlying farmers from delivering food to the British line and he shall do all he can to keep foragers harassed. And Howe must widen his defence arc to keep Washington far enough away. Our supply of goods from the far counties shall be blocked by a British defence perimeter. We'll have no milk, butter, cheese, or meat from the Germans at market, and the farmers close by will have their stores exhausted very quickly. Do you understand?

"I have bought more firewood than usual but it shall not be enough. I want you three and Josiah to tear down our garden fence now. And I want the chicken coop dismantled."

A loud protest rose up from all three. "The fence? The coop? With no fence, the Smith's hogs shall root up the garden. They are always without their yokes."

"Smith's hogs and Whittles' hogs, and every other hog in this city, will be slaughtered and smoked in the next week. Our chickens shall be stolen any night. Do you not understand? Things are different now. Listen, and listen carefully. Buy every bit of cheese you can find—every bit. I have seen men live on cheese longer than you might think. Wrap it well and store it in the lower cellar. Katherine, buy what nuts you can and what meat you can. Salt the meat heavily. Also, find a full bale of straw. Store everything in the lower cellar and cover it with the straw and say no word of it to any. Buy small quantities in many trips and buy from different vendors. Do you understand?"

Katherine nodded.

"Good. Then we need to find a way to cover the lower cellar so no one knows it is there."

A knock on the door interrupted the conversation. All heads turned and Dr. Browne whispered to Thaddeus. "Take mother's rifle and step around the corner. You, Kate, you, Penny—follow."

Dr. Browne drew a deep breath and opened the door. Standing before him was a British officer. By his uniform, Archibald knew he was a major in an artillery regiment. "Good day."

The man saluted politely. His blue eyes shone kindly under sandy-coloured eyebrows. He was small and genteel, but strong featured. "I am Major Oliver Crippen of His Majesty's Royal Artillery."

Archibald returned a salute. "Dr. Archibald Browne, field surgeon, Roger's Rangers, retired."

Major Crippen removed his hat. He was wearing his dress uniform—a plain, gold coloured frock-like coat over a smart shirt, a tricorn hat dressed with gold lace, a crimson sash wrapped neatly around his waist, and buckled shoes with silk stockings. Escorting him were two privates in their regimental blue coats, faced with red trim. "I have marked your door sill with chalk, as you can see."

Archibald stepped outside and stared at a yellow chalk line scribbled along his stoop. He couldn't imagine why he had not noticed it before and he didn't like it. "Is there a reason you have defaced my property?"

The soldier smiled patiently. "Dr. Browne, General Howe is preparing to bring the rest of his army to the city. The officers are to quarter in civilian houses. Citizens are to shelter and feed their guests for a reasonable payment."

Archibald turned red with rage. He stomped about on his wooden leg like a madman chasing ants. "No. This is my home, you have no right."

Major Crippen waited as the doctor raged about the sidewalk. Finally he spoke. "Dr. Browne, if you do not quarter me, you shall be quartering another. I fear if you refuse another, my superiors shall evict you. Your neighbour's house is empty and has been taken by a few privates of my own regiment. Several cavalry officers are taking occupancy in the home of an unhappy Mrs. Franks a few doors down. She has asked to take residence with you, as well. She fears for her virtue."

Dr. Browne nearly fell down. "Mrs. Franks. That overstuffed busybody, that witless, swag-belly gossip, that miserable matron, that—"

"Husband." Katherine's voice was calm. "Husband, might I help?"

"This fashionable toady plans to take quarters in our house and make it home to that—that Mary Franks as well."

Katherine winced but remained steady. She turned to Major Crippen. "Sir, I am certain there is a mistake. My husband is a doctor and brings diseased and corrupted bodies into his office. I am certain neither you nor Mrs. Franks wish to be exposed to the grotesque, seeping sores and terrible lesions of the city's infirmed."

The major did not flinch. "Mistress, as for me, I should live elsewhere, except I believe it to be in your best interests that I reside here."

"What possible reason would you have for caring about our best interests?" barked Dr. Browne.

Major Crippen was unflappable. Perhaps it was five years standing by the roar of cannon. "I have here a letter for Mrs. Browne." He handed Katherine a wax-sealed letter. She opened it curiously and read it.

"Husband, it seems Major Crippen is to be welcomed."

Archibald was astonished. Katherine handed him the letter and curtsied. "Major, thank you for your kindness."

The man bowed. "I am so very sorry for this inconvenience but I know of no other way to serve you and so honour my father's request—and your father's."

Archibald adjusted his new spectacles and read the letter. When he had finished, he sighed and welcomed the major into his office. He turned to his children. "It seems the major is the son of a business partner of your grandfather Henry. Old 'Gadfly' sent word to Mr. Crippen to be sure to seek us out and provide some protection if Howe enters Philadelphia."

Major Crippen smiled. "I've carried this letter from Rhode Island to Boston, then to New York, through New Jersey, Maryland—and now here."

Dr. Browne put down his spectacles. "You have done your duty and made your offer, but we respectfully decline."

Major Crippen nodded. "I understand. However, I assure you, if I do not quarter here, you shall house others. Majors are permitted to house alone and have more advantages than lesser officers. I shall honour your dismissal, but I fear you shall in the end be pressed by five or six lieutenants."

Archibald groused but Katherine drew him aside. "Dear husband. You warned us that things would be different. Now they are. I'd prefer one major who is given to our welfare than a house full of others who are not."

Dr. Browne was exasperated and weary. He stared at Major Crippen for a long while and shook his head. "And what of Mary Franks?"

"I do not order her here, sir. She bade me ask on her behalf. It seems she fears for her reputation and she says she attends church with you."

Archibald wanted to shout a resounding "No."—But a sudden sense of Christian duty chilled him like iced water on a winter's day. He spoke as if he were a good soldier about to enter the field of certain death. "Is she in any danger from her 'guests'?"

"I should think not. General Howe has ordered Lord Cornwallis to hang or shoot looters and any guilty of carnal crimes. A few men were executed in Germantown yesterday.

Her boarders are gentlemen and more likely to provide her protection than offer her insult."

His conscience eased, a relieved Dr. Browne replied. "You are permitted residence. Please tell Mrs. Franks we respectfully decline her request and assure her that her impeccable reputation shall remain intact."

CHAPTER 6

Yearning for Relief

IT WAS AROUND noon on the 23rd of October when the city paused. Cannon fire from the river batteries had become common, but on this day the sound was very different. It was a distant rumble, more like an explosion than cannon fire.

The British had been failing in their attempts to clear the Delaware River of the American defences that were preventing their ships' entrance to Philadelphia's docks. Their navy needed to sail up the river from the south so that it could supply their occupied city with necessary food, ammunitions, medical supplies and the like. The councils of their generals were now filled with desperation as the approach of winter grew ever closer. It was not unusual for the river to begin to freeze as early as late November, and if the Delaware was not open to shipping soon, residents and soldiers alike would be faced with a winter that would defy description.

The Americans had constructed a series of bank batteries from which they maintained constant fire against British ships, but most of these batteries were inaccurate and easily destroyed. However, two forts and an amazing water defence remained between the city and Lord Richard Howe's fleet. Fort Mercer stood on the New Jersey side of the Delaware, just south of Philadelphia. It was a large, earthen fort with nine-foot parapets but inadequately manned. Directly across from Fort Mercer lay Mud Island and the four towers of Fort Mifflin. Located about six hundred yards from the shore on the Pennsylvania side, this fort was built of stone and wooden stockades. Together, the forts provided a powerful crossfire against any ship attempting to sail between them.

But it was an ingenious, unseen defence that most frustrated and confounded Admiral Howe. Beneath the grey, heavy waters of the Delaware were scattered rows of *chevaux-de-frise*—huge, box-shaped wooden frames bearing sturdy, iron-pointed timber spears that faced downstream. Typically thirty feet square and twenty feet tall and made of heavy logs and thick planks, their centres were filled with stone and rock, and anchors held them fast to the river's floor. Floated to their destinations by barges during the summer past, they were connected to each other in their gloomy depths by massive iron chains. The heavy British ships that sailed the river would warp deeply into the water and, upon heaving atop the submerged spears, would be held fast as if run aground. In this predicament they would be prey for the forts' batteries or the attack of lighter American galleys and sloops whose keels did not plough the water as deeply. Removing the chevaux-de-frise was a painstaking and slow process that required many hands and much patience.

The sound that startled the city on the 23rd was the spectacular explosion of the British man-of-war, the *Augusta*. Windows rattled in Philadelphia and in the dozens of villages and towns along both banks of the wide river. Cannon balls had landed squarely in its powder magazine, blasting the ship's smooth decking and tall masts high into the sky. Encouraged by their victory, the Americans at Forts Mifflin and Mercer were inspired to sustain an even more determined defence.

The Brownes spent the rest of that day with ears cocked. It was a strange thing to endure the sounds of the day knowing that brave men were floating to watery graves with each distant rumble. Katherine did what she could to keep some sanity in her home.

She spent part of the afternoon with her daughter, escaping the troubles by playing with charcoal and a candle. Each took a candle and cast the shadow of the other's profile upon a part of the painted wall. One then sketched the outline of the other with charcoal, and before long they had created a washable gallery of silhouette art. But entertaining interludes were short-lived. There was simply no time for triviality.

Penelope's time in the hospital had quieted her some. Her spirit was tempered by the suffering and death that filled her eyes and her ears. One late afternoon she walked into the fresh air of the rear yard, where Josiah was busy splitting fence boards. Sighing, she said, "Josiah, you really must live with us. Your home is in a dangerous place now."

The Grackle nodded and split a few more fence boards before pausing to look around the garden. Mrs. Browne's

The List

purple, yellow, and red mums had been badly trampled and someone's hogs had rooted through most of the side yard. He wiped the sweat from his head and looked at the trees. Philadelphia was usually glorious in autumn, its many trees boasting brilliant colours in the crisp air. But this season the leaves had been lethargic and disinterested. Penelope told him she thought the times had stolen the trees' joy, for their colour was lacklustre and their leaves had fallen early. Most of the city's hardwoods now stood bare-branched and gaunt.

"Mr. Byrd? Did you hear me?"

"Aye, but 'tis my home."

"It's a *cave*. I mean you no disrespect, but really."

Josiah lived in the Cave of Kelpius, about a seven-mile walk straight north of the city. The cave was hidden in the heavy forest along the Wissahickon Creek and had once been the secret home of Johannes Kelpius and his followers, the "Mystic Brotherhood." Kelpius had been a scholar and his followers had been renowned for their skill in medicine and music. They considered themselves monks for whom the number "40" was filled with meaning. Forty of them built a forty-foot-square tabernacle from which they predicted Christ's Second Coming. But, as with false, end-times prophets of every era, they and their vain prophecies had faded away.

The cave, however, had provided Josiah with shelter for nearly twenty years. He loved spending hot summer days deep within its cool recesses, and in winter he snuggled warmly within, well shielded from cold and wind. In springtime and in autumn he often sat comfortably at its mouth while he whittled and smoked and sang with the birds fluttering all about. The long walk to the city was through a wonderful ancient forest filled with fox, deer, squirrel, and rabbit, and his strong legs carried him with ease. He loved his home.

Penelope pressed. "Mr. Byrd. Your cave is near the lines. You need to pass through pickets in the night—you'll be shot for certain."

Katherine came into the garden. "Please stay with us. Your cave shall surely be home to deserters, robbers, and the dregs of both sides. It is no longer a safe place. And Dr. Browne learned that the State Assembly now requires loyalty oaths from every inhabitant of Philadelphia who is over sixteen. Anyone caught travelling beyond the British line must carry a proper passport or be jailed without bail. Liberty indeed. You have no passport, Josiah. I implore you. Please stay with us until these troubles are past."

"Mrs. Browne, I knows the trails from the city more than any man alive. I knows how to hide; I walk like an Indian. I can sniff the air like a fox and run like a deer. I've no fear at all." He smiled.

Major Crippen suddenly emerged from the privy. "I am sorry, but I could not help but hear your conversation. Mr. Byrd, I am Major Oliver Crippen of the Royal Artillery."

Josiah bowed politely.

"I am told most of the free Negroes live on Lombard Street not far from here. Why do you not live with them?"

"I never has, and why should I?"

Oliver paused. "This man is a friend of yours, Mrs. Browne?"

"Indeed."

"Mr. Byrd, do you have any skills?"

Josiah was sceptical of the man's intentions. "What sort?"

"Can you tend a horse, repair a wagon, stitch a button, and shine a boot?"

"Mostly I whittle."

"Carve, Josiah," corrected Katherine. "The man's a brilliant artist in wood," she said to the major.

"Ah. Hence the belt full of knives lying over there?"

"Aye."

Major Crippen thought for a moment. "I am afraid I've bad news for you. Apparently you have not been to your home for a few nights. You see, I know of your cave, and it is directly along the defences. The quartermasters have filled it with powder and shot to supply the redoubts we are building all along the line."

Josiah stared sadly. "I–I've not been home for four days. Too much to do here."

Oliver nodded, compassionately. "Perhaps you ought to stay here until these troubles are past, and—" He turned to Katherine and spoke in a low voice. "Would you release him for other duties?"

"Release him? He is no slave."

"No, but it seems your family's affection binds him by the heart. If he is truly your friend, I may be able to help. It would be a way to repay your kindness toward me."

C. D. Baker

Katherine looked at the major with suspicion, but his soft eyes eased her fears. "Say what you will."

Oliver turned to Josiah. "You are a friend to this family, as am I. Frankly speaking, you may be able to sell some art to a soldier here and there, but I fear your winter shall be very lean.

"Your knowledge of the land beyond the city may be a great help to General Howe. Furthermore, I know his staff is searching for dependable, loyal workers to serve his head-quarters. They are seeking groomsmen, stable hands, boot-blacks, tailors, woodchoppers, cooks, and others with useful skills. I would be happy to recommend you to the general's aide, Major André, and to Secretary Serle for a position that pays in British sterling. I think that your service to General Howe could bring great advantages to you as well as to the Brownes."

Josiah Byrd was not concerned for his own well being. But he reflected for a few moments on what good the ma-jor's offer might bring his beloved Brownes. He turned to Katherine. "Do you think it a good idea?"

"I think it is."

"And could I sleep here if they've no room for me?"

"Of course," blurted Penelope.

Mrs. Browne smiled. "As she said, of course. You are al-ways welcome in the loom-room. The major is upstairs in the front parlour. The kitchen is yours to use with us or at your own time. Only, do not interrupt the doctor when he is with a patient, or the children when they are sleeping. The chamber pots are dumped in the privy, not the street, the—"

"Mother," laughed Penelope.

Few things pleased Katherine like good order.

Josiah turned his head wistfully toward the sky. He would surely miss the peace of his quiet cave.

→━● ●━←

A week later, Josiah Byrd was employed at the busy Market Square mansion of General Howe. True to his word, Major Crippen had found the man a position as a carpenter and general labourer. Josiah found the work interesting and he was pleased with his decision. The general's paramour, Mrs. Loring, was kindly and gracious and spent her time overseeing the affairs of the house. Like Howe, she had a fondness for Americans and particularly enjoyed the wise and gentle ways of Josiah. She also learned to appreciate his skill with wood as he repaired broken furniture, stairway spindles, and picture frames. In days, the man became her favourite house worker.

Six blocks away, Mrs. Browne was having a bad morning. "More rain," she exclaimed. "Days of wind and torrents of rain—oh, what of poor Cameron in this."

Dr. Browne overheard her. "Hush, woman. The lad's young and strong. You mustn't spend your days fretting so. Now, Thaddeus and I have calls to make. We should return by the supper hour." The man gave her a peck on the cheek and called for his son. They pulled their hats tight to their heads and wrapped themselves in their woollen cloaks. "Where is Penny?"

C. D. Baker

"I sent her to the church. She left her fan in the pew yesterday, and it's not the first time. The reverend Coombs is patient, but I do not want the girl thought of as idle-minded or slothful."

Katherine had hardly finished her sentence when the door flew open and Penelope blew in with a gust of pelting rain. She slammed the door behind her, her face ghost-white and dripping wet, and her eyes strained with terror. "What is it?"

Penelope burst into tears and collapsed against her father. Dr. Browne held her tightly and stroked her head. "Shh—shh, good girl," he said calmly. "Quiet, my pumpkin."

Finally the quaking girl began to settle and her mother wiped her eyes. The family circled around her as she moved toward her father's office fire. "Y–you would not believe it."

Archibald and Katherine exchanged glances. Dr. Browne paled. "Did someone—hurt you, girl?"

She shook her head. "No, father. It's not me. I saw something horrible, something more horrible than any nightmare."

Katherine wrapped a gentle arm around her. "Go on."

"I went to the church as you told me. The rain is like I've never seen it. I felt like I was walking under a waterfall. I got to Pine Street with my hood pulled over my head so far I could barely see. No one else was about and I felt so alone. The gutters were full like wild rivers and I tried to jump over one, but my foot landed on—" She trembled. "It was a body, a soldier's body. I fell on top of him and my face was against his. Oh, father. It was so white and—his eyes stared back at me." She buried herself in her father's breast.

"But there were others. I screamed and jumped to my feet. All around me were bodies—Hessians, I think. Men with moustaches, blue uniforms still muddy—they are floating all over Pine. They are this way and that—face up, face down. Some are tangled together around lamp posts and fences." The girl spoke faster and faster. "I ran between them but they floated toward me as if they were after me—"

"Shh," hushed Archibald. "Enough. You are safe—always safe with us. Mother, can you fetch her some coffee? She is soaked through and through and shivering. Thaddeus, go get your sister warm clothes and a quilt." He held her tightly and hummed a tune from the days when she was a little child.

In a half-hour, poor Penelope was warm and comforted in front of her father's hearth. She was quiet and still and stroking Cromwell, who was purring on her lap.

Dr. Browne beckoned his son and the two pulled on their goloe-shoes atop their leather walking shoes. "I am sorry, daughter, but we need to attend several patients. Are you well enough?"

Penelope nodded. "Please see about the bodies. I should hate to think it is another of my dreams."

Dr. Browne secretly wondered the same thing. The girl was given to fanciful thoughts and night time dreams. He bade her an affectionate, though reluctant, farewell and led his son into the blustery street. The two made haste toward Pine Street and in a few moments were staring aghast the sight before them. "Cursed, lazy dogs," shouted Archibald over the crashing rain. "The gravediggers put these Hessians too shallow. Look." He pointed toward Pine Street Presbyterian Church. Its sanctuary had been converted into a hospital a month prior and its graveyard had been filled with dead Hessians. But the unusually heavy rains had flooded the graves, and many of the hastily buried bodies were floating away. Archibald shuddered and shook his head. "We will leave this mess to the ones that caused it. Come, Thaddeus, we need to go to Whittaker's."

Dr. Browne and his son turned down Pine and walked toward the market. They quickly arrived at the corner of Second Street and entered St. Luke's Garden, the apothecary shop owned by his friend Whittaker Yates.

Greetings were exchanged, the shocking story of the floating bodies related, and a brief business conducted. Archibald purchased a number of medicinals, a few dried herbs, and a bottle of turtle oil. He had Whittaker blend a concoction of bear grease and alum for a woman suffering chilblains. Whittaker was deeply grateful to his friend for his support during the patriot occupation. Loyalist apothecaries were a constant target of the Whigs, for they were believed to deliberately poison patriots. Many had been arrested, and most of the others had been driven out of the city. If it had not been for the resolute protection of Dr. Browne, Whittaker would have suffered similarly. Now, with the British in possession of Philadelphia, Mr. Yates was in a position to prosper. Furthermore, it was his turn to assure the Loyalists that Dr. Browne could be trusted in spite of his politics.

The foursome chatted briefly about other neighbourhood news. Thaddeus learned that his friend Richard

Davis had enlisted with Washington. Braddock Nester and Timothy Thomas had left the city with their respective families. It was rumoured that they were living in the Lehigh Valley with relatives. Archibald told Whittaker that Eliza Thomas, Katherine's best friend, had written that she and her husband would stay in New York City, along with Mrs. Browne's other friend, Mrs. Sarah Wilkinson. Since the Wilkinsons and the Thomases were also friends to Whittaker, the news disappointed the apothecary nearly as much as it had Katherine.

Finished with their business, the Brownes returned to the rain and sloshed their way along the flooding city streets to treat a widow for dropsy, a new-born infant for yellow jaundice, three housewives for burns, a new mother for bleeding, and an old man for catarrh. Finally, a runner found them along Third Street and summoned them to Mr. Whiting's house.

"Please wait here," said the house servant, as the two arrived.

The exhausted doctor and his young apprentice removed their overshoes and their wet coats. Ensconced in comfortable chairs, they held their palms toward the snapping fire of the front parlour.

"Brr," shivered Thaddeus. "I'm cold all the way through."

"You've done well today. So many physicians are tending soldiers and prisoners, I fear many citizens have been neglected. You shall learn more in this winter than in five years as an apprentice."

The two stared at the fire and rested for a few moments.

"This Quaker suffers fever, we are told. Tell me again the likely treatment, and why."

Thaddeus sighed. He had been over this time and time again, but would recite it once more. "Yes. The body must be kept in balance. The ancients taught us of the four bodily fluids, which are blood, phlegm, black bile, and yellow bile. Excess or deficiency of any results in disease. The moderns teach us that nerve stimulation keeps the body in its balance. Fever and diseases of excess are from too much stimulation, whereas lethargy and diseases of debility are from too little."

Dr. Browne nodded. "The object of our diagnoses?"

"To determine either excess or debility. Then a course of treatment is prescribed."

Archibald cleaned his spectacles. "Mr. Whiting complains of fever. Your expected plan?"

Thaddeus continued. "Fever is from too much stimulation. It can be from bad air, spoiled food, a dramatic change in temperature, injury, or from an excited emotion. His nerves are too active and causing imbalance. To quiet his nerves, we need to remove this irritability by bloodletting, blistering, or a soft clysters. We may add medicinals or purgatives, diuretics, or emetics, depending on symptoms."

"Well done, lad. The man's age, his other complaints, and his history shall guide us."

A soft voice interrupted the two. "Please, doctor, this way."

A plainly dressed woman led the pair upstairs to a dark bedroom in the rear of the house. Thaddeus noticed that the house was furnished simply and that no pictures hung on the walls. They entered the room and stared down at a wigless, shaved-headed man of middle years. He was sweating heavily and breathing with difficulty.

"Good day. I am Dr. Archibald Browne, and this is my apprentice."

The man nodded.

Dr. Browne turned to the woman. "Are you his wife?"

"Yes."

"He has suffered this state for how long?"

"Five days. All the physicians are busy with this horrid war. Thou art most gracious to come."

Archibald nodded and examined the patient carefully. "Notice, Thaddeus, that his eyes are yellowed slightly and he breathes with difficulty. Mrs. Whiting, have you a fresh chamber pot of his?"

The woman reached under the bed and handed the doctor the brass container. Archibald raised it to his nose and sniffed. He passed it to his son. "Smell. You learn much through the nose."

Dr. Browne thought for a moment. He whispered to Thaddeus and in a moment was holding the man's wrist over a pewter bowl. "Mr. Whiting's fever is excessive. It is good he is sweating, because it reduces the irritation of his nerves. We need to bleed him of about two-thirds of a quart." Archibald requested a bowl of hot water, into which his patient's un-suspecting hand was placed. With the man's veins swollen, Thaddeus tied a leather cord tightly around the wrist and took a sharp lancet from his father's hand. Archibald nodded and the lad cut along an enlarged vein and laid the patient's hand into the water once again.

A rivulet of red streamed into the clear water. It swirled dark and thick until the whole bowl was coloured. The doctor watched carefully as the bowl slowly filled. At last, he lifted Mr. Whiting's wrist from the water and bound it tightly with a cloth.

"Beginning tonight, administer this medicinal three times each day. It is an elixir of camphor, ipecac, rhubarb, and several Indian roots that should increase his sweats. I recommend barley water and a thin gruel. In the morning you must wash him with cold water and again on the evening next. I am confident his fever shall ease within two days. If not, send a runner."

"Thanks to thee," said Mrs. Whiting. "I shall pray for thee at meeting, and may God save the King."

The three descended the stairs and the woman handed Archibald a Spanish dollar coin. The man stared at the silver disc, so generously given. Each colony valued its money differently, and many nations' money was used for payment. It was difficult to keep track of the varying exchange rates of each against the English pound, but the Spanish dollar was always welcome. Its edges were milled, so no one could shave off any silver, as was so often done with other coins. It was valued at almost eight shillings—more than a third of an English pound. Considering a common labourer earned only three or four shillings a day, Dr. Browne had been paid handsomely.

⊷⊶⊷ ⊷⊶⊷

November began unusually cold. Its early winds were as bitter as the city's spirit. Washington's army stubbornly defied the British navy on the Delaware and his pesky soldiers continued to annoy and threaten the picket lines of the British army that were spread in an arc around Philadelphia. Daily patrols of the British were surprised by ambush and British sentries were on constant alert. Only a trickle of supplies was entering the city from the river, most coming across the ferries from New Jersey.

Food was rapidly becoming scarce, wood was being burned at an alarming rate, and money was in short supply. The rest of Howe's army was poised to enter the city in a couple of weeks, and when it arrived the city's resources would be further pressed.

Philadelphia's leading newspaper, the *Pennsylvania Ledger*, scolded the American army for limiting the access of the city's beleaguered population to the farms of the outlying counties. Indeed, Washington continued to tighten the cord around the city and had curtailed the travel of Philadelphians beyond the British lines. Even wives of his veterans were no longer given permission to forage for badly needed food or fuel. Spies, it seemed, had compromised the safety of his men and he could no longer permit the risk.

The markets had little to sell and scanty portions of bad meat or mouldy bread seemed the only options. Sick and wounded soldiers had displaced the poor and the mad in various almshouses and hospitals, and these unfortunates wandered the streets in desperate need. Any number of charitable societies offered what help they could. The Masonic Lodge and the Quaker Meeting House on Fourth Street were opened as shelters, but nearly every other public building had been commandeered for the use of the army. Unfortunately, a black market of stolen property had begun to grow, as plundering soldiers sold their loot to crafty peddlers wandering the market places. General Howe tolerated no such disorder and insisted on a rigorous enforcement of military justice. A soldier caught pillaging was subjected to a penalty of six hundred lashes—or more. Some were executed by hanging.

General Howe kept his soldiers busy by having them spend their days making fascines—bundles of tree branches that were bound by heavy twine and stacked for infantry defences along the British line. Considering the need for firewood, the quota of forty fascines per day per battalion seemed outrageous to the cold citizens of the city.

Philadelphia's neighbourhoods had grown quiet and gloomy. Fences had been torn down, sheds were gone, windows shuttered. The trees were bare, gardens stripped, markets empty. The army had taken horses and oxen; chickens and hogs had mostly been slaughtered and hoarded away. Schools remained closed; church bells were missing. The colourful trim of the city's houses seemed dull and lifeless. The songbirds were gone, the laughter of children silenced; the only sounds were the constant thuds of cannon along the river.

November 11 was a frosty day. Katherine paused to blow a smoky breath into the chill of her bedroom. The family rationed their wood and no fire could be burned in any fireplace other than the kitchen's. Firewood had virtually vanished from the city. Mrs. Browne limited the food at meals. She and Penelope had spent their day rummaging about the city like a pair of paupers. They had not yet felt hunger—at least not the kind that gnaws in the night. But Katherine knew their stores were low. She had one basket of potatoes and four pounds of smoked meat. She thanked God each morning for the ample reserve of cheese and nuts, but served them with measured care. What little food she was able to find was outrageously priced.

"Imagine, Penny," she said, "I paid a Spanish dollar for two pecks of flour. We need to venture out toward the lines and find some brave farmer." Actually, the farmers of the surrounding counties were quick to violate Washington's commands. Many were Loyalists; others were businessmen. They took their wares close to the British lines in the night and hoped to find cash-paying customers sneaking toward them.

"But, mother, General Washington forbids you to leave—"

"General Washington is not my general. He is a rebel soldier who is making our lives miserable."

The two were descending the stairs toward the cellar when Major Crippen entered the back door. He was shivering. Katherine greeted him and led him to the hearth. "Sir, drink this tea."

Penelope looked at her mother incredulously. "Tea? I thought we drank coffee."

Katherine's face hardened. "I have some tea; be glad for it. Major Crippen would prefer English tea to rebel coffee."

Oliver nodded. His lips were blue from standing at his batteries all the night before. "Thank you. I shall have your board money next week. Of course, if the river is ever opened, things should improve."

Katherine wrapped a blanket around the young officer. "You are in summer uniform."

"Aye, Mrs. Brown. Our winter clothing is on a ship somewhere, along with food. The commissioner's secretary told us we've six months supply of beef, pork, bread, butter, and oatmeal for twenty thousand men out there. And we've a seven-month supply of rice and rum. But it's all on the victuallers" ships. The army is given the rum confiscated from the taverns, but I fear we continue to make more enemies with every swallow."

Penelope stood nearby and nodded. "I've heard the army has burned houses of Whig and Tory alike outside of Germantown. And that it's taken sheds and even privies wherever they were to be found to build huts and stables."

Major Crippen nodded. "Aye, it is true, I am sad to say. Most of us think we are here to help save our American cousins from the rabble. I fear we are becoming the rabble. I know that Captain Simcoe and the Queen's Rangers have been very frustrated by the Pennsylvania militiamen. They are foraging for the army just beyond the lines, but I fear their zeal turns King's men into patriots every day."

Katherine sighed. "Washington makes me so angry I could spit. He's bound us up in this awful place without wood and winter is fast coming. He says he is a Christian man but he revolts against his own King in direct disobedience to Holy Scripture.

Then he treats his fellow Christians like this."

Penelope stiffened. "What about the beating father took just weeks ago? That was in the name of the King."

"No. The King's army protected him from an angry mob. And can you blame them for their anger?"

"I can hardly believe my ears. You are defending them?"

Mrs. Browne hesitated, and then pursed her lips. "No. I am just saying that some people have reasons to be angry."

Major Crippen interrupted. "Forgive my intrusion but I think the patriots have reasons to be angry as well."

Katherine was surprised. "I do not know how to answer you."

"I am not defending their cause, Mrs. Browne, but I think I understand their grievances. When an arrogant government fails to hear its people, conflict is inevitable."

"Your temperance astounds me. I would have thought you to wish them all dead."

"No. I wish them all to yield their arms and return to their mother. I, like General Howe, have a deep regard for you Americans. You are kin to us and are our friends. I am angrier with Parliament than with your Congress. Its members have not listened to the sufferings of their own family. I fear we are reaping what we deserve."

Penelope stared at the young major in wonder. She had imagined all the British to be her enemy—vile rakes with ears deafened to sound reason. Instead, the man was thoughtful and fair-minded. He had considered the matter carefully and was humble enough to see the flaws in his own cause. She asked, "Then why do you kill your cousins? Why do you spend long hours aiming your cannon against our pitiful galleys?"

"I am an Englishman and have a duty to my King and Parliament. Under God, I have the grave obligation to preserve the order of tradition and the rule of law. I assure you, Penelope, that when we end this revolution I shall be equally dutiful in seeing that justice is properly recovered."

The man's reasoned perspective made Penelope suddenly uncomfortable. She had spent the past two years immersed in the rhetoric of Thomas Paine and Sam Adams. Her own views were characterised more by emotion than by reason and now her emotions were unsettled.

Hearing the officer talk of killing Americans in the name of tradition and law, however, did not sound as good to Katherine as she supposed it would. She had stated a similar position over and over in her own mind for the past several years, yet hearing the major's words made her feel differently. Perhaps it was because the Americans he reluctantly killed included her own Cameron.

A soldier burst in through the upstairs door and called for the major. A handsome young man crashed down the steps. "Sir." He saluted. "We are ordered to the batteries at once. General Howe has ordered the assault to continue."

Major Crippen stood and straightened his uniform. He bowed gracefully to his hostesses and followed the soldier out.

⇢⊨⊚ ⊚⊨⇠

For four long days the defenders at Fort Mifflin stubbornly endured a withering cannonade by the British. General Howe had been so frustrated by weeks of costly defeats that he had finally requested to be relieved of duty; however, it would be months before his request was granted. For now, the general had one goal and that was to open the river—at any cost.

Conditions inside Fort Mifflin were abominable. Each day the fort was nearly destroyed by cannon from the shore, and each night its brave American soldiers worked at rebuilding, under the orders of their French engineer, Major François Louis de Fleury. A freezing rain had fallen for several days and, by the eleventh of November, a half-inch of ice lay across the river. High winds had protected the forts from the approach of British men-of-war, but on the morning of November 15, the sky cleared. Six British warships picked their way through the remaining *chevaux-de-frise*. On the clear dawn of that new day they were positioned in a semi-circle and preparing to destroy the beleaguered fort.

Rallying to Fort Mifflin's defence raced a pitiful little fleet of American galleys. In a hopeless contest, these small ships engaged the earth's most fearsome navy with courage. Shelled by the British batteries on shore as well as by the heavy cannon on board the mighty British men-of-war, they suffered terrible casualties. The patriots fought on, nonetheless, until the sun set on both the horizon and on all hope. What few American ships survived slipped away in the night, and the exhausted defenders of the fort accepted their fate.

The valiant American commander of Fort Mifflin, Major Simeon Thayer, sadly ordered most of his garrison to row-boats and sent them through darkness to the safety of Fort Mercer. He remained with forty others, torching everything of possible value to the British—including the fort itself. With the American flag flying proudly in the centre of the flames, he and his company then rowed across the black waters of the Delaware to join their comrades at Fort Mercer.

Meanwhile, as Fort Mifflin was falling, a force of 6,000 British and Hessian troops had ferried across the river to attack the American defenders of Fort Mercer. The fort was the final obstacle to the British navy's entrance into the port city. The citizens of Philadelphia were filled with anxiety through these days for they heard only rumours and rumbles, and knew little of either side's condition. They had grown accustomed to a certain level of uncertainty and surprise, yet no one was prepared for what occurred at seven o'clock on Saturday morning, the 22nd of November.

The Brownes had been awake for two hours. They had eaten their morning fare of oatmeal and stale bread. The doctor and his apprentice were busy reviewing patient records in their chilly office while the women were trying to heat water in an iron kettle suspended above a scanty fire.

The distant bell of Christ Church could be heard striking the hour when the Brownes' house began to shudder.

"Katherine!" cried Archibald.

"The sound of a thousand hooves," as Whittaker Yates later described it, roared through the frightened streets of Philadelphia as the earth shook and quaked. The Brownes stumbled and fell; bowls rattled along their shelves. A porcelain figurine crashed atop the office floor and windows cracked. A cry rose up from the cellar; then the house was still again.

Dr. Browne and Thaddeus charged toward the twisting stairs that led to the cellar kitchen and flew to the aid of Penelope. The hot, greasy water that had sloshed from the kettle had scalded her arms. "Quick, Thaddeus, balm and a clean wrap."

Archibald's eyes swiftly scanned his daughter's tender skin. He breathed a sigh of relief. "Penny, you shall feel discomfort, but in a few days you'll be as good as new. No scars."

She nodded, in pain, and turned to her mother. "A few minutes ago I was angry that the pot wouldn't boil. Imagine if I had had my wish."

"Aye, dear daughter," Katherine answered calmly. "I think some weary angel must have been blowing cool air into our kettle. It is a good thing our demands are sometimes restrained by the One who knows better."

CHAPTER 7

Penelope's First Adventure

THE EARTHQUAKE SHOULD have been news enough to excite the whole of the city for weeks. Twenty-two years prior, an earthquake in Lisbon, Portugal, had been felt across the ocean in New York, Boston, and Philadelphia. That little quiver caused such a stir that taverns buzzed for days.

But the 22nd of November brought other news as well. Smoke could be seen rising in the north, near Germantown, and riders galloped through the city announcing that the British had torched dozens of country homes and barns. The magnificent estates of both Loyalist and patriot were destroyed by Hessian and English soldiers who were ever more frustrated by the sniping of American militiamen hiding within. Farms that had strained to provide much needed food to the hungry city were in flames as well. The citizens of Philadelphia were outraged. They set to work cleaning up after the earthquake, casting jaundiced eyes on the British soldiers sent to help them.

By late afternoon yet more news arrived. Weary and terribly outnumbered, the American army defending Fort Mercer had retreated from Lord Cornwallis' army. With the fall of the second fort, the Delaware River was open.

Shouts of joy suddenly filled the streets of Philadelphia. Fear and uncertainty yielded to revelry and the cold, hungry citizens laughed and sang. The abuses, annoyances, and injustices that had so embittered the city's people immediately gave way to a spirit of forgiveness and gratitude.

Admiral Howe promised that his ships would fill Philadelphia's wharves with potatoes and meat, flour, rice, rum, salt, bolts of cloth, trays of medicine, firewood, leather, sundry dry goods, ale—and hay for the poor beasts of the army.

In the midst of this jubilation Dr. Browne stood quietly at his doorway. He watched happy citizens parade the street and hurrah King George. He nodded politely to the smiling officers ambling up Union, but his heart was filled with guilt. Food and fuel would now provide his family with relief, and the cold winter ahead would surely be less desperate, so part of him wanted to cheer and sing with the others. Yet his son and their mutual cause had been defeated; their enemy also would be warm and well fed. The struggle within the man was a painful one and all he could do was weep. Such can be the nature of hope in a world clouded by dilemma.

⊷⧟ ⧟⊶

As promised, the Delaware River was soon crowded with ships racing to unload their wares at the wharves. As early as the evening of the 22nd, sloops began to dock. A few days later Penny counted twenty-six sails approaching the docks. Of course,

King Street—or Water Street, as the patriots preferred to call it—was jammed with eager customers bidding up every item, forcing prices to soar. Either limited supply or increased demand always drives prices upward—a simple principle upon which men of business build wealth. A pound of sugar now cost twelve shillings instead of two, a bottle of wine cost ten instead of one. A common worker needed to work four days to pay for one pound of sugar. Rum, the favoured drink of most men, cost four English pounds a gallon. At twenty shillings to an English pound, this meant that a gallon of rum cost eighty shillings, or about a month's wage for a worker.

In all of this, the army was concerned to protect its own supplies, and Quartermaster General Sir William Erskine took immediate control of the situation. He had no objection to enterprise, but greed was out of bounds. He ordered all private merchantmen and masters of vessels to provide an inventory of their cargoes. Anyone not complying would be subject to confiscation. Informers were handsomely paid. Furthermore, the waterfront was quickly fenced off and 250 marines assigned night patrol to guard against thugs, looters, and smugglers. But, despite high prices, the city's citizens breathed a collective sigh of relief, for they knew that more ships would quickly arrive and warehouses would be well stocked before the river froze.

In addition to food and countless other commodities, the ships brought the return of many a Loyalist. Hundreds of Philadelphia's wealthiest families had fled to New York the year before and had spent the last month bobbing on the choppy waters of the Delaware Bay. They cheerfully descended their ships' planks to reclaim their homes and their businesses. Along with them came a colourful assortment of musicians, artisans, caterers, and adventurers eager to serve the King's army in the New World's most splendid city.

The Brownes had little time to enjoy the newfound bounty heaped along King Street. Thaddeus spent two days helping Webster and Whittaker Yates restock their apothecary shop. The earthquake had shaken bottles and jars loose from their shelves and the catastrophe required a trained eye to sort the many teas, roots, and dried berries that had spilled into one another across the floor and counter. Dr. Browne was busy buzzing up and down the neighbourhood streets serving the many residents who had been burned, or injured by glass or toppling bricks. His wooden leg could be heard clicking along the cobblestones in daylight and in darkness. It was a sound that gave comfort to many in the night.

Penelope's arms were healing quickly. She was fortunate to have been spared worse. Any doctor would agree that he lost as many women to the kitchen hearth as to childbirth. Nearly a quarter of all women died from each of these most dangerous causes. Penny helped her mother as best she could to repair the damage that had been done by the earthquake.

The next day Katherine returned to duties at the State House, where a new heap of wounded American prisoners had been dumped. These wretches were survivors from the assault against Forts Mifflin and Mercer and had been roughly handled by their captors. Most arrived at the hospital near death. Those who were not mortally wounded were beset by fever and chill from the cold, unsheltered journey across the Delaware. Having embarrassed the British so badly by their admirable courage, the men were treated with an angry vengeance. Katherine wondered that any survived the rage of the British at all.

Mrs. Browne spent long days tending wounds and comforting spirits. Her husband returned from other duties to extract shrapnel and musket balls, bind bones, and stitch wounds. He worked tirelessly into the night, like the other angels of mercy hovering all about. It was not unusual for the Brownes to retire to their home at daybreak, exhausted by the death and misery of that awful place.

Early one morning, about two hours past dawn, Mr. and Mrs. Browne were awakened by the tiptoe of Major Crippen. The weary soldier had not wanted to disturb his hosts, but the creaking of the front door and the groan of the wooden steps sounded his presence like a loud warning signal. "Major?" called Katherine.

"Aye, Mrs. Browne. Sorry to wake you."

"Might I fix you some porridge and tea?"

Archibald yanked his wig on to his head. "Tea?" he groused.

Major Crippen answered. "Yes, it would be wonderful."

Dr. Browne led the officer to the cellar and plopped into his favourite ladder-back chair. He stared aimlessly at the snapping fire of the hearth. Penelope and Thaddeus came down the stairs and reported some news they had garnered at New Market.

"Yesterday a Frenchman defeated the Hessians across the river," grumbled Thaddeus.

"Aye, lad," answered Major Crippen. "He's that rascally Lafayette. Our own Major André hates him. I think he's a bit jealous. It seems Lafayette is a favourite of the ladies and André wishes to be the same."

"So, perhaps you ought to lay a trap for this Lafayette."

"I've heard some talk of it at headquarters, but I think we've other matters more pressing. Seems Washington may quarter his men in Whitemarsh for the winter. That's not far from our present lines and the thought of it makes Howe nervous. From there the rebels could torture us fairly well until springtime."

Katherine listened very carefully. She had learned from a wounded soldier that Washington's main army was indeed planning to winter at Whitemarsh and most of his army was there now. It was likely her Cameron was close, very close. "Major, do you think we will attack Washington before spring?"

The major thought for a moment. He had warned his junior officers and men to be careful what news they shared with civilians. Spies were a constant concern. He looked at Katherine. *She did say, 'we' will attack*, he thought. "Mrs. Browne, you understand I am bound to discretion?"

"Of course. I withdraw my question."

Oliver hesitated. He did not want to insult his hosts by insinuating they might betray his trust. "Let me simply say

C. D. Baker

that I believe it is a very likely option. Ah, but I've other news for you. The navy is paying a bounty to the artillery for our part in the capture in September of the American frigate, the Delaware. Admiral Howe insists the matter be settled before he sails to Rhode Island for the winter. So, Dr. Browne, I am happy to say that I shall receive a significant payment and shall be pleased to furnish this household with a table befitting the gracious character of your family."

Archibald darkened. Pursing his lips, he removed his spectacles, but said nothing. The cellar became very quiet except for the crackling of the fire as the man stared at his porringer filled with steaming oatmeal.

Major Crippen shifted uncomfortably on his chair and nervously fidgeted with the buttons of his coat. "Did I offend you?"

Dr. Browne looked up. "We'll not be wanting the advantages of your blood money."

"I see," answered Oliver sadly. "I—I truly meant no offence. With all the privation you have suffered, I only thought to offer some pleasantries."

"Pleasantries? I can only imagine what pleasantries my son is enjoying. I say again, I'll not share in your booty as long as you aim your cursed cannon at my son."

Oliver looked around the room at the faces staring at him. He nodded and politely excused himself from the table.

The family remained silent until Dr. Browne offered thanks for the simple meal placed before them. Katherine laid a hand atop his and squeezed it lightly. She understood.

⇢⥮⥮ ⥮⥮⥮

Penelope was troubled. She worried about Cameron for all that day, especially while tending the wounded with her mother. Katherine, too, seemed distracted and irritable. She was uncommonly tense and preoccupied. She cared little about the news of the day. She shrugged when she learned of tighter restrictions on citizens foraging beyond the British line. She cared even less to learn of some "Articles of Confederation" being considered by the states. And when a patriot woman whispered that the American Congress approved the confiscation of Loyalist property, she turned away.

The Browne women left the hospital at mid-afternoon and walked up-town toward Market Street. Katherine had been worried about Josiah, for she had not seen him for over a week. The man was supposed to be sleeping in the loom-room at night, but no one had seen him or the wood shavings that always seemed to follow. While walking up Sixth Street, they came upon Mrs. Mary Franks.

"Ah, good day, neighbour," the woman said curtly.

"And to you, Mrs. Franks," answered Katherine. "You are well?"

"Aye." The woman's face was drawn and she stood stiffly.

Katherine paused a moment, then smiled politely as she began to walk on. "Have a good day, Mrs. Franks."

"Mrs. Browne?" the woman called.

Katherine rolled her eyes and stopped. "Yes?" She turned around.

Mary Franks looked miserable and sad. Penny thought the woman would break down in tears at any moment. "I am sorry to trouble you, but I am trying to find news of my husband's regiment. Is there any chance you've heard any mention of it?"

"Mr. Franks is in the Pennsylvania Loyalist regiment, if I recall?"

"*Sergeant* Franks."

Katherine thought for a moment and recalled a comment from a wounded American. "I heard from a prisoner that his regiment was active in New Jersey in the week past."

"New Jersey? Ah, New Jersey, of course. That is why I haven't heard from him. Well, with General Howe sending another twelve thousand soldiers into the city today, I am sure I shall finally see him."

"I believe he said the Loyalists suffered very few losses."

"Oh, thank you, Mrs. Browne." Mary's face was suddenly beaming. Her pouty lips were spread across her chubby face and revealed more gums than teeth. Penelope clenched her jaw so she would not laugh.

Katherine smiled. She was pleased to bring a little joy to anyone. "I am happy for you, Mrs. Franks. I hope your husband is well enough."

Poor Mary Franks. No one ever was happy for her and to hear those few tender words brought tears. She lunged at a very startled Katherine and embraced her. "It has been so very hard, this war," the woman sobbed. "I fear it has taken my Melvin's affections, and it may take his very life."

Katherine stood stiffly but charitably and held the woman while she cried.

Finally, Mary backed away and dabbed her eyes with a kerchief. She took Katherine's hand. "Mrs. Browne, I am planning a Christmas dinner at my home on the 23rd of December. It is an occasion to welcome home some friends that we both know. I should invite a few officers as well—it is important to keep in good stead with them, you know. Would you and your husband join us?"

Mrs. Browne's mind raced. She'd enjoy seeing old friends and a social affair would be such a joy. But she was uncertain of her husband's approval. "I am humbled by your kind and most gracious offer, Mrs. Franks. I–I must ask my husband."

"Of course. Tell him I forgive him for closing his home to me. Actually, perhaps it was for the best after all. When my Melvin comes home he'd surely rather sleep in his own bed." She winked.

"Aye, indeed," smiled Katherine. "I shall be sure to tell him. Thank you and good day."

Katherine released a long sigh and laughed with Penelope as they rounded the corner at Market Street. "Can you imagine telling your father that Mary Franks forgives him?"

"That ought move him to accept her invitation. And, mother, your words were very kind. You know nothing of casualties."

Katherine shook her head. "I did not want to give her false hope, but sometimes it is better than none."

The two soon faced the imposing Deshler mansion at Market Square and stared in awe, pulling their cloaks around them against the cold and bitter air of late November. The busy Deshler home was large and immaculate and eminently suitable for the temporary residence of the commander-in-chief of Britain's forces. A stately, red brick structure standing three and a half stories tall, the upper story was lit by two dormers. Each sidewall was topped with a wide chimney, while eleven large windows and an impressive door graced the front wall. On the left side was a walled courtyard and the likely workplace of the Grackle.

Katherine led her daughter toward the bustling mansion and was immediately addressed by two grenadier guards. "Your business?"

"We are here to see a worker in General Howe's employ, a Mr. Josiah Byrd."

"What is your business with him?"

"He is a good friend and we are concerned for his wellbeing."

"Can you not see we are busy? The general is in council and visitors are not permitted on the premises."

"But—"

A merry voice called from the front door. "Mistress Browne." It was Josiah.

Katherine and Penny smiled and waved. They brushed past the soldiers and greeted their friend. "Mr. Byrd. So very good to see you. Are you well?"

"Yes."

"Where are you sleeping?"

"Here. Mrs. Loring lets me sleep in the garden house most nights. I've a stove, and good food. She takes proper care of me and the general likes my whittle-work."

"You are happy, then. Wonderful. We have been worried." Katherine was relieved.

Josiah grinned mischievously. He whispered in the ear of a guard by the door. The young soldier chuckled and allowed the three to pass indoors. Josiah waved to the house servants standing along the walls of the centre hall. He had made friends of all of them. "These are the Brownes. They are good Tories." He winked slyly at Penny.

Katherine stared about the foyer in awe. The ceiling was very high and decorated with ornamental plaster in the Rococo style. The floor was slate, and great mahogany doors opened to rooms on either side of the massive stairway in front of them. She stared into the smoky front parlour where some officers were bent over a table. The room was panelled from top to bottom and accented with fluted columns and wide, ornate crown mouldings. Its hardwood floor boasted an oily, satin shimmer, hand-rubbed to perfection by the strong hands of Josiah Byrd. The furniture was of fine quality wood, mostly cherry, and the windows were shaded with wooden Venetian blinds. Oil paintings of William Howe's family hung boldly next to simpler watercolours of England's green pasturelands. A knot of officers appeared at the top of the stairway and Josiah hurried the ladies to the rear of the house.

"This is the kitchen," he said. It was very different from Katherine's cosy, unpretentious kitchen. Large, spacious, and well equipped, it could easily serve the needs of dozens of guests. "We daren't go upstairs but come, follow me to the yard."

Josiah led the pair into the adjacent courtyard, where the remnants of the summer gardens lay unattended. Perfectly ordered squares filled much of the yard, each providing herbs or vegetables in their proper season. To the far side, by a well, grew half a dozen fruit trees. At the back side stood a row of buildings that were used as repair shops, drying sheds, and quarters for the five slaves who served the house. The three walked quietly along the outside wall of the house, admiring the grounds. They ambled to the side window of the front parlour and leaned against the brick wall. They surveyed the garden while Josiah told them of his duties. The Brownes were content to know the man was happy and well provided for. Katherine thought it was ironic that he was in a far better position than themselves.

Perhaps it was the smoke, or perhaps something else, but for whatever reason, the window near them had been opened a crack. The three hushed. General Howe was speaking. "He can not be allowed to winter in Whitemarsh."

"Agreed. But we must strike, and soon."

"The Americans have been joined by some four thousand troops from the north and may be easily tempted to enjoin us in a final battle for this place. Washington's present position is strong at the centre, but his flanks are weak and supported only by militia.

"Lord Cornwallis, how many days' expedition do you calculate you will need to draw Washington from his heights? My objective is to defeat him on *my* ground."

General Cornwallis was a faithful field commander whose judgement was valued. "Four days."

"Good. Have the quartermaster prepare provisions for four days. The rank and file shall engage with packs. I do not wish to be slowed in this rainy, miserable season with wagons. This is the 1st of December. It is my order that we advance no later than by dawn of the 4th. I shall entrust the welfare of the city to you, General Leslie. You shall use companies of convalescent soldiers, each with one officer and enough non-commissioned officers to keep order. I want Mirbach's regiment and two battalions of Hessians holding the trenches in our rear. Prepare the army, gentlemen."

Josiah and his nervous companions pressed their backs hard against the cold bricks of the house. The poor man had not expected the general to be holding council here, for those matters were typically held at the general's working headquarters on Second Street. If he and the Brownes were seen here under the window, it would surely seem they were spies.

Inside, the officers were discussing the particulars of the campaign. At one point a heated argument engaged several of them and Josiah seized the moment. "Quick. This way," he whispered. The three dashed through the mud and rounded the corner. They ducked into the summer kitchen wide-eyed and panting. Josiah's face was taut. Neither he nor they were thinking clearly—judgement so easily yields to feeling. "There, you needs to get out the back gate. Quick."

Instead of simply cleaning their shoes and re-entering the house, the frightened three hurried through the rear lawn, past the slave quarters and to the rear wall. Josiah opened the gate a little and ventured a peek. What he found was the end of a soldier's musket.

"Who goes?" barked a sergeant.

The Grackle knew how to play the fool. He stepped into the rear alley with a big smile and rolling eyes. "I goes. I goes to the market, I goes to the privy. I goes to church."

The Redcoat lowered his weapon and studied the old man. "Are you a slave to the Deshlers?"

"Yes, indeed. For 'bout thirty years."

"Hmm. What's your business out here?"

"Why, I—I needs find young Eliza. She's gone off for groats and corn-mash and she's not come back."

The soldier poked his head into the courtyard. Seeing nothing suspicious, he growled, "Go on. Get about it."

Katherine and Penny squatted quietly behind a hedge as Josiah meandered down the alley. They could see another gate at the street side but were sure it was guarded as well. The house would be impossible to enter without Josiah, and their shoes were clotted with mud. Katherine's heart raced. Penelope pointed to the sidewall of the garden, behind the fruit trees.

"Mother," she whispered. "Could we climb the trees and—"

Suddenly they heard the sound of a shrill whistle and men's voices shouting in the back alley. Horses galloped by and a company of boots could be heard squishing through the mud. Katherine didn't know what the commotion was, but she knew it was now or never. She hurried to the rear gate and opened it ever so slightly. A tardy private tripped past and shuffled away.

The alley was clear and the two slipped away.

⊷══ ══⊷

That night, Archibald and Thaddeus collapsed into their beds where they lay still as a couple of corpses. Their day had been filled beyond all reason, including another bleeding of Mr. Whiting. By contrast, Katherine and Penelope tossed in their beds through the whole of the night until dawn beckoned them to their duties in the kitchen.

As the new day began, the Brownes sat quietly before a warm hearth. Major Crippen entered the kitchen silently. Ever since Dr. Browne's rebuff, Oliver had become respectfully distant. The doctor was not an uncharitable man, however, and offered a few kind words. He even invited the officer to give thanks for the meal before them.

Relieved and a bit more relaxed, Major Crippen complimented the women on their fresh-baked bread. He then cleared his throat. "Sir," he began. "I wish to apologise for my poor manners and inexcusable insensitivity toward you and your family the other morn." He extended his hand.

Dr. Browne willingly grasped it and nodded. "On behalf of my family I accept your gracious apology. Now, no more of it."

The five ate quietly for a long while, enjoying every bite of the warm bread. Even the porridge tasted better. "Salt, Archibald—the difference is salt." Katherine could always read her husband's mind.

Oliver finished his tea and set his cup down. "Mrs. Browne, perhaps tomorrow I might enjoy some coffee?" He smiled at the doctor.

"Indeed. We'll make you an American yet."

"I could do far worse—I could be French." Oliver laughed and began buttoning his coat. He was thankful his winter uniform had arrived. As he stood to leave he casually mentioned an incident of the prior day. "I suppose you have heard about the commotion caused by your Josiah fellow at General Howe's home yesterday?"

Katherine and Penelope chilled.

"It seems the old fellow saw some spies running down Fifth and he called the whole block into action. He said he had seen *two* men in the garden earlier but gave it little heed. But he said he later saw the same two sneaking up the alley toward the house and he was sure they were up to no good.

"The villains escaped, but I am told that the guards found footprints in the mud by the parlour window. It seems the footprints were facing forward, indicating a position where the rogues' backs would have been set against the house to listen. But there were three prints, not two; a woman and two men. Josiah says he saw no woman-—but he may have missed her. I find it most interesting. I think I should have preferred investigations to cannon."

The Browne women were white and nervous. Katherine's heart was pounding. "So—so Josiah is—is—"

"He is a hero in the household. But begging your pardon, I must see to my duties. Godspeed to each." The officer disappeared up the steps.

"Imagine, Josiah a hero," laughed Thaddeus. "A hero for the Crown, father."

"Enjoy your fun, lad. I just wish the old man would stay clear of trouble."

Katherine breathed a sigh of relief and leaned close to Penny. She nodded toward the girl's big feet and whispered, "One woman and two men." Katherine giggled.

Archibald and his apprentice were off to another day's busy labours while Katherine began a day of weaving. Penelope was preparing to go to the hospital again but paused to watch her mother, thinking how much the woman had aged in the past few months. Streaks of grey now striped her hair and her face had grown gaunt and taut. She pedalled her loom and threw her shuttle with increasing impatience, as if she were driven by deep thoughts of other things. Poor Katherine was troubled. Her son was in Whitemarsh and her King's army was preparing to strike. Penelope, too, was given to thoughts of Cameron. Was he sick, was he wet and hungry, cold or injured? Did he know the British were planning to attack him in two short days? Two days.

The girl felt nauseous. She wanted to warn him: she must warn him.

Penny's heart began to race and her breath came quickly. She gathered her cloak and hat as she calculated a plan. General Howe permitted residents to cross the lines between 8:00 a.m. and 5:00 p.m. It was already approaching 9:00 a.m. and she would have six or more miles to travel to get past the lines. Then she'd have to find an American patrol or sharpshooter. She must hurry. "Mother, I need to leave. Dr. Rush said he'd be doing amputations all day and needs more nurses."

"Good, dear. Hurry along, then." Mrs. Browne's voice was odd sounding.

Penny had a strange feeling come over her. She looked at her mother carefully. "Is everything all right, mother?"

"Aye. You'd best make haste. The surgeons start early." The woman's body was tight and tense.

Penny shrugged and backed into her father's office. She wrapped herself tightly in her wool coat and stepped into her goloe-shoes. "Big feet, indeed. These over-shoes make them bigger still," she muttered. With that she disappeared into the busy streets of the city. She walked quickly from Union to Second, then turned north through the very centre of the city, passing Christ Church, the Anabaptist meetinghouse and finally entering the German neighbourhoods and the road to

Germantown. Just as they did some eight blocks to the west, the cobblestones finally ended at the northern edges of the city and the frosty mud began. She pressed on for three miles, passing hay wagons, carriages, and companies of soldiers. She ignored a trio of swaggering Hessians and raised her nose at a wealthy Quaker with a sideboard.

Finally, she rested her aching feet for a few minutes against a wide-trunked sycamore. Surveying the barren countryside, she shuddered. Everywhere she looked she saw burned farmhouses and barns. Fences and sheds had been ripped apart for firewood and trees had been amputated as roughly as the poor wretches she had left behind. She shook her head and returned to the Germantown road through a slightly rising landscape now filling with patches of woodland and rolling hills.

She entered the narrow town slowly and looked sadly at the houses lining both sides of the road. Penelope had often heard of the place, but had pictured it very differently. She imagined the town had once been quaint and lively. Its deserted homes had a lingering, stubborn neatness about them, but they displayed the evidence of hard times. Most of the shutters were gone, windows were smashed, and fences all removed. Many were charred; others had been vandalised. In the cold grey of the day, Germantown suddenly seemed to be a horrible place.

Penny fell in line at the army checkpoint and waited impatiently for over an hour until those in front were permitted through. Hundreds were crowding their way toward the

C. D. Baker

countryside in hopes of foraging nuts or finding farmers with something left to sell. At last it was her turn.

A large grenadier stared at her for a brief moment. "Where do you be going, lass?"

"My father'd be a Scot—a Scot from Ireland, but a Scot indeed."

"I'll say again. Where do you be going?"

"To forage."

"You've no basket."

Penelope reddened. *How could I be this stupid?* She thought. "Well, sir, a cursed Quaker stole it from me."

"Quakers do not steal."

"Aye; well, this one did." Her voice faltered. The soldier had made a good point.

"Captain, come here."

A huge man lumbered in front of Penelope. "Aye?"

"The wee lass says she's to forage and a Quaker stole her basket."

The captain shook his head. "Quakers do not steal."

"I told her that."

The captain stared at the girl for a long moment. "What is your name?"

"Penelope Browne."

"You understand, Goody Browne, that the generals believe most spies to now be women? And here you come to forage with no basket."

Penny was trembling on the inside but set her jaw. "I am no 'Goody' Browne. My father is a physician. Please address me properly, sir. I have walked some six miles and had my basket stolen by a Quaker. I do not expect to go home empty-handed.

Besides, I should think a spy would not be so stupid as to leave a basket behind." Her green eyes flashed beneath her wool mobcap. A wisp of red hair drifted down her forehead and she blew it away in a huff.

The soldiers laughed. "She's a Scot—can you not see it?"

"Aye, private. But not so many Scots have big feet like hers." The two roared. "Go, miss, find an egg or a berry that fits in your pocket but be back before five."

Penelope nodded politely and hurried past the guards. She wanted to run but thought the better of it. She had travelled about a hundred yards and her heart had just begun to slow when a horse charged toward her from behind.

"Halt. You there, halt."

Penelope froze. *Me? What could they want with me?* She thought. An aged lieutenant dismounted and seized Penny's wrist.

He spun her around and stared at her feet. "Where were you yesterday?"

"Uh, uh, I—I can not remember, sir."

"We shall see about that. Guards, I want her arrested and taken to Howe's mansion."

"I—I don't understand, officer. I'm only—"

"I was assigned duty at the mansion yesterday. Three spies left their footprints in the garden by the general's window. One set of prints were small, two were large. We assumed them to be men, but our Indian said the man would need be very light—or else be a woman with big feet."

"But—but—" She wanted to cry out that it was her overshoes that made her feet bigger than they really were. Something bound her tongue. The girl was tied and tossed into a wagon like a bundle of sticks. Landing with a whimper, she spent the next half-hour bouncing atop the hard boards. She fought tears by fixing her mind's eye on Cameron's face. She imagined them both suffering for their cause and she became steady.

Before long, the brick and cobblestone of Philadelphia surrounded her once again. The sun was still high in the sky. It was about two o'clock, she reckoned. The soldier guarding her was nearly asleep as they passed Christ Church. The bell chimed twice, startling the man. Penny smiled; she was always good at guessing the hour.

In a few short minutes the wagon turned into the alley behind the Deshler mansion and her guards dragged her to the ground. "Your name, wench."

"I am no wench."

The officer snarled. "Your name, missy."

"I prefer to be addressed as 'mistress.' I am no commoner."

The officer turned to the private. "Go and find the slave. He was witness to this. Once again, your name?"

"I am Penelope Browne, daughter of Dr. Archibald Browne, granddaughter of Sir Reginald P. Henry."

The lieutenant paused. "Reginald Henry—the privateer?"

"Aye."

"I knew him once. He bought me rum in the islands."

Josiah came through the gate, wide-eyed and nervous.

The officer addressed him curtly. "You. You are the one who witnessed the two running away?"

"Yes, sir," he answered slowly. His yellow eyes fell on Penny.

"And the two you chased were the same two as you saw in the garden?"

Josiah nodded. "Yes."

"Is this one of them?"

"Oh, no, sir. I saw two men."

"Are you certain?"

Josiah nodded. "Oh, yes, sir."

The lieutenant circled Penelope. "Do you have a brother or father with the rebels?"

Penny paled. Her mind raced. "Uh—aye, a brother."

"I thought as much." He took Penny by the arm and dragged her into the garden. He stopped by the window and faced the prints perfectly formed in the mud. "Now, girl, we shall have our answer. Stand with your back to the wall and fit your feet into the prints—carefully."

Penelope was trembling and she bit her lip. She looked toward Josiah who remained some distance away. He needed to avoid the chance risk of his own boots being compared. The girl was sweating in the cold air and dutifully obeyed; first one foot and then the other. She stared straight ahead and waited.

The officer stooped to his haunches, then leaned on his knees. Another squatted by his side and an Indian was waved from the corner. The British soldiers yielded to the Indian, who bent low and studied the girl's feet carefully. He raised his head and fixed his eyes on Penny's. A chill ran up the girl's back and she looked away. The Indian stood and whispered to the lieutenant, then stepped into the background.

The officer cleared his voice. "Mistress Browne. Please accept the most sincere apology of the King's army. As you can see, your feet are—larger than the prints. We shall gladly escort you home."

Penelope almost burst into tears. How glad she was to have worn her goloe-shoes this day. It was incredible to her that no one thought to have her remove them. She glanced at the quiet Indian and wondered. Then she turned to the lieutenant and raised her chin indignantly. "I should hope that if ever you see grandfather again, *you* shall buy *him* some rum."

CHAPTER 8

Joseph Galloway

PENELOPE RETURNED HOME about four o'clock on the afternoon of December 2nd. Daylight was yielding quickly to the blue-grey of twilight and the damp air of Union Street chilled her. She sat on the cold stone of the doorway's stoop and grunted as she pulled off her overshoes. She beat them together, scattering chunks of dried mud over the brick sidewalk. Sighing with relief and happy to be home, she stood up and reached for the brass doorknob, but as she did, she noticed an envelope pinned to the door. It read, "For Dr. or Mrs. Archibald Browne."

Penelope gulped, certain it must be a notice from a magistrate regarding her day's unfortunate events. *Oh, no.* She thought. *More trouble.* Unpinning the note, she entered her home and set her goloe-shoes along the wall beneath the coat pegs. She was surprised to see that her mother's overshoes were missing—along with her mother. She stood still and listened. Not a sound could be heard in the dark, empty house.

Penelope set the envelope atop her father's desk and picked up the tinderbox. From it she retrieved a flint and some lint and started a small fire with which she lit a candle in each downstairs room. As the little flames began to rise and bend on their looping wicks, the girl paused in front of one and stared. Fire was sometimes a friend, sometimes not—but it always enchanted her, and it released her mind to fantastic fantasy. "Imagination," her grandfather Henry had said, "is the wing of the soul. It flies within reason and without, from things seen to things felt. It is the energy of creation and the very wonder of God."

The girl descended the steps to the cellar where a sleepy hearth yawned red and ashy. Placing a few dry sticks on the coals, she pumped the bellows. In moments, a happy, snapping fire danced within the gaping mouth of the fireplace, and the young woman stretched her opened hands toward its warmth. Relaxed, Penelope reached for a wooden pail and walked to the Union Street well for water. The well was about midway on the block and tucked neatly within Drinker's Courtyard. She walked quickly through the cold evening's air but noticed that the street had a certain nervousness about it. She looked about uneasily as she pumped water into her bucket until it was full, then hurried back to the safety of her kitchen.

"Still no mother," Penelope muttered, as she entered the front door. It was not like her to be gone this late. She knew her mother had a quota of weaving to fill, but when she checked the loom she found little work had been completed. Strands of waiting yarn still covered the frame, like rigging on a large ship. *And why are her overshoes missing?*

At seven o'clock Archibald and Thaddeus arrived home-land hurried to the warmth of the kitchen hearth. "Where is your mother?" asked Dr. Browne.

"I do not know. I've wondered myself."

"Was she not to weave today?"

"Aye, father, and she was when I left this morning."

"And where did you go?"

Penelope paused and glanced at Thaddeus. He seemed exhausted. "Uh—oh, just a busy day as usual. But father, there was a message for you tacked to the door." She trotted up the steps and returned with the wax-sealed envelope.

Archibald looked at it suspiciously and cleaned his spectacles. Penelope thought he looked old that night. His round face was drawn and dark circles hung in heavy bags beneath his eyes. In the firelight his skin looked like faded parchment. His fingers moved stiffly as he opened the letter.

> *Dear Dr. and Mrs. Browne,*
>
> *I beg the good Physician to indulge his Services in the care of my Nephew, Master Cedric Wigglesworth. He suffers numerous Maladies, having just arrived from New York, including, we fear, the Rickets. Given the pre-occupation of this city's Physicians, we find care to be elusive. Kindly advise of your Disposition in this matter. Your Fee shall be paid in the King's Sterling. I remain your most appreciative and humble Friend and Servant,*
> *Joseph Galloway*

"Joseph Galloway? *The* Joseph Galloway?" asked Thaddeus excitedly.

"Aye, lad. What of it?"

"He's the most important man in all of Philadelphia—after General Howe. He's to be made Superintendent of the City. And he's a friend to mother, and—"

"Humph. He's become a hardened Loyalist. He once shared sympathy with our grievances but he's become a toady for King George. He's a snobbish bore and—"

Penelope interrupted. "Father, it might prove a good advantage to be close to him. Thomas Paine says, 'We are often surprised into good reason by the mistakes of our enemies.'"

"You quote Paine to me? You forget I've little time for radicals like him, either. Nevertheless, this little Wigglesworth fellow is neither Tory nor Whig. Thaddeus, finish your supper and let us be off."

Joseph Galloway lived up-town on Sassafras Street, near the Northeast Square. The Galloway home was genteel but not pretentious. While the family was in retreat in New York City, it had suffered vandalism and had been partly burned. But the man was one of great influence and many hands had quickly restored it to its former condition.

The Brownes were cold and irritable by the time they arrived at the front door. A nine-block walk after a long day would weary anyone. Dr. Browne wished he still had his buggy and his little horse, The Bruce. Unfortunately, the Continentals had taken both over a year before, and the seizure had almost driven the doctor into the arms of the Loyalists.

Archibald stared at the large brass knocker on the Galloway door and, taking a deep breath, he rapped loudly.

A Negro manservant quickly answered the door. Dr. Browne and Thaddeus followed the slave into a small but pleasant foyer. The house was amply lit with candles and whale oil lanterns. A woman hurried down the centre staircase, relief visible on her face.

"Please say you are Dr. Browne?"

"I am. And you are—?"

"Mrs. Galloway." She turned to Thaddeus and smiled.

Thaddeus "made a leg" properly as his father introduced him. Pleasantries exchanged, the Brownes were ushered to a rear room upstairs where a large feathered bed hosted a small fevered boy.

Mr. Galloway heard them arrive and stepped from an adjacent office. "Dr. Browne, I can not thank you enough." He and Archibald clasped hands. Galloway's eyes quickly studied the doctor until they rested on his wooden leg. "A soldier?"

"Aye, a physician with the Rangers in Quebec."

Galloway brightened. "Ah, you served our King against the French."

Archibald removed his spectacles and wiped them with a kerchief. He was not exactly sure how to respond. It was the "our King" that troubled him. "Sir, it was a privilege to follow conscience."

"Indeed." Galloway nodded. The doctor's choice of words did not escape his notice. He turned to Thaddeus. "We've met—at St. Peter's."

Thaddeus beamed. Joseph Galloway remembered him. "It was my honour then, as it is now."

"You are your father's apprentice?"

"Aye, sir."

Galloway looked long and hard at the lad. "Good. Now, Dr. Browne, I must beg your pardon, but I've a meeting in my office. My wife shall serve you. Good evening and many thanks." He shook hands with the Brownes and disappeared.

Mrs. Galloway introduced young Cedric to his physician and proceeded to recite a long list of ailments. It seemed the six year-old was sickly by nature, though not weak-willed. He was pale, white-haired, and thin. His lips were ruby red with fever and his breathing was rapid.

Dr. Browne carefully studied the lad's misshapen elbows. "And you say he teeters and falls even when without fever?"

"Yes, doctor."

Archibald murmured his observations to Thaddeus and the two consulted quietly. Dr. Browne turned to Mrs. Galloway. "You say this lad is a nephew?"

"Yes. He is my sister's son."

"And where is your sister?"

"She is in London presently to attend her ailing father-in-law. I am afraid she's lost three children in the last four years. Little Cedric is all that's left. Her husband served under General Burgoyne and was killed by the rebels nearly two months ago in Saratoga. I do not know if my sister knows as yet. This little lad *must* live."

"I see. Well, Mrs. Galloway, we shall surely do all we are able. Your prayers are coveted, as the boy suffers a variety of ailments. He is afflicted with rickets to be sure, but I fear his recovery shall be slow and arduous. He suffers both excess and debility—most unusual.

"My trouble is that the whole of the city is in desperate need of my services. It seems very few Loyalist physicians returned to the city. The Whigs are mostly gone and those who remain are hard-pressed. You must understand."

"I do, doctor. But–but the lad cannot be left to die. He just can not." The woman was insistent.

Archibald nodded and reached for a quill and paper. "His debility makes me hesitate to bleed him—but his fever inclines me to do so. Instead, I prescribe the following treatment: You must find black cherries. When you do, I shall prepare syrup with molasses that must be served scalding hot thrice a day. It has found much success in New England. Furthermore, you need submerge him in icy water morning and night for three days. Each dipping is to be followed with snakeroot and rum. I shall be sending over medicinals with further instructions."

The woman stared at the man's notes with a look of helplessness. She bade the doctor wait while she entered her husband's office. After a few minutes, Mr. Galloway beckoned Dr. Browne and Thaddeus.

"Gentlemen, this is Sir Ambrose Serle, the secretary of General Howe, Mr. Robert Morton, Mr. Phineas Bond, Mr. Enoch Story, and Mr. Ebenezer Willing." The circle of men stood patiently and greeted the pair.

Thaddeus smiled, for he recognised Mr. Willing as a close friend of his great-aunt Margaret. Dr. Browne knew him as well and was pleased to be reacquainted. Ebenezer Willing was a kindly, generous, and virtuous gentleman.

Mr. Galloway walked to the small fireplace that heated his office. He set a generous log atop the andirons and then walked toward the partially opened window behind his desk. "The cursed woodcutters are selling green timber. Even I cannot seem to find dry firewood. And my hearth has a poor draught besides, so please forgive the smoke," he said, opening the window a little wider.

"This should help the chimney draw better. Now, back to business. Dr. Browne, as you can see, I am a man deeply immersed in guiding a city through a most difficult time. My responsibilities require me to keep odd hours and to remove myself to positions around our city at a moment's notice. I have been informed of General Howe's intent to appoint me as Superintendent of the City and, as you might imagine, I expect to be pressed on many matters of grave importance."

Archibald nodded respectfully. The man then proceeded to boast of the great weight of his newfound glory and babbled on about his duties in such a drone that his friends struggled to stifle their yawns. During the man's presentation, Thaddeus let his eyes wander around the well-appointed room until they fell on a yellowish sheet of paper with what appeared to be a long list of names.

"Added to these things, good doctor," the man continued, "is my godly duty to assist my King in our nation's struggle for order. We shall prevail. The rebels shall be stopped before they unravel centuries of proper law with their outrageous revolution." He turned to Thaddeus. "Lad, you are loyal to the King?"

Thaddeus was surprised. "Oh, yes, sir." The boy puffed his chest.

Galloway smiled. "You are the future. You are what we fight for. You are the lifeblood of our English tradition. We shall not fail you."

The hairs on young Thaddeus' neck raised his spine.

Galloway pointed to the table. "Young sir, it is your fellow colonists who shall rise up to throw off this nonsense. We are compiling a list of loyal men in the Middle Colonies, men of influence—men who can raise an army ten thousand strong to tip the scale. I promised General Howe months ago that the key to victory was here—in Philadelphia. Recruiting in the city has begun and the bounties are generous."

Dr. Browne was struggling to contain himself. He did not need Joseph Galloway inflaming his son's interest in joining a Loyalist regiment. "My son's not sixteen yet. I'll not be signing for him to join in *any* army."

His tone caused a murmur around the table. Joseph Galloway, for all his snobbery and pretence, was a gentleman, nonetheless, and gentlemen do not insult guests. Galloway paused and extended a hand to the doctor. "My apology, sir. I did not intend to stir your son against your will. And I did not mean to distract us from our purposes. I thought you needed to know the nature of my household's attentions and I thought your introduction to these men would help you grasp the weightiness of my present duties. After all, you are—well,

I am told, a wonderful physician, but not necessarily in a position to fully understand the responsibilities of a household such as mine." He led the Brownes into the upstairs foyer and to the top of the stairway.

"Neither myself nor my wife is in a good position to tend a sickly boy," Galloway continued. "My wife has many extra duties as a result of our many guests. She must arrange for dining, sleeping, transport, and the like. Surely, Dr. Browne, you understand.

"We have Negroes, but I'd rather not entrust my nephew to them. And we have an indentured Irish woman, Goody Cassidy. But she is a Roman Catholic from Acadia and—well, we'd be less than comfortable with her praying her popish nonsense over the lad."

Archibald was not one to appreciate pretence. In fact, few things annoyed him more. "Thank you. Without your charitable patience I doubt I could have grasped your situation." He spoke with a poorly disguised hint of sarcasm.

"To be sure." Galloway maintained his decorum. "Allow me to state my request plainly. I would like to hire you to serve my nephew exclusively, at least until he is restored to reasonable health."

Dr. Browne was not interested. "I think not. Good evening, Mr. Galloway." Archibald took his bag and headed down the steps.

Thaddeus blushed and stammered. "G—good evening. A—pleasure to meet you."

The doctor stormed down the staircase, deliberately smashing his wooden leg on the wooden edge beyond the steps' carpeted runner. Bang—step, bang—step. He snatched his coat from the servant in the foyer and headed for the door.

Mr. Galloway came stumbling behind. "Dr. Browne, have I offended you?"

"You offend a common man like myself? A simple dunderhead from Union Street? How could that be?" Archibald strode out the door and descended the two steps to the sidewalk.

Galloway followed, his frantic wife close behind. "Little Cedric needs you."

Archibald whirled about. Now that he was in the street he was not bound by the manners due a man in his own home. "Mr. Galloway. I think you are a piddling, empty-headed, puffed-up toady. You walk about this city like a goose boasting an air of consequence. I've been in the City Tavern when you have flaunted your money and your sway. You've spoken of our own good state as—'a mongrel breed of Irish, Scots, and Germans salted with convicts' is how I believe you put it. I am not impressed with your position or your importance to the Crown. As for the lad, I've given instructions to your wife and I shall attend him as I would any other sickly child."

Galloway lifted his nose high in the air. "Good evening to you."

The walk toward home was silent and quick. Archibald Browne clicked through the night air angrily, bristling with every memory of Joseph Galloway and his pretence. "Boy, it is exactly that kind of arrogance that leads to tyranny. The man sees the rest of us like your King and Parliament see us." He spotted the Bunch of Grapes tavern and headed for its door. Once inside he slammed his fist on a table and ordered a tankard of rum.

"Sorry, sir. General Howe has all m'rum."

Dr. Browne was furious. "Ale, then."

"Uh—sorry sir."

"What? Then what of whiskey?"

"Sorry."

Archibald tapped his fingers on the table and looked around the room. The Bunch of Grapes was never his favoured spot but the Men Full of Trouble was out of business. Here were groups of Redcoats hunched over rum and smoking clay pipes. A few Tories laughed with them. "What are they drinking?"

"Who?"

Archibald roared. "*Them*!" He pointed to a table of citizens.

"Apple-jack."

"Apple-jack, then. For two."

"Aye, sir. Uh, 'ave you sworn to the King?"

"What?"

"To the King, sir—'ave y'sworn to the King?"

Poor Archibald stood. He was tired and in no mood for this. "I have sworn *at* the King, if *that* is what you mean."

The tavern-keeper folded his arms. He was a large man with huge forearms and a grizzled face. Thaddeus groaned. "Are you a rebel?" the man growled.

Dr. Browne leaned forward. "Do I *look* like a rebel to you, you swag-bellied bowl of toady?"

The soldiers put down their pipes and watched closely. Thaddeus fidgeted and tugged on his father's sleeve. "Father, it's late. We ought go home."

The tall tavern-keeper bent over and placed his nose against Archibald's. "You *smell* like a rebel."

Without blinking, Archibald answered. "You just smell."

The keep had endured a bad day, too. With a bellow and a roar he shoved Dr. Browne backward over his chair. Archibald crashed to the floor with an oath and came up swinging a broken chair leg. It landed squarely on the man's ear, splitting it badly. But for Dr. Browne, the night would only get worse. In the time it takes a tall man to stride five paces, three drunken British soldiers pounced on Archibald and his yelping son. They tossed the pair about the tavern and drew a few lumps before dragging the Brownes to the city jail.

⇥⟐ ⟐⇤

Penelope lay in bed, worried about her missing mother. And she thought her father and brother should have returned. Fretting or not, the girl finally dozed, only to be awakened by the dawn of a new day. "Mother?" she mumble as she awoke. The girl pulled a robe over her linen shift and trotted down the stairs from her attic bedroom. Checking her parents' bed, she found no one in it. She felt the sheet and blankets. "Cold."

The girl quickly ran to the first floor, then to the cellar. There, huddled in front of a cheery morning fire was her mother. Major Crippen was eating a bowl of porridge and bread. Penelope hesitated to ask any questions in front of the officer. "Good morning," she said flatly.

Katherine was nearly asleep on her haunches and her daughter's voice startled her. "Oh. Penny, you frightened me. Where is your father—and your brother?"

Penelope looked at her mother's baggy eyes and tangled hair. She looked as if she had had no sleep the night before. "I do not know. They never returned from Mr. Galloway's last evening." She looked carefully at her mother and at Major Crippen.

Katherine's eyes met hers. "Y–yes."

"Galloway?" said Oliver. "*The* Joseph Galloway?"

"Aye."

"Well, I hope your father cured whatever ails the man. He's one whom you need as a friend."

"Actually, it was his nephew that needed tending."

"Ah. Well—whatever. Mrs. Browne, I suppose you've heard the rumours by now. We are hoping to surprise Washington. I am ordered to Whitemarsh tomorrow morning with the light artillery companies. You'll not need to feed me until my return."

The man spoke slowly and respectfully. They all knew he would be attacking Cameron.

"I see," answered Katherine. She spoke with no emotion.

"How can you hope to surprise him when the whole city knows?" blurted Penelope.

"General Howe sealed the lines yesterday. Tight as a ship's keel, I'm told. They've arrested a few attempted spies and we've sent some false information with others who are posing as rebels. We shall see."

Penelope looked at her mother carefully. She turned back to Oliver. "I wish you Godspeed and a very poor aim."

Major Crippen raised his brows. "Good day. I hope we may eat together again."

⊷⊱⊰⊶

It was Whittaker Yates and a familiar face that knocked on the door before noon. "Ah, Mr. Yates. Welcome. Please, do come in." Katherine wiped her hands on her apron and pushed some hair from her face with the back of her hand.

"And you are Mr. Benjamin Fielding."

The lawyer bowed deeply.

Katherine," began Whittaker slowly. "I am afraid I bear bad news, again."

The woman held Penelope's hand. "Yes, go on, please."

Whittaker fumbled with the edges of his wide-brimmed hat. "It seems Archibald and Thaddeus are—are in jail."

"Jail? It can not be."

Mr. Fielding interrupted. "It can be so, and it is so. Mrs. Browne, you need to understand that I am a good lawyer—a very good lawyer. But I do not work miracles. Your husband is a known Whig. Mr. Yates has laboured to protect his reputation in the face of—shall we say, dubious assistance from Dr. Browne. All known Whigs are suspect. The army is about to attack Washington, so the patience of the present government is thin—very thin. Bold acts of sedition in time of war are easily considered treasonous.

"In the last twelve hours your husband has not only disturbed the public peace by brawling in a tavern, he has also denounced the King publicly. Furthermore, he has resisted arrest by the King's soldiers, gouged the eye of his jailer, and spat upon our flag. Ah, but there is more: he insulted and goaded the civil head of this city, Mr. Joseph Galloway, to his very face."

Katherine collapsed in a chair and closed her eyes. Then she looked at Mr. Fielding. "And my son?"

"Well, I am pleased to say his charges are being dropped as we speak. The lad was caught in the storm, as it were. A witness claimed he made no seditious comments and did what he could to keep the peace.

"It is your husband who is in a difficult way."

"Have you seen him?"

"Yes. Whittaker and I have. He is in good health but poor spirits. He was not battered about like the last time, but understands his predicament."

Katherine thought for a moment. "And your counsel?"

"The court has refused bail. He is to be tried for treason, I fear, but not until the army's adventure is finished. Perhaps the result might temper the court's mood. You need wish for a major victory—one that smashes Washington."

Katherine wiped her eyes with a kerchief. Cameron's defeat might save her husband's life; Cameron's victory might take it. "Thank you, Mr. Fielding. Please do what you need to do. I shall see my husband and go about some business of my own."

The two men bade farewell and Katherine quietly closed the door behind them. The woman sighed and leaned her back against the door and closed her eyes. Penelope looked sadly at her poor mother's haggard face and a lump filled her throat. Her eyes then fell toward the floor beneath the coat pegs. She saw that her mother's overshoes had been returned to their usual place, but they were caked with mud.

⋇⟞⬤ ⬤⟝⋇

The battle of Whitemarsh began a day later than General Howe had planned. On the night of December 3rd, many numbers of British and Hessian troops deserted. Some simply wanted no part of another battle, but many, it seemed, had found their way to Washington's lines and would be pointing their muskets at their former comrades. Such desertion to liberty's cause was not new, nor were desertions that came from the other direction. But the numbers and timing of these losses were distracting to the British general and required him to delay his advance. Furthermore, it was learned that a reconnaissance officer, Captain Allen McLane, had received a warning of Howe's plan. Confident of the nature and timing of the British attack, Washington was furiously refortifying his positions on high ground.

By December 5th the British campaign was finally underway. General Howe pressed his army through the cold up the Germantown road. For that day and for more to follow, Commanders Cornwallis, Knyphausen, and Grey probed and engaged the American line in places such as Chestnut Hill, Edge Hill, Whitemarsh Heights, and Militia Hill—names denoting that the terrain was high and difficult. Dense woodland and cold rain made the engagements difficult and wearisome. To add to the misery of the Redcoats, General Washington was as clever as usual. As hard as Howe tried, he could not lure the man away from his high ground. The British First Infantry took heavy losses from Daniel Morgan's riflemen, though they finally drove the stubborn Americans from their positions. The Hessians fought bravely, as did the Queen's Rangers.

Light artillery caused damage to the Americans at Edge Hill, but by the 8th of December 1777, the expedition was ended. To his credit or to his blame, General Howe proved, once again, that he was both a man and a general. His compassion for his troops kept him from subjecting them to adverse conditions for long periods of time. It also kept him from aggressively assaulting a well-defended position. Perhaps he had learned a valuable lesson years prior at Breed's Hill in Boston. In any event, he withdrew his exhausted, wet, shivering army back to the comfort and safety of Philadelphia.

Washington's army was saved. But the general had been reminded of how vulnerable his men were to the better equipped, better fed, and larger British army. It was true that his position in Whitemarsh had been held, but it had been held at some cost. With winter fast approaching, he thought it prudent to create a greater distance between himself and his foe. So, with some reluctance, he scattered a line of reconnaissance companies in front of the British lines to harass and monitor them while the rest of his army followed him to a safer place, a place called Valley Forge.

⭑⭑⭑

Katherine and her twins received the news of the battle of Whitemarsh with mixed feelings. On one hand, Howe had failed to defeat Washington. The British commander returned to Philadelphia with little to show for his efforts. On the other hand, Washington had abandoned his position, and that gave more room for the city to breathe. Was it a victory or not? And what would be the mood of the court with regard to Archibald Browne?

The doctor sat in the Fifth Street jail, once again pressed on all sides by captives from a recent battle. Members of Morgan's riflemen seemed to represent the largest lot, though there were also men from various regiments from any number of colonies.

No one knew Cameron, but two said the boy's regiment was active and had been posted near the centre of Washington's line. Katherine had come to see her husband each day. He had no complaints about his food or treatment, but was remorseful for having let his pride impact the safety and security of those he loved. "At the end of the day," he said to his wife, "it is pride that is at the root of all my troubles."

The reverend Coombs of St. Peter's was faithful and prayed with the man each day. And, of course, Whittaker Yates was ever-present. Mr. Fielding petitioned the court for delays, for he believed the passing of time would cool heads. "Justice needs to simmer like a good stew," he said. "Not too hasty, not too slow." It was Fielding's conviction, however, that the man might be made an example of. It was believed that a city Whig had warned Washington. A city Whig had set fire to the Second Street barracks. A city Whig was thought to have poisoned an officer at the British Tavern. So, reasoned the lawyer, a city Whig would need to hang.

Mrs. Browne spent hours on her knees. She cared little for the news of Lord Corwallis' success at foraging in the west. He delivered thousands of sheep and cattle to the happy city. But an American soldier his troops captured did warm her broken heart.

"He knows Cameron," she said to Archibald through the bars of his cell. "I bandaged him slowly so he could tell me all he knew. He says our boy is fine and in good health. He says Cameron is a brave soldier and has been made a corporal. He's marched to Valley Forge with his regiment and should be fine there, far away from the British. Oh, Archibald. Thanks be to God."

Penelope stood close by and listened carefully. She wondered if the soldier was being kind to her mother in the same way that her mother had been kind to Mary Franks.

⇢▬◉ ◉▬⇠

It was Saturday, the 13th of December, when Katherine, Penelope, and Thaddeus made their way from the jail to the Market Street shambles. They usually shopped at New Market in their own neighbourhood, but it had been agreed that a change of scenery might be good. As they passed a group of sooty chimney sweeps, who were laughing and singing merrily, Katherine grumbled, "They ought to be happy. Ever since Galloway ordered chimneys be cleaned they've had plenty of business." Indeed, Benjamin Franklin's old insurance company, the Philadelphia Contributorship, had hired Christopher Apple and his men to sweep every chimney in the city. Next to General Washington and the pox, fire was Philadelphia's greatest fear. Soon the trio approached Michael Clark's tavern, where the Loyal Association Club was meeting.

The Brownes slowed to study a table set in front of the tavern, manned by a forlorn-looking fellow chatting with a gentleman of means. As the three walked by, the gentleman turned; it was Joseph Galloway. Katherine slowed, but it was too late. Galloway removed his hat and "made a leg." Katherine and Penelope curtsied, albeit stiffly.

Thaddeus bowed and received the man's extended hand. "Good day to you all."

"And to you," answered Thaddeus. He was assuming his manhood and now spoke for his mother. Katherine was surprised.

Galloway was uncomfortable but not ungracious. "We are recruiting loyal subjects to His Majesty's Provincial Corps. A two-year enlistment pays a bounty of fifty acres for a private,

200 acres for a non-commissioned officer. And we are adding gold as a special incentive to rebel soldiers who see the error in their ways. We are not without understanding. I have William Allen raising a regiment over on Second at Market, and Alfred Clifton is raising a regiment of Roman Catholics. I'm visiting each. Here, James Chalmers is seeking Maryland refugees."

The group looked around and didn't see a single face. Galloway continued. "As you can see, not many Marylanders are in the neighbourhood today."

"And how goes recruiting elsewhere?" asked Thaddeus.

Galloway shuffled a little. "Ah, well, I think as men understand more and more clearly that the rebels can not win, more shall join us."

Katherine interrupted. "Mr. Galloway. How is your nephew?"

He shook his head. "Not well, Mrs. Browne. I fear he worsens each day. Your unfortunate husband gave some instructions but no one can read his writing. In my position I am able to find other doctors but they are so distracted. My fee has lured one but—he seems a bit of a quack to me."

Katherine nodded. "I was interested to hear you say that you are not without understanding."

"Yes, I believe it to be so."

"Could you forgive my husband his insult?"

Galloway darkened. He pursed his lips. His long nose seemed suddenly hawk-like and his face turned mean.

A woman's voice broke the silence. It was Mrs. Galloway. She was dressed in a lavish, red silk dress and sported a high, outlandish new wig. "There you are. I have been shopping all morning. Eliza and Goody Cassidy have been sent home with three loads already." She laughed and fanned herself. Thaddeus thought her vanity could only be outdone by her husband's. The woman turned to the Brownes. "Oh. You are that doctor's family."

"Yes," answered Thaddeus. "This is my mother, Mrs. Browne, and my sister, Penelope."

The woman hesitated, then did a quick "drop."

Katherine and Penelope returned the curtsy. Mrs. Browne smiled. "Your husband tells me that your poor nephew suffers so."

"Yes. I think he may be near death. With all my husband's influence, one should think we could have a true physician at the boy's side night and day." She turned a hard eye toward Galloway.

"My dear, it is not that simple. British officers take the best—I cannot remove their physicians for a boy. You really must be more liberal on this point."

Katherine's mind was racing. "Mr. Galloway, Thaddeus, is nearly fifteen. He has trained under my husband for quite some time and is respected by physicians all over this city. And, like me, he is a loyal subject of the King.

"With my husband in jail for—excesses of temper—Thaddeus is needed to serve in his stead. Were my husband able to return to duty, Thaddeus might be free to tend your nephew."

Mrs. Galloway brightened. She slapped her husband on the chest with her fan. "Do it."

"But–but really, I must protest. Dr. Browne insulted me, spat on the flag, cursed the King—"

"Did anyone other than myself hear him insult you?" clipped his wife, impatiently.

"Well, no—but—"

"Then it never happened." She turned to Mrs. Browne. "Where did this other business happen?"

Thaddeus answered, "At the Bunch of Grapes tavern."

"There. There it is. He was drunk and not thinking clearly. And his accusers were drunk—see that they change their testimony. Now, what of this spitting and cursing business?"

Everyone shrugged.

"Joseph, fix that as well. See the jailer, see the judge."

Galloway stood speechless and confounded.

Mrs. Galloway turned to Katherine. "Now, we know your family and its reputation for integrity. Do we have your word that Thaddeus shall serve our nephew as needed?"

"Do we have your word that Dr. Browne shall be released?"

The woman turned to her husband. Joseph Galloway shrugged. "Yes, Mrs. Browne. You have our word."

Katherine brightened. "Then we agree. The day our husband returns is the day Thaddeus shall come."

On Monday, the 15th of December, Dr. Browne returned home.

CHAPTER 9

The Letter

JOSIAH BYRD SERVED his employer well. He mended furniture, brushed bright milk-paints across thirsty woodwork, shined silver, and polished boots. When he wasn't hard at work for others, he sat in the brisk air of the gardens and whittled. His only regret was his obligation to remain within the walls of the courtyard, save those few precious times he escorted other servants to the market.

Still a favourite of Mrs. Loring, the man was privy to conversations and correspondence that would have made George Washington drool. William Howe must have assumed the Negro could not read. He should have remembered that Christianity had made men literate, including Africans.

The Grackle's greatest joy was the routine visits of Mrs. Browne. The charitable woman drew little notice from the guards who now treated her with every respect. Even Mrs. Loring would smile and wave as if Katherine were a dear friend. On one occasion Mrs. Loring even offered Mrs. Browne a generous serving of sweet cake and tea while she waited for Josiah.

C. D. Baker

Katherine enjoyed the serene elegance of the mansion and longed for such calm and comfort to return to her own home. "Ah, Mr. Byrd, it is good to see you well," said Katherine one sunny afternoon.

"Webster Yates passed by and told of trouble." Josiah was deeply worried.

"Yes, but that is over now. Dr. Browne came home on Monday and is fully recovered. He spends long days and nights tending the sick. With Thaddeus gone he finds the time passes slowly. Occasionally Webster assists him but I fear the lad is a bit—thick."

"You mean in the head."

Mrs. Browne scolded Josiah playfully.

"And what of Master Thaddeus?"

Katherine chuckled. "He has found himself in the employ of Mr. Joseph Galloway."

"*The* Joseph Galloway?"

"The very one." Mrs. Browne was proud.

Josiah wrinkled his nose. "I whittled him a whistle for some little boy in his keep, but he never paid me."

Katherine laughed. "We shall see what Thaddeus can do about that. I wish Penelope would come and see you, but she is very busy at the hospital and with home chores."

"Aye." Josiah was careful. "The young mistress came by a few weeks back but the soldiers—they were rude and I think it good for her to stay away."

"She did not mention it."

Mrs. Loring stepped from her front door. She was an attractive woman who kept a pleasant company for General

194

Howe. Many in the city, particularly the Quakers, backbit and slandered her since she was not the general's wife. They felt it was not the sort of relationship that was proper for any Christian man, regardless of his standing. Katherine agreed on the point but chose to offer the woman a taste of grace— a gift that ought to spring from conviction. Mrs. Loring watched Josiah and Katherine exchange some hushed words, then called to the Grackle. "Mr. Byrd?"

"Aye." Josiah bade Katherine a hasty farewell and dashed to his duties.

Katherine waved and called after him, "Until Sunday, Josiah." She tied her heavy bonnet tightly beneath her chin, pushed her cold hands deep into her beaver muff, smiled at Mrs. Loring, and walked briskly toward home. Somewhere along Third she heard a familiar voice.

"Mrs. Browne." It was Mary Franks, the dreaded busybody of Union Street. The woman was cheery and rosy-cheeked.

"Good day to you, Mrs. Franks," answered Katherine politely.

"I've wonderful news—wonderful news."

"You have heard from Mr. Franks?"

Mary twisted her face. She did not want to be reminded of that particular mystery. "*Sergeant* Franks. No. He's said to be quartered in a redoubt along the line. I cannot understand why he is not allowed a few days leave, especially with Christmas and the Epiphany so close. I feel so bad for him. Imagine, crowded in some muddy little fort with foul-smelling men. Oh, it gives me shivers."

"I am sorry, Mrs. Franks. Perhaps he shall come soon."

"Perhaps. But, let me tell you of other news. My dinner is still planned for the 23rd. But my guest list is changed." The woman's black eyes twinkled. "A relative of yours is my special guest. Can you guess his name?"

Katherine paused. "Hmm. No, I do not think so."

"Try." Mary was nearly bursting.

"Really, Mrs. Franks, I—"

"Can you guess?"

"Um, um—I am sorry, Mary, I have no idea."

Mrs. Franks reddened and pursed her lips. "Well, you might have tried. No matter," she whined, and started to walk away.

Katherine thought for a moment, and then called after her. "Reverend Seabury."

"What?"

"My guess is the reverend Seabury."

Mrs. Franks' eyes bulged and her cheeks puffed. "Someone told you," she scolded.

"No, no, I assure you I only guessed. I knew he was friends with the reverend Coombs and—"

"I shall see you on the 23rd, seven o'clock sharp."

⇥⇥🌑 🌑⇤⇤

Christmas for the Anglicans was a cherished holiday but not as festive as the Epiphany soon to follow. Gifts would not be exchanged until the January holiday and only the Germans and the Hessian soldiers were bothering with evergreens. The Hessian camp was decorated with as many green things as the young men could find, but their songs were soulful and sad. They longed to celebrate the occasion with their own loved ones in the hamlets and walled towns of their homeland. About half of them sought out the Reformed churches; the rest were Roman Catholic.

As Christmas loomed closer, those Hessians of the Reformed faith had a reason to become sullen. The pastor of Philadelphia's German Reformed Church on Sassafras and Fourth was one Dr. Caspar Weyberg. He had built the graceful church building just five years prior, working hand-in-hand with Robert Smith, the famed Scottish architect. Unfortunately, the indomitable Dr. Weyberg had preached the justice of the patriot cause to his congregation, no doubt with the particular intent of influencing the Hessian soldiers who filled his sanctuary.

Considering the number of Hessians who deserted, the pastor's words had born fruit. Needless to say, the British commanders were not pleased. Dr. Weyberg was thrown into prison and his church converted into a stable. His forlorn Hessians would now be celebrating Christmas with the Swedes at the Lutheran church.

Though each of Philadelphia's many Christian branches enjoyed Christmas in its own customary way, all would agree that it was a time to reflect on the wonder of the Incarnation. Families looked forward to time spent together in front of cheerful hearths and did their best to set their tables with the delights of the season: dried fruits, roasted meats, sugary syrups, and pumpkin breads; grogs and heavy ales, brandy, and rum, all blended with laughter.

If it were not for the war.

With Christmas approaching, Penelope was given to melancholy and dreams. She missed her friends, Rachel Willing and Eliza Ewing. Rachel's family had left for Lancaster a year before. Her father was a harness maker and had feared the city was destined to become the centre of the storm. Eliza Ewing had died about the same time. The poor girl had contracted diphtheria and succumbed after a short illness. When times were quiet Penelope thought of them both.

One dark night Penelope was staring wistfully out the little dormer of her attic bedroom at the stars sprinkled far above. Her favourite constellation was the beautiful, twinkling Pleiades, perhaps because she would have loved to have seven sisters of her own. Christmas was a week away and she looked forward to the simple joy of having her family around the parlour table. Her mind began to drift to happy memories and happier days. She thought of her childhood and the troubles she had often caused. She saw her friends in the garden playing hide-and-seek, or blind man's bluff—her favourite. Then she laughed as she saw Thaddeus bravely grimacing as their father's willow rod exacted penalties for misdeeds that had been hers. *Thaddeus is a good brother,* she thought. *"And Cameron, too."*

Penelope leaned her elbows on the window's deep sill and rested her jaw on the heels of her hands. She closed her eyes and imagined herself flying by night above the city's crooked rooftops, then over the treetops of the nearby forests. She smiled as she swooped over the glassy Schuylkill River and up the steep face of its western banks. She pictured a distant huddle of timbered huts gathered closely together in a snowy field. She flew closer and closer until she hovered just above their smoky roofs.

In her mind she descended, slowly, very slowly, until her feet touched the snow like an angel's slippers lighting upon a cloud. Facing the wooden door of one particular little hut, she heard the muffled voices of men and a cough and a sneeze. She opened the door and peered into the yellow firelight of a small, log-sided room. A chorus of cheery voices greeted her, but one was the most pleasing of all. Cameron. *Ah,* she thought. *Just to tell him how proud we are, how proud I am—just to give him a kiss on the cheek."*

Penelope could see herself smile at her brother, but then she noticed tears in his blue eyes.

"Where have you been, sister? His voice sounded wounded and even angry.

Penelope followed the tears now running down her brother's face. His voice became unfamiliar.

"I am so alone, so afraid. I am so hungry, and so very cold." He shivered and turned away. The fire dwindled to grey ash; then all was black.

Penelope ran to her bed and cried aloud. She was frightened and heartsick. "He must know we care. He *must.*"

⊷⊨⊜ ⊜⊫⊷

Poor Cedric Wigglesworth was a sickly boy. Thaddeus dutifully tended the little fellow with the care of a seasoned physician and made the boy's recovery a matter of personal reputation. But the young master showed little improvement.

As instructed, Thaddeus dipped the boy in icy water day and night. Then he served him the hot cherry concoction of his father's as well as several variations of the medicinals. Dr. Browne came by every other day to review the progress of both patient and apprentice, but was noticeably worried. "Father, he shows opposing symptoms."

"Yes, he does, and has from the outset. His body shows signs of nerve excitement and of lethargy. The fever is stubborn and must be reduced; yet if we reduce it, we contribute to his weakness. In your opinion, Thaddeus, which ailment is the larger?"

Thaddeus had never been asked his opinion before. He fumbled for words.

"You must never hesitate. When you do not know you keep silent." His father's tone was scolding. "Now, I ask you again: which is the greater trouble, his excitement or his weakness?"

This time Thaddeus maintained his composure. He faced his patient calmly and answered, "Weakness, sir."

"I agree. Well done."

The young man beamed.

"Your recommendation?"

The lad did not falter. "For his lethargy I believe the patient needs abrasive clysters every two days and a diet of stimulants with brandy or other liquors."

"And for his fever?"

"It is my opinion that he can withstand an increase in fever while we excite the body, but we must keep it within some manageable range so as to lessen it at a moment's notice."

"And how shall you do this?"

"I have noticed that the fever can be manipulated with his ice baths, though it does return. I should prefer to delay icing until he shows some improvement in his strength, then I shall begin again. As long as his strength remains, I shall increase steps against the fever, adding blistering first and bleeding if need be."

Dr. Browne nodded. "Well done, Mr. Browne. Soon you shall be examined for your certificate. And I think you've the mind to go on to be a surgeon."

The young man smiled. "Father, you'll administer the clysters?" Thaddeus grinned. Clysters—enemas administered through a most menacing and fearsome instrument—were common procedures but unpleasant for patient and doctor alike.

"Good try, lad, but I need to be off. I leave the patient in your skilful hands." Dr.

Browne laughed and left the room.

Descending the stairs, Archibald encountered Joseph Galloway. It was the first time they had met since their unfortunate introduction several weeks before. The two faced each other in the foyer as Goody Cassidy trotted past. She had become Thaddeus' able assistant.

"Good day, Dr. Browne." Galloway bowed, stiffly.

Archibald returned the gesture. "And to you. Your nephew is not improving as I wished, but is no longer worsening. Thaddeus is giving him excellent care."

"Your son impresses me. I fear our last physician, if he truly was one, did much harm. He filled both ends of the poor boy with every horrid concoction I have ever had the displeasure to smell. Tars and runny meats, insect parts and weeds. All most disagreeable."

"Aye. The city is full of charlatans. Thaddeus has snatched Cedric from the edge of his grave, but I fear he needs care for some time. However, my son could use a day or two of relief. Might you release him from your home for the days before Christmas? I would attend Cedric twice daily and Thaddeus tells me that Goody Cassidy is an adequate nurse."

Joseph Galloway nodded. The request was reasonable, he supposed. "I should like your word that the lad shall return the day after Christmas and if Cedric worsens, that he shall return at once."

"Done."

"Fine. Christmas is five days hence. Perhaps Thaddeus' respite might begin three days from now, on the twenty-third. Of course, he shall miss the executions."

"Executions, sir?"

"Aye. General Howe is to be hanging two looters and five deserters at the State House grounds. I am to order the citizens to watch so they understand the devotion to law the general requires. He wants this city to know he is committed to their welfare. Looting, plundering, rapine, and arson—all of these crimes shall be dealt with harshly, especially when committed by his own soldiers. I should think treason is on the general's mind as well." Galloway narrowed his eyes at the doctor.

Archibald nodded. "I see. Well, it is settled then. As long as Cedric shows a little improvement in the next three days, Thaddeus shall be released from duty until the twenty-sixth."

"Agreed. And one other matter, doctor. Here is your payment to date." Galloway handed Archibald a leather pouch. "The lad has watched faithfully for six days. I am paying you ten shillings sterling per day. You should find three pounds sterling in the sack."

Dr. Browne was pleased. Most of his patients were paying him with eggs, strips of bacon, or bartered services. Cash was in short supply and Mr. Galloway's payment in coin would serve his family well. "Thank you, Mr. Galloway. I believe the lad is earning every silver coin."

Archibald dropped the pouch into a pocket of his coat. But something else was weighing on his mind. He stepped toward the door in battle with his pride. Victorious, he turned around and faced Joseph Galloway squarely. "Sir, I owe you an apology.

I was uncharitable to you in front of your wife and judged you for your pretence. I have concluded that in that moment my pretence far exceeded your own. I am sorry."

Galloway was indeed a pretentious man. Filled with every vanity, puffed with pride and self-importance, the man strutted through his days with one eye down his nose and the other staring at a looking glass. At this moment, however, he struggled for words.

An upstairs scream suddenly filled the house. Galloway lurched with a start. Archibald smiled. "Clysters, sir. The dread of all."

⟿⟾ ⟾⟿

Philadelphians crowded onto the State House grounds in the early morning of December 22nd. Built during the 1730s in the elegance and balance of Georgian style, the State House had been witness to many important events. It was here that the business of the colony had been conducted. It became the meeting place of the Continental Congresses and in its east wing the Declaration of Independence was signed. Four days after the signing, its immortal bell, named the Liberty Bell, rang in the building's stately tower. Here General Washington was appointed commander-in-chief of the new nation's army and it would be here that an American constitution would be created.

The State House halls had echoed with the genius of men such as Thomas Jefferson, George Mason, Benjamin Franklin, James Madison, John Dickinson, and Alexander Hamilton; also John Witherspoon, John Adams, and John Hancock. Its hallowed chambers resounded with the prayers and the groans of other champions of liberty as well. For here were laid scores of nameless wounded and dying American prisoners who suffered in the very place their champions had urged their cause—farmers, blacksmiths, teachers, pastors, woodsmen, clerks, cabinet makers—men from every corner of a New World. The roll of heroes that had assembled within this most amazing edifice would mark a standard of character, courage, and brilliance never attained in the centuries before or after.

On this day the hallowed grounds of Pennsylvania's State House were jammed with the soldiers of the King and with Tories. Not unlike their patriot counterparts, they, too, revered law and the decency of order. General Howe was sincere in his concern to honour the traditions of a common past. The criminal treatment of his American cousins would not be tolerated and two of his soldiers would hang for their crimes. Desertion would exact a price as well. It was a spectacle that all sides could honour.

But the Brownes were not interested; they had other matters to attend. Major Crippen had delivered a letter from Mrs. Browne's father that very morning. The British military postal system was intact, even though the civilian postal system was in tatters. As recently as 1775, Benjamin Franklin had been the King's Postmaster General of the colonies. He had made amazing improvements in road surveys, corrected systems of delivery, added nightriders, and instituted other such needed change. But after the "Declaration," the Americans were suspicious of the British postal system, and Congress had appointed Franklin the Postmaster General of the United Colonies. Two systems now operated, each opening or closing depending on the proximity of opposing armies. It made for utter confusion.

Archibald and his daughter leaned over their mother's shoulder as she opened the letter at Dr. Browne's desk. Her hands trembled with excitement.

23rd October, 1777

My Most Beloved Katherine,

I write with a Heart bursting with Affections for you, dear Daughter, and for your most brilliant Archibald, your beautiful Children: Cameron, Thaddeus, and Penelope. It is with a sincere Regret and most humble Apology that I confess my grievous delay in this tardy Correspondence. You and yours are in my Mind each passing Day and I entrust you to an all-wise and merciful Providence. I send this by way of my faithful Friend and Partner, Lord Stanbury Crippen, in the resolute hope that he has forthrightly directed it across his muddy Shire by way of the King's Post to his good son for delivery to yourselves.

My present Situation prevents me from standing by your Sides in this present Distress and I beg your kind and gracious Forgiveness. My Jailers (I presently am contained in a reasonably agreeable Circumstance near Madrid) inform me that the King's army is likely to assume your fair City for Winter. I am no Stranger to such inconveniences and

I uplift you each by name in my daily prayers. As for me, know that I am in good Health and content in my present Condition.

I am permitted only one piece of this poor paper, so I leave You with these final thoughts: Firstly, love one another, for you have no higher Cause; it is your Duty under God. Never weary in the Pursuit of Justice, Law, and Mercy. Be brave and Resolute in the defence of all that is Good. Defend our English Constitution, for it is our Heritage and the Order God has called us to honour. Serve Friend and Foe with Christian charity and delight in the Liberty of God's most wondrous Grace.

I write in the hope of seeing you soon and do remain faithful
to the Hope of that good Day.

With fondest Affections,
  Father

Tears filled Katherine's eyes and she handed the letter to her husband. Archibald folded it neatly and placed it in a drawer for safekeeping. "Your father is a remarkable man."

Mrs. Browne nodded and smiled. "Thank you. He loves you, dearly, as he does his grandchildren. Ah, but what trouble is he in now? In prison in Madrid. He never liked the Spanish—or the French. I wonder if he sank one of their ships with his Prodigal? He always had a way of finding captains with more boom in their cannon than brains in their heads."

Dr. Browne smiled. He paused for a moment while he reflected on the letter. "Dear wife, it seems your father is a patriot."

Katherine's face changed. "I think not. Why ever do you say so?"

Archibald withdrew the letter from his drawer. "He says, 'pursue justice, law, and mercy. Defend what is good, defend our English Constitution—delight in liberty.' How else could one understand that?"

Katherine was intelligent, well educated, and not unaware of the world around her. "No, husband. You are wrong. My father has been a faithful subject since before he served against the French. We Loyalists want nothing other than justice, law, and mercy. Good heavens, Archibald, you know that the customs and the laws of our forefathers are based in liberty. Our whole Constitution is nothing less than centuries of just rules that give order to our rights as free Englishmen—and women."

Dr. Browne shook his head. He had had this discussion so many times with his wife and others that he knew it by heart. "Katherine, I shall no longer argue with you. Your government—aye, both Parliament and King, have broken faith with those same centuries of custom you and I *both* honour. This war is about reclaiming what is already ours against those who would steal it away. Can you not see it?"

"No. Your radicals have blinded you."

Dr. Browne chose restraint. "We disagree, again. It is clear to me, wife, that your government has surely violated the spirit of all we hold dear, and I think your father agrees."

While her parents talked, Penelope walked to the front window and stared at the barren streets. Cromwell leaped on to the windowsill. The girl stroked the cat's back as she thought of her grandfather. As her green eyes fell to meet Cromwell's, she drifted into distant memories of the man. "Grandfather was thoughtful and kind, rascally but mild of manner." Indeed, the man was an adventurer who had sailed much of the world in search of what wonders he might discover. He always had a ready coin for any in need or a word of wisdom for any that asked. Brave and strong, he stood hardjawed and immovable against injustice. But Reginald was one quick to forgive and ever willing to offer mercy. He enjoyed a good joke and loved to laugh. He had few vices, but English ale and Carolina rum were among them. His ability to spirit others to adventure and his restless, unfettered ways had earned him the nickname "Gadfly." Grandfather Henry enjoyed the title and even gave the name to his shallow-keeled sloop. Unfortunately, the French had sunk it off the coast of Florida some years past.

"Penny, are you listening?"

"Uh, oh, yes, father."

"You've need to help your mother with some chores. Webster and I are going to deliver some of Mr. Yates' medicinals to the hospital, then check on Thaddeus and Cedric. You and mother need buy some firewood from the cutters at market. Make sure they put it in the cellar. Wood is still in short supply and is easily stolen."

Penelope nodded, but she barely heard him. *Grandfather said we ought to love our own above all things.* She thought. *'Tis almost Christmas and he is all alone.* She remembered her imaginations of the other night and shuddered. "Father, when is Thaddeus coming home?"

"In the morning."

Penelope Browne had a plan.

⇥⊜ ⊜⇤

The morning of the 23rd of December was a pleasant one. Thaddeus strode into the cellar in time for a wonderful breakfast with his family and Major Crippen. The lad looked healthy and glad-hearted. And why not? The Galloways treated him with respect and fed him well. He handed his father another bag of silver with a smile.

"Thanks be to God, son," answered his father.

"Aye, and to Joseph Galloway. Cedric is improving. Hews laughing with Goody Cassidy last evening. Old Galloway actually wiped away a tear."

"I would have liked to have seen that," muttered Oliver. He brushed Cromwell away from his porridge and chuckled. "I'm told the man's a bit of a crank, but in fairness I have only met him once. Yesterday I saw him begging three sour-faced lads to join his Loyalist Regiment."

"Did they?" asked Penelope.

"No. They called him an old fool and walked away."

Thaddeus shook his head. "Mr. Galloway is surely convinced he can turn the tide with his list."

"What list?" blurted Penelope.

"He and some others are making a list of 'men of influence,' as he calls them. He says he can raise an army of ten thousand loyal subjects here in these middle colonies. I think it was his certainty that caused Howe to take Philadelphia instead of staying in New York. The man's very persuasive."

Major Crippen agreed. "I've heard the rumours as well. If Howe had stayed in New York, he could have relieved General Burgoyne and saved the northern army. Instead, Burgoyne was beaten by that American devil, Benedict Arnold."

"I thought Burgoyne was beaten by Gates," said Archibald.

"Only officially. Your Arnold is raging about—complaining he's not been properly honoured."

Katherine nodded, sleepily. She looked very weary. "I hear he is short-tempered and proud. And he has an eye for a cousin of mine, Margaret Shippen—Peggy, I used to call her."

"Peggy Shippen is kin to you?" Major Crippen was suddenly interested.

"Yes. She's about—seventeen, I should think. And that rascal Arnold is twenty years her senior. But he'd have his hands full with her. I've seen her eyes flash with greed."

Archibald belched. "Beggin'pardon. Aye, she's the favoured little grey-eyed bird of the gentry—a social butterfly with high tastes." He winked at Oliver. "You'd best keep a distance."

Major Crippen blushed.

Katherine had plenty of chores waiting for her, so she hurried the men out of her kitchen and began rinsing her pots, wiping the porringers, and setting all to order. "Penny, tonight is Mrs. Franks' dinner. I fear you and Thaddeus are not invited to attend. Had I known your brother would be here for these two short days I'd have gladly declined."

"I am happy not to attend. That chubby gossip is—"

Mrs. Browne set her fists on her hips and gave her daughter a stare that held the girl's tongue.

"Yes—well, I am pleased to spend some time with my brother. Perhaps we might stroll the downtown. It seems many are having dinners, and I'd enjoy peeking into a few windows."

⇢┉●◎ ◎●┉⇠

"Thaddeus, we need to talk," whispered Penelope. Thaddeus bent his ear to her lips. "Aye?"

"Follow me." Penelope led her twin into the rear yard. "Father and mother have a dinner engagement at Mrs. Franks' this evening."

"And?"

"And I think they shall be gone for five or six hours."

"And?"

"I told mother you and I would stroll uptown to see the parties and the dances in the gentry homes. We could leave at dark—say five o'clock."

"Oh." Thaddeus seemed very disinterested. He glanced at his sister's fingers. "You've been writing. I see ink on your fingers."

"Aye."

"Well, what were you writing? I thought the tutor left the city."

"He did. I—I wrote a letter to Cameron from all of us," Penelope said.

Thaddeus was confused. "Well—how shall he get it? Do you think Major Crippen will fire it from his cannon?" He laughed.

"No. You and I are taking it to him, tonight." Penelope stared hard at her brother.

"Taking it to him? Are you mad? He's at Valley Forge, nearly twenty miles away. You'd freeze or be shot."

Penelope was serious. "Listen, I have an American pass—I've sworn to the nation. You have a Tory pass—you've sworn to your cursed King. We use yours to get out of the city and back again, we use mine amongst the patriots beyond the lines. I'm told there are cavalry companies riding between here and Valley Forge all the time. They might take us."

Thaddeus stared at his sister and groaned. He knew if he did not go she'd go alone. "Well—well, I think you're mad. We'd be lucky to get home by dawn. We need to cross the Schuylkill River—it really is madness. And no cavalry is going to take us anywhere."

Penelope preferred to follow her heart; her brother followed his mind.

Thaddeus began to think. "We could take a coach out of the city. If we could get past our lines, we could probably find a rebel scout easy enough. He could take your letter for us and then we could turn around."

"But I want to see him."

"Aye, me too, but then he'd be worrying for months whether we got back. He knows how dangerous it is between the lines."

Sometimes logic and passion find each other. Penelope nodded. "I hadn't thought of him worrying. Fine, we'll do it your way. If we can get through the lines in three or four hours…then find a picket. We wouldn't have to go all the way to Valley Forge; yes, this could work."

CHAPTER 10

Dinner Plans and a Dangerous River

"OH, MY, MY, my. Mrs. Browne, would you be so kind?" Mary Franks was flustered and frantic, and beads of sweat were scattered across her brow. She wrung her hands as though they were two damp rags.

Katherine was calmly holding Cromwell in her arms.

"Please, Mrs. Franks, do come in."

Poor Mary's face was flushed and puffed like a ripened tomato. She swished her wide-hooped skirts past Kate and paced the doctor's office like a nervous, waddling goose. "My caterers are late. They arrived just moments ago, and they say my kitchen is too small. I–I think I shall faint." The woman staggered backwards into a chair.

Katherine could not remember having seen an actress more convincing. "How may I help you?"

"Oh, would you?" Mary hung a set of sad eyes toward Mrs. Browne in a way that nearly made Katherine laugh out loud. She had seen an old coon dog once and she suddenly pictured it again.

"Yes, Mrs. Franks. I should be happy to help."

Mary Franks sat upright and beamed. "Well, then please allow us to use your kitchen. We are only three doors away, and Samuel, the caterer, says his men can run back and forth. Have you wood enough for a good fire?"

"Aye."

"Wonderful. You shall enjoy a most splendid meal this evening. I insisted that Samuel follow Mrs. Hannah Glasse's book, *The Art of Cookery*. It was given to me as a wedding gift and her recipes can be trusted. She is my husband's favourite. I also have *The Compleat Houswife* by some Mrs. Smith, but I find the colonials simply lacking the fine points of good English taste."

Katherine smiled politely. She was considered a fine cook, but her skill was the result of dozens of recipes committed to memory as a child. *"Perhaps I should make a book of them. After the war,* she thought.

"Mrs. Browne? Are you listening?"

"Yes, Mrs. Franks. I am sure the dinner will be excellent, and Dr. Browne and I are looking forward to joining you."

Mary's body swelled like a bellows filling with air. "You shall not soon forget such a Christmas feast as this. Samuel is a master caterer. He and his men live on Lombard with the others. These Negroes have a way with food that confounds me. And he has the finest delftware and pewter—porcelains and china. Oh, my heavens, I have spent a fortune on these rentals but—" She lowered her tone and glanced about the room as if someone might hear. "But I am paid handsomely by my British officers—and their friends buy my lace for their sweethearts."

⇢⊨⊙ ⊙⊨⇠

While Mary Franks and Katherine Browne were chatting, Penelope and her brother were busy conspiring for their night's adventure. Climbing to their attic bedroom, they wrapped themselves snugly in their quilts, as their room had no heat. On a cold winter's day their breath often froze along their noses and mouths. The wooden shingles of the roof had shrunk, leaving room for slivers of light to shine through the scattered spaces.

"I think we should bring some food and a blanket for Cameron."

Thaddeus nodded. "A good idea, but I doubt he'll get anything other than the letter."

"Well, even if another steals them, they will serve a good purpose."

'Good purpose' was a matter of opinion, but Thaddeus did not want to argue. He glanced across the room at Cameron's bed. Atop it lay a blanket his mother had made many years before. It was a good woollen one and the moths had only eaten a few holes in one corner. "There, sister," he said, indicating the blanket with his eyes. "He should have his own. And I have a pair of wool socks and a good linen shirt, the red scarf from Aunt Margaret, and—and he shall have my rabbit mittens."

"He always loved that scarf of yours. And there—Cameron has a canvass bag beneath his bed. Let's stuff it. Mother has dried apples, pear preserves, salted pork, and bacon in the cellar. I suppose eggs—no, forget the eggs."

"Some porridge meal could go far."

"Do you think he hasn't any porridge? Good heavens, Thaddeus, they must eat better than that. But probably no baked bread, at least not regularly, so let's add a loaf, and what about some honey?"

Thaddeus was thinking. "If we make the bag too tempting, it shall surely be stolen."

"How much temptation is too much?"

"Sounds like a question for Parson Coombs."

Penelope shook her head. "I say let's pack the bag with plenty and hope for the best." Agreed, the two descended the stairs to assist with the day's chores.

This day was the slowest Tuesday they had ever endured. Finally, by four o'clock, they received permission to dress for their own night's fun. But as they each faced their clothes pegs, they realised their dilemma. A night walking through the city would require hoops and petticoats for Penelope, silk stockings and knee breeches for Thaddeus. But a night in the forests required quite another outfit.

"Penny," said Thaddeus, "we need to wear the good stuff to get out of the house. But we'll need the other once we're out. Look—wrap what you need in a bundle with mine. Drop it to me from the window and we'll change in the garden." It was a reasonable plan.

It was nearly five o'clock by the time the two were nearly ready to leave. Thaddeus hurried down two flights of steps. Mrs. Browne met the young man as he entered the loom-room first. "Let me look at you." She surveyed the boy from top to bottom. He was wearing his best coat. "You've grown again. The tails ought to fall behind your knees and they are at mid-thigh. Good heavens, lad, you should have told me. You'll be seeing the tailor next week. Why the tricorn? I thought you liked to sport that flop-hat of yours."

"I suppose."

"You are not children any longer, so I expect your behaviour to be above reproach," began Mrs. Browne, as she handed the boy his hat. "If you intend to stroll the city, be on your guard. Stay away from the enlisted men. I hear the Second Street barracks lacks in virtue and in decency. Keep to the better streets, near the homes of gentry. I suppose the taverns might be of interest, especially the City Tavern, but enter only where you see officers' uniforms or gentlemen. The wharves and the shambles are no place for anyone at night."

Thaddeus smiled. He knew he'd always be his mother's little boy.

"Your father should be home soon. I expect he would want you to return by ten o'clock. Please make an entrance at Mrs. Franks' so we know you are home. Is this understood?"

The lad hesitated. Ten o'clock would be impossible.

"Good. Here is some silver that you earned. I think two shillings each should do. Take your sister for a nice meal. I'm told the Yorkshire Club has wonderful meat pies and puddings—and good ale."

Having passed inspection, the boy pecked his mother's cheek. "I'll wait for Penny on the walk."

He hurried out the door into the deep blue twilight of early winter. He stared upwards and whistled lightly. The attic window was creaking outwards when a voice suddenly startled the lad. "What are you looking at?"

It was Webster Yates. Before Thaddeus could answer, a black bag came hurtling toward the sidewalk.

"Move."

Webster jumped backwards with a yell and the canvass bag landed hard on the bricks. "Wha–wha–what?" stammered Yates.

His words had barely left his lips when another bundle crashed to his other side.

"Shh–shh, Webster. Quiet." Thaddeus pulled his friend from the street. "Follow me."

Meanwhile, inside the house Penelope fluffed her petticoats, straightened her hoops, reset her hairpins, and donned a green bonnet. She looked at her feet and wrinkled her nose at the thin leather shoes that bound them tightly. She feared they were still growing. The young lady came down the stairs looking very much like a fairy princess. As she entered her father's office, she paused to bid her mother farewell.

"Ah, my dear. If only your father could see you. You look stunning. You have the red of your grandmother's hair, I am sure of it—red like a robin's breast. The bonnet brings the green of your eyes to life, even in this candlelight." Katherine pointed to Cromwell. "His eyes and yours are a nearly perfect match. Now daughter, listen well. Avoid the soldiers. By all means, stay away from King Street—"

Penelope interrupted. "You mean 'Water Street'?" She smiled.

"I mean 'King Street.' Now just listen to me. Officers are most likely gentlemen, but rum takes the virtue from all of them. Be careful and keep your brother from fighting."

"Thaddeus isn't much of a fighter. Ask a Mennonite." Penelope giggled. "And you take care of father. He'll be out-numbered at dinner and you know how that can make him."

"I think his last time in the jail mellowed him some. We can pray for it. I only hope he is home soon. Mrs. Franks demands perfection and promptness. Ah, well. Now, run along and promise me you shall make your introductions by ten o'clock."

"Ten o'clock?"

"Aye."

Penelope hesitated. "Don't be cross if we're a little late. Only Christ Church has a bell and we may lose our time."

Mrs. Browne thought for a moment. "We'd prefer ten o'clock sharp, but at Christmas I suppose we ought leave a little room for mercy."

~•➤=◉ ◉=◄•~

Mary Franks was struggling to attain perfection. However, her caterer, Samuel, was gifted with more talk than culinary skill. The woman should have wondered why he was available when every other caterer had long since been claimed by Philadelphia's high society. But on the morning of her special day, Mary did not yet know the difference and was flitting about her house singing merry ballads. Mary's house was similar to the Brownes'. It was a row house, built between two larger homes about fifteen years prior. Like the other homes on the street, its cellar was home to her kitchen and opened to the street. And, like the Brownes', her hearth was a cavernous five feet tall and six feet wide and filled with roaring logs resting on sturdy andirons. On this day the fireplace was cluttered with the caterer's pans, pots, and iron baskets that he had hung on hooks or chains from the swinging crane. Of course, Mary's own ever-present iron kettle squatted in the coals atop its four stout and stubby legs.

In the rear of the hearth was an ornate fireback—a large plate of iron that reflected the heat of the fire back toward the room. Standing by the stone wall was the long handled "peel," or shovel, and two sets of iron tongs. Scattered about the kitchen was an assortment of trivets, waffle irons, roasting "kitchens," and baking pans.

On the first floor of the Franks' house was Mary's millinery shop. From here the woman made and sold fine brocade, laced doilies, stockings, and ruffled collars. Hers was the pleasure of trimming the gentry with the smoothest silk and finest cotton appointments from Europe and the East. A side door led to the second floor, which contained two rooms. One hung out beyond the first floor, creating a shaded garden beneath. It was a tiny room, but served as the bedroom for the Franks. The main room of the second floor was ample and was used as their parlour. It was here the dinner would be served that evening.

Unfortunately, Mrs. Franks now slept in the attic. Her British officers had taken the parlour and the rear room for themselves. However, the men were kind enough to clear the parlour of their gear so Samuel and his caterers might prepare the room for entertaining. A nice fire now burned in the small fireplace and the caterers had spent some time outfitting the room with a long table, some benches, and a serving table.

Soon after a hasty lunch, Mary began to prepare her face. Her mother had often said, "If your presentation can endure the test of sunlight, it shall surely be pleasing 'midst candles." With regard to Mary, most doubted the former and denied the latter.

Mary spent the whole of the afternoon preparing for the "test of sunlight." She mixed white flour and cornstarch in a pork-fat base and applied it generously to her ample face until nothing showed except her lips, her nostrils, and her black eyes. When the mixture had dried, she applied beetle rouge to heighten her cheekbones and redden her lips. Then she brushed a carbon powder on her furry eyebrows and accented the whole project with a round "beauty patch" on her chin— a black, circular patch that looked like a mole.

In the late afternoon, Mary began to dress. She had become heavy over the years, a condition not as easily concealed by her hoops as she assumed. But plumpness alone did not make the woman unattractive. Blessed—or cursed—by blindness to her own vanity, the woman's heart beat happily. She knew the ladies of the neighbourhood kept a distance from her. It was her husband's younger sister, the beautiful Rebecca, that drew smiles and waves from everyone. And her husband seemed popular enough with others. She knew she had not yet claimed a position of worth in her world, and thought a dinner worthy of note might serve that purpose very well.

Mrs. Franks was in the business of textiles, so her own wardrobe was generous and befitting a lady whose enterprise involved the gentry. She selected particularly uncomfortable stays, or corsets, and, as her husband was away, enlisted one of Samuel's girl-servants to tighten it until she cried out in pain. Made of whalebone and heavy linen, it lifted her otherwise stooping back into a proper posture.

Around this the woman hung her pannier, a cloth-covered basket frame. This one had been imported from England a few years prior. She had noticed that society women were beginning to wear hoops that were a bit narrower, and although concerned that style had passed her by, she had little choice for this evening's gala. Atop her pannier she draped several under petticoats and finally, a bright yellow over-petticoat from Portugal. Atop the petticoats she donned a scarlet Christmas gown of velvet, open in front from the waist to the hem to show the petticoats beneath. The gown was Spanish and adorned with gauze and lace imported from France and the Netherlands. The white silk gloves she would later wear were from India.

By four-thirty, Mary was pleased. Holding a looking glass to her face, she smiled. She must have seen something no one else could have. She checked the new wig waiting by her bed stand. Outrageously expensive, it had arrived from New York just one week before. A high, cylindrical mound of blond, human hair, it would surely stop the hearts of her guests.

Indeed.

Fortunately, Mary had abided by the advice of the wig seller and set a mousetrap deep inside. After it had been cleared of a little corpse, the wig was ready. Content in her vanity, round Mary bustled about her house, checking on this and that. She straightened the sampler hanging on one wall of the parlour. It was a needlecraft of the alphabet surrounding the Lord's Prayer. In the centre, at the top, was the face of the British lion. She paused to survey her room one last time. One wall of the room was wallpapered with thin, leather sheets bearing a rich design of flowers. The other walls were painted with glossy milk paint in a brilliant yellow. The chair rail was red. Mary suddenly realised her evening's dress matched her room and she was delighted. She wondered if anyone would notice.

Believing it to be nearly five o'clock, Mrs. Franks thought it wise to check on her caterers. She paused one more moment in front of the rippled mirror hanging over her fireplace. Though yet wigless, she was thoroughly pleased with what she saw. She sighed and smiled contentedly. "I love Christmas."

⤙⚬ ⚬⤚

Penelope joined her brother around the corner of the house. "What's he doing here?"

"I forgot. I was to spend the evening with him."

Penelope turned to Webster and shook her head. "You can't come."

"Come where?"

"It is just a–a brother and sister thing." Penelope had mixed feelings toward Webster. She thought he was too soft and fearful. But he had a heart as big as the whole of the New World. "I hope you understand."

"Oh. Well, I'll just go home then." Webster's tone betrayed his hurt.

Thaddeus hesitated, then grit his teeth. "Well, maybe—"

"No," blurted Penelope. "We have little time as it is. Webster shall slow us even more."

"Slow you at what?"

The twins whispered together. "We have to tell him now, else he'll slip and tell; he always does." Thaddeus was insistent.

"I can't believe this. He is fat and slow."

"I'll ask him and I think he'll say he won't want to go. I know him better than you, remember? Now, go get your clothes changed, and quickly." Thaddeus turned to Webster. "You need to keep a secret for us. We are going through the line to give a letter and supplies to Cameron."

Webster was silent.

"Did you hear me?"

"Aye."

"And?"

"When do we go?"

"We? Webster, you're not dressed for a march through the forests, and—well it's a long way."

"All I need is m'overshoes and an old coat. I can be back before you're ready. I promise I'll keep up with you. Cameron is your brother, but he's my friend."

Thaddeus was annoyed. "But Webster, you can't come, it's too far and—"

"Wait for me, Thaddeus. I won't be more than five minutes." With that, Webster bolted down Union.

Penelope called from behind the privy. "Thaddeus—is he gone?"

"Aye. Now hurry." Thaddeus stood behind the chestnut tree and threw off his fancy coat, knee breeches, stockings, and buckled shoes. In their place he donned a hunting outfit of Cameron's. It was a little big, but not too big. He pulled a buckskin shirt over his head and leather trousers over his legs. On his feet he put his brother's shin-high Indian moccasins over wool socks. Unlike his shoes, these were cut for one to fit his left foot, the other the right. Atop his shirt he wore a brown work coat his father used in the garden.

Penelope was happy to tie her fancy clothes in a bundle. She wore a working gown that she had pinned up at the hips to free her ankles. Covering herself in a woollen, homespun coat, she pulled on a pair of softer shoes. "My blasted goloeshoes again—I forgot them."

"You forgot them? How could you forget them? You'll need them in the wood."

"Aye. Wait here."

As Penelope slipped through the alley to the front door, Thaddeus looked nervously down Union. He wanted to hurry and leave before Webster returned, and he surely didn't want his father to appear. He calculated it was at least a quarter past five.

Penelope peeked into the front window carefully, very carefully. She assumed her mother was getting dressed upstairs. Though Katherine would not bother with so much face-flour as Mary Franks, she still had an hour or two of work ahead of her.

Penelope saw that the room was empty. Only one little candle flickered by her father's desk. Reaching for the brass knob, she pushed lightly on the door. It opened with a creak.

Mrs. Browne called from upstairs. "Archibald, is that you?"

Penelope gulped. She pushed the door open further. It creaked louder.

"Archibald? Answer me."

The girl stretched quickly, reaching for her goloe-shoes. Her fingers tumbled along her father's overshoes, then a space, then Cameron's, then Thaddeus', and finally her own. Each was always in its proper place leaving her to wonder where her mother's were.

"Archibald." Katherine's tone was harsh.

Penelope lunged for the far pair and pulled the creaking door shut as quietly as she could. She hurried around the corner to the frantic whispers of her brother. They heard footsteps running up Union and groaned. "Webster."

But just when the boy neared the house, Mrs. Browne flung open her front door.

"Halt!" she screamed.

"Don't shoot!" Webster stood quaking on the sidewalk, hands raised.

"Webster? What are you doing here?" Katherine lowered her rifle and closed the hammer.

"I–I–I—"

"Relax, boy. I thought someone was sneaking into the house."

Thaddeus and Penelope hugged the wall and held their breaths.

Webster took off his hat and bowed, dutifully. "Good evening."

"Master Yates," laughed Mrs. Browne. "No need for that. Did you see anyone leave my house?"

"No."

"Well, I suppose it was Cromwell making noise. So, are you looking for my twins?"

"Uh—no. I–I wanted to know if Dr. Browne had any— red pepper to spare for a mix?"

"Who is sick?"

"Uh—I think a child by the wharves. My father is preparing a remedy but was a bit short."

"I see. Wait a moment." Katherine withdrew from the doorway while Webster gained his composure.

Penelope was furious. "You said he'd never go. You said you knew him. Now, do we hide until he leaves, or do we take him with us?" she whispered.

Thaddeus nodded but felt badly for his friend. "I think we should let him come."

Penelope grumbled an oath.

"There, Master Yates. That should do." Mrs. Browne handed the lad a small, folded paper containing grindings of red pepper.

The boy tucked the paper neatly into the pocket of his breeches. "Many thanks, Mrs. Browne. I shall see you at prayers on Christmas Eve?"

"Indeed, lad. Now have a good evening." The door closed.

"Psst. Psst. Over here. Webster." Thaddeus reluctantly beckoned his friend from the corner of the alleyway.

"Aye?"

"Are you ready?"

Webster nodded.

Thaddeus and Penelope looked at their unlikely comrade in the yellow light of a smoky street lamp. The earnest boy smiled back and waited. "Fine," Thaddeus said. "Now let's be off."

--⇥●⟡ ◉⇤⟡--

"It is five o'clock!" shrieked Mary Franks. "It is five o'clock and you have yet to roast the beef. You know it takes an extra hour in winter. It shan't be ready until eight o'clock."

"Aye, but I thought it was for second course and —"

"No, you dimwit. The beef is first course—with the eel and the puddings. Are your puddings ready?"

"What puddings?"

Mrs. Franks staggered backwards into a chair. She fluttered her face with a new silk fan. "Good heavens, Mr. Samuel—what puddings? You are to have Yorkshire pudding in the first course, and orange in the third."

One of Samuel's helpers hummed his way through the kitchen. "Hallo. A good night for a party."

"Do not speak to me, you—you sooty fool." Mary snatched a paper from her bosom. "You, Samuel. If you ever want to work in this city again, you had best look at this."

The man stared, blankly.

Mrs. Franks pointed to the order of her meal and the various dishes she had paid for. "There—roasted beef in the first course, with stewed eel, Yorkshire pudding, raised pork pie, pea soup, pickled asparagus, fairy butter, and wheat bread. Why are you staring like that?"

"I cannot read."

"What? Do you not go to church?"

The man shook his head.

Mary Franks nearly fainted. Sweat began to bubble beneath her face-cake. "Can *any* of your helpers read?"

"No."

Mary pursed her lips. "Then how do you read from Mrs. Glasse's book?"

"Who?"

It was more than the woman could bear. She closed her eyes and pretended she was dining at Mayor Powell's with *real* caterers in a *real* hall.

"Mistress—mistress? Are you fainted, mistress?"

Mary stood on wobbled legs. It was hopeless. "Do I look 'fainted,' Mr. Samuel?"

"No."

"Then I suppose you have answered your own question."

Samuel nodded.

A group of his cooks gathered around, variously holding spoons and knives, mixing bowls, and pitchers. Mary gawked at the semi-circle of black faces. "None of you have read to-night's bill of fare?"

They stared blankly.

"Pity." The poor woman was beaten. "Good evening, Mr. Samuel. I shall see you in the parlour at say, seven o'clock?"

Samuel smiled. "Yes. Seven bells."

—▸▣◅ ◐▣◅—

Thaddeus, Penelope, and Webster rushed west on Pine Street where they hired a coach to rush them out of the city. The afternoon was cold. A thin layer of snow covered most of the city walkways and alleys, but the cobblestones were cleared. The lamplighters were beginning their routine but each block westward had less street lamps than the one before until by Sixth St. they were gone. At Eighth the sidewalks ended and the streets were no longer paved. "Somewhere out here is where Thomas Jefferson stays while in the city," commented Penelope. "I thinks he likes the gardens and the quiet."

By Fourteenth St. the streets were no longer numbered. They were at the outskirts of the city, near the Quakers' Bettering House. There they dismounted their coach and hurried away on foot. Penelope estimated the time at about three-thirty or better by the time the final few homes of the city were behind them. By choosing a westerly route directly to the Schuylkill River, the three knew they were adding time to their journey. In darkness, however, none trusted their sense of direction. Thaddeus had properly reasoned that the less travelled westward roads could lead them the short distance to the Schuylkill, and then the river could be followed northward.

The three finally arrived at the banks of the Schuylkill River. The river was about a quarter as wide as the Delaware and only deep in parts. It had ample fords for armies to cross and numbers of working ferries. Thaddeus had heard Joseph Galloway remark that Washington's troops had used their wagons, set end to end and covered with planks, as their bridge in the retreat from Whitemarsh. In the December twilight the frozen river shimmered silver and grey.

The three paused for a very brief respite. Thaddeus calculated the distance to the river at about half their total distance. He hoped to follow its eastern shore northward to the mouth of the Wissahickon Creek. Then they would follow the creek a short distance, cross it, and sneak through the British lines somewhere just west of Germantown. "Which way is Valley Forge?" asked Penelope.

Thaddeus pointed northwest. "About fifteen miles from here?"

"Do you think Cameron is well-fed and warm?"

"Mr. Galloway says Washington had plenty of time to gather food in Whitemarsh. I should think he is fine, but I'm sure he'll be glad for what we've brought."

"I hear Washington is crude and cares little for his men," offered Webster.

"I doubt that. His men love him."

"Well, it's what they say in the taverns."

"It's what *who* says?"

"British officers."

Penelope shook her head. "They say that because Howe is so easy on them."

"He loves his men."

"Aye, perhaps, but they may lose for all his love of them." Penelope turned to Thaddeus. "And, speaking of your Galloway, tell me more of his list."

"He told me he could offer the British three hundred names. These would be wealthy men who could pay for an army of Loyalists if asked—an army ten thousand strong. He says their only hesitation is their fear that Washington is still too close and the rebels would make their lives very difficult if they ever found them out."

"I should think so," blurted Penelope. "They'd likely be tarred or killed. How many names does he have?"

"I'm not sure. I thought Mr. Bond said they've about two hundred so far."

"Is that Phineas Bond?" asked Webster.

"Indeed. He is amazing. He is as fiery a speaker as—as Penny's Patrick Henry."

"I doubt that. But tell me, Thaddeus, what do you think of this list?"

Thaddeus shrugged. "I don't know as yet. But we should talk of it another time—we need to hurry on."

The trio followed the icy river carefully. Penelope glanced over her left shoulder. She stopped. "Thaddeus, why don't we just cross?"

"I don't think it is thick enough."

"Why don't we try? It's been very cold."

Webster didn't want to interfere, but an uneasy feeling filled his belly. "What if it breaks and we're half-way?"

"Then we die." Thaddeus was worried.

"I say we try," said Penelope. "We could shave two hours off this trip. You've got such big ears, Thaddeus, that you'd never sink anyway." The three chuckled, nervously.

Thaddeus stared across the ice. "I'm not sure about this." He stood still and looked about the deepening darkness. He took a deep breath. "Fine, I'll lead, you two follow, but keep a good distance." Thaddeus shook his head. "Penny, you take the bag; I shouldn't add the weight to myself."

"But what of *my* weight?" complained Webster.

"Just—just listen for creaking. I'll be in the front. If it doesn't crack for me, you'll be fine. But if you hear a creak, stop and back up slowly. If the ice gives way, spread your arms as wide as you can."

"But—but—"

"You were warned not to come," scolded Penelope. "Now either go home or come with us."

Thaddeus eased on to the ice. A layer of crystalled snow crunched. He paused and drew another deep breath. "Penny, there can't be more than an inch of ice." He stepped a little farther, then farther. Soon he was twenty paces off shore and he waved slowly for the others to follow.

Penelope came next. She hefted Cameron's bag on to her shoulders and stepped on the ice as lightly as she could. She and her brother then crept forward in the night while Webster trembled on the snowy shoreline. Finally, the boy found his courage and stretched one stubby leg as far as he could on to the river. With one leg on shore and the other on ice, he made his decision. He leaned forward and stood on two shaking legs. His friends were in view but quickly disappearing in the silvery darkness.

Suddenly, all three heard the sounds of nearby soldiers laughing. Webster began to whimper. "What to do?" he muttered. He knew he could not stay but he feared to go forward. He turned his eyes toward the shrouded moon and saw its cloud slowly drifting away. Soon the moon would shed its full light on the river. The frightened fellow feared the troops more than the ice. He wasn't sure why—after all, they were his troops. But he doubted he could ever explain his presence on the river at night, headed toward the enemy. *Surely they would hang me as a spy.* Stout Mr. Yates crouched low and slid his slipping feet quickly toward the far shore.

Thaddeus and Penelope had heard the soldiers as well. Though not yet halfway across the river, they were in no position to return. Thaddeus quickly whispered to his sister to lie flat and not move. She immediately fell to her back, facing the night's sky. As he spoke, he eyed Webster slumping rapidly toward them. *Get down. Down, you dunce,* he thought. Unable to call out, Thaddeus sprawled face down on the ice.

The British knew the frozen river was a temptation for spies and deserters, though an unlikely point of surprise attack. On the far shore were a few redoubts, or earthen forts, and scattered patrols to keep any large force at bay. This western defence was much less heavily manned than the land to the north of the city, where the line was comprised of a series of redoubts and miles of fascines, trenches, and stockade walls. But it was a plain fact that the river was patrolled regularly and well defended nonetheless—a fact the three should have considered.

As recently as the day before, the river had been dangerous for crossing. Apparently two Hessians had fallen to a cold, watery death while attempting to join the Americans on horseback. And downstream, a small company of deserting Americans had met a similar fate. So the British were not yet as vigilant as they might have been otherwise, and, with Christmas fast approaching, ale and rum were the order of the day. While patrols were supposed to be sober, something about the holiday softened the rules.

The Redcoats were surprised to see anything suspicious on that night's ice. In response they sent a soldier forward. A small-framed private stumbled on to the snowy crust and trotted lightly toward poor Webster. The man paused once to test the ice, then cocked his weapon and advanced.

Webster was gliding well for a clumsy fellow. His fears had found a way to drive him hard past his comrades. He gave no heed to Thaddeus' urgings to lie down, instead pressing on toward the far shore, faster and faster.

Thaddeus lifted his head just enough to see the silhouette of a soldier slipping his way towards them. He strained to see a huddle of others laughing and snorting on the bank. "Penny," he whispered. "Lie still. If I say 'go,' get up and run for the west bank. If we are separated, get your bag to a rebel and find your way to the mouth of the Wissahickon—a mile or so north. We'll meet there."

"Right."

The two lay still. Thaddeus' mind was whirling. He peered into the darkness and saw the soldier getting closer and closer. He turned his head and saw Webster still scooting away. The ice beneath Thaddeus' belly began to shake as the Redcoat's boots beat steady on his trail. He pressed his face tight to the ground. He heard the ice yield a mournful groan, then crack—but it held.

In a moment, the soldier thumped within a few yards of Penelope, and then by him, then went past him. The man's eyes were fixed on his prey.

The low moon burst from behind the clouds and lit the river with its silver light. Thaddeus lifted his head ever so slightly and watched Webster's bulky form struggle toward safety. But suddenly, not twenty paces from himself, the Redcoat stopped and snapped his weapon to his shoulder. It was no short-barrelled musket but rather a sharpshooter's rifle. With his comrades hooting from the other side, the man took aim.

CHAPTER 11

Tension Mounts

"When this war is over," grumbled Archibald, "I shall purchase another pocket watch. It is bad enough we need to attend this miserable dinner at that most awful Mrs.

Franks,' but now we need fear tardiness too."

Dr. Browne's mood was sullen and broody. The very last thing he wanted to do was pretend a glad heart at a table surrounded by his enemies. He sat at his desk and poured himself a glass of Madeira wine while he waited for Katherine. He stared deeply into its deep, caramel colour. *Enemies,* he thought. *Imagine. Same history, same language, same God—yet enemies.* Archibald shook his head.

"I am ready." Katherine entered the doctor's office and curtsied.

Her husband smiled and rose to meet her. "Ah, my dear. You look—delicious. You are still the sparkling jewel I married so very long ago."

Mrs. Browne blushed in the candlelight. The shy turn of her eyes drew the man close. He took her hands in his and kissed each one.

"I shall always love you, Kate Browne."

The woman's pale blue eyes swam in pools of tears and she embraced her husband. "And I you," she answered softly. Dr. Browne escorted her to the door, pausing to survey her one more time. Katherine was wearing her favourite gown, a square-necked, green velvet dress from the Netherlands, edged with lace and ruffles. Simple in design, it fell to her ankles with a quiet elegance that so befitted her. She wore no wig, but had tied her own red-brown hair atop her head in braids, covering all with a cream-coloured bonnet.

Archibald had donned his Sunday best: a French-made silk shirt with ruffles, a brown English waistcoat, green breeches, one white stocking, a silver-buckled shoe, and a blue coat cut away at the hips, with tails tapering to his knees. His wig had been freshly powdered—at no little expense— and sat neatly underneath his well-worn tricorn hat. He took a moment to oil and buff his wooden leg, and then smiled at his wife.

The pair admired each other for a long moment before Katherine entreated her husband one last time. "Archibald, I beg you to be longsuffering and restrained tonight."

"Aye."

"Please. This will be very difficult for you; that I understand. You will be dining with men who oppose your conscience and who may offend you. I believe one or two may even be pretentious."

"For you, my dear, I shall bind my tongue with coils of steel. I shall sew my lips together with leather cord and—"

"Enough, Archibald," sighed Katherine. She smiled and took his hand. "I confess another reluctance. I think of Cameron and the difficulties he must now suffer. And here we are, preparing to stuff ourselves at a Christmas feast." The woman hung her head.

Dr. Browne set a tender finger beneath her chin and lifted her eyes to meet his own. "I, too, think of the lad. I think of him shivering and hungry. But, my dear, he would surely be content to know he is not forgotten. He would smile to see his beautiful mother happy and warm."

Katherine dabbed her eyes and nodded. "For Cameron, then. Now, shall we?"

"Aye. Indeed. To dinner."

The two stepped into the night's frigid air and hurried quickly to Mary Franks' front door. Dr. Browne grasped the brass knocker and rapped the door firmly. It was opened at once by a well-dressed Negro servant, who smiled and welcomed the two, taking their overcoats and escorting them through Mary's shop to the stairway. The Brownes ascended the curling staircase and entered the front parlour.

The room was aglow in a forest of flickering candles and lamps. A fire snapped and danced cheerily in the hearth and a circle of contented faces turned to greet the doctor and his wife. Mrs. Franks rushed through the crowded room and curtsied. Katherine returned the courtesy.

Dr. Browne returned his hostess' welcome by "making his leg" with high drama. He always liked to extend his wooden one and, while doing so, tap it hard upon the ground as he bowed. Unfortunately, the house-cleaners had polished the wide-planked floor that very afternoon. His wooden leg skidded to one side and Archibald found himself doing something of an Irish jig. Somehow—the surprised guests could not imagine how—the man avoided a fall. With a red face and a pumping heart, the doctor made a quick retreat toward a corner and a brandy.

"Good evening, sir." A finely dressed gentleman extended his hand toward Archibald. "My name is Mr. James Humphries, and this is my wife, Ruth."

"The two clasped hands and bowed. "I am Dr. Archibald Browne, and this is my wife, Katherine."

Katherine curtsied and lowered the fan from her face. She smiled politely. It was a ritual the pair would repeat throughout the early evening.

"You are the editor of the *Pennsylvania Ledger*?"

"Aye."

Katherine stiffened. The *Ledger* was a Loyalist newspaper that regularly rankled her husband. *Please—please,* she thought.

"Ah, yes. Well, then. A pleasure to meet you."

Mary Franks shuffled close. "Please, doctor and mistress, come meet the others." The woman was buzzing and bustling, her voice giddy and shrill, yet pinched with nervousness. She whispered to Archibald ever so politely, "Doctor, the floors are a bit slick; do be careful."

Dr. Browne scowled and followed his hostess o a cluster of British officers standing by the table.

"Gentlemen, I should like to introduce Dr. and Mrs. Archibald Browne, neighbours of mine."

Each officer bowed in turn, and greeted the Brownes with the courtesy of his tradition and breeding. One of the soldiers was Major William Cunningham of the First Battalion, British Grenadiers. The man was tall, dark-haired, and stern. His white vest and red coat hung neatly over his broad shoulders and followed his tapered torso like fine, tailored garments should. He wore a wig, dress white gaiters (heavy stockings), and polished, shin-high boots. The second officer was Major Richard Stanton, of the Queen's Rangers, a Loyalist regiment. A thick-chested, short man of middling years with fiery brown eyes and a curt manner, he wore the green coat and white breeches of his regiment. The third officer in the group was the Brownes' own Major Oliver Crippen.

Mary Franks had hoped the city's flamboyant Major André could have come, for he was a friend to Major Cunningham. But the major was spending the evening at the prestigious City Tavern with pretty Peggy Shippen.

Mrs. Franks led the Brownes to the other side of the room. "May I introduce Dr. and Mrs. Archibald Browne?" The pair greeted Katherine's distant cousin, the reverend Samuel Seabury, recently arrived from New York.

"Good evening. I understand we are related through your mother's side, Mrs. Browne?"

"Yes. My mother was Hannah Shippen Howell."

"Of the Philadelphia Howells?"

"Yes, the same. My grandmother was Penelope Seabury, married to William Howell."

"So, cousin, your grandmother and my grandfather were brother and sister. Yes, yes, now I see." The man smiled kindly. He was in his late forties and well seasoned. He had a pleasing, broad face with strong, balanced features. His dark eyes peered powerfully from beneath arching brows and conveyed a quality of confidence.

Katherine was pleased. The reverend Seabury was a man of stature both in the colonies and in England. His sermons were often quoted as eloquent defences of the Loyalist cause, and his essays, later combined under the title *Letters of a Westchester Farmer*, were considered among the best works published on the matter. To be in the company of this "man of great good sense," as he was called, was a thrill for the woman.

To have him call her "cousin" was even better. She was flushed with joy. "I believe we once met in Princeton, as I recall. I was about twelve years of age and I remember you had just returned from London. I remember how impressed I was that you had trained as a physician before becoming a minister. I was amazed at a man that could be a healer of both body and soul."

Seabury laughed. "Ah, yes. I had come home for a brief respite and to consider a church in Hempstead. I am humbled that you would remember me from so long ago."

Katherine nodded shyly. Anxious to turn attention away from herself, she asked, "And is your wife here?"

"I am sorry my wife could not attend. She is ill with a devilish cough."

Dr. and Mrs. Browne turned to greet a familiar couple, the reverend Coombs, of St. Peter's Church, and his wife, Lydia. Formalities completed, Mrs. Franks begged her guests to gather at her table. The reverend Seabury was escorted to the high-backed chair at the table's head. On one side the reverend and Mrs. Coombs, the Brownes, and Oliver Crippen were to sit. On the opposing side Mr. and Mrs. Humphries, Major Cunningham, Major Stanton, and Mrs. Franks would take their places. The guests stood in front of their appointed positions and waited quietly as the reverend Seabury stared at the ceiling and began a prayer for the company.

Archibald thought it was a tedious ten minutes or so that followed. The reverend's words wandered over all the colonies and the various conditions of the King's army in each. He then crossed the sea and blessed King George, the Parliament, Lord North, the Prime Minister, and the Archbishop of Canterbury. He laboured earnestly over the peace negotiations being considered by the British government and entreated the heavens for order and reason to rule the day. Finally, his prayer returned to Philadelphia and the little gathering on Union Street, for whom he begged God's eternal mercies. Archibald looked about the table in hopes the man's appeals were finally finished but was called, by name, to join the others in a final plea to their common Lord:

"Oh Lord, show thy mercy upon us."

The assembly answered, "And grant us thy salvation."

"Oh Lord, save the King."

The group answered, "And mercifully hear us when we call upon Thee."

"Endue thy Ministers with righteousness."

"And make thy chosen people joyful," they responded.

"Oh Lord, save thy people."

"And bless thine inheritance."

"Give peace in our time, O Lord. Amen."

"Amen," responded the company.

The scowling Presbyterian remained quiet throughout. He was not familiar with the liturgy of the Anglicans, and did not appreciate the personal invitation by Seabury. His silence did not go unnoticed. As the diners were invited to sit, James Humphries cleared his voice. "Ah, Dr. Browne. Are you well this evening?"

Katherine braced herself.

"Why do you ask?"

Mr. Humphries smiled wryly and set a napkin neatly on his lap. "I thought perhaps some cause prevented you from joining our prayer."

Archibald's jaw tightened. An Irish-born Scot dining with a table of Englishmen was bound to be served a portion of stress. " 'Tis true enough. I did not join your prayer—for cause."

Major Stanton bristled. He was an ill-tempered, poorly bred man from New Jersey. "And what is your cause?"

Katherine pinched her husband's thigh. Dr. Browne winced and bridled his tongue. "I sir, am ignorant of your liturgy." The words fell stiffly from between clenched teeth.

"Then, sir," asked Humphries, "what liturgy do you follow?"

"I am a Presbyterian man, sir. Born to it and bound by conscience to my doctrine."

A few grumbles rumbled round the table. The Presbyterians and the Anglicans had suffered their differences for more than a century. Many of the British called the present troubles a "Presbyterian Revolution."

Mary Franks was suddenly as nervous as a Christmas goose. She desperately wanted this evening to be a success. She did not need discord to ruin it. She slid from her chair and hurried the caterer toward the table. With a tense smile and a squeaky voice, she cried, "Everyone, please, it is time to enjoy our first course."

Major Crippen was anxious, too. "May I offer a toast to our hostess and kind neighbour, Mrs. Mary Franks." He stood and turned toward the woman and raised his glass as the others also stood. "May you and yours be blessed with a greater bounty than you have set before us in this most glorious Advent season."

The woman feigned a swoon. She fanned herself and smiled with so much insincere humility that Dr. Browne almost laughed out loud. Of course, her drama, added to the overabundance of hair heaped high on her head, the shocking scarlet of her ample gown, the surplus of rouge, and the excess of her face-cake, made the unsuspecting woman a target of secret mockery on the part of nearly every soul gathered.

The guests raised their glasses of fine, French claret and tilted their heads for a quick swallow. Major Stanton of the Queen's Rangers then added another toast: "To Sergeant Melvin Franks, good husband of this lady and the provider of our Christmas feast. May God protect him as he serves his King."

"Huzzah!" cheered the guests.

The reverend Coombs passed the wine. "Fill once more," he said. "I should like to offer a health to the reverend Mr. Samuel Seabury. May the wisdom of your preaching soften hearts to temporal and eternal righteousness."

The group lifted their glasses again. The massive Major William Cunningham then spoke, holding his wineglass toward the others. Katherine thought the glass looked like a thimble in the grip of a giant. The man's weathered face was sullen and hard and his bearing was that of a man who had dealt death to many. His voice rang out clear and strong, and somewhat threatening: "God save the King."

Katherine chilled. It was exactly the moment she had dreaded. She felt her husband's shoulder tighten and knot against hers as he set his glass hard atop the table. She raised her glass half way as the others hurrahed the King. *Do I honour my King and dishonour my husband?* She thought. She lowered her eyes *and* her glass. The table fell silent.

Mary Franks' jaw dropped. Mrs. Franks was aware of Archibald's position, but she knew Katherine to be a Tory, a devoted Loyalist. *Oh, why did I invite them? How foolish.* The woman fluttered her fan nervously. "Please, all, be–be seated. We've a wonderful first course waiting—and I have a surprise."

The diners seated themselves uneasily. Mary knew it was time to reveal the special addition to the evening's experience. Ebenezer Pidcock stepped shyly from the rear room and bowed. Sitting himself on a stubby stool, he began to blow a buzzing drone on his badly tuned bassoon. The old man had objected to playing a solo performance, arguing that the instrument was intended to accompany singers or violins.

But Mary wanted music, and he was all she could find. Reverend Coombs, the man's pastor, closed his eyes in dread. He knew the kindly bassoonist was an earnest and pious old fellow, but he had been the bane of the choir for decades. God had gifted him with a tender heart, but had denied the man any measure of rhythm or pitch.

So, as Ebenezer began punishing the composer of his first sonata, the guests of Mary Franks faced the untested creations of Samuel, the caterer. The smiling Negro lifted the lids off the serving dishes arrayed the length of the table. The diners nodded and whispered and studied the fare before them. But none studied the table more than Mrs. Franks.

To her great relief, however, she found much of what she had ordered: roasted beef, pink on the inside and well-charred on the outside, just as requested; raised pork pie, stewed eels, pea soup, and pickled asparagus. There was also fairy butter, white bread—made the "London way"—and currant jelly. In the table's centre, of course, was a fine- looking Yorkshire pudding. Mrs. Franks was surprisingly pleased.

The conversation soon settled into things of little note—the sort of idle chatter that neither edifies nor injures. It was a prattle of things common though not uninteresting. The Brownes remained quiet while the soldiers spoke of battles past and conditions in other places. For a while the diners reflected on the issue of the Indians. The reverend Seabury thought them to be untrustworthy and barbaric. "No amount of Christian teaching seems to touch their hearts," he said.

"But Mr. Seabury," objected Major Stanton, "with few exceptions they remain loyal to the Crown. If I am not mistaken all the Iroquois are with us. Only the Mohicans of Stockbridge and the Oneidas have joined the rebels."

Oliver Crippen answered. "We need to be careful of them. I'm told a lieutenant in Burgoyne's army was delivered his fiancée's scalp just months ago."

Mrs. Humphries choked on her eel. None were sure if it was the slippery stew or the conversation, but talk graciously turned from Indians to the Church.

The reverend Seabury posed a question to the reverend Coombs. "Sir, tell me about our reverend Jacob Duché. He once was a most respected rector of Christ's Church and of your own St. Peter's—is that not so?"

The reverend Coombs was a gracious man and not one for gossip. He preferred not to discuss matters of others unless it was for their advantage. The Duché matter was a problem. "I believe the man to be repentant and in good stead."

"I thought he was arrested."

"Yes. That is true."

"And what of his letter to Washington?"

The reverend Coombs hesitated, but Mr. Humphries was quick to fill the void. "The Duché scandal was a matter of great interest to my readers, and I doubt these officers know of it." He turned to the soldiers. "This rebel reverend had been the chaplain for the Continental Congress. It seems he learned of that cursed Declaration of Independence the Sunday before it was to be signed.

"Well, he thought himself more clever than he was. On that particular Sunday he took the *Book of Common Prayer* from his own pulpit and cut out all references to the Crown."

The British officers were aghast. They shook their heads in disbelief as they gnawed on beef. Humphries continued. "The minister then shocked even the Whigs of his church by reading his prayers void of any reference to the King. He thought he was quite the clever hero of the rebel cause until our army re-entered the city this September past. The man was not so clever after all. He conducted the next service in front of a church full of red coats with all the words added back in."

The group then laughed.

"Then, after the morning service he was arrested and sent to jail."

"'Tis where he belongs," grumbled Major Stanton.

"Ah, but there is more. From jail he repented of his rebellious ways and was released. He then sent a letter to Washington, informing the rebel general that the cause was lost, that men of dignity and character were returning to their King in droves. He told the general that his army was filled with only commoners and ruffians."

The guests chuckled. "True enough," added Stanton. "That rabble of an army is little more than a group of desperate villains and greasy rebellious rogues."

Humphries paused to swallow an asparagus spear. It was pickled, indeed, and the man's mouth twisted and puckered so that he could not go on. The reverend Seabury cast an annoyed look at the struggling Mr. Pidcock, while the table waited politely for Mr. Humphries to continue.

Mary gulped.

Dr. Browne kept his mind on the food before him rather than the conversation. He pretended he was picnicking with his family on the banks of the Schuylkill on a warm summer's afternoon. He reached for the fairy butter. It was a delightful spread made of hard egg yolks, sugar, orange-flower water, and fresh-churned butter. He wiped a generous portion atop a slice of hot white bread. "Hmm. This one Samuel failed to spoil." He rolled each bite around his watering mouth. It was pure joy.

Just as Archibald was swallowing, the caterer whispered in his ear, "Eat no eel or pickled onions."

The doctor turned and stared at the man.

Samuel winked.

Humphries continued. "So, it seems the reverend Duché's letter drew loud complaints from General Washington. So, received by his forgiving King and our most gracious

General Howe, the reverend boarded for home. So, to Jacob Duché—a health: May his conscience be restored and his mind refreshed in merry England."

⊶⧫⊷

On the dark, icy Schuylkill, poor Webster had no idea that his silhouette was filling the eye of a British sharpshooter. The Redcoat slid a shaking forefinger to his trigger, but his chest heaved and his arms began to tremble. The sharpshooter was a smooth-faced boy from Liverpool who, because he had been too small to manage a bayonet, had been assigned by a merciful officer to a sharpshooter's company in the light infantry of the 1st Battalion. He had just arrived from England via New York, and though he was a superb shot when knocking down clay bottles, he had never so much as fired on a squirrel.

But for all Thaddeus knew, the soldier was about to slay his innocent friend. The Browne lad scrambled to his feet with a yell and charged through the darkness toward the surprised Redcoat. Spinning around, the soldier fired a wild shot in Thaddeus' direction. The lead ball whistled past Thaddeus' ear, singing through the cold air with a high-pitched whine.

Unscathed, Thaddeus tackled the startled Redcoat and the two slammed on to the cracking ice. The sharpshooter's rifle spun away in circles. After a few grunts and rolls on sagging, creaking ice, the two realised their common predicament and suddenly lay still on the groaning, tentative ice.

"Hold, Yank," begged the terrified soldier. "Hold, else we both swim."

Penelope slipped and slid toward them, threatening the British soldier with every foul word that had ever soaped her mouth. She grabbed the lad's rifle off the ice and stepped lightly toward the two. "I'll bash your head, Redcoat," Penelope shrieked.

"Easy, sister. The ice is cracked all around us."

Faithful Webster Yates suddenly appeared. The brave little fellow knew his comrades were in danger and he had returned to help. Penelope called to him. "Stay where you are. The ice is cracking."

Webster froze as stiff as the river. His eyes widened and his mouth dried. "Aye. Can I help?"

Thaddeus' mind was racing. He was larger than his foe and had the soldier pinned on his back. But he could feel the ice slowly giving way. "You—have we your word that you'll not follow?"

The Redcoat nodded.

"Say it!" roared Penelope.

"You've m'word. I'll no' follow."

"And shout to the others that the ice is too thin."

The boy was so frightened he could not yell.

"Say it."

"Sergeant!" he cried. "The—the ice is too thin. Hold where y'be."

The company of soldiers had been moving gingerly toward the four. They stopped and called to their comrade. "Are ye fine?"

"Nay—hold fast," he shouted.

Thaddeus rolled softly to one side and belly-crawled ten paces away. The soldier lay still on the ice, eyes fixed toward the shadow of Penelope Browne standing near with the butt end of his own rifle poised to crush his skull.

"Sister—come," begged Thaddeus.

The girl joined her brother and Webster and quickly moved toward the far shore. The young lad of Liverpool was left behind, still and quaking in the puddle of icy water creeping around him. He had no interest in following anybody.

The western bank of the Schuylkill was steeper than the eastern one. It was tree-covered and rocky. The three scrambled off the ice and hurried deep into the woods before they huddled in a tangle and gathered their wits. "We'll talk of this later,"

Thaddeus ordered. "Penny, you have the sack?"

"Aye."

"Good. Webster, are you all right?"

He nodded.

"Good. Thanks for coming back. It was brave of you."

Thaddeus looked to the sky, bright with stars and a setting moon—bright enough for shadows in the wood. "Listen." Muffled shouts and jingling buckles could be heard in the brush behind them. Thaddeus whispered. "We need to follow the river, else we'll get lost. But we need stay inside the forest enough to hide. Penny, give me the sack. Webster, follow in the middle. Penny, from time to time call to me with a loud whisper so I know you're still with us."

The three made their way north along the river's rising bank. It was difficult to see in the dark, despite the light of the sky. Darkness was, in fact, the enemy of the times. Most people considered it to be a dreadful thing, for, without the protection of light, it was easy to fall into a well, stumble over a rock, be assaulted by a highwayman, or lose one's way.

Fortunately for the threesome, most of the British sentries were busy celebrating Christmas, and those few who had heard the warnings of the soldiers on the river gave half-hearted heed. On this night they preferred rum to vigilance. Last Christmas Washington had used this vice to his advantage when he took his army across the Delaware and successfully defeated the Hessian troops stationed at Trenton.

Climbing through the barren hardwood forest, the three pressed on for two or three miles. Penelope estimated the time to be past six o'clock. Thaddeus crept to the river's edge and peered across the ice to the eastern shore. Judging by the firelight, he was confident they were now at a point directly opposite the British line. He could barely make out the movement of men along a hedge of fascines. Turning his eyes northward in hopes of spotting some evidence of an American camp, he saw only an endless black, barren wasteland of leafless trees. A loud snap to his left dropped him to his haunches.

Snap. Snap.

Someone was edging closer and closer.

Penelope and Webster heard it, too. They were waiting for Thaddeus about fifty yards inland. They lay close to the ground.

Snap. Snap.

The sound passed between Thaddeus and his comrades. The lad held his breath.

Snap. Snap.

It finally faded away. Thaddeus led his company northward for another half mile or so. Confident he was through the British line, the young man began to seek a rebel scout. "Webster, Penny—sing."

"Sing? Are you mad?" Webster was whispering.

"We want to be found. Sing."

Webster shrugged. "Fine." He struck up a whining rendition of "God Save the King."

Penelope shrieked. Thaddeus scolded his friend loudly. "Now who's mad? We're trying to find rebels, not Englishmen. Sing that and we'll get shot for sure."

"Oh, uh, that's right. Shall I sing a Psalm?"

Penelope groused. "I'll do the singing." With that, the girl cleared her throat and struck up a merry "Yankee Doodle."

The young Tories winced but joined in. The three then climbed the rolling hills along the Schuylkill River singing and laughing, shouting and hollering like mad fools.

"God save George Washington," roared Thaddeus.

"Heaven bless Thomas Paine," Webster giggled.

The three blessed and re-blessed Jefferson, Hancock, Mason, Washington, Franklin, the Adams cousins (Samuel and John), Dickinson, Hopkinson, Henry, and Witherspoon until at last—at long last—they were stopped dead in their tracks.

"Halt."

Four soldiers encircled them. Their muskets were raised and cocked. They inched closer and closer until one of them spoke. "Who are you?"

Thaddeus spoke. "We are looking to give a message to a soldier."

The four stared for another minute. They eyed the rifle Penelope was still carrying. One soldier yanked it from her hand. A large fifth figure emerged from the darkness of the forest and said nothing. "Follow us," the leader barked.

The group formed a column behind the fifth man and quickly trotted along a dark deer path. The moon had set and none could see more than a few feet in front of themselves. The leader seemed familiar with the trail and in about fifteen minutes they reached a dish-shaped clearing where three small campfires glowed. A group of shivering soldiers were huddled close to the fires, but rose as the column appeared, pointing their weapons.

"Corporal Harding, we've prisoners."

The three were pushed to one of the fires where a rag-tag officer faced them. Wrapped in a threadbare blanket, a battered tricorn pulled over his unruly hair, the man looked tired. The yellow light of the fire threw heavy shadows across his gaunt face. "What is your business?" His tone was firm but not unkind.

Thaddeus answered. "Sir, we are family to a patriot soldier.

We've a Christmas letter and a bundle."

The officer looked at the bulging bag hanging by Thaddeus' side. "How do we know you are not spies?"

"'Tis why we sang our way to you, sir."

"Eh?"

"Aye, captain. We found them singing and shouting in the forest," said Corporal Harding.

"Who is your soldier?"

"Cameron Browne, 2nd Pennsylvania."

"Never heard of him. Of course, there's some ten thousand of us, so that means little. You'd be from Philadelphia?"

"Aye."

"Who are the others?"

"This is my sister, Penelope. And he's a friend, Webster Yates."

A sergeant ambled close. "Captain, we've a Philadelphia boy due back from patrol soon—that new lad. He may know them."

"Show me your passports."

The three stared at each other. Penelope was the only one to carry an oath to the United Colonies. The others were carrying oaths to the Crown in case they had trouble on the return "If you have no passports, the Congress requires me to arrest you as spies."

Penelope rummaged through her coat and found the inside pocket where hers was hidden. "Here."

The man read it by the fire's light. "Seems in order. Now, you two."

The young men gulped.

"Your passes?"

Thaddeus answered. "Uh–uh, we have no passes. We did not know we'd leave the city and there's been no way to get one since—since Washington abandoned us to the Redcoats."

The captain ordered Penelope's bag to be opened.

While the men were smelling the bacon and rubbing their hands along Cameron's thick, red scarf, Penelope watched the strange, tall man that had led them on their path. The man stood perfectly still, facing a different fire, his arms holding his blanket tightly around his angular frame. Penelope, always curious, walked slowly toward him. He did not look up until the girl was directly across the campfire from him. When he lifted his head, Penelope gasped. "It's you."

The man grunted with a nod.

"But—who—how—"

The man faced the fire again. He was the Indian who had studied Penelope's goloe-shoes in General Howe's garden. A whistle sounded from the forest and the soldiers readied their muskets. "Corporal Scott with my patrol," cried a voice.

"Enter," called the captain.

Six weary, shivering soldiers hurried to the fireside. The captain ordered a sergeant to retrieve one of them. In a moment, he returned with a shuffling, exhausted young private. The lad was dirty, trembling with cold, dressed in torn clothes, his feet wrapped with rags. "Private, do you know these people?"

The lad looked up from smoke-squinted eyes. He rubbed them once, then again. "Thaddeus? Penelope? Webster!" He lunged toward the three and laughed. It was Richard Davis, their neighbourhood friend.

"Richard!" the threesome squealed. Thaddeus slapped the boy on his back and held him by his shoulders. "I haven't seen you since—since the fight in the shambles."

"That German farm boy gave you a real beating." Davis assured his captain that the three were safe.

Captain Robertson nodded and then studied Thaddeus carefully. "Why aren't you with us? You are old enough, and fit."

"He's an apprentice doctor and helping patriot prisoners," blurted Penelope.

"Is that so?"

"Aye."

The captain turned to Richard. "Is this so?"

"Yes, sir."

"I see." The officer rubbed his cold hands together. "Fine. Now, a question: how do I pass over my own men with these blankets and this food?"

Penelope looked at the faces staring back at her. It was a pitiful circle of young boys and one very old man. Their clothes were thin and tattered; most had no shoes. Few had gloves. All were coughing and shivering. "Sir, I–I wish we could outfit the whole of your company."

"We could put it to a lot," grumbled a soldier.

Thaddeus answered. "You could. We cannot stop you from taking our brother's things. But he is your comrade and we did not think you would steal from each other."

The young man was right; they would not steal from one of their own.

The captain repacked the bag. "We may not look like much, but know this: we are men of honour and we are joined together as brothers in a common cause. Your Cameron's things shall be sent to him. You have our word on it."

There was a quality in the man's tone, a ring of character that moved Thaddeus. He was reminded of the determined faces that had marched past him when Washington's army swept down Second Street. These were tired, cold, hungry young boys and old men led by others just as weary and threadbare. Yet something greater than their resources was alive within them. For all their plenty, for all their pomp, and all their puffery, the British lacked such spirit as this. At that moment, the young man's suspicions were affirmed: these rebels would surely win.

Thaddeus extended a grateful hand to the captain. "Thank you on behalf of my mother and father, as well as from us." He then turned to Richard. "What is it like for you in all this?"

The boy shrugged. For a lad who had just turned fourteen, he had seen a lot in a few short months. "I am hungry, cold, and tired. But I am not dead. I shot two Hessians and I think a Redcoat officer at Whitemarsh. There was no joy in it. Some of m'mates were killed."

"Have you seen Cameron?"

"Yes. He's a good fighter. He was in the centre line at Whitemarsh. They held. I passed him on the march to Valley Forge. He's thin, though. But steady, like you. He's made sergeant."

Penelope beamed. "Sergeant Browne."

The captain returned. "*That* is your brother? Sergeant Browne, 2nd Pennsylvania, Company D?"

"Aye."

"Ah, of course I know him. He is a tough fighter. Brave as they come. And good with a bayonet."

Richard asked about other things in the city. He was astonished to learn the details of the occupation. His house, Thaddeus told him sadly, had been taken by Hessian officers. The fence was gone, and the stable.

"Firewood—everyone is in a panic for firewood. And Richard," asked Penelope with a smile, "whatever happened to your bully friend from the market—that Gilbert Oakely?"

"Oh, him. He is in my division, the Pennsylvania 3rd. But I think he deserted at Matson's Ford. Cornwallis made things pretty hot for us, and I saw him scamper away. Haven't seen him since."

Thaddeus nodded. "So, it looks like the army's not feeding you so well—or clothing you."

The boy shrugged. "Yep. It's not too good. Shoes don't last and Congress can't seem to find more—or coats, gloves, hats, ammunition, or medicines, either. They made us celebrate a day of Thanksgiving just a week back or so. They bragged up the generous portion for the good day and then we were each given a half-gill of rice and a tablespoon of vinegar. I could hold the whole of that mighty portion in one hand. Then we were sat down in front of a minister who preached us a pitiful sermon. A hundred of us called Scriptures to correct him from where we sat. Thanksgiving indeed. But the cause is just, and that is enough."

The threesome listened sympathetically. Webster groaned for the plight of the suffering patriots staring at him in the firelight. Thaddeus would have liked to have spent the whole night learning more of Cameron and of the army, but time was running short. Penelope mumbled that it was surely nearly eight o'clock already and they had no hope of returning home on time.

Thaddeus turned to the captain. "If your men can get us to the river, we shall be on our way."

Captain Robertson lit a long clay pipe. "If you crossed downstream, you are mad. The river's not yet hard enough."

"Aye, sir. It is just hard enough, but barely."

"How did you penetrate the line?"

"We hugged the shore tight."

Captain Robertson thought carefully. "The river's wider and deeper near to us. The water freezes quicker where it moves the slowest. It's where some of our scouts cross. But you'd be crossing north of the British line and on the other shore it's nearly solid with fascines and redoubts. I'm not sure there's a single hole."

Richard nodded. "Sir. I know of one—a mound of rocks with a sentry on top. We could distract the sentry and they could climb past."

"Can you find it in the dark?"

Richard shrugged.

The captain tapped his fingers on his knee. "Running Fox, do you know of this rock pile?"

The Indian nodded.

Penelope was nervous and uneasy. *But he's with the British?* She thought.

Captain Robertson drew a long draught on his pipe. He released the smoke slowly. "Good. Running Fox, Private Davis—and you, sergeant. Get them home."

CHAPTER 12

Pickled Onions, Fairy Butter, and Red Pepper

"AH, MRS. FRANK, delightful." The reverend Seabury smiled as Samuel and his caterers delivered their second course to the table. "I say, brandied peaches?"

Mary surveyed her table and nodded. "Indeed. I am told they are a favourite of yours." She turned to Mr. Humphries. "And for you we have pickled onions and pickled white walnuts."

James Humphries grinned from ear to ear. "But, *Madame*, how did you know?"

"Ah, *Monsieur*, it is the privilege of your hostess to keep that a secret."

The guests chuckled as Samuel uncovered the remaining dishes. Set before the well-pleased guests were boiled pigeon garnished with turnips and dried beans, a bowl of mashed pumpkin, apple dumplings, and stewed turkey with gravy. Dr. Browne raised his eyes and winked at his wife. Perhaps dining with the devil was not so bad after all. He was reaching for the pickled onions when a voice whispered in his ear. "I think not." It was Samuel.

Dr. Browne passed the bowl, curiously, and shook his head at his perplexed wife. "Pass them," he whispered.

Mr. Humphries crunched away on his walnuts while Mary Franks gulped a spoonful of the little onions. Humphries then reached for the platter of pigeon and commented, "I was quite surprised to learn of General Howe's request to resign his command."

The table became quiet. Not everyone was aware of that fact. "Ah, yes, 'tis true. And I think we've our own Joseph Galloway to blame." "How so?" asked the reverend Seabury.

"It is well-known that Galloway has promised more than he can deliver—again." Galloway and Humphries shared little other than ambition.

"Are you referring to his Loyalist army?" quizzed Oliver.

"Indeed, young man, indeed I am."

A murmur circled the table. The reverend Seabury sat back in his chair and swallowed a long draught of wine. "I am ignorant of this matter, Mr. Humphries."

"Your pardon. Mr. Galloway promised General Howe an army of Loyalists from these middle colonies. Most believe the general changed his strategy in trust of Galloway's knowledge. But no army has been raised—the recruiting offices are empty. Some say he is frantically compiling a list of influential men who have the means to hire an army, but it seems Howe may have lost interest. The general believes he has erred and must retire from his command."

The reverend Coombs added, "I wonder if this is the reason, or if it is that the uncanny resolution of the American army has frustrated the man."

Major Cunningham's lips curled with fury. He stood to his feet. "You give that rabble of Welsh coal-heavers and Gaelic bog-trotters too much credit. They are little more than unwashed, rebellious rogues, and talk like yours swells their heads. We shall squash them like slippery worms under our boots—with or without our kindly general."

The room was silent. Cunningham's face was tight and he sat down slowly.

The reverend Coombs cleared his throat nervously and dabbed his dry lips with the corner of his napkin. "I meant no disrespect to His Majesty's forces, I—" His wife tapped him softly on the knee and the man fell quiet.

Major Crippen spoke calmly. "Major Cunningham, a man who fails to know his enemy is bound to suffer defeat. I think you underestimate these rebels."

Cunningham reddened. He leaned toward Oliver. "You fire your cannon from safe distances. All you see is a blur of distant men. I bayonet them. I see the terror in their faces. I feel their brittle bones break in these very hands."

Katherine felt sick. She set her spoon and knife atop her trencher. Archibald held her hand and fought the rage building in his chest like a furnace readied to blast iron.

Oliver was not impressed with Cunningham's bravado. "You butcher the body. But they keep coming. You may break their 'brittle bones,' but it is as if they live again. In their places soon stand other kin or countrymen. We chase them from the field and they run and hide—but only to fly at us again. We have not beaten their hearts. They have something they believe in and unless you can bayonet *that*, sir, we shall never win."

Humphries was aghast. "You of all people—an officer of the King. Your tone suggests there is virtue in their cause."

Mary Franks wanted nothing to interfere with the evening she had envisioned. Loud voices and short tempers were not on her menu. Her reputation was at risk, and as she began to panic, her breathing became short and she began to fan herself rapidly.

Sweat collected beneath her make-up and large wart-like bumps began to appear on her cheeks and forehead. Her nostrils flared and her eyes fluttered—her party was in jeopardy.

Major Crippen refrained from comment. He poured a glass of wine and wondered if he had unwisely exposed the doubts that troubled him so. His remarks had quieted Archibald, however, and the doctor was grateful for the major's courage in the face of the menacing Major Cunningham.

Humphries squirmed in his seat as he blustered and grumbled. He turned to the reverend Seabury, who was quietly reflecting upon the conversation. "Have you thoughts on this 'something' the rebels hold to?"

Seabury grunted as he reached for an apple dumpling and the sugar cone. "Indeed, Mr. Humphries. I have thoughts on most things."

The diners chuckled, awkwardly. The man's voice was reasoned and calm and his demeanour restored the table to a more comfortable mood. "First," Seabury began, "let me say that I deeply respect the marketplace of ideas. It is a rare privilege to break bread with men of—differing views who still share a devotion to civility and respect." His words were chosen wisely.

A great relief came over Mrs. Franks and she released a long held breath with a trembling sigh.

"I think this unfortunate rebellion is founded on a deception. The rebels contend that our British government is in conspiracy to violate the liberties granted to all free Englishmen. Yet they cannot point to a single shred of evidence. This 'thing' they hold so firmly to, Major Crippen, is a figment fabricated by the rhetoric of the likes of Sam Adams and Tom Paine.

"I can not tell you how desperately I have argued the cause of sanity. I believe liberty to be a good thing—a very good thing. Liberty under my King and Parliament is as good as under their Congress, and slavery under either is a bad thing. All men should have a right to as much freedom as is consistent with the security required to maintain order and civility. Now, I grant that an empire requires more order than a small nation. But our empire is a good empire; it serves us as no other empire in the whole of history. I know of no better balance of liberty and order in all humankind. To put it at risk for these—these frivolous grievances is outrageous.

"The rebels give little heed to the care Parliament has provided in birthing and nurturing these colonies. The motherland has wept great puddles of blood in defence and support of these lands, but all we hear of is abuse and neglect.

"The rebels claim that 'natural law' gives them 'natural rights.' I say, 'hurrah' for these rights, as far as they may go. But yet they do not claim the 'natural right' of a government to maintain the peace, to regulate trade for the benefit of all, to secure her citizens from her enemies, nor to tax as is necessary for its very life.

"The rebels speak of 'taxation without representation.' Yet, their Congress does not represent each person any more than does Parliament. In fact, I would contend that the Congress is formed illegally, without regard for the lawfully established colonial assemblies. Nay, friends. It is order and decency that must prevail. Tradition and law—these are words upon which our liberties must draw. If these rebels prevail, none shall enjoy true liberty. Imagine if each colony were to govern itself—none would benefit. Our empire would dissolve into many petty kingdoms, each ruled by a republican tyrant."

Major Crippen cleared his throat. *Dare I enter this?* "Some believe it is the King, not Parliament, who created the colonies through his granting of charters. These charters were to provide certain protections and guarantees so that men could leave their homes and settle in a far away place in good faith. Parliament's violation of the rights and privileges delineated in these charters is seen as a breach of trust, a broken compact, if you will. And the King is now seen as an accomplice in this betrayal. Hence, the rebels believe they are free to declare their independence. For them, it is a matter of law."

"Law. I am aware of their argument; you need not educate me. I ask you to show me one example of how the government has violated the law."

Oliver thought for a moment. "Are not tradition and customary law related?"

"Indeed."

Oliver paused. Dr. Browne leaned forward as the company waited. "Then does this follow? The rebels claim that Parliament always had a right to tax their ocean trade, for it was related to issues of protecting an empire that spans the seas. And they claim they have no objection to the government's right to raise revenue in this way. But from the time the colonies began, no taxes were ever taken from them *directly*. Parliament had never taxed them for things such as buying and selling between themselves. Only their own elected assemblies did that—a process consistent with the English Constitution. The Stamp Act of just a dozen years ago was the first time the Parliament had ever taxed them directly. Hence, they claim, the government has broken the law by violating the established custom."

Seabury nodded. "Yes. An old and weary argument. Of course, I find it almost amusing that the indulgence of the motherland would be turned against her. It is preposterous to imagine that Parliament is expected to defend these spoiled children, only to be denied the right to tax them for it."

"Sir," Oliver pressed, "*if* Parliament has the legal right to directly tax them, what do you say to those who claim the colonies are taxed without representation in Parliament? Is this not a violation of our Constitution?"

The reverend Seabury narrowed his gaze at the young major and answered in a strong voice. "I have addressed this point. Of course, no Englishman—or American—is bound to any law but one that has been approved by the representatives of the nation.

It is the fabric of our English Constitution and the essence of the liberty our forefathers passed to us. But to say that *every individual* is to be represented is fantasy. No English farmer is exempt from the laws of the empire, even though he is not *personally* represented. We are a people who are represented *indirectly* by those to whom the nation has entrusted its care." Seabury stabbed a chunk of turkey and stuffed his mouth.

The guests remained quiet until the reverend Coombs spoke. "With all respect I admit that I find it troubling that our present government endorses *direct* tax by *indirect* representatives. What would you say to those who argue that those who represent the empire do *not* care for us?"

Dr. Browne raised his eyebrows. He was impressed that the reverend of St. Peter's would raise such a question. Samuel Seabury turned his head in surprise. "Are you making that charge?"

The reverend Coombs lowered his eyes. "No. However, I know that there are some in my congregation that do, and I sometimes am at a loss to answer."

"I see. Show me, then, Mr. Coombs, where Parliament or the King have not cared for us."

The group was silent. Archibald cleared his throat, but Katherine quickly pinched his leg. Oliver spoke. "If I may answer. I observe that the colonists are troubled by the *spirit* of the many acts passed against these colonies. Our laws have hemmed them within the boundaries of the Alleghenies in order to keep them in a manageable area, we now require them to house our officers, we monopolise tea, we support tyranny in Quebec, we toppled the Massachusetts charter, and we withdrew our defence of that colony—by statute."

"Major Crippen," roared Cunningham. The grenadier stood to his feet and towered over the table. "Are you loyal to the Crown?"

Amidst a volley of grouses Oliver stood to face the giant. "How dare you ask such a question?"

"Gentlemen, please." Mary Franks was faint and beginning to tilt off her seat.

The two officers stared at each other as the room quieted. Mary was given a swallow of quince juice by the kindly Mrs. Coombs. It was tart and she puckered her lips. Ebenezer Pidcock thought it a good time to bring calm and he began playing his bassoon once again. His decision proved unwise, for he had barely savaged the first few notes of another opus when the reverend Seabury begged him to stop. "Sir," Seabury hissed. "The room is tense enough without the grating drone of that—that instrument of torture you blow in." The old man blushed. He nodded, bowed, and quickly disappeared.

Archibald watched the reverend Seabury close his eyes and grab his belly. He was sure the man must have been praying for the night to end. He wondered whether Seabury regretted accepting this invitation in the first place. The doctor smiled. He looked at Mary Franks and thought her to look like some overstuffed beetle gawking at Seabury from wounded eyes. Along both sides of the table was an assortment of faces twisted or bound in various expressions of fear or outrage. He turned as the caterer delivered the third and final course.

"Ah, Samuel," Mary said nervously. "You have our final course. Look, everyone, look." The woman pointed to each pewter dish as the caterers uncovered them. "Oysters in roasted butter, Dutch cole slaw, orange pudding, and lemon honeycomb."

The diners applauded politely.

"And for you, Mr. Seabury, Queen's Cake."

"Ah, a true delight. Many thanks." His words lacked sincerity.

Mary flitted about the table, smiling at her guests and barking at her servants. "And Major Cunningham, a little bird told me you had a soft spot for cherry preserves." The woman tittered and giggled as the grenadier grunted. "And for you, Major Stanton—baked custard."

The officer nodded and impatiently tapped his spoon on his forearm.

"Samuel, do not forget the port and the clotted cream for tea." Surveying her table, Mrs. Franks smiled. All was in order once again.

The well-stuffed diners reached half-heartedly for the table's treats. Dr. Browne bade his wife hold her spoon until he received his instructions from the caterer. In short order, Samuel passed behind him. "And eat no custard."

Curious, Archibald nodded and instructed his wife.

In the meantime, the reverend Seabury seemed more and more agitated; he had not put to rest the comments of the obstinate artillery major. At the risk of upsetting the other diners, he cleared his throat. With a mild apology he began. "Major Crippen. I believe I have failed to adequately address either your comments or those of my colleague, Mr. Coombs."

Seabury leaned back into his chair and gripped his lapels with both hands as he faced Oliver Crippen. "Let it be said that each event the rebels characterise as points of grievance have a reasonable explanation. The mother country has no interest in restraining the flexing muscles of this new land, nor does she wish to inconvenience, exploit, terrorise, or abandon any of her colonies. On the contrary, each of these actions has been a necessary response to keep the rule of law. And the rule of law is necessary for order, and order, major, is necessary for liberty."

The reverend turned to Coombs. "As for guiding the sheep of your flock, Mr. Coombs, I say this: the Holy Scripture is plain enough. We find in Romans and in I Peter specific instructions for a people to obey the powers that be. One might argue all the night about natural law and the delicacies of our English Constitution, but at the end of it this point remains: it is our Christian duty to support and defend the government that is."

Crippen listened carefully, but was not convinced. "I should note that the question remains: what constitutes a *valid* government? What do you say to those who would argue that the present government has usurped the spirit of English law? Is not 'Law' our true government?"

Seabury, feeling ill, was becoming short-tempered. Slamming his palm atop the wooden table, he thundered, "I say such claims are undefended. And as for your second point, I say that the King and Parliament are essential components of our law, just as much as their statutes and prerogatives. You can not separate them."

Oliver nodded. "Yours would seem to be a reasonable position. Yet it seems our empire has ever evolved toward a state of increasing liberty for each person. During our Glorious Revolution, Pym and Hampden wrote that liberty was the highest goal of human effort. It would seem the increase in empire is requiring a change in the momentum of five hundred years of English law. It seems we are reversing the cause of liberty in favour of the order you so highly esteem."

"I say again, young man, that you shall have no liberty without order. And I remind you once more, that Christian duty requires obedience to the order that is."

"Some might answer you that the order you require comes at the cost of the very liberty it is intended to protect. And I do wonder if the government our Christian duty calls us to obey is the rule of Law as established over time and tradition, or the persons who occupy Westminster. I should think that the Whigs in Parliament are, at the least, right to seek reform."

Seabury tapped his fingers impatiently and answered, "There'll be no reform with anarchists and rebels tearing at the heart of decency. This revolution must be crushed and this crabbed race culled of its treasonous toads. We must root out those who belch sedition from the pulpits and end this most pernicious nonsense. You, Major, have become entangled by Tom Paine's cobweb of deception. You need to avoid the malicious snares of these greasy, rebellious rogues who weep and rail at petty grievances that they imagine ought to draw tears from stones."

Oliver took note that the reverend Seabury had suddenly chosen rhetoric over substance. The young man was wise to note it, for it meant that further discussion would prove fruitless.

Major Cunningham was flushed with anger. He pointed his long arm at Crippen.

"Tell me this, major, and tell me plain. Are you loyal to the Crown and to Parliament?"

"Indeed I am. I am proud to serve the empire. That does not mean that I turn a blind eye to our failures. Nay, major, I am a free Englishman, free to give my nation honour and free to beg it to make changes. My heart breaks at my every command to fire on these Americans. I am slaughtering my cousins, free men like myself who share my heritage, who worship my God. These decent people speak our language, eat our food, sing our songs, and still call Mother England 'home.'

I think we have wounded them, neglected them, exploited them, and denied them the rights and privileges they are due. I abhor their rebellion, but I love them and their land."

Cunningham was silent. He shifted uncomfortably in his seat until James Humphries finally stood. "All, please fill your glasses and rise with me. It is plain to see that we have our differences. Yet we share much. First, a health to General Howe. While we dine on sumptuous fare, this very night he leads seven thousand troops to forage for our benefit. Hear, hear, General William Howe."

All glasses were lifted, save those of the Brownes.

"Secondly, a health to Mr. Seabury. Your wisdom and your insight—" Humphries paused to let a cramp pass through his belly. "Your wisdom and your insight give us needed guidance in these most difficult times."

The Brownes toasted politely.

"Lastly, though we differ from point to point, we all serve the same King. God save the King."

All eyes fell upon Archibald Browne. He held his glass in his hand hoping to respect his hostess without violating his own conscience. His wife followed in kind.

Major Stanton had kept a suspicious eye on the doctor and his wife for most of the evening. As the diners took their seats, he fired a volley. "You are a rebel?"

Katherine closed her eyes as Mary's fan began to flutter.

"I ask again, are you a rebel?"

As Dr. Browne prepared to answer, Oliver Crippen interrupted. "Major, the man does not need to be a rebel to share sympathy with their cause. Lord Pitt in Parliament, as well as

Lord Chatham, Colonel Barre, Lord Dartmouth, and many other respected men of distinction, agree that these colonies have just claim to their grievances. I beg you leave this gentleman out of the conversation."

Major Stanton abruptly stood to his feet. "Major Crippen, I was willing to put my doubts about you to rest, but to hear you defend your rebel host makes me wonder more." He turned to Archibald. "I–I ask again—" The man's eyes suddenly bulged and he bent forward. "I–I—" With a wave of his hand, he turned and ran from the table. In a moment he disappeared into the darkness of the stairway and thundered into the street below.

"Well—whatever is wrong with the major?" quipped Dr. Browne.

Mary Franks began to perspire again and pleaded with her guests to finish the treats still lining the centre of her table. "Please, eat—drink. 'Tis Christmas."

Few were interested. Cunningham turned toward Archibald, but as he prepared to engage the man, the reverend Seabury begged him to restrain himself. "Major, in the spirit of the season, let us have peace."

The officer assented and the conversation quickly turned to lesser things. Over the next quarter hour the guests left the table and gathered in groups of two and three throughout the candlelit room.

"Archibald," whispered Katherine. "I am so proud of you. You were wise and patient, self-controlled and even-tempered."

Dr. Browne smiled. Two trips to the city jail had mellowed him a little.

Major Crippen walked up to the pair, sipping a good Portuguese port. "I am sorry for this evening."

"Sorry?"

"My colleagues lack breeding and good sense. I fear they are the tyrants the Americans speak of. They would strip these colonies of their souls if they could." The man spoke sadly. He was troubled.

Katherine laid a hand on his shoulder. "Thank you, Major. You deflected a most uncomfortable moment for us and you did it with grace and skill. And you spoke with courage and great honesty. You are what is good and right about England."

The man blushed and bowed, but bent suddenly in two. He grimaced and clutched his belly. "Mrs. Franks," he said. "Have you a latrine in the yard?"

Mary was aghast. "N–no, sir. You need use the one across the street in the courtyard, it's—"

Poor Oliver stumbled across the room, as white as the snow now falling on Union Street. He crashed down the stairs and out the door. The room became very quiet and a sense of dread quickly filled each face. Seabury was next. The righteous parson belched and groaned, then swore an oath and hurried for the stairs. In moments, the Humphries, the reverend Coombs, and a most mortified and humiliated Mary Franks were stampeding toward the stairway and the far too distant latrine. Mrs. Coombs was left staring at the Brownes and Major Cunningham.

It was only a matter of time. The giant grenadier growled and rolled his eyes, then charged toward the stairway like a desperate schoolboy caught short on a long walk. Then there were three, and Dr. Browne knew. He smiled patiently at poor Mrs. Coombs until the frail woman curtsied and sprinted for the stairs.

Dr. Browne laughed and held his wife, imagining the horror a the neighbourhood latrine. He filled two glasses with good red wine and handed one to his wife. He raised his own in a toast, "To our warrior cook, Samuel the patriot—to Samuel, the saboteur."

⸻

Penelope remained anxious about the Indian. If the man were a British agent, they were at grave risk. But if he were a double agent—like others she heard of—then she was safe. Penelope prayed a quick prayer, took a deep breath, and accepted the fact that she would just need to accept whatever happened.

Looking at the sky, she saw that the stars were peeking between the dark shadows of unseen clouds, and the moon had settled low in the sky. The night air was cold, and she shivered. *No matter what else happens*, she thought, *it is enough to know Cameron will be happy.*

Captain Robertson ordered Sergeant Dickson to lead the trio to the British line. Joining them were Richard Davis and Running Fox. "Davis, you take the rear," ordered the weary young sergeant. "Running Fox, you lead; I'll follow with the girl, the pudgeling, and Thaddeus, in that order. Do you understand?"

Thaddeus looked carefully at the soldier. The lad was probably fourteen or so, the same age that he was. It was hard to see him clearly in the light of the low campfires, but it was apparent that he was a broad-shouldered, lanky boy with the bearing of one much older. The soldier poked Yates in the belly with his musket. He then mumbled to Penelope. "And you, girl. Keep up or we leave you behind."

"My name is Penelope Browne, Mistress Browne to you. And I'll have no trouble keeping up with the likes of some smart-mouth westerner."

Dickson stepped toward Penelope and growled. "I'm no westerner, I'm from Carolina. And ain't no wench of a girl goin' to talk to me like that."

Richard Davis interrupted. "Sergeant, you'd best leave things be. She's got a good left fist and a really painful bite." He laughed.

Dickson grumbled and set his company in proper order. "Now listen. Running Fox'll cross us over. The ice is hard enough, but keep ten paces between. Redcoats patrol both sides of the river, but when we're over there'll be even more. Once we leave, you can't talk. Just follow Running Fox. I'm ordered to get you through the fascines—at the rock pile. Once yer over, yer on yer own."

Penelope felt the eyes of the Indian upon her and she was very uncomfortable. Her mind whirled as she took her place in line. *If he's a spy for the British,* she thought, *he'd kill us all once we leave, unless he is exposed now. If he's a spy for us, then there's no harm in the telling.* She decided to march directly to the man. "You, Running Fox."

The Indian stared at the girl, blankly.

"Tell me now. I saw you with the Redcoats in the city. Are you with us or them?"

The Indian stood motionless for a long moment, then pointed to the girl's feet. "Big feet for a girl—made bigger by goloe-shoes." He waited.

Penelope felt relief through her whole body. The man had known all along it was her footprints under General Howe's window and had said nothing. "I am sorry, then."

Thaddeus was confused. "What on earth—?"

"Never mind for now. Let's get home."

The sergeant checked his column one more time and confirmed his orders with Captain Robertson. With a reluctant salute the young soldier took his place behind Running Fox and the troop disappeared into the darkness of the forest.

The Indian trotted quickly through the trees and heavy brush toward the riverbank. He paused from time to time to cock his ears and raise his nose. Thaddeus thought he was well named, for the man had the instincts of a hunted fox. Before very long he led them to the steep bank that fell toward the silvery ice below. The six slid in the thin blanket of snow that brightened the forest floor, then stepped gingerly on to the frozen river.

A fresh snow was falling and Running Fox grunted his approval. Falling snow blurred the images of silhouettes crossing the river's expanse and was a veil of protection that the group needed badly. Each in turn stepped gingerly onto the ice and proceeded across in single file at ten pace intervals.

They gave no heed to the occasional groan or crack the ice yielded beneath them as they hurried toward the far shore.

Once the group had climbed onto the Schuylkill's eastern bank, Running Fox gathered them in a circle. Sergeant Dickson squatted on his haunches and rubbed his ungloved hands together. "Now," he began in a low whisper, "you must be very quiet. No talking, no coughing. Step lightly and keep close. If Running Fox raises his hand, stop. We've reckoned to go some one mile east of here, then another mile south to the line. Between here and there are patrols and scouts—sometimes by twos, sometimes more. If we get in a fight, you'll needs be on yer own. Just move toward the campfires and find a hole to poke through. If you can't see, follow yer nose—the campfires are plain to smell. And you needs get through 'afore dawn 'cause you've some four miles to the city from there.

"The best place through is the rock pile. Usually one or two guards sleep on its top. The fascines stop at each side. You needs climb over about halfway up. Understand? We'll get you to the rocks and watch you go over. If you've trouble we'll make a diversion—but it's all we can do."

The group nodded nervously and entered the forest behind Running Fox. Before long they found themselves slipping their way across the Wissahickon Creek, then through more clearings and woodland in the snowy darkness. The land was a rolling forest and heavy with brush and large trees. The sky was dark and the company could see little but the shadows of those in front. The Indian snaked his way through increasingly difficult terrain. The ground beneath their feet was snow-covered and slippery. The six slid along the steep sides of deep ravines and clawed their way up rocky slopes. Fortunately, the falling snow helped muffle the sounds of cracking sticks and tumbling stones.

They were near the British line when Running Fox raised his hand. His panting, shivering company stopped. The man lifted his nose and sniffed. Penelope did the same and shrugged. "I don't smell a thing," she whispered to Thaddeus.

"Three hundred yards," pointed the Indian.

Richard Davis had an uneasy feeling. He kept his head turning in all directions as he hurried to keep up with the others. Suddenly, Running Fox stopped and turned toward the rear. He collected his group and motioned for everyone to squat in the snow, then whispered to Richard and Sergeant Dickson.

Thaddeus suddenly smelled what the Indian smelled. "Pipe—I smell pipe tobacco," he whispered to his sister.

Dickson ordered Davis to move thirty paces to the right. "Hold fast 'til we whistle you back. Running Fox, circle wide. I'll move left. Let's see who comes. You three, stay here."

The three civilians huddled close together in the falling snow. They heard no sounds other than the feathery sound of snow dropping lightly through the woods. Their comrades had vanished like shadows at dusk and only the white haze of the forest floor kept the three from utter darkness. As time passed, the trio became nervous and shuffled closer together. It was so quiet—dead, stone quiet. The forest seemed to come alive with an eerie presence that haunted the abandoned three.

The snow fell faster and Penelope grew anxious. "Thaddeus," she whispered.

"I saw the Indian before—with the Redcoats. What if he really is one of them? He may be killing Richard and Dickson now—then he'll hunt us."

Webster trembled. "He could do it. It would be easy for him."

Thaddeus thought about it. "But we all smelled the smoke. He didn't need that to turn against us."

"But he needed something to separate the soldiers," answered Penelope. Her heart was pounding and doubts gripped her. The three peered into the blackness around them. "Nothing. I see nothing and I hear nothing."

"Do you smell pipe smoke anymore?" asked Thaddeus.

The others sniffed. "No," answered Webster.

"Then—then they should be back—soon."

The three waited longer—still no sound. Thaddeus drew a deep breath. "I'll move toward Richard's position and see if I can find him."

"Careful," warned Penelope. "He may think you're a Redcoat and shoot you."

"Aye. Wait here."

The lad inched his way toward his right. *Twenty paces,* thought Thaddeus. *'Tis only a few more feet.* He looked back toward his sister and his chest seized. He could see nothing. He whispered into the snow-filled air, "Richard—Richard." There was no answer. He turned his face toward where he thought the others were. "Penny. Penny." Again, no answer.

Thaddeus felt a clammy sweat break beneath his buckskin. He tried to retrace his steps, whispering for his sister all the way. He thought he heard a noise behind him and he stopped. He listened carefully. He was sure he heard a heavy thud. His heart raced and he strained to hear more. He stared about the darkness, then realised he was lost. Panic seized the young man and he suddenly bolted between the columns of tree trunks closing in around him.

Thaddeus crashed through the snow-laden underbrush like a terrified sheep pursued by a pack of ravenous wolves. He whimpered and gasped until he was felled to the ground by the weight of a large body. Strong, groping fingers muffled the young man's scream. He felt his neck bend back and he struggled to breathe. His eyes widened and his mind whirled as he pictured Running Fox poised to kill him.

The lad was held firmly in his place until he stopped thrashing about. Hot breath hushed into his ear, "Hold fast, boy. Stop and make no sound."

Thaddeus trembled. He quivered until he finally yielded. He nodded and grunted. The man's hand released Thaddeus' mouth. It was Running Fox. The Indian rolled the boy over and pulled him to his feet. "You run the wrong way. Follow me."

Shaken and still trembling, young Thaddeus picked his way through the forest behind Running Fox until the two arrived at the shivering huddle that was Penelope and Webster. As they stood to greet their missing comrade, Running Fox delivered a warning. "Boy, when you are in the eye of the hawk be still. It is the rabbits who run that are taken."

Richard Davis and Sergeant Dickson shook their heads. They handed the three each a coat and hat taken from the British patrol they had just ambushed. "Here, wear these. They'll help on the other side of the line."

The Brownes and Webster removed their coats and offered them in return. "Take ours to your camp," said Thaddeus.

"You've about two hundred yards to the fascines. Stay close and be quiet. When yer told, begin your climb over the rocks—then you'd be on yer own." Sergeant Dickson was firm.

The company crept behind Running Fox until they could see the glow of sleepy campfires yellowing the forest walls. They hoped many of the soldiers were already asleep and the others drowsy or drunk. The young Americans felt confident as they approached the line, but Running Fox was not sure.

Thaddeus was surprised to see that the "rock pile" was more than the simple heap he had expected. He faced a foreboding mound of large snow-covered boulders and deep, dangerous crevices. Davis told him the guard on the very top was alert, for it was a dangerous place to doze. At the base of the rocks was the end of the fascine wall, over which two soldiers' heads could be seen peering toward them.

Running Fox then said, "They are waiting for the scouts we killed."

"Aye," said Dickson. "'Tis a problem."

The group sat quietly and thought. Richard spoke next." We need make a diversion down the line. We could stand some fifty paces away and fire on the wall. They'd never catch us."

"What of other patrols behind us?" asked Dickson.

"In this snow they'll never find us either."

Running Fox grunted and the plan was set. It was simple enough, thought Penelope, but she was uneasy. The group bade each other a hasty farewell. Richard paused to cast a final look at his friends, and then disappeared in the darkness with his comrades.

Thaddeus, Penelope, and Webster moved quietly toward the boulders. They knew they'd need to climb some distance quickly so that the diversion would give them enough time to get over the rocks and through the line. They had been told to begin their climb about thirty paces from the edge of the fascines, and then to skirt the side of the mound and avoid the guard at the top. They did just that.

But the snowy rocks were slippery and in the first few feet Webster slid into a crevice and caught his foot. He wanted to cry out in pain but he grit his teeth and remained silent. Thaddeus crawled to his side and strained to pull him loose. The two struggled with no success for many minutes. Penelope had gone ahead and was waiting in the darkness for the others. "Where are they?" she wondered.

Suddenly, a troop of British soldiers came ambling through the forest not ten paces behind the three. Thaddeus and Webster lay still as the men walked past them, but groaned silently as they realised that the Redcoats were moving in the direction of Richard and the others.

It was only seconds later when the three heard Sergeant Dickson and his comrades fire at the British line. With that, the surprised British patrol charged into the forest with bugles blowing the whole of the line to the alert.

"Hurry, Webster!" cried Thaddeus. "Hurry!"

All three slid across the boulders on their bellies closer and closer to the British camp. Shots could be heard in the distance as the trio descended into the shadows of the army's fires. They scampered through the snow and hid behind a log as more men tramped past.

"Keep moving," whispered Penelope.

The three slumped their way further and further from the camp, hiding behind trees or rocks as soldiers followed the sounds of sporadic gunfire. Finally, they found themselves out of the reach of the campfires' light and paused to listen. They heard no more shots but a loud voice echoed through the snowy forest, "I shot me a rebel boy."

"Richard or Dickson?" Penelope began to cry.

"Save your tears." Thaddeus' face was hard set and determined. It was time to move on.

The three said little as they hurried the four remaining miles to the city. They hoped they were travelling in the right direction, but they had no way to be sure. No stars could be seen, though, even if they could be, these city dwellers had little experience in following them. They had the good sense to keep the British line directly to their back but, as the distant campfires vanished, they were left to trust their instincts.

At long last, Webster pointed dead ahead and exclaimed, "There." The lanterns of the city blurred yellow in the distance. To see them brought such joy to the Brownes and Master Yates that they soon forgot the aches in their weary legs, which were dragging them through the deepening snow. At last, they found themselves pushing through sleeping neighbourhoods of Philadelphia, and visions of a safe hearth filled their minds' eyes.

A loud voice frightened them. "Halt."

Three hearts stopped and the trio froze in their steps. A suspicious soldier moved toward them. Penelope's mind raced. "Move away from the lantern," she whispered. The three shuffled deeper into the shadows.

"Who goes?" barked the soldier.

Thaddeus answered boldly, "Sick to the infirmary, sir."

"Aye? What company?"

Thaddeus thought quickly. "Private Jones, Private Smythe, Private Yates—all of His Majesty's 71st, sir."

The guard walked close and strained to see the three. All were standing at attention. "And where'd be your weapons? And you're out of uniform…"

"Orders, sir. We…we were sent away right quick."

The soldier moved closer. "You'd be no soldiers." He jerked his musket to a shoulder.

Thaddeus and Penelope could only gawk, but Webster reached a trembling hand into the pocket of his breeches. "Aye, s–sir, but we'd be delivering an important message."

"Eh? What 'ave you in your hand?"

"Uh–uh, a note, sir, for Lord Cornwallis."

Penelope and Thaddeus both chilled. *What is the fool doing*" they wondered.

Webster slowly opened a wrapped paper and held it on his palm. "If you read it, sir, it shall explain."

The unsuspecting Redcoat bent his face close to Webster's opened hand. The soldier strained to see what was written. But before he reached his fingers toward the paper, Webster blew at it with all his might. A cloud of red pepper flew into the man's eyes, blinding him and sending him howling into the street.

"Run!" shouted Thaddeus.

The three raced away. They flew down Eighth, and then turned right on Pine. They threw their coats and hats away as they charged toward Union. At last, they rounded the corner of Third, then turned again on Union—blessed Union. Then, with tears of relief, they slipped into the Brownes' front door.

CHAPTER 13

Christmas and a New Year

"And that's the whole truth," Penelope sobbed.

Dr. Browne, Katherine, and Whittaker Yates sat dumbfounded. After several minutes of silence Archibald and Whittaker laid their hands atop each of their children's heads and thanked God for sparing them.

"Amen," murmured Katherine.

The group hoped Major Crippen had not wakened. Providentially, the man was exhausted from his bout with food poisoning and was collapsed with fever and a whirling head.

The Brownes bade the Yates a hushed farewell and watched the two disappear in the first light of dawn. Content that all was restored to order, Mrs. Browne hurried her family to their beds and soon all were fast asleep.

A loud rap on the door awakened Dr. Browne early the next morning. He stumbled through his cold house and opened the door to find two members of the city patrol and three Redcoats holding his favourite garden coat. He rubbed his eyes.

"You are Archibald Browne?"

Dr. Browne nodded.

"This coat has the name, 'Arch. Browne' stitched inside. Is this your coat?"

"Let me get my spectacles." The man pulled the familiar wires around his ears and thought quickly. His heart began to race. "Let me have it." Archibald took the coat and turned it over in his hands. "Aye. 'Tis mine, sure enough. It was stolen from the privy some weeks back. Thank you so much for returning it. I hope you caught the rake that took it. Good heavens, what is this city—"

"Enough," bellowed a soldier. The man was a lieutenant with the look of ambition etched all through his craggy face. Archibald was familiar with the type. "We took this off a dead rebel shot near our lines. We want to know how he came by it."

The officer snatched it from the doctor's grasp.

Dr. Browne shrugged. Lying was not his greatest gift, but he could muster a good one from time to time. "As I said, it went missing weeks ago."

"How many?"

"Perhaps three."

"I see, about the time of the earthquake, then?"

Archibald relaxed. He knew the man thought himself clever. It was a snare that would not snag the shrewd doctor. "Ah, no. It was nearer the week of the Whitemarsh battle. At the time I thought some rogue must have imagined the distraction a good opportunity for petty theft. Perhaps the thief sold it to some farmer passing through?"

The soldiers grumbled. Archibald was about to invite them in for coffee when one of the city patrolmen arrived to apologise. The company turned to leave but Dr. Browne called after them. "Might I have my coat back?"

"What?"

"My coat."

The lieutenant stared at Archibald's steely eyes for a moment, then tossed it to him. Dr. Browne thanked him politely and closed the door. With a deep breath and a heavy sigh, the doctor hung his coat neatly on its peg and prepared for a quiet Christmas.

Christmas morning, 1777, was restful for the Brownes. Archibald readied his family for church and invited the recovering Major Crippen to join them. The officer was weak and pale but relieved to have survived Mary Franks' party. Mrs. Browne was melancholy, for her mind was with her Cameron. She was pleased to imagine him warm in the blanket, socks, scarf, and mittens her twins had smuggled to him. And she prayed he was enjoying the bread, honey, pork, and fruit preserves. But her thoughts were also with Thaddeus and Penelope. Both were deeply troubled by the price of their adventure. She believed they were forever changed.

After morning services at church, the family returned to their damp home and stoked the fire until there was a friendly blaze in the kitchen hearth. The upstairs parlour was more fitting for a Christmas meal, but the household was weary from their recent adventures and they were all quite content to gather in the cellar—the cosiest part of the house. Whittaker Yates and his son had been invited to join them, and by noon the group of friends was snuggled in a half-circle before a cheery blaze.

Archibald recounted to all the events of Mary Franks' party. He wheezed as he told and retold the story of the "belly rush" to the courtyard privy. He mentioned that neither poor Mary, the reverend and Mrs. Coombs, nor the Humphries had been in their pew boxes that Christmas morning. News had filled the church of Samuel Seabury's gastric distress and Archibald told how he had amused himself by looking down on the whispering heads that tittered from pew to pew, like bending grasses rippling through a summer's field. To Mary Franks' great horror, the Advent event was to be forever known as "Franks' Debacle."

Oliver Crippen was not particularly amused, though he chuckled at the picture of Mary Franks thundering her way into the privy next to his own. "Ah, Dr. Browne, you should have seen what I saw in that horrid place. The King's mighty Major Cunningham did little to honour that throne."

Archibald laughed until tears streamed from his eyes. The Brownes had come to appreciate their tenant. Humble and well bred, the officer now commanded their respect and had earned their growing affection.

"We are pleased to celebrate this occasion with you and we pray God's blessings on you."

Oliver sat quietly for a moment. His eyes moistened and he could not speak. The man longed for home but these people had become dear to him. He had so hoped they would consider him a friend, but it was a hope he dared not cling to. After all, he was an officer in the army opposed to their son. How could they open their hearts to him? Katherine laid a gentle hand on his shoulder; it was the touch of forgiveness.

"So, now—shall we eat?" Archibald smiled and welcomed all to his table. He prayed a joyful prayer and bade all to partake.

The household later settled into a comfortable afternoon of reflection. It was good to enjoy some measure of normalcy, though their thoughts and conversations were ever set on the mighty struggle that had forever changed their world.

"Hard times, they were," said Whittaker. "My shop was more than half empty of product by mid-November. I feared for the city."

Oliver nodded. "The American navy is a stubborn lot, and I admire the men who defended Forts Mifflin and Mercer so nobly." He turned to Archibald. "I believe Parson Coombs was on to something when he remarked about the determination of this rebellion. I think it is wearing down the government."

Thaddeus' ears cocked. From the day the American army had marched through the city he had been convinced the rebels had some undefined quality that would win their war. "Sir," the lad asked, "do you believe the rebels have a chance to win?"

Oliver sat quietly as all ears turned toward him. He swallowed a draught of applejack and nodded. "A chance? Indeed, young sir. Is it likely? I cannot say. I have fought them in Massachusetts, Rhode Island, New York, New Jersey, and in your own Pennsylvania, and it is always the same: we drive them off only to face them again and again. They have a will to win. Whether they have the means or not, I do not know."

Whittaker listened carefully. He was a peace lover—a gentle man cheerfully predisposed to hope. "I have heard of peace overtures from time to time. Do you know of this?"

Oliver shook his head. "Only that Lord North has made some inquiries, but—"

"Peace overtures?" exclaimed Archibald. "Whittaker, have you forgotten? The American Congress approved John Dickinson's Olive Branch Petition over two years ago, but the King rejected it. And that petition, friend, was followed the next day by Dickinson's and Jefferson's explanations of our position in the Declaration of the Causes and Necessities of Taking up Arms. This document explicitly declared Congress' *opposition* to independence. Even in the face of his loyal subjects' pleas for reform, your King *still* made war against his own people. If the British want to make peace now, I fear it must be on our terms."

Major Crippen listened carefully. "You say that your Congress offered a concise explanation of your grievances in a spirit of allegiance?"

"I do. And it was not the first time. Three years ago, George Washington presented a resolution drafted by the most honourable George Mason of Virginia to the Virginia convention in Williamsburg. This document is known as the Fairfax County Resolves and most respectfully outlines the American perspective of how the compact between King and colony has been violated. It was written in the spirit of kinship and affirms our preference to remain as loyal subjects, but not slaves. It is a masterful work."

Crippen was surprised. "I must confess we are told mostly of the treasonous rhetoric of your radicals. I have read Paine's *Common Sense* and even the rantings of Philadelphia's own Charles Thomson. I simply cannot go as far as they in their understanding of 'natural rights' as rooted in Enlightenment philosophy. I am not ignorant of their thoughts, for I have read John Locke. But I believe they go past the ultimate authority of Holy Scripture and run, instead, to their dubious idol, reason."

Archibald nodded. "With due respect, you should be reading John Dickinson instead of the radicals. Here is a man my heart follows. He is a lawyer of impeccable honour and reputation. He is well trained; he studied in London for some four years, unlike our Patrick Henry, who got his licence to practice law after six weeks of schooling. Read the words of this Christian gentleman, and you shall understand why reasonable men take arms against you.

"But, Major Crippen, I do share your concern. The radicals fly to reason as if it is the final Authority. I do not share their opinion. But I, like the reverend John Witherspoon, believe the Bible does establish the existence of natural rights. After all, we are commanded not to murder—hence, the natural right to life. We are commanded not to steal—hence the natural right to property. We are commanded to worship only God—so, the natural right to true religion. We are commanded not to bear false witness—hence the natural right to justice. Inasmuch as these rights require a certain liberty to enjoy, I say we have a natural right to liberty. I concur, however, that even that right is not absolute. And I believe that Scripture grants government 'natural rights' to rule and to defend itself. But the rights given governments to rule are not absolute either. Can a government murder, steal, or violate just laws? I think not, major. The question remains whether *this* government is doing just that."

Whittaker nodded. "I freely admit that if all the rebels were of similar sway and character as the likes of Dickinson and Witherspoon—or even yourself, I might have joined them. Dickinson championed your cause but his conscience would not allow him to sign the Declaration of Independence. For that he paid a high price in reputation and respect. Yet, once the Congress approved the Declaration, he continued to follow his conscience and now finds his duty with the new nation's army. Such integrity is most persuasive."

The apothecary tapped a long forefinger against his chin and continued. "Dickinson argued his points well in his *Letters from a Pennsylvania Farmer.* He defends the rebel position as a conservative Whig—he makes a constitutional argument more than an argument based in philosophy. He sees the colonies as part of a stream of history rooted in our ancient Saxon past, therefore eligible for legal guarantees. On this point I am almost persuaded to join your cause. But, like King Herod Agrippa, I am *almost* persuaded. What keeps me loyal to the Crown are two things. First, the voices of those cursed radicals who would separate us from our past, strip us from our birthright as Englishmen and set us on an uncharted course using 'reason' and 'natural law' as our rudder instead of heritage and custom. I fear them, Archibald, more than I fear the excesses of a government I have always known. Second, my Christian conscience requires me to honour and obey the 'powers that be.'"

Archibald and Whittaker had battled over this middle ground for years. Whittaker remained close to the fence, but not *on* the fence. Archibald was near the fence but was gradually moving further away. The doctor was not the radical his daughter was, but he was becoming ever more committed to the patriot cause. It was the very fact that middling men like Archibald Browne were moving further from the centre that would ultimately insure the success of the patriot cause.

Archibald answered. "We have fenced over these matters for a decade. I parry, you thrust; yet we both yearn for the same things—peace, liberty, and justice. We each want to serve God in ways that please Him. I can think of no better way to love my neighbour than to oppose tyranny. You believe our obedience to God requires submission to the established government. I say, your King and Parliament have violated the compact under which they serve. In so doing, they have forfeited their rights to our submission. Law is our government and God is our King—not Parliament and not George III. We are not in rebellion, sir. We are defending our rightful, God-ordained authority—the law of our forefathers. Your present government, old friend, has broken trust with that Law and it is more than our right to protect it, Mr. Yates: it is our duty. For that reason I have little choice but to endure the excesses of the radicals in my own camp and pray we can restrain them.

Oliver listened intently. He furrowed his brow. "Dr. Browne, there was a time these colonies embraced us instead of shooting at us."

"Aye."

"Then when did matters change?"

Whittaker interrupted. "I point to that cursed war with the blasted French. Most of the grievances stem from the time following that."

Archibald agreed. "Most, Mr. Yates, though not all. The Molasses Act was long before, and some think it was a fore-shadow of things to come."

"But, Archibald," protested Crippen lightly, "the loudest complaints seem to be over the Stamp Act and the Quebec business, the tea troubles, and the like."

Dr. Browne nodded. "Yes, perhaps, as well as the Declaratory Act, in which Parliament declared its absolute authority over us, the Mutiny Act, in which you imposed the threat of force by requiring the quartering of soldiers in our homes, or the Boston Massacre, where you slaughtered free men. And also we suffered your attempted theft at Lexington, where you would have illegally stolen the arms and ammunition of our militias and, of course, there was the attack on the men of Massachusetts at Bunker Hill."

Major Crippen scratched his head. "As I understand things, the French and Indian War, as you call it, cost the

Parliament a shocking amount of money—money spent on the defence of her beloved colonies."

Archibald darkened. He was a veteran of that war and was painfully familiar with the details. "And your point, major?"

"My point, doctor, is that the mother country has a right to recover her expenses for providing the protection you needed. It seems that every one of your grievances follows a line back to that simple fact. Laws were passed to raise revenue, and then more were passed in response to the colonies' resistance. The cycle continued until we are where we are. If we could look back to the beginning perhaps we would see that the colonies' original reaction was wrong. And now, I wonder why you claim the government has no right to regain its rightful authority in whatever way it requires. Even your most moderate, reasonable spokesmen do not move me on this point."

Katherine and Penelope paused. The young major's voice had become suddenly firm and laced with a tone of indignity. Perhaps the applejack had loosened his tongue.

Archibald removed his spectacles and began cleaning them. "You were in soiled diapers when I was marching through the mud of Quebec." He spoke with a hint of sarcasm. "Do not presume to tell me, young man, who protected these colonies.

Aye, to be sure a good number of British lads fell to French muskets, but we Americans died there as well.

"And I will remind you that what we call our French and Indian War was little more than a part of your wars with the French over the whole of this New World, Europe, and even of Asia. Your eternal hatred of them keeps you in perpetual warfare that spills from this place to that. Do not tell us that we are responsible for replenishing your treasury for a century of wars we did not begin. And do not tell me that our rights were not violated.

"These colonies have furnished wealth and prosperity to the mother country for generations. Your Parliament has reaped bounty from the trade and duties we have provided. Your present shortages are due to the generous peace you offered the French at their surrender. *That* is not our fault. But no matter what the expense, Parliament has no right to tax beyond lawful limits." Archibald's eyes blazed and a stern look from his wife did little to quiet them. He was drinking rum.

"With due respect, Dr. Browne, I do not agree." Oliver Crippen's tone had softened. "Our government has faithfully protected these colonies from invaders within and without. It is true she has benefited from the labours of her subjects, but she has also provided the means and support for them to thrive and prosper. Mother England has nurtured you well. She has been a good mother—a worthy lioness—and when wounded or weary, she is entitled to expect help and support from her growing cubs, not rebellion."

The kitchen remained uncomfortably quiet for a few moments until Whittaker Yates cleared his throat and raised his tankard. "As iron sharpens iron—may our differences be forged into ploughshares of peace." He smiled and coaxed Dr. Browne to lift his tankard. Major Crippen lifted his and together they toasted the season.

Outside, the air was cold and clean. Shin-deep snow swirled in the breezes of a cloudless sky and the setting sun laid an orange hue across the red brick city. Inside, Katherine and Penelope stoked the hearth once again and heated a kettle of cider. The wise woman thought it better to begin filling tankards with cider instead of rum.

Thaddeus had strained to follow the conversations of the three men, but his mind returned over and over to the events of two nights prior. He imagined three or four ambushed Redcoats lying dead in the snow. He pictured the faces of Richard and of Sergeant Dickson and he shuddered. The lad climbed the steps and stared at his father's coat hanging still and lonely on its peg. Just a little time ago it had been wrapped around the waist of one who was now dead and buried in the frigid forest. "But who did we give it to?" The young man closed his eyes. Neither he, Penelope, nor Webster could remember who received whose coats. "If only I could know."

Downstairs, Penelope and Webster were secretly suffering similar thoughts. Each was despondent, but neither dared raise the matter. They had been reminded that Major Crippen must never know. The two quietly reflected on the consequence of their adventure and they suffered for it. For them, as for Thaddeus, childhood was now a memory.

⊷⊷⊸◉ ◉⊶⊷⊷

True to his word, Thaddeus returned to the service of Joseph Galloway on the day after Christmas. Cedric Wigglesworth was still weak and sickly, but Goody Cassidy had done well by the boy. She had administered the doctor's heated black cherry remedy each day and had dipped the boy in icy baths twice daily. Cedric's fever came and went, sometimes abating for as many as two days. On those happy occasions the Galloways imagined the boy on the road to recovery. Unfortunately, poor Cedric had a fragile constitution.

The Galloway home was roomy and cheerful enough. High ceilings, portraits, heavy draperies, and thick-woven carpets made for an environment of prestige and understated elegance. Mrs. Galloway, however, was not nearly as understated as her husband often wished. Thaddeus enjoyed her boisterous collisions with Goody Cassidy. He laughed as the woman scolded her husband and he respected her for her genuine compassion for little Wigglesworth.

As far as Mr. Galloway was concerned, Thaddeus thought the man to be a bit overstated as well—at least publicly. The man had a pompous air around strangers and especially around those he considered his inferiors. But spending time in the man's house gave Thaddeus a different vantage point. He also saw a man sincerely troubled by the chaos of the world around him. He watched as Joseph wept over the deaths of two British officers he had known and quietly gave a young patriot's widow enough money to last the winter.

Little Wigglesworth coughed through most of the new year's first day, but he was on the mend. Under the instructions of Dr. Browne, Thaddeus had adjusted some of the boy's medicines and had lessened the ice baths to once daily. Archibald thought he ought to apply more stimulations because the lad's balance was drifting toward lethargy again, so Thaddeus iced Cedric only in the mornings, to quiet the slackening fever, then applied a variety of substances to irritate and redden the boy's skin. These rubefacients were thought to stimulate the nerves.

In addition, Dr. Browne sent Webster Yates with expectorant powders made of mayapple root, meadow cabbage, and bloodroot, to ease Cedric's unyielding cough.

Thus engaged for several more days, busy Thaddeus hardly noticed the celebration of Twelfth Day, or the Epiphany, and would have missed it entirely if Penelope hadn't come to call on him after services at St. Peter's. The Brownes didn't always attend church on Epiphany, as they were Presbyterians, but they did this year because they were attending the Anglican church. The Anglicans welcomed the day more heartily than even Christmas, and the morning of January 6 was always a favourite date for weddings. Mrs. Browne had been raised in the Anglican Church, so she was particularly pleased to celebrate the day with dinner and gifts at Whittaker Yates'.

"It is good to see you, brother," smiled Penelope, as she entered the Galloway's foyer. She pecked Thaddeus on the cheek and looked about the house. She had not been there before and she stared in wonder. Goody Cassidy invited her for tea in the rear parlour.

As Penelope removed her wool bonnet, the house servant smiled. "You'd be Irish?" The woman pointed to the girl's red hair.

"Scottish and English. But by your speech, you are."

"From Dublin. I am called Goody Cassidy, but m'Christian name be Erin—Erin Cassidy." Erin set a tray of biscuits and jam by the teapot. "Mr. and Mistress Galloway'd be spendin' the day out. So—if you'll not tell them, might I 'ave a bite with ye?"

"Of course," said Penelope. She handed the Irishwoman the tray. Erin was about twenty-five, Penelope guessed. She had shocking red hair, freckles, twinkling blue eyes, and a thin frame.

Erin took a small biscuit and heaped a large spoonful of raspberry jam atop it. She smiled at Penelope and knew she had made a friend. After the biscuits disappeared, Erin vanished into the pantry and returned with another tray. This one was filled with slices of an Epiphany cheesecake, marzipan, and a bowl of rock candy. The three laughed and gorged themselves, hoping their host and hostess would not later object.

Erin then led her new friend into the front office used for public matters, then to the kitchen in the rear of the first floor. The kitchen was appointed with the customary utensils of the time and its hearth was well draughted and clean. Upstairs was a small foyer with a bedroom to the rear. It was here that Cedric lay. To the left of the stairs was a large parlour for entertaining; to the right was Mr. Galloway's private office.

"In here, Penny, is where the real business of the city takes place." Erin pointed the girl to the large wooden table surrounded by a half-dozen ladder-backed chairs. Along two walls were bookcases filled with the classics.

Penelope studied the office. Her eyes were drawn to a large yellowed paper held flat at all four corners by paperweights. It lay on a cluttered desk by the windowed wall, a stained quill pen lying next to it. She walked to the desk and looked at the paper carefully. "Erin, this is the list I hear so much about."

"I pay little attention to Mr. Galloway's time here. But I think he meets other gentlemen from time to time, and I hear 'em discuss names and the like."

Penelope leaned over the desk. She dared not touch the thing. "Ah—Mr. Smythe of Kent, Benjamin Walpole of Annapolis, Elijah Simons of Baltimore, Timothy Burnside of Trenton—Look. 'Tis Thomas Williams of the city, and Ebenezer Pidcock, our bassoonist. I never knew he was a man of wealth." *I must show Thaddeus.*

At dawn on Sunday, the 7th of January, the pounding boots of Oliver Crippen and the thuds of cannon fire along the city wharves rolled the Brownes out of bed. The artillery major charged down the steps in answer to a panicked summons from criers on the street.

"Good heavens, Archibald. Would Washington attack in mid-winter?" cried Katherine.

Dr. Browne stumbled through his shadowed house. He grabbed a woollen blanket and wrapped it around his shivering wife. "I can hardly imagine it. The Delaware is not yet frozen all the way across, but it is not possible for the American navy to be sailing against Howe's fleet."

Penelope scampered down from her attic bedroom and stared at her confused parents. "What is happening?"

"We do not know, pumpkin," answered Archibald. "But it seems there is some kind of attack underway by the river."

The three arrived at Whittaker's shop, St. Luke's Garden, but found themselves surrounded by a growing crowd of spectators kept at bay by a street full of dragoons. The whole of the British river defence was firing furiously at the sluggish water, and midstream, the British men-of-war were frantically firing their ships' cannon at some unseen invader. But as the sun rose higher, the only presence on the Delaware River was the rocking masts of the British navy and the nervous bows of merchantmen.

Katherine studied the river. The cannon had ceased and longboats were rowing their way through the lingering smoke to the city docks. It seemed that a large conference of officers was being called. "What on earth was this about?"

Archibald shrugged. "Perhaps it is a new way to fish?" The three laughed.

A group of seamen stowed their oars and climbed from their longboat tied at the dock below the Brownes. They ambled toward the wharves with looks of irritation and annoyance, their faces black with soot. Katherine was surprised that her husband interrupted their oath-filled conversation.

"What's this business about?"

A short, stout seaman turned a grizzled, fleshy face toward the doctor. He was dressed like the others: red and white striped pants, buckled shoes, red waistcoat, and blue jacket. He removed his flat, round brimmed hat and bowed facetiously. "M'lord and ladies. His majesty has saved yer city from the dangers of driftwood and floating rubbish. Seems Sir Erskine thought we'd be under attack; he thought the whole rebel army were floatin' in barrels to attack the city. But there weren't no devils in the barrels—only powder. The Yanks be clever rakes. Seems they made a way to set a spring in the barrel, so's when it bumped a ship it'd blow. I expect they floated a whole fleet of 'em down from upriver in Jersey. Those Jersey rebels'll pay for that."

Archibald Browne laughed, loudly. And for the shivering soldiers of George Washington, news of this "Battle of the Kegs" would soon prove to be a much-needed boost.

CHAPTER 14

The Call of Duty

"CURSED, PERVERSE KNOT of Jersey rebels. Would the King could send the British lion to tear that troublesome colony from our city's shore and float it to the centre of the sea." It was a bitter day in early February and Joseph Galloway was not happy.

A ballad written by John Hopkinson was circulating throughout the city. Famous for his wit and his brilliance, Hopkinson was a signer of the Declaration of Independence and a designer of the nation's new flag. "Listen to this disrespect, wife. It's supposedly sung to that awful tune, *Yankee Doodle*:

> 'Gallants attend, and hear a friend,
> Trill forth harmonious ditty;
> Strange things I'll tell,
> Which late befell, in Philadelphia City.
> 'Twas early day, as poets say,
> Just when the sun was rising,
> A soldier stood on a log of wood,
> And saw a sight surprising.'

"I can hardly read on. Oh—hear how he mocks General Howe—and scandalises him with Mrs. Loring. Egad, woman. Then the rake assaults Sir Erskine—and even the royal bands. Oh, I must read you this:

> *'The fish below swam to and fro,*
> *Attacked from every quarter;*
> *Why sure, thought they, the devil's to pay,*
> *'Mongst folk above the water—'*

"And hear how he finishes:

> *An hundred men with each a pen,*
> *Or more upon my word, sir,*
> *It is most true, should be too few,*
> *Their valour to record sir.*
> *Such feats did they perform that day*
> *Upon these wicked kegs, sir,*
> *That years to come, if they get home,*
> *They'll make their boasts and brags, sir.'"*

Joseph Galloway flung the paper across his office, sputtering. Thaddeus interrupted. "The ballad is an outrage."

Galloway released his breath. "Now, tell me, how is our patient?"

"It is my opinion that my services will soon be unnecessary. Master Wigglesworth is better every day, shows fever only mildly, and is laughing—as we speak."

"Why?"

Thaddeus hesitated. "Uh—he heard the ballad, sir."

"Humph. You'd think a little lad could hardly grasp such a thing. What say you, Master Browne?"

"Of what?"

"The ballad."

"I find it troubling. These rebels are stubborn."

"I give that to them." Galloway sighed and seated himself. He picked up a small letter and stared at it. His eyes strayed to the paper on his desk and its lengthening list of names. "Young man, we must strike a decisive blow—and quickly. As you are aware, I have been in counsel with prominent men of this city to compose this list of loyal champions. I wanted three hundred names—I have two hundred and eighty. By heaven, I shall have my three hundred by the first of March."

Goody Cassidy rapped lightly on the office door.

"What is it, girl?"

"You've a guest, sir. Ambrose Serle."

"Eh? Well, show him up at once."

Thaddeus excused himself and returned to the bedside of his improving patient. The little fellow was feeling chipper and staring out the rear window at the snow-covered alleyways of the neighbourhood. The apprentice settled into a chair by the door and strained his ears to listen. Ambrose Serle was General Howe's personal secretary, and whatever was to be discussed would certainly be of grave importance.

The city's acting mayor and Lord Serle clasped hands and took their seats by Galloway's table. Erin brought them a good Madeira and two glasses, then pulled the door behind her, leaving it open just a crack. She winked at Thaddeus as she descended the stairs to other duties.

Thaddeus listened to a variety of administrative details. More money was needed for the poor, contraband goods needed to be controlled, spies were scheduled to be hung, and matters of refuse, firewood distribution, and night patrols were reviewed. With the city's business finished, Lord Serle cleared his throat. "You received our communication?"

"Yes, just this morning."

"Sir Henry Clinton shall assume command of the armies of North America within the next two months. General Howe shall remain in the city and shall serve Sir Henry in matters of transition and planning until he sails for home."

"Yes. I assume I shall retain my position?"

"Indeed."

"I am yet perplexed why General Howe has refused every request to meet with me, save one."

"I am not at liberty to discuss this."

Galloway paused and tapped his fingers lightly on the desk. "I shall be seeking an immediate opportunity with Sir Henry to present my list. I assure you we *can* win this war and *these* men can make that happen."

"Perhaps." A twinge of condescension sharpened his words. It did not go unnoticed.

"I see." Galloway's mood shifted.

"Two more things, Mr. Galloway. First, we are told Lord North shall be proposing a plan of colonial reconciliation with Parliament very soon. We are told it is most liberal—it offers the suspension of all acts passed since 1763. They are giving the rebels everything they want." Lord Serle was sullen and dejected.

Thaddeus' heart stopped.

Galloway was stunned. "That would be nothing short of capitulation. We shall never have the respect of this rabble again—never. What of loyal subjects like myself—like these on my list? The mobs shall have at us."

"Agreed. And the second point: It appears the French are about to recognise the independence of these colonies. That is tantamount to a declaration of war."

Galloway stood to his feet and shouted, "It can not be. Those pasty-faced Romanists. Those swarming, popish demons. They are determined to drive the Crown from this land one way or the other. They could not defeat us twenty years ago—they think they can now? How dare they. We shall sink their fleets and drive their Catholic hordes into the sea."

Ambrose Serle rose. "You must see the importance of the timing between the peace offering and the French alliance. This business is become quite a game of chess."

Galloway lifted his list in the air. "Then this is the move we need to make."

⇥⇤

It was Monday evening, the second of March, when Thaddeus was summoned by Erin Cassidy to the front parlour. He had been digging through Cedric's toy chest with the happy little scamp. They had removed two jack knives, a wooden broadsword, a bow, several blunt-tipped arrows, a pair of wooden ice-skates, and a willow whistle before locating their prize—a leather pouch of marbles. The boy had an eye-opening collection of agates, bull's-eyes, alley-taws, and dubs. But Thaddeus would have been content to play even one game with a fist full of commoneys. Unfortunately, Goody Cassidy was insistent.

"Aye," answered Thaddeus. He descended the centre stairway to find Mr. and Mrs. Galloway dressed in their finest. The hands on the clock by the door showed the hour of six and the two were pacing about the foyer restlessly. Thaddeus bowed.

"Yes, Master Browne," began Mr. Galloway. "My wife and I are late for the theatre. With the shortage of horses we are relying once again on the sedan chairs. But it seems the worthless porters are behind schedule."

"Husband, the play begins at seven o'clock sharp. I do not expect to be late. You are the mayor." Mrs. Galloway was indignant. Her face was powdered as white as the snow yet piled on the city's lawns. She boasted an extravagant gown, and a monstrous red wig was mounded high atop her head. "I tell you, Mr. Galloway, these porters shall be punished."

Joseph Galloway bore few burdens more wearisome than the one he had married. "Indeed, they shall bear my wrath." He turned a bloodshot eye to the young Browne. "Now, lad, take this to your father as final payment. You and your father have served young Cedric well. I believe he is no longer in need of your services, but I shall call upon you from time to time to look in on him. I commend you both and shall see to it that your medical career is properly advanced." He tossed Thaddeus a generous bag of silver coins. Then the man held a gold Spanish dollar between his thumb and forefinger. "This, young man, is for you. You have served us with dignity and with respect. You are the future of the realm, a worthy subject of our King."

Thaddeus received his reward with a deep bow. "You are kind and generous and it has been my great pleasure to serve you." The young man had enjoyed his time at the Galloways.

A rap on the front door drew an angry snort from Mrs. Galloway. "At last."

Goody Cassidy opened the door and the strutting pair stepped into a chilly, twilight wind and climbed into their wicker sedan chair. The Galloways settled into their positions awkwardly and wrapped themselves in heavy woollen blankets. Poor Mrs.

Galloway screamed and cursed at the wind that was having its way with her mountain of hair. Much to her dissatisfaction, Mr. Galloway was as helpless against the forces of nature as he was against the forces of liberty. With a holler and an oath from the mistress, the litter was lifted from the ground and carried toward the theatre by four silent Indians.

Erin and Thaddeus were now free to laugh at the spectacle trotting down the street. "Did y'see her? Did y'see the mistress climb into that thing?" roared Erin.

"She looked like a plump bird being stuffed into a small pot," said Thaddeus.

Goody Cassidy shook her head. "Ah, vanity. I'm not sure who the actors are at the theatre—is it the ones on stage or the ones in the seats?"

"They're going to the Southwark?"

"They are."

"'Tis near my home. I've heard its overseer is that peacock, Major John André."

"So 'tis. He's opened an office by the hatter on Front Street. He's done some of the scenery with his own hand. Ah, I hears he's a man to make a woman swoon."

Thaddeus wrinkled his nose. "Whatever are they holding theatre for in the middle of a war?"

"I hear General Howe wants to raise money for the widows and orphans of his soldiers. And Mr. Galloway says some money will be used for the poor of the city. He says the building holds nearly seven hundred patrons, so I think there's some money to be had. Seems a good thing."

"It strikes me as strange that Washington's men are freezing to death at Valley Forge while we English are attending theatre in sedan chairs."

⸻

The Brownes were happy to welcome home their son. He returned in time to share a simple supper of salted pork and boiled rice with them. Dr. Browne was particularly pleased to have his helper restored to him. The man had been busy tending the city's sick. It had been a difficult year. Many of the midwives had left the city, leaving the doctors the task of delivering newborns in addition to their normal duties of treating disease and injury.

Winters were particularly infamous for their high rates of burn accidents. This winter it seemed that the doctor was treating at least one severe burn victim each day. He insisted that his wife and daughter wear simpler, more tightly fitting clothing while working in the house. Hooped skirts or full skirts worn over many layers of petticoats were more apt to catch fire than skirts that fell from the waist without any added fullness.

After dinner, the family members retired to their various rooms. Dr. Browne settled at his desk with a long pipe and his commonplace. From time to time the man liked to revisit the truths life was teaching him. He stroked Cromwell, who was purring softly on his lap, and looked at his forlorn son. "You know, Thaddeus, I can read a proverb or consider a truth on one day and it means little, then the next day it means a lot. I like to read my commonplace regularly, like my Bible, so I can glean what my soul needs for that day. This morning I was too late to save a young child who had drowned by the docks. This afternoon I failed to save a woman who had been badly burned, and then I attended a young mother who died in childbirth. By three o'clock I had over bled an old Quaker man. I walked home begging God's mercy on my pitiful service. So tonight I am relieved to find this: 'We do not offer God our perfection, we bring him our need.' Such things comfort me, boy." The man wiped a tear from his eye.

He closed his book and looked at his son. "And what of you, Thaddeus? How are you?"

"I am troubled too. I feel as if the ghosts of those who died when Penelope and I were at the lines haunted me. I lie awake at night and think I see their faces in the snow staring at me. And I think I must do what I can to keep others safe from harm."

Dr. Browne grew anxious. "Are you thinking of joining the Loyalist Regiment?"

"I have thought of it, but I want no part of more killing. And I—well, I think the Crown's cause is just, but I think it is destined to fail. Killing patriots will do nothing more than make more widows."

Archibald was relieved. "Then what do you think to do?"

Thaddeus already knew what he could do, but he dared not share his plan with his father. "I–I must pray for wisdom."

The front door opened and Oliver Crippen entered with a big smile and a cheery greeting. He removed his high black leather boots and draped his red overcoat over his forearm. "Good evening, gentlemen." The major removed his tricorn from his wigged head and stepped close to the office fire to warm his hands. "It was a delightful evening at the theatre, just delightful. We saw *The Constant Couple* and it was marvellous. Next week we shall see a double show, *The Inconstant*, and *Mock Doctor*—a farce. You might enjoy that one. And after next week's performance we are to be entertained with fireworks. I say, these performing officers and their mistresses are most talented."

Neither Archibald nor his son were interested in the epicurean excesses of the British army. They turned away. Oliver's smile disappeared and he bade a hasty good night.

Archibald drew a long draught on his pipe. "You know, son, the British and their toadies will have Hell to pay if the rebels win. I fear for them. Actually, I fear more for you Loyalists than the army. The soldiers shall scamper away—or claim they were simply following duty. But the civilians who helped them shall be seen as turncoats against their own. They will be branded as worse than traitors. Imagine if you were with Cameron and you took this city, only to learn that its finest citizens danced and dined with your enemy whilst you froze and starved. I pity them all."

Thaddeus knew what had to be done.

⇥⊶ ⊷⇤

Penelope nodded. "Agreed."

"And we mustn't tell another soul."

"Aye."

"Good. I can't do it alone."

"You'd have been caught and would have hung for it. I am amazed, though, Thaddeus, for I was thinking of doing the same thing."

"And you are agreed that we destroy it?"

Penelope thought for a moment. She'd rather give it to Washington, but accepted a compromise. "Aye."

Silence filled the cold attic. It was deep night on the tenth day of March 1778. Neither Thaddeus nor Penelope could

longer postpone what their consciences required of them.
Duty had called. Yet for each the reasons were different.
Cross-purposes had found a common goal.

Thaddeus now believed the war was lost for the British.
It was a destiny that defied logic, yet rang as true to his soul
as the bell of Christ Church. If his belief proved to be true,
he knew that the men on Joseph Galloway's list would suffer—and perhaps die—for their very appearance on that roll
of paper. If he would contribute one thing to the welfare of
his fellows, it would be to rescue these honourable men from
the hands of angry, vindictive rebels.

On the other hand, Penelope believed the cause of the
patriots was hanging in a delicate balance. She admired the
spirit and the determination of men like her brother, but
she could see firsthand the power and might of the world's
most powerful military force. Once General Clinton had
Galloway's list in hand, he would surely believe these men
could raise the Loyalist legions that were promised. And with
10,000 new regulars for the Crown, the patriot cause would
surely be lost.

So, the twins agreed that the list had to be destroyed.

"In six days the city is having a St. Patrick's Day parade," Penelope said. "The soldiers are so bored I think
they'll use it as an excuse for a grand day of drinking,
horse-racing, cock-fighting, and dice. Galloway shall be
sure to be among the officers somewhere—as shall his
wife. We ought to be able to get Erin to let us in. She likes
me, and I can find an excuse to get into Mr. Galloway's
study for a moment."

"We can't go in during daylight. He often has a guard at the front door."

Penelope scratched her head. "Do we know if the list is even still at the house?"

"The day I left it was on the table. He had had a meeting the evening before, and had added the final names."

"Aye, but that was over a week ago," said Penelope.

"I heard him say that Howe refused to see him. He said he wanted to present the list to General Clinton as soon as possible, but I don't know if Clinton is in the city or not." Thaddeus was puzzled.

"He's waiting for Clinton? I heard Oliver say General Clinton was not coming to the city until early May."

"I wonder if Galloway knows that? He would want his list put to use before then."

Penelope shrugged. "Well, it seems it is likely the thing is still in his office."

"But we should be sure before we go barging in."

Penelope brightened. "We don't need to 'barge' in. You can say you are to check on Wigglesworth. I am coming as your assistant. This is easy."

Thaddeus nodded. "So, we've a plan—St. Patrick's Day."

⇥▬◉ ◉▬⇤

As plans go, the Browne twins had a good one. As is to be expected, however, good plans seldom are. At dawn on the morning of March 16, Evan Jones, the cobbler, pounded on Dr. Browne's door.

"Sir!" he cried. "Sir, come quick."

"What is it, man?" Dr. Browne was bleary-eyed.

"M'wife, doctor. She's with child and havin' troubles—bad troubles."

"Did you not summon a midwife?"

"No—don't know one."

"What? Your wife's been with child for nine months and you didn't bother to think this through?" Archibald's tone was scolding. "I'll bring Thaddeus."

Thaddeus stared at Penelope and shrugged. In moments he was running alongside his father to help the suffering Mrs. Jones.

⟶▬◉ ◉▬⟵

Hours passed and finally Penelope announced she had some errands to run for Mr. Yates. She hurriedly wrapped herself in her woollen coat and pulled on a pair of garden shoes. She bade her mother a hasty farewell and stepped on to the brick sidewalk and rushed toward Joseph Galloway's.

The girl walked quickly down Philadelphia's busy streets. It was mid-afternoon and, just as she and her brother had imagined, the city was enjoying a day of parades and revelry. Several companies of Irish grenadiers had led a raucous procession through the city's centre and the mob it had created was spilling into the taverns and the teahouses. Shouts and laughter echoed on to the street as Penelope Browne marched past the taverns. News of horse races at the squares drew merry-makers into their carriages and sedan chairs. In alleyways and sheds the squawks and curses of cockfights rose above the din. The prestigious City Tavern was filled to its capacity with officers and the gentry playing cards or dining on Philadelphia's most delicious fare. The sky was blue and the sun was warm for mid-March.

Penelope saw the Galloway house just ahead and paused to adjust her clothing. She reset her bonnet and tucked her hair beneath it, brushed the wrinkles from her coat, and stamped a bit of mud from her shoes. Staring at her big feet, she realised she should have dressed better. After all, to call on the mayor's house in work shoes was an offence. "Well, let's hope they are not at home." She took a deep breath and approached the door.

Her hand had barely released the brass knocker when Erin Cassidy flung it open. "Happy St. Patrick's Day to you." Penelope smiled.

Erin giggled.

Penelope felt confident. The woman was drunk and would be easy to manage. "Might I come in?" asked the girl.

"Why?" When Erin Cassidy drank, she changed moods like others change hats.

Penelope was caught off guard. "I was sent to check on Cedric."

"Who sents ya?" slurred Erin.

"Thaddeus."

"I cannots let ye in. Mr. Gall–Galloway says so." She hiccupped.

Penelope stiffened. "May I please speak to Mr. or Mrs. Galloway?"

"Not home."

"Then, Mistress Cassidy, you must let me in." Penelope's tone was firm and commanding. Her eyes flashed and she set her jaw hard.

Erin Cassidy's eyes were half closed. "Oh, well that'd be fine, then. Why didn't you just say so?"

Penelope brushed past the servant. Her opinion of the woman had changed considerably. She hurried up the stairs and turned around. She pointed a finger at Erin. "You, Goody Cassidy. Just wait there."

The woman waved and collapsed on to the first step.

Upstairs, Penelope turned quickly into Galloway's office. Her eyes scanned the table as her heart beat faster and faster. It was not there. She stepped deeper into the room and fixed her eyes on the badly cluttered desk. There, by the window lay a half dozen or so yellowed scrolls, each tied with a ribbon of cloth—some blue, some red. "I don't remember it being tied. I–I—" She took three steps toward the desk when a voice behind her locked her in place.

"Hello, Miss."

It was Cedric Wigglesworth. Penelope whirled around.

"Uh–uh, hello, Master Wigglesworth."

"Why are you in my uncle's office?" The little Englishman was dressed in a smart suit of a matching red-and-yellow-striped waistcoat and trousers. He had the bearing of a young lord.

Penelope's mind raced. "I–I was looking for you."

"For me?"

The girl nodded.

"And why in here?"

The girl wanted to choke the little imp. "I didn't see you in your room, so I thought you might be hiding."

"Did you open my door?"

Penelope blushed. *Outfoxed by a shrimp.* "I listened at your door and heard nothing."

"Are your ears waxed?"

"What?"

"Father used to say—"

"I just didn't hear you."

"I was reciting my catechism."

Penelope snarled. "Is that so? Then, which question?"

"Guess."

"What?" Penelope was frustrated. "So anyway, now that I have found you, I am supposed to report on your health. How do you feel?"

"I was reciting the Ten Commandments...when you say you heard nothing at my door. Do you know which I said the loudest?"

The girl drew a deep breath. "Tell me."

"Thou shalt not steal." A cunning smile toyed at the corners of the boy's mouth.

Penelope felt a shiver go up her spine. "What?"

"Thou shalt not—"

"Yes, yes. Why are you saying that to me?" Penelope's voice betrayed a hint of guilt.

Cedric folded his arms.

Flustered, Penelope Browne turned away and hurried down the stairs. "I shall report you are in perfect health." With that she brushed past Erin Cassidy and returned home.

CHAPTER 15

Thieves for Conscience

THE NEXT MORNING Thaddeus and Penelope discussed a new plan for obtaining the list. They decided that St. George's Day would be the next best chance and, fortunately, it would be celebrated on the following Saturday. The problems, however, were that Penelope had probably damaged her friendship with Erin Cassidy, and her reappearance might raise the suspicions of the clever Cedric.

"But if we go together, Thaddeus, I think it would be fine. You can occupy the brat while I sneak into the office."

Thaddeus was not so sure. "I fear you spoiled this whole strategy. Why did you go there without me?" He shook his head.

"You say they were all wrapped by ribbons?"

"Every one."

"I don't recall ever seeing it wrapped like that. And there was a pile of scrolls by the window?"

Penelope nodded.

Thaddeus sighed. "Well, I can't think of another plan. So, I guess we need to try this one."

The week passed slowly for the twins, groaning along with a series of unpleasant chores for each of them. Spring was fast approaching, and Katherine was impatient for its arrival. Even though Easter would be late this year, she was already calling on the twins to help her with the beating of the carpets, the scrubbing of the walkways, and the raking of leaves from the gardens.

At last, Saturday arrived. Now, Thaddeus was not one to lie. Yet, he reasoned, he had lied already, when he had sworn allegiance to the American Congress, and this would be a matter requiring a similar bending of the rules. So, when he told his father he had been summoned to Joseph Galloway's house, Archibald believed him.

Penelope was not one to lie either, at least not without a twinge of guilt. Her conscience was tender on the point, and she found it troubling to inform her mother that Josiah Byrd had sent for her.

"So what did you tell mother he wanted?" Thaddeus was confounded.

"She didn't ask. In fact, she said to tell him she'll be by for her visit soon."

Thaddeus wrung his hands. "I don't know about this business. There is always an ash in the pudding."

"Come on, brother, let's be off."

It was nearly midday when the two slipped away from Union Street. Penelope had dressed more appropriately for this deception than she had for the other. This time she wore a nice black bonnet and a green dress over several layers of petticoats, but she had wisely left her hoops off and loosened her corset in case the adventure required some agility. Thaddeus had donned a tight-fitting pair of breeches, silk stockings, and his blue coat. He strutted the bricks of Philadelphia like quite the young gentleman.

Just as it had been the week before, today the city was alive. St. George's Day was dearer to the British army than St. Patrick's, so the parades were larger and the mood even brighter. The army was particularly joyful, for in the past week it had defeated the New Jersey militia in two punishing battles.

The Brownes reached the Galloways and Thaddeus knocked boldly on the door. A new Negro slave answered. "Yes?"

"Hello, is Mr. Galloway or his wife here?"

"No, young master, they left."

The twins were relieved. "Is Goody Cassidy here?"

"No, sir. She was dismissed last week."

The twins looked at each other. Thaddeus removed his hat. "I am Thaddeus Browne, the apprentice physician who cared for young Cedric. I am here to check on the boy."

The servant looked carefully at the two. "I am sorry, sir, but Mr. and Mrs. Galloway are not home and they said I should ne'er let anyone in."

A British soldier appeared from within the house. Thaddeus maintained his composure. "I am certain Mr. Galloway would not object to my examining the boy."

The soldier stepped forward. "If you tended young Wigglesworth, I am sure he would recognise you."

"Indeed, sir."

The soldier turned and called the boy down. Penelope held her breath. Things were not going according to plan. Cedric appeared with a big smile. He was glad to see Thaddeus. "You've come to check on me?"

Thaddeus nodded.

"Last time you sent her." He pointed his finger and wrinkled his nose.

"Yes, well, I was very busy helping another, but I was concerned about you, too," Thaddeus answered.

The soldier interrupted. "You can see the lad is in good health, now be off."

"But—I really should examine him properly, I—"

"I said, be off. You must make proper arrangements."

Thaddeus nodded and turned to leave. He and Penelope travelled a few steps when Cedric's voice called to them. "Come back. He says you can examine me—but make it quick."

The two brightened. They walked to the front door where the guard held a hand on Thaddeus' chest. "The lad says he felt fevered last night—'tis the only reason I'm letting you pass. But don't dally—and does *she* need to join you?"

Thaddeus thought quickly. "Aye, sir. She's in training and—"

"Ah, fine. Just get on with it." The impatient soldier waved them inside and returned to his post on a comfortable chair.

Once upstairs, Cedric giggled. "I told the soldier I was sick last night—but I really just want to play the game of marbles you promised."

Thaddeus smiled. "Fine. But are you well?"

"Of course. Does she have to be here?" Wigglesworth had a particular distaste for Penelope Browne.

"Where would you like her to go?"

Cedric thought for a moment. "Downstairs."

"With that nasty soldier?" asked Thaddeus.

Penelope had an idea of her own. "Master Wigglesworth. Remember when I was here before—I was looking for you in your uncle's office?"

The boy nodded, suspiciously.

"Well, it seems I lost a bracelet—a thin silver one my mother bought me. Might I see if I dropped it in there?"

The little gentleman looked at Thaddeus. "What say you?"

Thaddeus scratched his head. "I don't know. I wouldn't want you to be in trouble with your uncle—I know how frightened you are of him."

"Frightened? I am not frightened of anyone."

"Well, then I say you might let her look." Thaddeus waited.

Cedric sat on his floor and crossed his legs. He reached for his bag of marbles and rolled a few in his hand. "Fine. Go then."

Penelope curtsied sarcastically and slipped away. While the two boys began their game, the girl quietly stole into Joseph Galloway's office—again. Her eyes raced about the room. A scroll lay alone on the dusty table and she immediately flew to it. She unrolled it and saw it was nothing other than some accounting records. She stepped lightly to the desk by the window and sorted through the pile of ribboned scrolls. She peeked in the open end of one and read a line or two. "Not this one," she muttered.

Then she checked another, then another. The girl frantically held tube after tube to her eye. "Nothing!" she exclaimed. Her fingers trembled as she neared the bottom of the pile. "Please, oh dear God above, please." She knew Cedric would soon wonder about her, so she turned an ear toward the door she had wisely left ajar. Listening for a moment, she heard Thaddeus chuckle. Turning again to the papers, she began fumbling through them, only to begin dropping one after another to the floor. "Oh, no," she muttered.

Suddenly, the downstairs door opened and she heard a man's bellowing voice. It was Joseph Galloway. Penelope's heart raced and she felt faint. She grabbed at this roll, then that—one, then another, until she held a lap full. Then she rolled the whole bundle onto the desk. With palms held out, she steadied the pile and prayed. Footsteps climbed toward her from the stairway and the girl whirled about the little room. "Where to go?" The girl wanted to scream.

Penelope bounded silently behind the door as it opened toward her. She stood with her back pressed against a plaster wall and her chest flattened against the wooden panels of the heavy door. From her dark crevice she faced outward and held her breath.

Joseph Galloway was in a hurry. He and his badgering wife had been on their way to a business luncheon at the City Tavern, but the busy man had forgotten a document. Four long strides took him across his office to the desk, where he rummaged through his papers. He cursed and grumbled as the pile of scrolls tumbled to the floor. Penelope dared to crane her neck closer to the edge of her shelter.

The man hastily re-ordered his desk, and then opened a folded paper to scratch some notes. Murmuring a few words, he sealed the paper with dripping wax. He then paused, deep in thought, and surveyed his room for a moment. Penelope watched him walk toward an empty bookshelf and retrieve a blue-ribboned scroll. The man stared out his window, tapping the scroll against his leg. He seemed distracted and spoke aimlessly at the slight reflection of himself in the thick, blue-tinted glass. "Do I give this to the secretary now, or wait for the general himself?" He stood motionless for another minute or so, then set the blue-ribboned scroll on top of the others. As he turned to leave,

Penelope straightened up and pressed herself against the wall.

Did he see me? She wondered. *Will Cedric say something?* The girl began to perspire. Galloway took a step or two, and then paused. Penelope heard him turn and mutter another oath. She heard the tapping of glass on glass, then the tinkling sound of pouring.

After a few second's silence, she heard a contented sigh and sounds of glass and bottle being returned to their places on some wooden thing.

"'Tis good." Galloway walked through the doorway and pulled the door closed behind him.

Penelope dared not move. She heard Galloway's voice in Cedric's room. *Please, oh God please...*

"Thank you for your care, Master Browne."

Penelope held her breath. The mayor was standing not six feet away, bidding her brother and Cedric farewell.

"Uncle—" Cedric's voice called after the man.

Penelope closed her eyes.

"Aye, lad?" answered Galloway from the middle of the stairway.

"I wonder if–if you—"

"Go on." Galloway was impatient.

"I wonder if you would hear my catechism before Sunday?"

Galloway continued down the stairs. "Of course, either Mrs. Galloway or I will be glad to do so. Now have a good day, lad." The door shut behind him.

Penelope breathed again. Trembling, she dashed toward the scroll perched atop the others—the one with the blue ribbon.

"What are you doing?"

Penelope froze. Her arm was extended toward the window and her fingers were stretched. She did not move. "Uh—I'm–I'm–I'm admiring my bracelet—in the sunlight."

"Let me see it." Cedric walked briskly to her side. He stood at attention and waited without expression until she lowered her hand. Fortunately, the bracelet she had claimed was missing had been on her arm all along.

"It is nice. Where did you find it?" The young Wigglesworth spoke in a suspicious, accusing tone.

"It was on the floor, just by the desk."

"So my uncle met you in the foyer?"

"He was in a hurry. I curtsied but I fear he did not notice."

Cedric narrowed his eyes to a squint. "I see. Perhaps I should ask him at dinner."

Penelope hated the squeaky little fellow. She wanted to take him by the throat and shake him. Instead she smiled. "Perhaps." She turned to her brother. "Well then, Thaddeus, how goes your marbles?"

Thaddeus was as white as a ghost and too nervous to reply. He smiled half-heartedly and motioned for Cedric to return to his room.

The stern voice of the Redcoat below foiled the plan. "Enough," he said, impatiently. "You've had enough time with the boy, now out of the house—the both of you."

"Aye, sir," answered Thaddeus respectfully. He patted Cedric on the head and promised to return another time. "Keep in good health."

Penelope scowled and knocked the imp to one side with her hip. "Oh. Pardon, Master Wigglesworth—and good day to you."

In a few moments the Brownes were standing empty-handed and exhausted on the cobblestones of Sassafras Street. "Tell me how you did not get caught."

"I hid behind the door."

Thaddeus looked at his hands. They were still shaking. "Now what?"

"I heard Galloway mutter something about presenting the list to Clinton's secretary. That could put things in motion any day."

"And who did you hear Galloway tell this to?"

"Himself."

Thaddeus started toward home. "We need a new plan."

"If you are thinking of waiting another week, you need to think again. Today is the day, brother. We have no time."

"But we have no plan."

Penelope thought for a moment. "I know exactly where it is and what it looks like. It's on the very top of the desk and tied with a blue ribbon. And it is by the window—the window."

"A *second floor* window." Thaddeus was agitated and anxious.

"Come, follow me." Penelope led her brother through the city's busy streets. It was mid-afternoon and Philadelphia was bustling. Street peddlers, groaning wagons, rushing carriages, swaying sedan chairs, swaggering soldiers, and tailored dandies filled the streets and walkways with colour and sound.

The Brownes soon arrived at the walled gardens of General Howe's residence. Penelope gathered her wits and walked directly to the front door. Thaddeus was confused. The general and Mrs. Loring were, of course, dining or engaged at the horse races. But Josiah Byrd was delighted to welcome his old friends. "Mistress Browne—and Master Browne. Glory be. I think of you near to every day. Come—come follow me to the gardens. Very few is allowed in the house anymore—they say there'd be spies everywhere. Frightened rabbits they be."

Josiah led his friends through a small wooden gate and invited them to sit on a bench under the leafless limbs of an apple tree. "See—some buds. Buds mean hope. Now, tell me 'bout everything. I do see your mother from time to time. Mrs. Loring took a liking to her and lets her sit in the parlour for tea. She's been a good friend. But I've not seen Dr. Browne much."

Penelope finally said, "Josiah, we need your help. We need to borrow a ladder from your orchard. I saw one when I was here before."

Josiah was confused. "A ladder?"

Penelope waited.

He turned to Thaddeus. The boy nodded.

"Children, I think you are about some mischief. Is this for your father?"

Thaddeus answered. "No, Josiah. We just need you to let us borrow an orchard ladder for an hour or so."

Josiah was worried. "Follow me." He led them out of the garden and the three huddled on the sidewalk. "You knows I love you two—like you was m'own children. But, I can not do whatever thing you've planned."

Penelope stiffened and spoke directly. "Josiah, if you do not help, we shall climb over that wall and steal it."

Josiah Byrd stood silently. He stared at the twins with eyes all the more yellowed in the twilight. "Tell me what you are doing."

The Brownes quickly told the Grackle their plan.

As expected, Josiah Byrd was more nervous after the disclosure than before. "But you'll be caught and no one will be able to save you then. They'll hang you as a spy. You can't climb into Mr. Galloway's window."

Thaddeus hardened his tone. "Mr. Byrd, you can help us or not, but we *are* going to do this."

Josiah's breathing grew shallow and quick. "But–but— you'll swing for sure. There must be guards 'bout the place— and the window's sure to be locked."

"Thaddeus says the window's never locked—and the only guards are usually inside." Penelope was equally firm.

Poor Josiah wrung his hands. He bit his lip and his eyes widened in fear. *I'll swing too*, he thought. The man paced about the sidewalk. He concluded he'd not be able to deter the two. But more than that, he saw their plan as one that might serve the patriot cause—his secret cause. He loved William Howe and had served the man's household honourably. But he had overheard other officers speak of "crushing the colonies," and "stripping liberty from the rebels' wagging tongues." He longed for the day when the Redcoats would be chased from his city.

And then there was Cameron and the other suffering Americans he knew were starving and shivering at Valley Forge. *They* surely deserved his help. Josiah nodded. "The general sends me through the city sometimes. I carry dispatches to his officers at the prisons and hospitals. I see the patriots there and they have not lost hope. *We* may be that hope."

Penelope hugged her dear friend. "Thank you, Josiah. Now, the ladder?"

"We needs more than a ladder. If the window be locked, we needs my knives to cut the glazing and pry out a glass. It would be a quieter way than breakin' it. And, we needs a lantern to see which scroll to take—and a tinder box to light the lantern."

Thaddeus was disappointed to learn his friend was a rebel sympathiser, but he would *never* betray him, and Josiah knew it. The lad rubbed his hands together in the cold, damp night air. "His fireplace has a poor draught so he opens his window a crack to help the chimney draw better. But, you're right to bring a knife—just in case."

Josiah thought for a minute or two. "We needs to travel up to Sixth, then over to Sassafras. If we stays to the alleys it might work. If we're caught, I'll say your cat's up on a shingle and I'm goin' to help to catch it."

All agreed, the Grackle led the twins through the darkness of the alley behind General Howe's mansion. He had them squat behind a shed as he disappeared. It seemed forever before he returned with the equipment they needed. "Here," he whispered. "A lantern, tinder box—the ladder. But I'm not sure it's long enough." The ladder was an orchard ladder, the kind with rails spread wider at the bottom than at the top. It stood about twelve feet tall and that meant it would barely reach a second floor window. "It's the only one we has."

The three thought quietly for a long moment before Penelope said, "What do we do with the list when we have it?"

"We burn it straightaway," answered Thaddeus.

→⊫◉ ◉⊨←

Penelope closed her eyes and calmed herself as she pressed her back to the wall of Joseph Galloway's brick house. She had dashed and darted, crouched and crawled through Philadelphia's alleys alongside her brother and friend. The bell of Christ's Church pealed nine times. She and her two accomplices collected their wits as the final clang echoed over the wood-shaked rooftops of the candle-lit city.

The three were positioned carefully along the back wall of Galloway's house. A small garden with a shed and privy nearly filled the rear yard. The lack of fences had made their approach easy and Thaddeus imagined that would facilitate a hasty escape as well. They surveyed their surroundings under the starlit night until they were content they had their bearings; then, the three tiptoed to the corner and crept along the sidewall of the house until they were beneath the window of Mr. Galloways' study.

Thanks to William Penn's city planning, the Galloway house had a generous side yard between itself and its neighbour, which was dark and apparently vacant for the evening. The Galloway house was quiet, but a glimmer of yellow candlelight spilled through its front windows onto the red brick sidewalk. Thaddeus presumed the servant or a guard was in the front parlour. Fortunately for the three, the house had no side window on the first floor.

Penelope looked up. "Seems like a stretch for your ladder."

The three squatted quietly for a short while before Thaddeus said, "We'll only know if we try."

Josiah set the ladder lightly against the brick wall. "Let me goes up first and see if we can reach." Without a word he crept upwards, slowly. In the meanwhile, Thaddeus crawled along the building and twisted his head around the front corner of the House to keep watch. Galloway's guard was sleeping on a stool by the front door. His musket leaned against the wall, as did his head. Thaddeus studied him for a moment.

Good, he thought. *The fool is snoring.* He returned to his sister as Josiah descended the ladder.

"No good, Master Thaddeus. I can barely reach the bottom of the window with m'hands. I was able to push against it and it ain't locked. But I was too low to see inside."

Penelope muttered an oath. The three retreated to the rear yard and squatted close to the house.

"Now what?" grumbled Thaddeus.

The city was quiet. Most of the gentry were settled into long dinners or were engaged at St. George's Day parties in the distant taverns.

"When we hear carriages, we needs be somewhere else," whispered Josiah.

Penelope was not about to have the cause of liberty suffer a defeat because of a too-short ladder. "Enough of this. Mr. Byrd, how much higher must you go?"

"'Bout two more feet."

"And we can't straighten the ladder more? Could we hold it near to straight up?"

Josiah thought. "Uh, no. I already has it too tight to the wall."

"Fine. Then this is our plan." The girl leaned forward and whispered an uncompromising, unyielding, not-to-be-questioned order.

"Fine," said Thaddeus. "I'll hold the bottom."

Now in command, Penelope continued. "I'll need the lantern to be sure I've the right scroll. "

With shaking fingers, the frightened old man struck his flint into the tin box of thread. The tinder caught a spark and he pinched a tiny flame together, set it against the wick of his whale oil lantern, and then turned the wick very low. Josiah handed it to the girl. "Here, Mistress Penelope. I hope you can see blue."

Thaddeus scanned the rear yards for any sign of movement, and then swung his head around to scan the neighbour's side yard. Content all was well, he stole through the darkness to the front corner of Galloway's house and peeked at the sleeping guard.

Then he peered into the street, and raised his hand as a city patrol passed along the other side. The lad held his breath. The patrol paused on a corner, then turned in another direction. Thaddeus exhaled slowly and signalled the other two that all was clear.

Josiah squatted and took a firm grip on the ladder. Penelope climbed upon his shoulders and wrapped one arm firmly around the man's sweating forehead. He grunted and pulled himself slowly to a standing position as Penelope secured herself by hooking her feet behind his back.

She was ready.

Josiah lifted one shoe to the first rung. The two wavered slightly. He stepped to the second, then the third.

Returned to secure the ladder, Thaddeus was beginning to shake all over. Above him, Josiah climbed higher, step after step—slowly, so very s-l-o-w-l-y.

As the two neared the top, Penelope set her eyes on the twelve-pane window coming closer and closer toward her. She rocked a little and swayed. Josiah quickly squeezed the ladder rails harder and stopped to regain his balance. Penelope urged him on with a nudge with her feet.

The man obediently strained to take another step. His legs burned and his back ached. He wanted to cry out in pain. Josiah was a strong man, but he was old. His shoulders felt numb. He stared at each rung and the pattern of dark bricks between them.

At last he took his final step.

Penelope carefully released her grip on poor Josiah's head and tentatively moved one hand to the smooth, painted wood of the window frame to steady herself. With her other hand she lifted her lantern to the glass and pressed her face against the window. She could see nothing but blackness within.

Moving ever so slowly, Penelope placed the wire handle of her lantern in her teeth and turned the wick higher with her free hand. The raised flame cast a brighter light into the room. *There*, she thought. *I see it.* She prayed it was the right one. The blue-ribboned scroll lay perched exactly where she remembered it to be. She narrowed her eyes and fixed them on her target.

Penelope pushed upwards on the bottom window. It moved easily and rose with barely a sound. Leaning forward, her chest pressing against the windowsill, she stretched her hand through the window. With the lantern swinging from her teeth and her eyes staring at the scroll just a few inches away, she stretched her open hand forward. A moment later she felt the stiff pulp-paper roll fill her palm and she closed her fingers around it.

Josiah was squeezing the ladder with all the strength in his old hands. His rider was scrunched awkwardly on his pain-wracked shoulders, forcing his face hard against the ladder's rung. He prayed for strength and begged God to stop his legs from shaking.

"Mr. Byrd," Penelope mumbled. "Get ready."

"Hurry."

With her heart pounding, the girl gently lifted the scroll from the desktop and drew her hand back until it was outside the window. She immediately dropped the scroll to the ground below and quietly closed the window. She extinguished the lantern. "Go!"

Josiah Byrd came down the ladder with his heavy cargo as fast as his tingling, half-numb, quaking legs could carry him. When he arrived on the ground Penelope tumbled off his shoulders with a grunt and landed in a heap. She picked herself up as Thaddeus snatched the scroll from the ground. Josiah quickly tucked the ladder under his arm and the trio raced for safety in an empty carriage house.

"Do you have it?" asked Penelope. She was jittery and panting.

"Yes," said Thaddeus.

"Are you sure you took the right one?" asked Josiah.

"I think so." She was near tears.

"Are you *sure*?" Thaddeus was insistent.

Penelope licked her lips. "Josiah, light the lantern again."

The old man struck a flint into his tinderbox and soon the lantern was casting a yellow glow across the dirt floor of the building.

Thaddeus' shaking fingers fumbled with the ribbon. Finally he got it untied and opened the scroll. He turned it to face the dim light of the lantern.

Penelope clapped her hands, lightly. "Yes. Look—the names. It is the right one. There's Elijah Thornton, Benjamin Hampstead, the banker…"

"Good—we have it…"

"Shh." Josiah's keen ears had heard something. He doused the lantern with a quick turn on the wick-wheel. "Patrol."

The three sat still as mice as the murmuring voices of a group of men drew close. Josiah crept to the doorway and peered into the darkness. "Coming this way," he whispered.

Thaddeus took Penelope by the arm. He could feel her muscles tense and he knew she wanted to run. "Remember Running Fox," he whispered. "When you are in the eye of the hawk, be still. It's the rabbits that run that are taken."

The patrol walked along the alleyway looking into the few sheds that had survived the winter's firewood shortage.

They paused to lift their lanterns casually into the dark carriage house where the threesome was hiding, but they did not see them pressed breathlessly against the rear wall. The men walked on.

"We need to burn this at home," said Penelope Her mind was racing. "Thaddeus and I can go by way of the streets. If we are stopped we can say he was tending a patient—Wigglesworth if we're stopped here, or—"

"Or Mrs. Jones if we're near to home."

"Good. But Mr. Byrd, you be careful." Penelope pecked the man's cheek with a kiss. "Thank you, and Godspeed."

The old man clasped hands with Thaddeus. Josiah peered into the alley and gave the twins a final wave. With his ladder tucked tightly under one arm, he vanished.

Thaddeus flattened Galloway's list and helped his sister slide it inside the back of her dress. "See, all those years with your backboard serve a purpose."

Penelope grumbled. The two knew that if there were any kind of trouble it would be less likely for her to be searched than Thaddeus. The girl had loosened her corset earlier, but now pulled hard on its strings to be sure the paper was secured tightly against her back. The pair checked the alley and then walked quickly toward the street.

Emerging from the alley they stepped confidently on to the red brick sidewalks of Sassafras Street, then hurried eastward toward the river and turned south on Third. Trembling, they waved politely to other citizens strolling home from dinner and even greeted two British officers singing at the corner of Chestnut. They soon crossed Walnut, and as St. Peter's bell tolled ten o'clock, they faced their own front door.

"Crippen is probably at a party, but mother and father are surely awake and waiting for us," whispered Penelope. "I don't know what to tell them." Penelope was anxious.

"Let's burn the thing first. See, father's office is dark. They'd be either in their room or in the cellar."

The two walked quietly along the side alley into their rear yard and stared up at their parents' bedroom window. "The lamp is lit." Thaddeus was certain they were in their room.

The twins then tiptoed into the house through the rear door and descended slowly into the cellar. The kitchen was heavy with shadows and smelled of green wood and burnt bread. Penelope hurried to dig the list out of her dress as Thaddeus set some kindling on the red coals of the smouldering hearth.

"Here," whispered Penelope. She was still nervous. She stared at the flattened scroll and handed it to her brother as though she were Washington surrendering his sword to a British general.

Thaddeus unscrolled the paper and surveyed the list now illuminated by the small fire. His eyes rode along the curls and knots of Galloway's quill, picturing the faces of many whose names appeared. Handing the list back to his sister, Thaddeus hoped he was doing the right thing. "Here. You should do it."

Penelope took the paper with a trembling hand and stretched it toward the hearth without a word. She laid a corner of the list into the rising fire, and watched with her brother as the hungry flames licked their way along a quick-spreading path. The heavy paper blazed and smoked, rolled and fell away as name after name was sucked into the mouth of the gaping chimney and forever lost in the night's sky. And when the final flame flickered and fell, all that remained of Joseph's Galloway's grand design was a handful of grey ash.

⤙━⧳ ⧱━⤚

It was Easter Sunday, the 19th of April, before Dr. Browne permitted himself or his wife to forgive their twins. The obstinate pair had refused every attempt to pry from them an adequate explanation for their mysterious disappearance on St. George's Day. In response to every deprivation, entreaty, shaming diatribe, scalding tongue-lashing, or extra duty, the two simply declared their right to "follow conscience." It was a great frustration for Archibald to find his youngest children out of reach of his discipline. But at last, after morning services on that triumphant Sunday, the man relented. He offered his children the "peace of the Resurrection," and he gave them the liberty to stand before the "high Judgement of the Maker," Who, he assured them, had no limits to persistence.

"Oh, Katherine," Archibald sighed when they were alone. "I've not the wisdom to know the right time to let these two stand on their own. Their birthday is June 13th, less than two months from now. I had hoped to keep them in their yokes 'til then."

"Well, husband, each child has its own time to bloom. And each season is different. There are those carrying muskets that ought to be flying kites or playing stickball. The war has changed things, Archibald, and it has changed people."

The man looked lovingly at his wife, but he had been secretly troubled about something else for months. He took Katherine by the hand and escorted her into the garden. Daffodils were in their full yellow bloom and the apple tree was covered in fragrant white flowers. The sun was warm and the grass bright green. It had rained every day for nearly twenty days, beginning soon after St. George's, and the earth was ripe and well watered.

"Katherine, I am a trusting man and I beg you to forgive my question, but—" He paused.

Katherine paled. She stood stiffly and removed her hand from his. "Yes, husband, go on."

The doctor reddened and fidgeted with the lace of his silk shirt. He removed his spectacles and wiped them on his kerchief. "Well, I have noticed from time to time that you seem preoccupied and distant."

"I think often of our son."

"And I as well. I have said nothing, but I know that from time to time you slip away from our bed and do not return until the hour before dawn—and sometimes you do not return at all. Sometimes I find you in the kitchen, and it seems you are pretending you awakened just before me."

Katherine stared, blankly. "And is there more?"

Archibald was firmer. "Aye. Your goloe-shoes move about."

"Eh?"

"Your overshoes—I find them here, then there. They sit under the pegs for days and then I find them at the rear door."

"Is there still more?"

Archibald sighed. "Sometimes I see figures near our door in the night. They seem to hover and glide about the darkness. Sometimes I hear them in here—in the garden."

"And?"

"And now I would like your explanation."

Katherine Browne was a wise and patient woman. Born and bred of English gentry stock, she had always valued an impeccable reputation. She shook her head and sighed. "Husband, my thoughts are often with Cameron and his welfare.

They are with the others whom I love as well—you and the twins. I see the weight of all the world mounded on your shoulders day by day and so I keep my own miseries to myself. I often walk at night. I find the stillness of the sleeping city to be a comfort.

"As for my goloe-shoes, I can tell you that I loan them from time to time to Goody Hawkins, an old woman moved to St. Mary's poor house since the army's come. I think she helps herself to them as well. I cannot explain the strangers by the house. I have seen them too."

Dr. Browne nodded. He had listened carefully to every word but her tone and her tightened shoulders troubled him.

"I see. Well, then, I beg you to forgive me. You are a good wife and I do love you so." The man embraced Katherine with his strong arms. He could not see the tears that filled her eyes.

CHAPTER 16

The List

"THERE'S TO BE a parade." Whittaker Yates was pleased. He stood in his apothecary shop with Dr. Browne and Thaddeus and stared out the large window on to Second Street.

"When?"

"Today."

Thaddeus and his father smiled. Parades were a simple pleasure that cost nothing. Webster climbed out of the cellar with a basket of items for the doctor and joined in. "Parade? What kind of parade?"

Whittaker rolled his eyes and held his nose. "A German parade, of all things. They want to bid a fitting farewell to General Howe, so they're marching the entire Hessian army past him."

The four decided it was a sight worth seeing, so off they ran. And they were not disappointed. Pressing their way into a crowd of fascinated citizens, they watched the spectacularly bedecked General Knyphausen lead his mercenaries in perfectly ordered ranks past the British officer corps. It was an impressive sight. Row upon row of red-trimmed blue coats swept by atop their white legs and long black boots. Whittaker laughed and swallowed a long draught of English ale he had quickly bought from a street vendor. He offered a quick sonnet:

> *"Fusiliers and musketeers,*
> *Cavalrymen, and grenadiers,*
> *In rigid blocks march forward.*
> *Above them flags of gold and red,*
> *They serve our King though Hessian bred*
> *And not one acts untoward."*

The Germans paraded to music unfamiliar to Thaddeus and somewhat displeasing to his ears. It seemed heavy and morbid. The faces of the Hessians were hard-set and moustached. It wasn't long, however, before the city was brought to tears of laughter. The jovial General William Howe was enjoying his day. He was happy to be yielding his command to General Clinton and was dreaming of leisure time on his English estates. He sat atop his horse and waved to the passing troops and, from time to time, enjoyed a swallow of his favourite wine.

But Philadelphia had one last humiliation for the general. As a company of Hessian musketeers marched past, they raised their weapons to the blue, spring sky above and fired an unexpected volley at the heavens. Poor gentleman Howe clutched the reins of his startled horse and desperately struggled to remain in his saddle. But to the delight of the patriots scattered throughout the crowd, the English lord fell from his rearing mount and crashed to the street, where he lay in a heap on Philadelphia's cobblestones like a bundle of laundry dropped by a washwoman. Even the Quakers howled.

A gaggle of aides hastily stood the general to his feet and steadied him until he had straightened his wig, reset his hat, and remounted his horse. It would be the last parade of the Germans.

→➤◉ ◎◀←

As the wonders of springtime filled the city with the fragrance of fresh flowers and tender grass, the trees lining each of Philadelphia's ordered streets opened to full bud. Their green leafed branches spread wide and softened the hard lines of the city's brick and stone. The citizens were renewed by the warmth of the season and set about their many tasks with the enthusiasm that oft' comes with sunshine and blue skies. Coopers and blacksmiths, tanners, rope makers, sail makers, cabinet makers, masons, tinsmiths, jewellers, printers, weavers, ship builders, clerks, teachers—all were coming to new life like the flowers opening everywhere in the garden city. Philadelphia was beginning to live once again.

The river had been ice-free since mid-March, and ships' stores filled the wharves with goods coming from England, the Caribbean, Spain, Portugal, Africa, and Pennsylvania's sister colonies. Ships unloading their cargoes, however, were not able to reload with the bounty of products as they had done in the past. Ever since the British occupation of the city, manufacturing for export had virtually stopped. What production of cloth and dye, iron goods, brick, handcrafts, or foodstuffs that did occur was ravenously devoured by the city itself. Yet, many of the merchant ships were ordered to stay in port—a command that raised the suspicions of most.

The soldiers occupying the city were bored with their dinners and their parties. The weather was making the theatre uncomfortably warm, and it was about to close for the season. Its closing mattered little to most, however, for it had become a tiresome distraction. Even horse races and gambling had lost their appeal to an army that had been overindulged and was now growing more restless every day.

Of course, not all of England's soldiers had expended their time in leisure or excess. Major Crippen and others had spent some of the past winter attending a very popular lecture series offered in natural philosophy at the city's college. Oliver had frequented the various bookstores sprinkled throughout the neighbourhoods, and once he toured the orrery—an apparatus that configured the solar system— of David Rittenhouse, the famous astronomer. But even he, like his comrades, longed for a change.

For some units of the British army the monotony of the Philadelphia occupation was finally interrupted on the first of May, when a detachment was sent against an American force at Crooked Billet. The Redcoats returned joyfully, having defeated the patriots. A week later, the British navy sailed upriver and surprised a fleet of small American vessels, sinking forty-four of them. A day after that, eight hundred British regulars savaged parts of New Jersey. And finally, the routine of a fearful Sergeant Melvin Franks was changed as well—he was ordered home to his happy wife.

On May 11th, General Sir Henry Clinton assumed command of His Majesty's forces in North America from General William Howe. The transfer went largely unnoticed by the citizens of the city, but within days rumours were flying about the bricks that the British were going to abandon Philadelphia.

"Preposterous," Dr. Browne argued.

Whittaker was insistent and anxious. "I tell you, Archibald, I have it on good authority. And I am frightened. The American Congress continues to pass more loyalty laws. What am I to do? I am still bound by conscience to the Crown. And now my own government may abandon me to the rebel army." The man was drawn and pale.

"Ah, were it so. But listen to me, friend. Howe recently fortified his positions near Germantown. He would have no reason to do this if he were planning to evacuate the city. And Oliver tells me that Clinton is continuing the work."

Whittaker shook his head. "I hope you are right, Archibald, but I fear it is a ploy. I believe my son and I shall soon be in harm's way again. I've heard that Galloway was ordered to do an accounting of the city's rum, molasses, brandy—even salt. He has his friend, that lap dog Enoch Story, in charge of the inventory. Some think the army is going to strip the city. I believe they are running on account of the French."

"I would not expect them to run from anyone. And we are not absolutely certain of the French."

"But remember the cannon we heard so far in the distance a week ago or so?"

"Aye."

"A customer told me it was Washington's troops celebrating their treaty with France."

Archibald nodded. "If this is true, then I am surprised." He lowered his voice. "You do understand that the would change everything."

Whittaker agreed. "Aye—the break is complete. If the Crown wins, these colonies shall be forever treated like a conquered nation." He was frustrated. "I remember not long ago a lot of Whig talk about England's betrayal of her colonies because the King was softening toward the French in Quebec. Now, these same rebels embrace the popish dandies. I tell you, Archibald, it is a confusing time. But I believe this— with the French on Congress' side, the United Colonies shall surely win. And then what of loyal subjects like myself and my boy?"

Dr. Browne reached for a glass of sherry. "In the beginning of these troubles I did not side with the radicals—you know that. I wanted to reform the way things were done. Even Galloway wanted a new 'Plan of Union,' as he called it. In those days the most ardent Loyalists agreed that our rights were being violated. Why wouldn't Parliament listen to reason then? The matter kept getting worse—men died on both sides, and still some of us wanted to make peace and remain as loyal subjects. Whittaker, I have never wanted to abandon my motherland—never. But the government kept pushing at us—denying even a hearing—rebuffing and scoffing our petitions. What did they expect?

"Now this. I lost my leg fighting the French—I hate them. Now they are my allies? I can hardly bear the thought of it. But truly, now there is no turning away from our course. We have broken with our past." The man sighed and stared away for a moment. He turned back to Whittaker and laid a hand on the shoulder of the unhappy apothecary. "No matter what, Whittaker Yates, I remain your friend."

⇢⊨⊚ ⊚⊨⊰⊱

"That Major André is an extravagant, mollycoddled peacock if there ever was one. He spends his days and nights at the theatre or dining. I hear he courts that society flirt, Peggy Shippen," said Katherine Browne. She wiped soot from her forehead and handed Penelope the hearth brush. "It confounds me that the government would let him spend revenue on some kind of farewell to General Howe."

"It's to be called the 'Meschianza,'" added Penelope. "I think it means 'The Medley.'"

"It does. I was listening to Mrs. Galloway go on about it at the market. She had quite a crowd around her, including Mary Franks."

"Mrs. Galloway?"

"Yes."

Penelope measured her words. "I haven't heard much of the Galloways lately. Have you?"

"Only that some say Mr. Galloway's gone mad as a drunken cock bird. His wife sent Cedric to New York… something about the two of them sharing some sort of poppycock. Oh, and you remember the supposed list of names he bragged about?"

Penelope bit her lip.

"Now he claims it is missing. I wonder if it all was just madness all along."

Penelope's heart was beating. "And father says he hears talk of the Redcoats leaving the city."

Katherine dipped a kettle in a barrel of water. "I overheard Major Crippen speaking to a lieutenant this morning. He said nothing of an evacuation."

Penelope pressed for more.

Katherine turned her head. "That's all I know," she said.

Penelope's mind was racing. "Do you think Galloway really *had* a list—and do you think it's really missing—and do you think t*hat's* why the Redcoats are leaving?"

Katherine chuckled. "What I think girl, is that you are dreaming again." She walked to the front of the cellar and stepped up the short flight of stone stairs. With a grunt she raised the narrow double doors leading to the street. In warm weather Katherine loved to keep the door open. It provided a pleasant draught through the kitchen as well as some welcome light.

Penelope Browne called from the hearth. "But tell me mother, what else did you learn about the Meschianza?"

Katherine shrugged. She dried her hands on her apron and beckoned her daughter to join her on the steps. It was time for a short break.

The two sat atop their cellar way and enjoyed the warm, Saturday afternoon sunshine. They nibbled on a platter of cheese and waved to neighbours passing by. Katherine pulled her mobcap tight to her head and fluffed its floppy brim to shield her skin from the sun. "It is scheduled for this Monday. I am told it's to be quite the affair. Mrs. Franks told me that twenty-two officers each donated 140 pounds sterling to off-set some of the costs. She says the banquet shall cost some 900 pounds, and Mr. Coffin and Mr. Anderson—those merchants near Christ Church—sold silks and starched stockings, shirts, ruffles, and the like, in the amount of 12,000 pounds. Can you believe it? In a city where the poor go begging, these officers lavish such luxury on themselves. The Quakers are in fits."

Mrs. Evan Jones suddenly appeared at the Brownes' door. Katherine and Penelope rose and greeted the young woman with happy smiles. Mrs. Jones was beaming, her newborn held tightly in her arms. Handing Mrs. Browne a basket, she said, "Please give this to yer husband as m'thanks."

Katherine looked in the basket to find a lovely conserve of spring flowers. The conserve, made by blending beaten flower petals and sugar, was a lasting treat, and would be a delight on the family's table for many years. "Mrs. Jones, 'tis so very kind." Katherine knew the sugar alone had cost the struggling family more than a month's wages.

"Yer husband saved me and m'little Thaddeus. 'Tis a small gift."

The two embraced and the happy mother pulled the homespun blanket from her child's face. Little Thaddeus Jones smiled.

->==@ @==<-

Monday, May 18th, was a day of dismay for some and of excess for others. Archibald, Thaddeus, Whittaker, and Webster were standing dumfounded on the city's docks as the Meschianza began. At four o'clock in the afternoon of a breezy, but rain-free day, a procession of decorated watercraft began to sail downstream on the rippled Delaware. Three flotillas of ten barges were each led by a galley as their flagship. The vessels were bright and colourful, sporting flags of the empire, regimental colours, and buntings.

The first galley to lead was the *Ferret* and on board was an assortment of general officers and their ladies. Behind followed three barges of bands playing music and several others packed with officers and ladies of Philadelphia society. The city's homes and docks had been decorated as well. Streamers and flapping pennants covered the buildings lining King Street, and King George's loyal subjects crowded the riverbank, shouting and singing in jubilation. Sailors invited many into small boats and proceeded to row into the midst of the flotilla. The resulting clog of oars and hulls slowed the procession even more.

Cannon belched smoke and noise, cheers and laughter filled the waterfront, and when the bands played, *God Save the King*. "Archibald, I love my country," choked Whittaker Yates. The towering, spindly apothecary waved his Union Jack proudly.

At six o'clock the flotilla finally arrived at its destination. It had travelled a mere mile downstream to the estate of one Joseph Wharton, where the company was to be entertained by a tournament of medieval knights, including an ever-popular joust. Having passed through a number of gaudy arches, the gape-jawed guests were escorted to the tournament grounds. Here they found seven young ladies known as "The Knights' Ladies" seated inside a small pavilion. Surrounding the jousting field was an assembly of vanity never matched in all of America's years. The tournament lasted for hours, and the dandies so impressed the ladies that all competing knights were dubbed the victors.

As night fell, the guests were then escorted to the large banquet hall that had been built for the occasion. As they walked along a gravel path that passed through lush flower gardens, the sky was lit with a display of fireworks that brought cheers of approval from the indulged. Each guest was presented a personal greeting by the event's organisers and then escorted through the breathtaking dining hall, brilliantly illuminated by hundreds of fine white candles.

Columns of the elite were led through the hall and into the parlour rooms of the mansion. The panelled walls of the banquet room were painted to look like Sienna marble

C. D. Baker

and boasted fine works of art. Finally, at midnight, dinner was served in the grand hall where guests sat along two long tables, each set for 450 diners. On the tables stood twelve hundred dishes and fifty pyramids of jellies, cakes, and sweetmeats. Courses included lamb, buttered hams, veal, Yorkshire pies, puddings, and soups.

Serving the guests were thirty Negro men dressed in gaudy oriental costumes consisting of silk turbans, white shirts, blue silk sashes, and silver bracelets.

The meal lasted for hours and when the meal was finally over, the guests danced until daybreak. And thus, General Howe bade his farewell.

⋅⊱⊰⋅

Archibald Browne stared blankly before him as his wife stoked the kitchen hearth. It was an hour before dawn, and he wondered why she looked as if she had been awake for hours, but he asked nothing.

"Good morning, husband." Katherine stated flatly. "I am wanting to bake bread today and I need to heat the oven before the day's too hot."

"I see." Archibald wiped his spectacles. A courier had wakened him, requesting that he hurry to the prison hospital. "Seems there was some attempt to break out of the city jail last night."

"Oh?"

"With the Redcoats so engaged in their extravagance, I suspect some thought it was a good time for distraction."

"Seems logical."

Archibald watched his wife for a moment and reached for her cup of tea. It was cold. Setting it down, he slowly climbed the steps. He met a sleepy Thaddeus in his office and the two passed out into the dark streets of the sleeping city. They walked quietly toward the Fifth Street Jail. The only sound that could be heard was Dr. Browne's wooden leg clicking steadily on the brick sidewalk.

Inside the jail the doctor and his young apprentice found a loud and chaotic scene. Apparently, just hours before, Captain Allen McLane of the American army had organised a night's entertainment of his own. He had sent four detachments of twenty-five men as well as a company of mounted dragoons to the British fascines. At a given signal they—like Gideon in the Bible—shouted and threw their fire in the air in hopes of igniting the wooden defences. So, while the dandies of the empire had tasted fancy cakes and delicate wines, McLane's rugged patriots had been thrashing about the Pennsylvania forest in their persistent pursuit of liberty.

The surprised British had rolled their drums in near panic as their bundled fences began to burn. They thought the whole of Washington's half-starved army might be upon them. But they soon learned that it was not Gideon, nor the arm of the Almighty. It was only that scoundrel McLane, who had spent all winter harassing them from his hideouts in Bucks County. Though the scare did little more than singe the wooden wall, it had been meant to serve another purpose. It had been planned as a diversion to assist a cadre of patriots who had organised a jailbreak. Unfortunately, the attempted release had failed, and many of the imprisoned American soldiers had been injured or killed in the mêlée.

Dr. Browne entered the torch-lit jail and stepped carefully over the bodies strewn about the floors. The city's patriots had killed several of the guards before order was restored. Two cells had been opened and some of the prisoners had gotten as far as the front walkway, but an efficient company of grenadiers had handily captured all of them and exacted a severe penalty. Groaning and whimpering men were now huddled against the walls.

The doctor immediately began binding limbs and sewing open wounds while Thaddeus confirmed several deaths. The two worked through the dawn and far into the day before they finally paused to rest. A young American shuffled toward them. "Thanks to ye, doctor."

Archibald grunted.

"I'd be from Georgia." The boy was thin as a skeleton. Thaddeus thought he was no more than sixteen. "Ye saved m'friend o'er there."

"You're welcome, lad." Dr. Browne sighed.

"I been with Washington at Valley Forge nigh all winter. Got caught by the river last month."

Archibald became interested. "Do you know any from the 2nd Pennsylvania?"

The soldier thought carefully. "Uh—no, can't say as I do. I thinks they'd be o'er the hill from us."

Thaddeus asked, "Did many die?"

"Lots died. Some come here for the bounty. They takes the oath to the King and gets paid and some food—and a deed to land. Then they comes back to the army. Then when they gets hungry again they comes back here. That's what I was tryin' when I gots caught."

Archibald shook his head. "Clever trick...the sort of thing that makes the Redcoats wild. They think we're barbarians as it is—men without honour, they say."

The young man grunted. "I've honour sir. But none to spare on tyrants." Then he smiled a large, gaping, toothless smile.

"And we've another trick for 'em."

"Eh?"

"We've been trained good now. Some German fella—General Von Steuben—made us march day and night. Back and forth—in straight lines. He learned us commands an' fornications—"

"That would be 'formations.'"

"Formations, right. By God, I feel like a soldier."

Archibald brightened. He bade the lad Godspeed and finished his day's tasks. At early evening father and son walked home exhausted but encouraged by the prospect that Cameron was alive.

Thaddeus said, "Talk is that ships are being loaded with rum and molasses. Rumours are all about the city that the army is going to evacuate. Do you think so?"

Dr. Browne shrugged. "A few days ago I thought not. But I hear it everywhere. Merchants are meeting and talking of how to make amends to the Americans if the city is abandoned. I fear they shall have a high price to pay."

The two walked in silence for another block until Thaddeus said, "Did you hear of Galloway's burglary?"

"Aye."

"I heard his list was taken—the one he bragged of to so many. Do you think the British are retreating because it is gone?"

Thaddeus was suddenly worried that he was the very cause of the distress he had hoped to prevent.

"I think the French have them scared. My guess is they are being directed by a new strategy from London. I suspect they'll move to New York and regroup. They may leave the middle colonies and take the war to the south."

Thaddeus was relieved, but not convinced. He wondered if he had done the right thing after all.

→━◉ ◉━←

"Confounded Frenchy," snorted Major Crippen. "We almost caught him. Someone warned him; I know it."

The officer was tired and frustrated. His artillery company had been ordered to support a British force led by General Howe against the Marquis de Lafayette just across the Schuylkill the day after the Meschianza. Apparently, the Americans had felt emboldened by the extravaganza, and the wily Frenchman had positioned himself precariously. The trap had been cleverly designed by General Clinton, but had been undone by information received through the ever-meddling Captain McLane. Oliver collapsed on a kitchen stool and pulled off his boots, then gratefully took the fresh bread and jar of jelly offered to him. A tankard of ale followed.

The Brownes sat quietly as the man swigged a long draught. "I was a guest at the Meschianza and dined and danced 'til dawn. On my way home I was ordered to gather my company and sleep in the barracks at Fifth Street to await orders. Then off we went after the slippery frog, and to no avail. So, please forgive my disposition."

The Brownes continued with their evening meal but Katherine was nervous. She spilled ale on her lap and left the table. She returned wringing her hands. "I am sure you must be very tired, major."

"I truly am. I look forward to lying on my bed, but I am even happier to enjoy this meal with all of you." He ate ravenously for a few minutes, and then paused. He set down his spoon and turned to the doctor. "Sir, I have something to tell you."

With his eyes on his wife, Archibald wiped his mouth with a napkin and set his knife and spoon aside, waiting.

The officer straightened and spoke slowly. "It is not officially known but I know, and I want you to know. Please do not tell others."

The doctor looked at the soldier.

"We shall evacuate the city soon."

The Brownes stared.

"We are ordered to New York and we are to strip the city of rum, sugar, medicines, and the like. I am certain we shall also be ordered to torch any ships that remain, as well as any stores that might serve the American army. Rumours have begun and soon they shall be cause for panic. When the news is made public…"

"The Congress should grant them amnesty. That would preserve the city and lessen the resolve of Tories everywhere." Dr. Browne was now on his feet.

"Perhaps they shall. But I need to say this as well." The weary soldier drew a deep breath as Archibald sat down. "You have treated me with every Christian kindness. I have grown to love you all. I thank you from the bottom of my heart. I have learned to love this land and have learned much from you. I confess I do serve my King with some confusion.

"While marching this morning I reflected on the nauseating spectacle of the overindulgence I wallowed in at the Meschianza…and I am ashamed. I suddenly pictured myself serving a gluttonous empire greedily grasping at the destiny of your New World. Few know it, but there are those in our army that are defecting to your cause. They believe our traditions have been scandalised by excess and corruption. I pray it is not so, but I fear perhaps they are right." Oliver Crippen turned a sad face to the table. "May God bless you."

Few cared about the royal salute for the King's birthday on June 4th. And few gave much regard for Lord North's peace commission that arrived on the 6th. The fact that the commission offered everything the Americans demanded except independence served only to frustrate and confuse the Loyalists of the city.

And these overtures seemed to encourage an alarming number of British soldiers to desert and join their American cousins. As for Oliver Crippen, none knew. He was gone one morning and no one knew his whereabouts, including members of his own company. But as Oliver had predicted, all ships under construction were set ablaze, as were excess blankets from the hospitals, warehouses of gun parts, sail makers' sheds, and shipyards. The entry of the French into the war had changed the game. The English army needed to concentrate itself and its resources in New York. It could ill afford to leave anything behind, so what it couldn't take with it simply had to be destroyed.

Panic gripped the citizens of Philadelphia. Late spring winds fanned the army's fires. Some became convinced the army was going to raze the city to the ground. Thousands jammed the docks begging passage to New York. Others crowded the ferries shuttling back and forth to New Jersey.

On the 13th of June, the birthday of the Browne twins, Whittaker and Webster Yates stood ready to board one such ferry.

"I love you," wept the heartsick Mr. Yates. He embraced Katherine and Penelope and grasped the firm hands of Archibald and Thaddeus. "I must leave the city. Webster and I shall meet a poor end if we stay."

Webster's round face was tear-stained and flushed. He was trembling and suddenly feeling very much alone. The motherless lad bade Mrs. Browne such a heartfelt farewell that the woman burst into uncontrollable sobs. He turned to the twins. Goodbye, Penelope—and Thaddeus."

Whittaker released his grip on Archibald's hand and the two fixed eyes for a brief moment. The gentle apothecary then laid a long arm around his obedient son and climbed aboard the heavy-laden ferry floating very low in the water. The chaos of the city swirled around the two families, but they gave it little notice. And as the ferry's ropes were untied, they waved to one another knowing that no nation's discord, no immeasurable distance nor deep despair would sever the cords of love that had bound them to each other.

⌐⊨⊨⊨⌐

For four more days the city of Philadelphia was in turmoil. Smoke hung heavy beneath her trees, and her cobblestones chattered loudly like teeth shivering in the bitter cold. Her ordered grid of streets were filled with frightened children and racing carriages. Vacant homes and shops were looted and some set afire. General Clinton was more concerned with the evacuation of his twenty thousand soldiers than the welfare of the city's residents.

Over three hundred ships jammed the Delaware, and onto these tramped the battalions of Hessians who were particularly suspect for desertion. They were joined by various British battalions and the sick and wounded. Other units of the army spent the days of June 15th through the 17th loading flatboats manned by some five hundred sailors, who shuttled them to New Jersey.

On the British line, grenadiers and the light infantry were moved into the redoubts, where they dozed nervously through the night of June 17th. The rest of their comrades were removed to the city and the waiting ferries. Then, at daybreak of Thursday, June 18th, 1778, they abandoned their defences and hurried to board the last ferries waiting impatiently at the city docks.

The Brownes awakened on that same day and stepped onto their stoop to survey Union Street. It was nearly empty of people and cluttered with discarded crates and broken wheels. The privy at Drinker's Courtyard had been left unattended and the whole of the neighbourhood was filled with stench. But more terrible than the odour was the silence. The family walked carefully down the sidewalk, staring at the shuttered homes lining the street. Turning on to Second Street, they looked at New Market. The shambles was abandoned to refuse and litter and only a handful of the homeless poor huddled in its recesses.

Archibald shook his head. "I wonder—" he said. "I wonder what would be if the Congress had accepted the King's peace?"

A shout and a sudden clatter of hooves startled the Brownes, and an advance company of American dragoons suddenly roared into the empty marketplace. "Quick—home," commanded Archibald. He hurried his wife and twins back up Union, and as they disappeared one by one into the house, a familiar voice suddenly cried to them from the street.

"Dr. Browne, 'tis me—Josiah."

Archibald turned hastily. He glanced past the old man running toward him to see another company of blue-coated soldiers crossing Union at Third. "Hurry, Josiah."

The Grackle scampered into the doctor's office and Archibald slammed the door. "Beggin' pardon," panted Josiah. "I need to find a place. Soldiers be all over General Howe's…"

"You are safe here," said Katherine. "Now come, all of you, we need to eat." As she finished speaking, gunshots were heard in the distance. The twins poked their faces against the glass of the front windows and watched small companies of Americans begin to filter through their neighbourhood.

"Come away." Archibald was insistent. "They'll be looking for Redcoat stragglers. I doubt they'll settle in the city yet. I've a hunch Washington has them chasing the Redcoats all the way to New York. But they are excited and confused. And they may take you for nosy Tories."

Katherine urged her household to the safety of her cellar kitchen. Securing the beam that locked the doorway to the street, she went about the business of preparing hot coffee, tea, and porridge. She seemed nervous and preoccupied, however, and nearly dropped the kettle she was lifting to the crane.

"Mother—if the army's coming, we should see Cameron." Penelope was beside herself with enthusiasm. "The Redcoats are beaten, father. And Cameron's to come home. What a day—what a glorious day." She paused and stared at the faces looking back. They all seemed anxious and she was confused.

Her look prompted a reply from her father. "Penny, my pumpkin. We would rather celebrate after Cameron comes home. We are hopeful, but it was a hard winter for him— many did not live through it." His voice faded.

Penelope's eyes fell. Indeed, the winter at Valley Forge had made many a widow and broken many a mother's heart. She sat quietly at her seat and reached for Cromwell as she waited for her porridge. Old Josiah stretched a hand toward the girl and rested it kindly atop her shoulder. His golden eyes offered her hope.

The quiet household ate their morning's fare and prayed together. They passed some time speaking of the amazing events of the past year, pausing from time to time to listen to the tramp of soldiers or the clicking of hooves just beyond the thin wood of their cellar door.

It was around noon when Archibald decided to read the words of comfort in Psalm 18. The family listened respectfully while he read. As he came to the forty-sixth verse—"The Lord liveth; and blessed be my rock; and let the God of my salvation be exalted—"

A loud rap on the upstairs door suddenly echoed through the house. Archibald set his Bible on the table and looked at his wife. He took a breath. "So it begins.

The family followed him upstairs and to the door. The doctor flung it open to find a well-weathered, war-worn American captain on his stoop. Behind him on the street stood two lieutenants and three foamed mounts.

Katherine clutched her hands to her breast and kept her eyes on the blue-coated soldier. *News of Cameron?* Her breath quickened.

Archibald braced himself. "Sir, how can I serve you?"

"Are you Dr. Archibald Browne?"

The man nodded, fearing the worst.

"Might I come inside?"

Archibald hesitated. "Have you news of my son?"

The captain faced him squarely. "I do."

"Then, come in."

The group backed into Dr. Browne's office as the handsome officer entered, removing his hat with a bow. Archibald took Katherine's hand and waited.

"First, your son is in good health."

Katherine burst into tears and clutched Archibald's arm. The twins cheered and Archibald bowed his head as he removed his spectacles. Wiping his eyes he said, "Thanks be to God." He pulled the wires over his ears and then looked squarely at the officer. "You've more?

The captain continued. "I am sent here by General Washington."

The Brownes waited.

"The general has a secret list of names of those who have protected the life and health of his army in this most difficult time. This list, Dr. Browne, is committed to my memory and known only to the general and two members of his staff."

"I don't understand." Archibald suddenly wondered if he was about to be cited for serving the American prisoners. He abruptly stood erect and squeezed his wife's hand.

"It is my honour to express the personal thanks of General Washington and the Congress to those who have risked much to smuggle information to our army through enemy lines." The officer then faced Katherine and stood at attention. "Mrs. Katherine Browne..."

To the astonishment of the woman's flabbergasted family, the man snapped a salute.

Archibald turned to his blushing wife, dumbstruck.

Katherine's chin quivered and she leaned against her husband sobbing softly in his ear. "I am sorry, dear Archibald. I could not endanger you." She buried her face in his shoulder.

Archibald and the twins stared speechlessly at their mother. Struggling to compose his thoughts, the doctor finally muttered, "A...spy? You are a spy for Washington? But..."

Katherine nodded and wiped her nose with a kerchief. "Under God, husband, it is my family whom I love and serve. Would I ever betray my Cameron for a mere King?"

Captain McLane stood respectfully and then cleared his throat. He smiled at the woman and she at him. "General Washington learned to trust your messages more than any others. And I trusted you, too." He turned to Archibald. "I met your wife twice, sir. Once near Germantown in the autumn, then just weeks ago. It was she who helped us warn Lafayette of the trap."

Archibald shook his head. It was too much to grasp.

Katherine squeezed her husband's arm. "I shall tell you all about it another time. But I did not serve alone." She looked at McLane. "Is there another on that list, sir?"

"Indeed. There's one whose name I do not know." McLane turned to Josiah Byrd and extended his hand. "My couriers called you 'the Grackle,' but I should like to give your real name to General Washington."

The old man beamed. "My name is Josiah Byrd."

Captain McLane snapped another salute. "When the war is over, you and Mrs. Browne shall be given citations from the Congress. Until then, Mr. Byrd, I have nothing to offer you other than the thanks of our nation." He turned to Katherine. "But for you, dear lady, I do have a gift." He opened the door and motioned to his lieutenants. From the corner alley came running a tattered, thin young soldier.

"Cameron!" squealed Katherine.

The happy patriot raced toward the family now rushing from their doorway. "Mother! Father…"

Wiping tears from his own eyes, Captain McLane then mounted his horse.

"Thank you, captain," wept Katherine from the joyful circle. "But do stay and eat…"

"I've duties to attend, but enjoy your evening. Your city is now under the protection of that courageous patriot, General Benedict Arnold."

The End

Epilogue

In the days that followed the British abandonment of Philadelphia, Loyalists and quick-thinking converts to neutralism wisely remained behind closed doors. Vengeful patriots returned to the city to reclaim their homes and they were all too anxious to exact a penalty. After all, they had suffered when *their* army had withdrawn the autumn before.

But the citizens of Philadelphia soon realised they were facing a problem of immense proportions. The people quickly recognised their need to co-operate with one another regardless of their differences, and soon Loyalist and patriot were working side by side to rebuild their broken city. Many of the houses in the northernmost neighbourhoods had been destroyed by fire. Those that remained were gutted of hinges, glass, windows, doors—even roofs. During the winter, many had been stripped of all things wooden. Churches, particularly Presbyterian churches, had been violated in every conceivable way. Their pews had been taken, their stairways and glass destroyed; most had been used as stables—or privies.

Heaps of reeking rubbish, maggot-infested garbage, and human waste filled the streets. In homes where many of the soldiers were barracked, human excrement was found piled in the basement. It seems the men resorted to cutting holes in the first floor planks so they might use the parlours as a more convenient privy. To add to the misery, the hot, humid, summer air was thick with stench and darkened by clouds of flies that carried infection and disease throughout the ravaged city.

Other homes had been disrespected in other ways. Patriots of means returned to find their houses pilfered of paintings, chinaware, clothing, and even furniture. Major John André had occupied Benjamin Franklin's home. The dancing peacock of the British army was apparently as light with his fingers as he was with his feet. He stole a good deal of Dr. Franklin's personal effects, including a portrait that the major then presented to a superior officer. In contrast, it should be added, the Hessian general, Knyphausen, conducted himself with great honour. He occupied the house of an American general, John Cadwalader. Knyphausen ordered his steward to write an inventory of the man's house upon his occupancy, and each item was then checked upon the German's departure. Everything was in its place, including every bottle of wine. And General Knyphausen left rent money for the returning homeowner.

Though the civilians of the city faced a daunting task, it was no easier for the withdrawing British army. Washington sent Lafayette and 14,000 soldiers across the Delaware to harass the Redcoats as they marched through New Jersey. The hapless British endured heat and persistent, pesky fire as they hurried along the sandy roads toward New York City. Most wished they could have joined their brethren on the ships that had sailed before.

By the 28th of June, General Washington was ready to fully engage General Clinton's army, and a battle was waged at Monmouth, New Jersey. It was here that the famous Mary Ludwig Hays—or "Molly Pitcher"—manned her cannon. The battle was deadly for both sides and somewhat inconclusive, but it was the first time the Continentals fought the world's greatest infantry on equal terms. Von Steuben's training had made a difference.

In the months that followed, General Clinton followed the King's strategy. He had secured New York City and Newport, Rhode Island—a critical port. With those two northern cities properly defended, the British army was then to attack the Americans in the south.

The next several years saw the heaviest engagements in the southern colonies. Savannah fell to the British, then Charleston. Battles raged all through the Carolinas and Virginia before the British increased their pressure on the north once again.

The French supported the Americans by land, but made a particular presence on the sea. They attacked the British navy off American shores and also engaged them in the Caribbean—a location of supreme importance to the British Empire.

Meanwhile, Spain declared war on England, and England declared war on the Netherlands. The entanglements of old alliances were drawing a noose around King George's neck. The war in America raged on and on through hot summers and cold winters. Loyalist militias battled patriot militias in fierce combat, particularly in South Carolina. On the frontier, Loyalists allied with Indians to sustain a brutal offensive at the nation's edges. But despite mutinies, betrayal, defeats, and exhaustion, the American will to win sustained its cause. Eventually the determined patriots won some significant battles, such as Cowpens and the Battle of Kings Mountain. Finally—miraculously—in October of 1781, a dumfounded and humiliated British army under Lord Cornwallis was forced to surrender at Yorktown, Virginia. The scales were forever tipped.

After Yorktown, the war sputtered on in South Carolina, Kentucky, and Georgia, as well as in the waters of the Delaware Bay. The British, however, had lost their resolve and the cost of this unending war was soaring. Finally, on January 20, 1783,

King George III signed the Treaty of Peace that ended hostilities, and, nearly a year later, on January 14, 1784, the American Congress ratified it. The War for Independence was over. Liberty as expressed in the spirit of the Magna Carta had endured.

In *The List*, numbers of historical characters were involved or referenced. Since these people really did walk the earth, it seems fitting to share something of their lives.

Major John André (1751-1780): Major André was the son of a Swiss merchant who settled in London. He was known as a debonair, dashing officer whose gallantry and courage earned him the respect of his peers. As adept with his sword as with the ladies, the officer danced and battled his way through the war in America with high honour. Unfortunately, he became involved in an adventure of intrigue and espionage that entangled him with Benedict Arnold. He was captured in civilian clothing carrying messages to Arnold and subsequently tried as a spy. He wrote to Washington and pleaded to be shot as an officer, not "hung like a felon." It was a request that was out-of-bounds in the law and the American general could not comply. Reluctantly, and out of kindness, Washington did not respond.

On the morning of his execution André put on his full dress uniform and expected to face a firing squad. Instead, he crested a hill to see his waiting gallows. Gallant as ever, he calmly stepped atop his own coffin that sat waiting in the wagon below his noose. He adjusted the rope around his own neck and pulled the kerchief over his eyes. He died with the respect of two nations and was honoured in later years by both King and Congress.

General Benedict Arnold (1741-1801): It is ironic that the city of Philadelphia was both home to the Liberty Bell, the Declaration of Independence, and the Continental Congresses, and yet was considered a "hotbed of Toryism." It was truly a divided city, and perhaps it is fitting that Benedict Arnold switched loyalties while its governor.

General Arnold had served the patriot cause with distinction and honour. Some considered him to be the nation's most brilliant general. But vanity and bitterness ultimately turned him to the Crown. While governing Philadelphia, General Arnold married the beautiful and very young Mistress Margaret (Peggy) Shippen. Considering Margaret's outspoken Loyalist sympathies, some believe the "whispers of Eve" were equally responsible for the general's ultimate treason.

By 1779 Arnold had begun considering desertion, and by 1780 he and his wife were involved in a plot to surrender information regarding the American fort at West Point, N.Y., to the British through Major John André. Upon André's capture, the general fled to the British army, where he was made a brigadier general and sent to Virginia. He fought for the British until 1781 and then sailed to England, where he lived the rest of his life in poverty and disgrace.

Katherine Browne: No, our beloved heroine was not an actual person. But one Lydia Darragh inspired her character. Mrs. Darragh and her husband William lived in a blue house on the corner of Dock Street and Second. The upper back room of her house was often used by British officers as a council chamber and on December 2, 1777, she was asked by those same officers to have her family retire to bed early. With a son in the American army, the woman chose to eavesdrop and she learned of Howe's plans for the Battle of Whitemarsh. Her information was sneaked past British patrols in Germantown and found its way to General Washington. Lydia was one of a number of Philadelphia spies, most of whom remain anonymous.

General Sir Henry Clinton (1738-1795): Commissioned as a lieutenant in the Coldstream Guards at age 13, Clinton ultimately became His Majesty's commander-in-chief of all North American forces in 1778. He enjoyed a stellar military career that included service in Germany during the Seven Years' War. He was a Member of Parliament in 1772 and 1774, and knighted for his part in the Battle of Long Island, 1776. After leaving Philadelphia, he quarrelled with Lord Cornwallis over strategy in America's south. After Cornwallis' defeat at Yorktown, Clinton resigned and returned to England. There he tried to vindicate his American strategy by writing a history of his campaigns. Few noticed. He was appointed governor of Gibraltar in 1794, but died before taking office.

John Dickinson (1732-1808): A quiet, often ignored hero of liberty, Dickinson was a gifted lawyer, statesman, and brave soldier. He championed the constitutional heritage of liberty and demanded redress of American grievances. As a member of the First and Second Continental Congresses, Dickinson inspired and encouraged many by his reasoned, thorough, convincing arguments. He authored the influential *Letters from a Farmer in Pennsylvania*, in which he expressed the cause of liberty with amazing effectiveness. He wrote a Revolutionary anthem entitled, "Song of the Farmer." At the loss of personal reputation, he could not, for conscience' sake, sign the Declaration of Independence. Yet, once the new nation was declared, he willingly joined the army and fought in its defence.

Jacob Duché (1738-1798): Born in Philadelphia, Duché served as the chaplain of the American Congress in 1776. After the British occupation of Philadelphia, he was imprisoned briefly. He quickly turned Loyalist and sent a letter to Washington urging him to do the same. Pennsylvania confiscated his property and Duché fled to England, where he served as chaplain for the Asylum of Female Orphans at Lambeth. Later he returned to Philadelphia and was buried at St. Peter's Church.

Joseph Galloway (1731-1803): Born in Maryland, Galloway studied law in Philadelphia, where he became a prominent attorney. He was elected to the First Continental Congress as a Pennsylvania delegate, and here he supported the colonists' concerns. He feared the rumbles of independence, however, and quickly proposed his Plan of Union, which would have reorganised the relationship between Britain and America.

Considering himself an aristocrat of sorts, he became an ardent supporter of the Loyalist position and ultimately expressed his disdain for the "rabble" that supported independence. He was convinced that the Middle Colonies could raise ten thousand Loyalist volunteers who would guarantee victory for Britain. He boasted to have developed a list of three hundred "men of influence" who could deliver such an army. Galloway's list disappeared and its fate remains a mystery to this day. After the British evacuation of Philadelphia, Galloway sailed to England.

A note: The author was unable to determine the exact location of the Galloway house; therefore, references to his home or address in the story are fictional.

General Sir William Howe (1729-1814): An illegitimate descendant of King George I, Howe served the British army with distinction. He led a courageous assault against the French in Quebec in 1759, just a year after he had been elected to Parliament as a representative from Nottingham. As a Whig, Howe was sympathetic to the American cause from its beginning, but obeyed his King and went to Boston to fight the Americans at Bunker Hill. In subsequent engagements he failed to pursue the patriots to his utmost advantage. Whether it was reluctance for his cause or natural indolence that contributed to his lack of zeal is not known.

Howe was loved by his troops, friendly to all, and charitable to those in need. After resigning his commission, he returned to England, where he retained the King's favour.

He had married in 1765 but had no children. His relationship with Mrs. Loring was well known, but did not seem to detract from his reputation as a man worthy of respect. General Howe died in Plymouth, England.

King George III (1760-1820): King George was committed to strengthening the power of the monarchy. In the hopes of rallying Britain around him, he and his Prime Minister, Lord North, proceeded upon a fatal course of heavily taxing the American colonies in the face of opposition from Parliament's Whigs. Instead of uniting Britain around him, it divided his own nation and fomented rebellion in his colonies. After Yorktown, King George nearly abdicated. He reflected on his decision and concluded that Washington would ultimately become a dictator and that the Americans would then seek shelter under his rule once more. Later, upon hearing rumours of Washington's resignation from the army, the King exclaimed that such an unlikely act would make the American hero the "greatest man in all the world."

King George loved the simple life of his country estate and was known by the English people as "Farmer George." He had a tranquil domestic life with his wife, Charlotte, but spent the last years of his life mad and blind.

Marquis de Lafayette (1757-1834): Lafayette's full name was Marie Joseph Paul Yves Roch Gilbert du Motier. Born in Chavaniac, France, this young, wealthy officer resigned from the French army to join the Americans at age 19. Serving at his own expense, he was commissioned as a major general by Congress on July 1, 1776. He fought in numerous battles and returned to France in 1779 to plead the American cause. He returned to America in 1781 and distinguished himself in battle until returning to France once again in order to assist Thomas Jefferson in political and military matters. He was a republican leader in the French Revolution from 1789-1791. Lafayette later rejected the radicalism of the French Revolution. He was imprisoned by the Prussians and the Austrians from 1792-1797. He was given a hero's welcome in the United States in 1824 and he died in Paris in 1834.

Captain Allen McLane (1746-1829): Captain Allen McLane was born in Philadelphia and later moved to Delaware. He was commissioned in the Delaware militia in 1775 and, when war broke out, he spent much of his inheritance raising a company of troops. His distinguished military career carried him through many major battles of the War of Independence, such as Long Island, White Plains, Trenton, Whitemarsh, and others up to and including the battle of Yorktown.

During the Philadelphia occupation, McLane was instrumental in collecting information from a small network of spies situated throughout the city. Courageous and daring, the captain harassed the British line from secret outposts in neighbouring Bucks County. It is said he was one of the first to suspect the loyalty of Benedict Arnold.

An ardent Methodist, McLane spent many years after the war serving his faith. In addition, this unsung hero served as Speaker of Delaware's House of Representatives, as a judge, as a U.S. Marshall, and as a delegate to the Constitution Ratification Convention in 1787.

Samuel Seabury (1729-1796): Samuel Seabury was ordained an Anglican minister in 1753 and served as a clergyman in New England. He was considered a man of "good sense and learning" and worked furiously to persuade the colonists to remain loyal to the Crown. In his *Letters of a Westchester Farmer,* he stated the Loyalist position with convincing clarity. He managed to stay safely behind British lines throughout the war, yet successfully retained the favour of his countrymen when the war ended. He became the presiding bishop of the newly organised Episcopal Church—the American counterpart to the Church of England.

George Washington (1732-1799): Farmer, soldier, statesman—the adjectives for this great American could fill volumes. For our purposes, the title "spy-master" needs to be mentioned. Few realise that the brilliant general was also a genius at espionage and maintained rings of operatives in Philadelphia and New York. He was also adept at leaking misinformation through double agents, constantly confusing his enemy with inflated estimates of his army's strength or false reports of its movements.

The Others: Suffice it to say that the author is unable to offer information on the other factual characters mentioned in our story. These include: Christopher Apple, the chimney sweep; Enoch Story and Phinneas Bond, Loyalist activists; James

Humphries, the publisher of the *Pennsylvania Gazette*; Charles Thomas, the outspoken Philadelphia patriot; Captain Roger Staynor of Company B, Second Pennsylvania; Dr. Caspar Weyberg of the German Reformed Church; and the reverend Coombs, the rector of St. Peter's Church.

Alas, these, like most of us, are committed to obscure destinies, having left only a vanishing print upon the sand of time.

Books by C.D. Baker

Bookends of Liberty Series: *Swords of Heaven*
The List

The Journey of Souls Series: *Crusade of Tears*
Quest of Hope
Pilgrims of Promise

101 Cups of Water
40 Loaves
The Seduction of Eva Volk
Becoming the Son; an Autobiography of Jesus
Seedlings

More information about the author and his work is available at www.cdbaker.com

43079321R00232

Made in the USA
Charleston, SC
13 June 2015